# Newton Cutter

LEE ANNE WONNACOTT WELTSCH

# DEDICATION

For all who go roaming

# 1 CHAPTER ONE

At first look, the town of Bradford was a motley gathering of different buildings and structures. The first building a traveler saw was Goldman's Saloon and the doorway boasted a painted sign of "Fresh Whiskey - Hot Food". The long bar inside spanned the length of the room with floor-to-ceiling shelves behind it exhibiting a variety of bottles, glasses, and knickknacks. Bert Goldman grew up as a con man, petty thief, and talented hustler who knew the art and science of brewing alcoholic spirits. A big man of six-foot-four with muscular arms and an ash axle handle, he kept the biggest saloon in town orderly and more of a meeting place than a drinking establishment.

The locals were confident that Goldman's was the place to find out news and happenings by sitting for a spell in the wooden chairs on the wide boardwalk in front.

Next to the saloon stood a gray weathered wooden building with two small windows protected by close-set iron bars. Bruno Stenson built and sold guns from his weapons store - for the right price, of course. An arms dealer before the war, he had brought his gun-making equipment to the wilds of the southwestern territory and supplied anyone who could ante up the price. The smell of gun oil, steel shavings and cold iron permeated the interior. A glass case of tiny to large blade knives meant for non-kitchen use caused many to stop and stare. Two dozen Sharps and Winchester rifles hung on the walls. If another war popped up, Stenson was ready.

Across the dusty lane was the official Town Hall building. Mayor William Watley maintained his desk and files there and the public room had seen several shouting matches over decisions over a calf or horse. Voted into office and given a modest salary, William Watley had served eleven years with no opposition. Any given afternoon could find the mayor reclined in his wooden chair sound asleep, resting his worn leather boots on his desk.

The small office of the sheriff tucked in the corner of Town Hall had been vacant for five years. A shooting near the corrals late one night had led to the Sheriff resulting in him being pronounced dead in the morning from an ugly bullet hole in the side of his head. The mayor's efforts requesting a replacement from Santa Fe were met with silence. Mayor Watley pressed the matter and he learned that there was no one to come keep the peace in Bradford. Court was up in Santa Fe and nobody wanted to risk transporting some criminal even in chains on that trail. The one jail cell door remained closed, the chairs and benches in their proper place and the shiny Silver Star badge rested under an inverted clear glass bowl. The only other occupant of the office was the half inch thick coating of undisturbed dust.

To the north of Town Hall spaced out about thirty yards was a single story wooden building belonging to Doctor Woodson Baines. A veteran of varied armed conflicts from the east coast to the west, Doc Baines had been on the verge of retirement for twenty years. Doc tended to the bleeding, broken, shot and mangled bodies of the unfortunate from mysterious unknown origins. North of Doc Baines was the jaunty two-story whitewashed Hotel Bradford which sat at a stately ninety degrees to the rest of the town. A trading post packed full of manufactured goods from points east sat a few yards from the street on the east side. Flint Carlson and his wife Hazel Kent Carlson were the senior residents of Bradford and kept the post full of salt and pepper, matches, several different elixirs, and assorted clothes and fabrics.

Chick Miller's Saloon sat like an old stone bear on the distant north edge of town. The Bradford Bank, run by William Huddleston, sat off by itself at least fifty yards from all the other buildings on the west side. Fastidious in a glaring whitewash with gleaming windows, the structure boasted dual safes: a Hall & Company square black safe and another heavy brass Yale safe.

The most beautiful building in the town was the Bradford Congregational Church sitting on a flat piece of grassy acreage maintained by Pastor Edgar Thurston. The mayor's wife, Addie Watley, gave assistance with sweeping, cleaning, planting, and such from time to time. South of the church stood the gray painted Bradford Stables and corrals run by Thomas Wood, partner to and friend of his immediate neighbor Newton Cutter, blacksmith. Situated in between the blacksmith shop, Town Hall and the hotel was a lush, grassy lawn area with benches and stone walking paths winding around a centerpiece of a huge old cottonwood tree that towered over the area.

Dawn White, the town seamstress kept her small dressmaking business building tidy with its lace curtains, flower boxes, and porch benches. This side of the plaza was quiet and this widow of ten years operated a successful business with sewing, mending, and tailoring. Shirts and dresses were her specialty, but her true calling was custom handmade gowns and ladies' clothes. About thirty yards to the east was the offices of Merle Doyle, Attorney at Law, which enjoyed a vantage point across from the rowdy Chick Miller Saloon. Several other abandoned buildings stood in various states of disrepair and decay to the east. The boom and bust of economies saw buildings sprout up in weeks only to be abandoned behind when fortune left town.

Beyond the west edge of town was a dried lakebed that coursed right up to the rolling hills. Several clusters of round boulders were strewn where a flood of water had pushed them. The rocks had become home to a noisy roosting of big black crows. Scrub brush sage and cacti dotted the hard ground and tiny insects and lizards darted in and out of shade.

A man riding out of town in any direction for eighty miles would find seven ranches with good grazing and plenty of free flowing water for their horses and cattle. To the northeast, the Pacific Coast range had virgin timber tracks for hundreds of acres and the snow melt fed the streams and rivers. Twenty miles up over the Flint Hills was a granite quarry along with a few abandoned gold and silver claims. To the east thirty five miles was Williams Creek and the Faraway Inn. To the southeast was the broad mesa of Table Bluff with its little community of Beatrice. The richness of the land and the industrious fortitude of its people was magnets for the scum and villainy of the west.

It was a colder, crisp morning. A slight mist hovered above the ground. Newton Cutter could see water droplets falling from the leaves of the old cottonwood to the side of the shop. This quiet, this peace made a sort of serenity not found any other time of day. He stood there in the quiet looking out over the land, taking in the glistening blades of grass, wildflowers drenched in moisture and the soft blue sky streaked with pinks and gold. The steam off the mug of coffee drifted and disappeared into the warming air. A gentle smile came upon his lips and he took in a deep breath of the cool air. The damp, musty perfume of the earth, animals, leather, and iron swirled about him as he opened the heavy wooden doors to the blacksmith shop.

Cutter laid his hand alongside the old forge finding it warm. He grubbed through the wood box and found the dried moss and rough tree bark. Tearing them in his strong hands, he tossed them into the forge and watched as the tendrils curled, bursting into flame. Shoving in several larger chunks, he shut the forge door and listened to the groan of the metal as heat started to build.

He had worked out most of the details in the night. Lying in bed he had made the decision, come to an understanding within himself that this was the right thing to do. This would be a welcomed change to his life and bring happiness into his future. He had determination and willpower and all he had to do was find a little help.

It was a quick walk across the green and the smell of cooking food engulfed him as he opened the door to the Hotel Bradford lobby. He could see a taller thin man with an older woman on his arm walking into the restaurant. Cutter stood in the doorway a moment as he looked about the room. Thomas Wood waved and grinned as he started to take a sip of coffee. Cutter reached to shake his friend's hand then seated himself across from him.

White tablecloths covered heavy carved wooden dining tables surrounded by tall wooden chairs with tufted seats. The cream colored walls hosted a display of paintings and photographs from this part of the country. Luxurious gold silk drapes were restrained open with ornate brass rods. The shining mahogany floors crossed the lobby, the dining room and onto the office. Over breakfast Cutter told Thomas Wood about his decision to build a house for himself, start a family and bring a much needed school to the town. Wood had become enthralled by the schoolroom idea and saw how it would benefit the community.

"Have you ever built a house before, Newton? It is a lot of work. And a lot of money," Wood said as he munched on a bite of bacon.

"I've got some money saved up in a bank up in San Francisco. When I was mining I tossed every cent I could into the bank knowing that I would invest it someday. I'll have to get an accounting of my money, but I am confident I have enough," Newton said as he took a bite of the savory home fried potatoes.

Wood was thoughtful for a moment, stirring his coffee. "Living here in the hotel for the past few years has made my life easier. From time to time, I am aware that I am giving my hard-earned money to someone and getting a roof over my head. You may be on to something, my friend."

"Myself, I would want a couple of acres outside town. Somewhere I could breed horses and raise good stock. It's what I know how to do and I am fond of them four-legged cusses, if I do say so myself," Wood said with a chuckle at Cutter.

A tall man in a white shirt and black jeans and boots walked into the dining room. Without looking around he seated himself facing away from the other diners. He took off his hat and placed it on the chair next to him and picked up his napkin. The young girl in a red gingham dress and white apron brought out a coffee pot and poured coffee. In a hushed voice, he gave her his order and she scurried away smiling into the kitchen area.

"Couple of strangers have come through town lately," Thomas was spreading jam onto his biscuit. "Lots of people stop and then continue on."

"Yep, there have been more wagon and carriage wheels getting repaired and most of them are from travelers, not the local folks. At least it makes business good," Newton nodded.

A movement caught Cutter's eye and he noticed the young serving girl carrying two full plates of food over to the lone man across the room. She returned and refilled his cup. She leaned a little closer and after listening, nodded with a smile, and hurried to the kitchen.

Wood saw Cutter watching the girl. "That's Miss Georgianna Caldwell. She is fourteen years old and niece to our own Tommy Boardman. Her mother and father are in Denver where they have their own business."

"Mr. Boardman never married and from what I hear, Georgianna is his favorite relative," Wood said as he turned to his left and gestured to the other side of the room.

"See those little pictures on the wall over there? That group of six framed pictures? Miss Georgianna is the artist," Wood raised his eyebrows and took a sip of coffee.

"How do you know all this stuff about her? You a nosy-nellie?" Cutter sliced the ham with a mocked disbelieving look on his face.

"Oh, you'd be surprised at the things I nose around about," Wood tapped the side of his nose and winked at Cutter who chuckled.

Again Cutter's eyes drifted to the man across the restaurant. The disturbing sense of knowing him from somewhere stole across Cutter again. He shook his head with a grimace and ate the last bite of his breakfast. The blacksmith stood up and reached into his pocket to get out his money. Miss Georgianna Caldwell had light brown eyes and tawny brown hair in a long braid. She started to object when she looked at the coins in her hand but he stopped her, with a wink. She blushed a fine rosy hue and stole a glance at Wood, then hurried to the kitchen.

The blacksmith and the stable master walked from the dining room, but not before Royal Benning, the lone man with the dark eyes and the hard mouth sized them up.

The doors to the blacksmith shop were open. Clay Dunagan had loaded in blocks of wood for the forge.

"Mornin' Clay," Newton said with a grin and reached for Dunagan's leather glove.

"Howdy, Boss," Dunagan set down a thick ring of iron and straightened up, gripping Cutter's hand.

"What is that you're workin' on there?" Newton leaned a bit to look at the black iron.

"That there is gonna' be a fancy candle holder called a can-dell-dabra or somethin' like that. Mrs. Watley described to me a circle made of five small rings with upright posts of different heights for candles." Dunagan stood with a small frown on his face.

"I can almost see it in my head, but I'm not sure if it is what she has in her head," Clay said, raised his eyebrow and nodded. The older cowboy had the tanned leathery skin of most range riders. He had dirty brown blondish curly hair, mustache, and goatee. His gray eyes were clear and he had that deceptive muscle strength found in smaller men. At fifty-five, Dunagan had proven himself to be an exceptionally talented man who enjoyed working part time in the blacksmith shop for Newton Cutter. His specialty was custom iron fittings and the occasional sculptured doo dad.

"For her house? Sounds big," Newton said as he walked over to the forge and put in a few more sticks.

"No, no, it's for the church. I had some bar stock left over from those grills I made last month and so I am gonna put it together and see what it comes out like. I've never made one so it might come out lookin' like a pile of metal, but I'm gonna try it."

Cutter's father had been a successful ironworker in North Carolina. Newton had learned the trade and gone on to the shipyards outside Boston. Now at thirty years old he had come to own a blacksmith business in a good town. He was a tall young man, at six foot four, heavy in the chest with black curly hair and blue eyes that crinkled up when he laughed. He wore a thick black mustache. From his years of swinging hammers and wrestling iron he had built up strong corded muscular arms. His slim waist went down into thick muscular legs and he walked with a spring in his step.

Cutter stood a moment rubbing his hands together thinking over his decision from the night. He was quiet and Dunagan turned to look at him a little closer.

"What's on yer mind, Boss?"

After a moment, Cutter leaned up against the workbench and looked at Dunagan with a little amusement in his eyes.

"I've decided to build a house, find me a wife and start a family, Clay."

"Well, that is a big decision. You been thinkin' on this for a while, Newton?"

"Yes, I have and it's time for something more in my life," Newton said as he gazed out the double wooden doors to the town.

The town's only practicing lawyer, Merle Doyle came out of the hotel, looked around and waved to Cutter and then walked to his office.

"Where you thinkin' about building this house? Here in town or out in the country somewheres?"

"Well, I have a thought about how I want to do this. The town ain't got no school and children here got to ride at least twelve miles to get over to the Salmon Creek School. I want two rooms on the bottom floor of my house to be used as a school until Bradford builds its own school."

"Well, that sounds right nice of you, Newton. You thinking ahead to the future n' all."

"Later on today I'm goin' over to see Cole over at the bank and find out what land is available here close to town."

He would also have to write to the bank in San Francisco and get a figure on how much money he had there. The majority of the mining claim profits had been put into the new Wells Fargo Bank in San Francisco.

Dunagan wiped off his hands with a wet rag. "You said somethin' about getting a wife? You got anyone in mind?" Dunagan started to grin.

Newton felt himself grin and his face warm up. "No, no. I will have to look and see who is whom. Well, I mean, what young ladies are here, you know what I mean!" Newton chuckled.

"Hmm. That is a good question. Now let's see here, Jeremy Ladd's daughter is not married, but she is off in the east at some lady's school. Bruno Stenson's wife, Angela, has a younger sister, but she might be a bit older. Hmm," Dunagan mused as he looked up at the sky, rubbing his chin, and trying not to laugh.

"An' if I was twenty years younger I'd marry that Chiatane LaCosta over in Williams Creek faster than you could rope a calf," Dunagan said as he turned with a serious look on his face.

"I have a lot of affection for Chi, too. But the only thing is, I see her as a sister, not as my wife and the mother of my children. That an' Charlie Winchester takes up a lot of her time anyways," Cutter said as he put on the heavy leather apron and wrapped the ties about his waist knotting them.

Cutter then realized that Dunagan had gotten quiet.

"What about you, Clay? Ever think about marryin' and all that?"

Dunagan said, "Yes, sir, sure I did, when I was a younger man. There was a time when I was working hard, building up something. Getting' ready and prepared for a wife and then the kids we'd have. But it never happened. I have suffered too much bad luck in my life, I guess. Newton, I'm a simple man. A poor, broken down cowboy with no thriving ranch or land. I ain't got nuthin' to offer a woman and no woman in her right mind would look twice at me. An' ya know I could never love a woman who was outta her wits." Dunagan slapped his knee laughing.

The ironsmith picked up the small iron rings and turned them over in his hands. "You are a strong young man with a good head, Newton. You have got a good business here and a mind for thinkin' ahead. I would lay odds you'll do well."

"Woman wants a house where she can put up curtains and make quilts. Women like to plant flowers and make a house into a home. Well, all I have are my tools and a good horse, Newton. And that is all I wish for now." Dunagan made a wry smile and laid the rings into a circle on his workbench.

Dunagan returned to the piece of hot iron in the forge and turned it once and then let it rest. Six short pieces of stubby blackened metal lay on the workbench. One at a time, Dunagan heated them up and curled them around the point of the anvil.

Cutter nodded as he watched Dunagan move the rings around into a design.

"Well, there's no doubt. I got some work cut out for me. I figure it is gonna take the better part of a year to get that house up. I will have to find an architect, a builder, suppliers for the lumber, and stone and the list goes on, I'm sure. I've never built one before so this is all new to me," Cutter said as he picked up a hammer and a wooden carrying box.

"If you will let me, Newton, I'd like to make the front gates for your house. Carl has some nice rolled iron out at the ranch that I can get and I have always wanted to make a matching pair of gates. My present to your new house and sort of a thank you for letting the folks here use it as a school." Dunagan said as he leaned against the workbench and smiled at the young blacksmith.

"That's right nice of you, Clay. Thank you for offerin' that. Come to think of it, I will be needin' front and rear gates," Newton said.

"There must be a couple thousand things it takes to build a house and that's one of them!" Cutter winked at Dunagan. He then pushed the tool cart over to the new farm wagon that he was finishing up for Harley Long.

***

There was a rising bustle of activity in the small town. A slow ranch wagon turned the corner of the auction house and the driver stopped in front of the Town Hall. A man on an Appaloosa horse rode past the hotel and then turned in between the buildings disappearing. The small town showed signs of life in the cool morning air. Birds chirped and fluttered about in the big cottonwood that stood over the blacksmith shop. The horses in the corral blew and stomped, swishing their long tails at the flies.

Bert Goldman's saloon was said to be the oldest saloon in the area. It had started out as a tent alongside the tent of the trading post. A little outpost in between two other places to be, it had sprouted up where there was money to be had for drinkable whiskey. The main saloon was large and spacious with tables and chairs scattered over the smooth plank floor. Another tale told was how it had been a shipbuilder who hammered together in the shiplap style of rough-sawn ten inch wood planks with a grooved overlap for strength. The years had seen gunfire in the saloon and several slugs were still embedded in the front of the bar.

Goldman had taken one look at the rundown business, once he was sober, and the businessman in him was thunderstruck with the opportunity. He had run moonshine from the Carolinas to Texas and set up dozens of stills from the Montana territory to the gulf coast. Goldman had rolled into Bradford with his last five dollars in his pocket. Nancy Williams gave him a job as bartender and Goldman's six foot four size and quick eye kept the roar down and the riff raff out. Within six months they were married and the country saloon that Nancy's father had left her started expansion under Goldman's trained eye.

Now at forty years old, Goldman had become a fixture in this local area. They had built a large room to the rear of the saloon and set up a copper still into it along with wooden storage kegs. Goldman grew with a reputation for decent whiskey, selling the wooden casks as far away as Santa

Fe and San Francisco and gave plenty of hauling business to the freighters coming into Southern California. Before she died, Nancy had taught him to always have a pot of chili on the stove and keep the hospitality tradition of a long running card game.

***

Cutter, Wood, and Dunagan leaned against the wooden bar, chattering with Bert Goldman about Cutter's new house.

"Nancy was always wantin' a bigger house, wanted more room. But we never did build one or buy another," Goldman said as he swirled his whiskey around in the little glass.

"Every time we got a little money ahead, we used it somewhere."

"Yep, I understand that. There's always boots to buy or a wheel to fix," Dunagan said with a nod.

"So have you decided what type of a house you want, Newton?" Goldman asked as he refilled their glasses with a light amber drink from a black jug behind the bar.

He popped the cork into it and set the heavy container down. Goldman grinned as he lifted the glass in a toast with the other men.

"To Newton's new house!" The men tossed back the drink then gasped for breath as they gripped the bar.

Wood tried to catch his breath as he said, "That's like drinking red hot silk!"

He picked up the empty glass and looked at it. "What is that?"

Cutter began to slap Dunagan's back hard to get the man to breathe again.

"Old shiner in Tennessee taught me how to run fresh shine into a keg. Used to burn up to half a ton of apple wood with a touch of sage to make the charcoal. He put a bucket of it into every keg. Up in Lake County there is an apple orchard and I go up there in winter and bring home a wagon load," Goldman said with a smile.

"I have Cushman bring in a couple bales of sage from the Arizona desert when he gets over there. Those two burnt up into charcoal is what gives it all that smooth, silk feel."

"Apple and sage, who'd a thought?" Dunagan chuckled as he tried to lick the inside of the little glass. Cutter downed another shot glass and gripped the bar, his eyes watering. After a moment, a small yelp came from his mouth as he stomped his right boot into the wood plank floor.

"I know a couple of crusty old timers up in the mines who could use this to blast with!" Cutter took a couple of deep breaths and shook his head hard.

9

"So what about yer house there, Mr. Cutter. Ranch style, bungalow, lean-to?" Goldman said with a chuckle. "Give us the details, boy!"

"Two stories, bricks all around, and a gate. I have gotten that far. Oh, and two fireplaces upstairs and one downstairs. Big kitchen, I suppose," Cutter said, looking thoughtful as he leaned against the bar.

"What kinda schemin' and connivin' is goin' on this here establishment?" Mayor Watley ushered himself in the door and up to the bar, putting his hat down. Without a word, a shining small glass of amber liquid appeared before him, making him smile in surprise.

"Don't mind if I do, Sir!"

The three men stopped laughing, stood with mouths agape and watched the Mayor.

Dunagan started to take a step closer thinking that he might come to the aid of the town official in case he should fall to the floor. The Mayor tossed back the shot. His eyes went wide as his face flushed, grabbed his chest, and his flat palm pounded on the bar three times.

"Are you gonna build close into town or out in the country somewhere?" Goldman said as he refilled the Mayor's glass and leaned on the bar.

Cutter nodded and said, "Here in town. My business is here and I don't want to be ridin' ten miles and then sweat over a hot forge all day. I have to get over to the bank and talk to Huddleston about any land that is available close to town," Cutter explained as he looked at Dunagan.

"How long did it take to build your house, Clay? Clay? Pay attention, boy!"

Dunagan had only sipped half the drink but was making those held in sneeze sounds like he was on the verge of exploding.

"My Dad started building our house right after I was born. He dug out the basement and put a big storm cellar in there. He was from Missouri where they had tornadoes and he was sure someday a twister would come along and he was gonna be ready. Then it took him and some other men almost a whole year to build up that house. Between running the hotel and working on building a house for my mother, that man wore down."

Dunagan was remembering the day that his father loaded up a small wagon and pulled out to return to St. Louis.

When Dunagan turned sixteen, Mr. Dunagan decided to sell the Bradford Hotel and asked his son if he wanted to take over and run it. Dunagan did not, so Mr. Dunagan sold it to Tommy Boardman and Dunagan senior relocated to St Louis, Missouri. Dunagan then lived alone in the huge twelve room house that had been his mother's pride and joy.

"Yours ought to get up faster than that, I'd think," Dunagan said with a nod and slid his glass down the bar to Goldman for a refill.

Another voice joined the mix. "I can hear you people all the way over inside the trading post. What the tarnation is going on in here?" Tommy Boardman walked in wearing a dapper silk vest over a crisp white shirt and brilliant peacock blue bolero tie. Nobody said a word but pointed to Goldman, who had already poured a shot glass for the newcomer.

Boardman thought it odd that they were all staring at him, but he was not one to pass up a shot of free whiskey. Especially the custom smooth delicious elixir that came from the mysterious depths of Goldman's bar. The whiskey went down and Boardman's head twitched to the left, his right eye shut, and a toothy grimace was stuck on his mouth. His fingers splayed out and his knees began to buckle. It started like a kitten's mew but after a moment, a gut-wrenching half-sob half-moan screech came from the hotelier and he could finally breathe again. Wood had to sit as he laughed so hard his legs could not hold him upright.

Cutter, Wood, Mayor Watley and now Tommy Boardman stood around the big wooden bar. Cutter was trying to draw out what he wanted in a house on a big piece of paper and the other men offered their two penny's worth. With every drink, the house got bigger, until it was one hundred feet long by one hundred feet wide. They were all laughing so hard, they had tears in their eyes.

"Oh look! You forgot a sewing room!" Mayor William Watley took out his handkerchief and dabbed at his eyes. A heavier man, he shook when he laughed.

The unmistakable sound of a shell being chambered into a rifle filled the room, silencing them and they turned to look at Bruno Stenson who held a big Winchester.

"And how could you forget a gun room!" Mr. Mayor grabbed the bar to keep from falling down, he was laughing so hard.

People peered in through the door to see the source of the laughter.

Cutter and Wood hung on to each other as the fateful glass made it way over to Bruno Stenson. "Oh no! You fellas ain't getting' me to drink fire. What'dya think I clean my guns with?!" Everyone roared with laughter.

Goldman poured another round.

Boardman leaned his chin on his hand that rested on the bar. He couldn't get his blue eyes to focus right.

"So what're you gonna do with them school rooms once the kids are gone, Newton?" Boardman rubbed his eyes and the other men still swam around.

"I don't know. I was figurin' they'd be filled up with my kids," Cutter said then took a sip as he winked at Goldman, who chuckled.

"Kids?! You ain't even gotta whiff," Boardman slurred as he could not get his tongue and mouth to work right. On top of that, the room started to spin and he hung onto the bar with both hands.

The Mayor's coat was gone, his shirt half unbuttoned and hanging out.

Cutter slapped Mayor Watley's back and exclaimed, "Better find me a whiff!"

Folks came in the door holding out tin cans, coffee mugs, globes off lamps, and anything that would hold an ounce. The word of free whiskey spread like wildfire and it was rumored that folks were coming up out of their graves to grab a sip. Outside on the boardwalk, more than one member of the female persuasion could not stand the curiosity and whooped and hollered at the taste.

The men laughed so hard, they didn't notice Boardman collapse onto the floor, passed out. Goldman noticed that Boardman was gone and walked around the end of the bar, peering down at the too-much-fun man.

"How 'bout a spare room for all yer friends who drink and can't walk?!" Another roar of laughter assailed the walls of the saloon.

A blood curdling scream for help pierced the noise along with a wagon rumbling by. Everyone's eyes went wide and the men dropped their drinks and raced outside. Stenson made it out of the saloon and raced down to the wagon. The driver pulled up in front of Doc Baines place and Riley Stephens leapt down to the street.

Doc threw open the door and came out to the wagon.

"I found him, layin' in the yard of the house. He's not breathin' too good, and he's been shot," Stephens said in a high-pitched voice full of emotion.

Doc stopped Stephens and looked at his wounds, trying to get the bloody man to hold still. The younger man bled from a vicious gash on his forehead. Overwhelmed, his tears flowed down over his cheeks and chin.

"Leave me be, take care of Mr. Long," Stephens cried out and tried to lift off the tailgate, but it fell.

Cutter braced his hands on the gate and lifted it, letting it drop to the side. With one smooth motion, the blacksmith leaped up into the wagon.

"He's unconscious. You want him inside, Doc?" The older man lying in the wagon, was coated in dirt, disheveled, and motionless.

"Bring him in, boys, and be gentle. I don't know what all's wrong with him." Doc led the way into the building and soon many lanterns and candles blazed from inside.

Both horses were down and Wood struggled to release them from the harness.

"Bert, I need your knife!" Goldman ran out and helped Wood cut the harness loose and rolled the wagon out of the way. It was twenty-six miles from the Long Ranch to Bradford and Stephens ran the team at a blistering gallop the entire distance with the hope of saving Harley Long. It would take all of Wood's equine knowledge and skill to keep these horses alive.

Stephens sat in a chair to the side and held a cloth up to the gash on his forehead and tried to explain what happened. Goldman brought over a bottle and after two drinks the ranch hand could finally tell them what happened.

Doc cut off Harley's blood-soaked shirt and there was an ugly bullet hole in his lower left side.

Doc cleaned the wound and probed the tissue. "It went all the way through so that's good. He's got a couple broken ribs, his nose is broken and he's missing a couple nails off his left hand," Doc said in a lowered voice.

Then he lifted one eyelid and frowned. "He's taken a couple good whacks on his head. That would be a concussion." The doctor grimaced.

"I was out to the hills, bringing in about twenty head of horses. When I got close enough I saw there were horses tied to the rail at the house. I didn't think anything of it until I got up to the corral and there were men there with guns on me," Stephens' voice trembled and broke. He took another sip of the bitter whiskey, his eyes on the floor.

"I woke up in the barn tied up. I still had my knife so I cut myself loose and ran for the house. I yelled for him, but there was no answer." Stephens bent over gripping his chest and when he straightened up, his eyes were watery.

"They'd tried to bury him, dumped dirt over him, and dragged some branches and stuff over him to hide him. The dog found him and set up barking so bad that I thought they were comin' back. He was still alive and they tried to bury him!"

Great sobs shook the young man and he doubled over. Goldman gripped his shoulder and helped him sit up to take another sip of whiskey.

"Harley is in pretty bad shape. He can't be moved with them broken ribs. There's a danger that one if 'em will puncture a lung and then there'll be nothing I could do," said the doctor.

Goldman watched the young cowhand. "Have you ever seen 'em before? They might have came out to buy cattle or horses?"

Stephens shook his head.

"I got a good look at two of 'em. But there were at least five others. I heard 'em shout to take the horses in the corral and then everything went black." Stephens grimaced.

"Riley, lie up here on the table for me. I need to get some stitches into that forehead of yours," Doc's voice commanded. The young man's nose had an ugly break and both hands were a red, bloody raw mess.

"Looks like you put up a mean fight there, Mr. Stephens," Doc said as he probed.

Stenson sat down beside his old friend, Harley Long with a grave expression.

"Newton, you'll want to go get Miss Dawn. Harley is her uncle and he just might need family right now," Doc said as he nodded towards the door.

When Cutter got outside, he saw the blood bay horse was still down and Wood wiped him down with a damp cloth. The bigger appaloosa stallion stood shaking and drinking water on wobbly legs.

Cutter broke into a run and ran over to the dressmaking shop. He burst in, scaring the daylights out of Dawn, and caused her to stab her own finger. Out of breath, he told her that Harley had been injured and that he was over at Doc's. She flew past Cutter with a high pitched scream and he had a hard time catching up to her.

Cutter stopped at the horses in the street and knelt alongside Wood. This past spring Cutter had put a new set of shoes on this young animal.

"Newton, can you take the Appie one over to the stables and get him bedded down. You'll have to make sure he has plenty of water and hay. If you would give him a double portion of grain, too, please," Wood stroked the head of the other big stallion still down on the ground.

"Sure, of course. Is he gonna make it?" Cutter knelt and patted the thick muscular neck. The horse was burning up yet shivering.

Wood asked, "And can you bring me a big blanket from the tack room?"

Cutter stood up and went to the Appaloosa. He stroked the big horse for a few minutes and whispered some words, then clucked to the horse to follow. Wood watched them walk off into the distance and then his eyes went to the bay on the ground.

The afternoon sun had gone down and the evening twilight was turning all the colors gray and purple. Lights here and there were showing up in windows and a few townspeople started to gather next to the doc's office. The quiet little town had been shaken by the trouble that had come riding in.

***

"How much longer?" Luke Iverson sat on the buckskin smoking, looking out at the rolling hills and trees in the distance. A rangy, young man in patched black chaps, a faded and mended gray shirt with a fawn colored hat. He had begun rustling cattle as a teenager looking for more money for his pockets. Iverson had been caught in the Oklahoma Indian territory but shot his way out and ran west long and hard. In Texas, he along with several no-account friends brought two hundred head of unbranded Mexican cattle across the border and put his father's brand on them under cover of night.

At twenty one, he was loafing in Kansas City, met another man who traveled with him to the New Mexico Territory where they stole a small herd of cattle by picking them off from a cattle drive. The other man got caught sleeping next to the fire. Iverson had slept up in the safety of a draw and made a retreat at the sight of trouble. Iverson was on his way to Denver when he stopped in Santa Fe and over a drink in a saloon found out that Angus Tolliver, who was looking for hungry men who were good with guns.

Four Southern California wealthy cattle ranches had been lined up and there was talk of retiring to San Francisco afterwards to live by the ocean. Iverson fell in with the boys. This sleepy horse ranch laid out before them was the first.

"We're waiting on the boys to get out the other side of the house." Royal Benning had knelt next to a boulder, the smoke from his cigarette a blue thread up into the air. Benning was ten years older than Iverson and a lifetime more intelligent. He was a tall, lean man with broad shoulders and dark straight hair cut short with ebony eyes. His mouth might smile but his eyes never did. It was a rough-hewn face with a two-day beard stubble. Benning showed a thoughtful face with a jutting chin to the world, but there was a small dark scar on his right cheekbone and a broken nose from long ago.

"Only the old man is there in the house. I saw the ranch hand ride out earlier this afternoon. Must be goin' after strays or something," Benning said as he squinted at Iverson.

"You watch for that ranch hand comin' in. We don't want no surprises," Benning's voice had irritation in it. He dropped the end of his cigarette and rubbed it out with the toe of his boot.

The afternoon heat waves danced in the distance. The hard packed ground around the old corral threw off a broad shimmering of warmth. There were some old hoof prints in the dried earth and a small stack of lumber half grown up with grass leaned up against a post. Buzzing insects darted in and out of the rocks and plants and cicadas were in their evening song. Bunches of fragrant wildflowers bobbed and waved in the grass.

Down through the boulders rode three men on horses and with a touch of the hat, they all started towards a big stone ranch house. Iverson tossed his smoke and trotted down towards the barn. Benning saw that they all carried rifles and had Colts strapped down. He wondered about all the fire power if there was only an elderly man in the house. One by one, they got down and walked towards the house.

Angus Tolliver had come through the Sierra Nevada and down into the Sacramento Valley leaving burned houses, dead bodies, and destruction behind him. A bitterly cold winter forced the outlaw to hole up in a snug shack on the outskirts of a prosperous mining town. Tolliver was skilled in separating miners from their gains and letting the bodies fall into snowy ravines where they would not be found until spring.

When the snow fell, everyone turned to drinking and gambling in the saloons, excepting the old timers with deep caves. Everything had gone well for the hustler until the town chose a young, strong miner to carry a badge and keep the peace. The sudden memory of Cutter's face shocked Tolliver and he knew at once that he was the man from that scrubby mining town.

Tolliver could not remember even the cause of what had started it. He had many blurry memories and brief slivers of color and sound streaked in front of his eyes as he tried to remember. He had landed a punch on the side of Cutter's head, knocking him down in a saloon. Using the butt handle of the Colt, he had beaten the young sheriff until he was a bloody heap on the wood plank floor of the saloon. Hands had pulled Tolliver off the unconscious Cutter and outraged miners tried to force him into the one jail cell. With quick knives and fast hands, Angus Tolliver slithered free. That night Tolliver saddled his dun and led two pack horses in darkness through snow, headed southwest. That was close to nine years ago and now here was the man that had sworn to put Tolliver in the ground.

Tolliver put down his coffee cup and sat gazing out over the swampy land. South Landing was down close to the shore of a vast lake. There was a low blue haze hanging over the low hills in the distance. Here was fresh air and a clear vision for miles around. Tolliver had returned to this old house many times in his travels to either heal from a wound or hide out from those who hunted trouble. The old man had built a still all the way out there and had set aside a few kegs of whiskey out on the rickety porch. It was cold and rusting now and Tolliver had other interests.

There were three more ranches in his scheme and after that he could stroll into San Francisco fat and happy. The main room at South Landing was long with high ceiling framed in thick, rough beams. A river rock fireplace radiated warmth, crackling as embers floated higher. Tolliver leaned against the wooden counter in the kitchen and stared to the furniture and fire. Scuffed work boots, a faded green shirt and denim pants he looked more like a ranch hand than a gang's fearless leader. Two years ago he had run off the old man that had lived here alone, forcing him out at gunpoint with whatever he could throw into the old buckboard. Tolliver chuckled at the memory of terror in the watery eyes of the elderly, hunched man.

He cooked for himself and for whoever else had rolled in. Breakfast was fried potatoes, bacon, and beans along with cornbread and coffee. Once in a while he brought in a couple cuts of beef or a ham if he was in town. He buttered the cornbread and watched the curl of steam rise off the coffee. A soiled gray towel was slung over his shoulder. For all the fancy dinners in New York and Chicago, he still preferred simple fare.

He could hear the pounding of a horse's hooves coming up the gravelly dirt road. Picking up the shotgun, Tolliver stood next to the door out of sight. Two strong loud whistles told him it was Benning. Easing his head around the window, he relaxed and walked to the fireplace and put the gun down. Royal Benning came to a halt in a whirl of dust and flying rocks.

"Howdy, Boss," Benning said with that smirking glint in his eye as he swatted the dust off with his hat.

Benning had never liked Tolliver, and at first refused to fall in with him. Benning had made his living with his fists and his guns and he was aware of the stories left behind him. If he could make serious money, he would ride with rough, lawless men and then disappear into the night. There was still the lingering tale of his four gang members that rode out for Mexico but ended up in a Denver jail. Benning did not like people, plain and simple, but that did not keep him from using them for his own benefit.

"What sort of interesting stuff have you found out? Anything useful?" Tolliver rolled a smoke with slow care, looking down at his hands. He didn't see the sneer across Benning's mouth as he turned away to a chair.

"Not much, you have anything to eat? It's a long ride out here," Benning asked as he went over to the washstand and wiped down his face and neck.

Tolliver ladled a bit of the stew into a pan and put it onto the stove to heat. Slicing a couple generous portions of the cornbread, he quartered up an apple and set it with the cornbread.

"I've been thinking about a man I saw in Bradford the other day. Blacksmith. Big man with muscle." Tolliver said as he turned and filled up a second coffee cup for Benning.

"Who is he?" Benning asked as he dried off with an old, ripped towel, looking at Tolliver.

"I was up north by Sacramento. Little scrubby mining town called Bear Valley with a dozen saloons and gold-rich miners. I was makin' out so sweet. The stabbings and shootings and robbing were gettin' so violent people were gettin' edgy. They elected that Newton Cutter to the Sheriff's office and he put on a badge and started knockin' heads together.

"I kept outta his way and out of his sights. Kept my head down and took my business to the far side of town where there was no trouble. Mining is a risky, dangerous business and when people go missin', well, folks just assume there was a mining accident." Tolliver 's voice had a cold glint in it as he talked.

"Had me a sucker with five ounces of gold on him. Caught him comin' outta saloon drunk and walked him into the alley and ready to lift those sacks when Cutter came down the other end. The old codger starts yellin' and Cutter came runnin'," Tolliver said as he examined his fingernails with a clenched jaw.

"What happened?"

"I got a couple of lucky punches in and he was down. I didn't wait for him to get up. That night, I saddled up and took my pack horses outta there," Tolliver drummed his fingers on the table watching Benning eat.

"I need to keep shy of that man. I don't need him causing any trouble about me. We are close to getting all this done and moving on out of this area."

Benning shoved his chair to the side and lifted his plate taking it over to the wash tub. After it was rinsed and stacked he turned around.

"He ain't no law man no more. You ain't got nothin' to worry about here, Tolliver," Benning said as he moved to the door. With a wave of his hand, he stepped out to the porch. The brow furrowed about this information. So Tolliver had been lifting gold off hard-working miners up in gold country. Tolliver wasn't the sort to drink it up or spend it on women. A dollar said he had it stashed somewhere.

Royal Benning looked at the damp shore with its lilies and cattails waving in the breeze. Something was getting his hackles up and after he rolled a smoke, he sat down at the table on the porch and began cleaning his guns.

# 2 CHAPTER TWO

Dawn White's eyes kept tearing up and her vision was blurry. Her hand was shaking and she had tried to write down her message but tear drops splattered onto the paper. A bleary-eyed Tommy Boardman took the pen and wrote out a quick message. He pushed it back to Dawn.

*'Brother Harley Long injured. Ranch robbed. Please come now.'*

Boardman patted her hand as she nodded. A white handkerchief dabbed at fresh tears and she nodded with a weak smile to Boardman as he turned away to run over to the telegraph at the hotel. Exhausted with emotional grief from the bedside of her older brother, Dawn trembled. He was breathing roughly in his sleep, grimaced in agony when he woke with nonsensical words from the laudanum. Doc Baines could only shake his head and squeeze her hand.

Her first husband had become deathly ill in the Pacific Northwest and succumbed to a lung infection after a horrific broken leg. A miner by trade Charles Milton Biggelo had brought in a profitable gold mine and at his death left Dawn a wealthy woman.

Dawn Long Biggelo met Graham White in a Seattle hotel. He was a timberman and a logger who had succeeded in felling and selling large tracts of timber across the Pacific Northwest. Unknown to Dawn, Graham White had actually met Charles Milton Biggelo and they had discussed the timber rights on the gold mine claim being sold to White.

Biggelo's attorney recommended she sell so Dawn sold the mine and claim to a gold consortium and White negotiated the timber contract, winning millions of feet of timber.

Dawn made plans to travel to southern California to be nearer her older brother Harley Long. She could no longer suffer the place that had brought grief to her and after fourteen days, three wagons took her entire life south.

Graham White never forgot the stout, full bodied woman with grayish hazel eyes and glossy wavy long brown hair she wore up around her head. After a year, he came looking for that reddish pink complexion and the quick smile of white teeth. They married and moved around wherever the timber fell.

Dawn White arrived in Three Corners on a bright, sunny May afternoon to join husband Graham White, who was felling aspen and lodgepole pine for a building project. White was a businessman about using every foot of the trees he took down. He had set up a complex sawmill and his bride cooked for the loggers and mill workers. Happy with life, she started a local library for the children of the workers and had a story hour twice a week.

It was during one story hour that a grimy man with a hat clenched in his bloody hands came to the door with a stricken look on his face. Graham White was killed by a swinging snag of a felled pine tree. At forty three years old, her husband left her the wealthiest woman on the west coast and alone.

The door to the seamstress shop opened and a head peeked in. Addie Watley brought in a woven wood basket with soup, cornbread, and fresh fruit.

"I was over to see him. There's no change, my dear," Addie said as she herded Dawn to the chair and put a spoon in her hand.

Dawn stared at the soup and her eyes squinted with her lips pressed together.

"Has Riley Stephens been able to describe the men that did this to my brother? Has anyone been able to figure out who tried to kill him?" Her voice was shrill and fresh tears welled up in her eyes. After a moment, she took a sip of the warm soup and a bite of the bread.

"Riley doesn't know who they were. He described one man as a blonde man with black chaps on an appaloosa. He said there were several men that had gone into the house and a couple of men had taken the horses," Addie encouraged Dawn to eat some more soup and sat down across from the pretty woman. The soup spoon was shaking.

"Riley is trying to determine exactly what was taken from the ranch. He is still pretty banged up, but no one could keep him from returning out to the ranch. There are some cattle there that were over across the river in a secluded valley. I don't know much else. Without a sheriff in this town, I don't know what can be done, I don't know who can help us," Addie rubbed her eyes and fussed with her knitted shawl.

Dawn looked up from her spoon. In a low voice, she said, "I've sent a telegram to my brother, Jackson, in San Francisco asking him to come. He is a strong man, a businessman and will handle the ranch until Harley recovers. I'm sure he'll bring Carmella, his daughter with him to help take care of Harley. She is a smart girl and very capable so I'm sure that he will be in good hands," Dawn sat in her chair and slender fingers rubbed her forehead.

"Dawn, go lay down. Get some rest. I'll wait here if you'd like so you won't be alone. I'll walk over with you when you are ready," Addie said with a strained look. "You're no good to him if you are exhausted, honey."

"You're right. I do need some sleep. Addie, thank you for bringing me some nourishment. I've been in a daze these last hours," Dawn said and wiped her mouth. She stood and wrung her hands.

"I'll lock the door behind you and then get myself into bed," She said with a weak smile.

Addie gave her a hug and then pulled her shawl around her as she stepped out into the late afternoon sun. Addie rubbed her hands together until she heard the lock slide shut. One by one the shades were pulled down and draperies slid across the windows. Addie admitted to herself that she could never understand the grief that had cursed Dawn White's life.

Riley Stephens walked a buckboard into town to pick up supplies and to check on Harley Long. After sitting over at Doc Baines with Dawn White, Stephens knew there was nothing he could do now for the injured man. Only time would be needed to help Harley now. Flint Carlson at the trading post gave over an extra can of coffee and a pound of sugar, thinking that every little bit of help was needed.

Stephens pulled the team over next to the blacksmith shop and watered the horses at the trough. He dropped a leaf of hay into the feed trough and secured the tarp over the supplies. His ribs were sore still from the robbery. His knee felt like something was loose inside it. The throbbing headache had never let up. Stephens opened the stable door, stepped inside, and closed the door behind himself. The cool darkness of the tack room was welcoming and the minute he hit the cot he was asleep.

Goldman leaned on the bar murmuring with Mayor Watley. Both of them were nursing a shot glass and shaking their heads. There were three local ranch hands torturing each other with a lazy card game over in the corner. Dunagan sat relaxed at a table drinking with Mac Kelly arguing over the finer points of iron working.

Outside in the dimness, three riders were getting down off their horses at the rail. Luke Iverson, Thornton Glass and Sammy Ramirez stepped to the bar and ordered a bottle of whiskey. Goldman lifted a clear tall bottle off the rear shelves and set it along with three glasses in front of the men.

"Three dollars, gentlemen," Bert said as he looked them over with both hands flat on the bar.

"Three? Why... we can get the same bottle down at that other saloon for a buck," Iverson's mouth was hanging open.

"I have to charge you for breakage," Bert said with a grim smile on his face and now one fist was clenched.

"Breakage? We ain't broke nuthin', mister," Thornton Glass said and held up a hand quieting down the younger man and tossed down three dollars. He picked up the bottle and poured three drinks. Goldman shoved the coins into his vest pocket and walked down to the end of the bar and started a fresh pot of coffee.

Mayor Watley turned to look over the men at the bar. "You gentlemen lookin' for part-time work or a real job?"

"We're lookin' to have a drink or two before movin' on, mister," Glass said as he turned the small glass in his hand examining it.

Watley realized then that this bigger, older man wore dual Colts strapped down. The younger blonde man wore a dark wood handled revolver, but the darker skinned man who hadn't spoken appeared to not be carrying any gun.

Half an hour later, the bottle on the bar was half empty and the three men sat unmindful and joking amongst themselves. Goldman went to the storeroom for something and Watley helped himself to a cup of hot coffee, with sugar. Watley had snatched up an old newspaper when Riley Stephens, a little better from his nap, stepped into the saloon.

Stephens smiled and nodded to Dunagan and took two steps before turning his eyes to the men standing at the bar and came to sudden halt.

"Hey, you're the snake-bellied bunch that jumped me out at the ranch!" Stephens glared at Luke Iverson. Eye contact was made with Clay Dunagan and Mack Kelly who stood up with their fists clenched. Goldman had walked into the main room when he heard Stephens' voice.

"Luke, stop!" the bigger heavy man had his grip on Luke's arm, but the hot-headed kid growled and tore loose, springing for Stephens. Clay Dunagan was a step ahead of him and crashed a right fist into Iverson's jaw, dropping him to the floor. Dunagan whirled around in time to catch a fist from the dark skinned man. The punch doubled him over. Goldman rushed behind the bar and eliminated the glasses and bottles from harm's way.

"Glass! Get 'em!" Luke was staggering to his feet when Thornton Glass drew a silver knife from inside his vest and lunged for Stephens. The ranch hand may have been stiff from sleep, but he was quick on his toes and sidestepped the flashing blade. Glass went past him and hit a table, kicking it to one side. There was an ugly sneer on the face of the big man as he swung around.

Sammy Ramirez gave out a shrill yelp and kicked into Dunagan's ribs. Dunagan slammed a fist into the side of Ramirez's knee throwing the man off balance. Ramirez groaned, limping a couple of steps. Wild black eyes found Dunagan. Ramirez' hands were grabbing claws raking at Dunagan's face with his lips like a snarling animal.

"Luke! Get Sammy outta here!" Glass yelled as he turned to swipe again at the ranch hand. A thundering shock filled the room from the Colt held by Goldman. Stephens had drawn a derringer and was bringing it up when he screamed, dropped the gun, and clenched his side. When the gun fired, Mac Kelly swung a wooden chair across Glass's shoulder, knocking the blade loose and Glass stumbled down to his knees.

Luke Iverson swung a mean right into Kelly's head, knocking him down. Luke jumped to Ramirez and got an arm around him, dragging him out of the saloon. Mac Kelly was down on the floor, groaning, holding his head. Cards went flying, coins hit the floor and all three ranch hands dove under the same table.

"Stop 'em! They tried to kill Harley!" Goldman was taking aim for another shot when Glass snarled something and stumbled out the door. Dunagan was trying to get Mac Kelly up off the floor and onto a chair. Watley was frozen in his tracks holding onto the ash axe handle with a white-fingered grip behind the bar. The sound of three racing horses passed the saloon and died off in the distance.

Goldman brought out a cold cloth for Kelly's head. "I heard one of 'em call that blonde one, 'Luke'."

"Yeah, that big man called 'em that. Luke. So now we got a name, at least. An' that dark Mexican-lookin 'man, the one that jumped Clay, they called him Sammy." Dunagan was holding his ribs with one hand, grimacing.

"Luke, Glass and Sammy is what I heard," Watley said as he released his death grip on the axe handle.

Goldman lifted the axe and put it behind the bar. The bartender poured a shot for everyone.

Stenson walked in the alley door carrying a shining Colt down low, looking around at the dull blue haze floating overhead.

"What's goin' on in here? Sounded like a gunshot."

"Riley recognized one of the men in here drinkin' as one of the holdup men from the ranch robbery," Goldman poured a cup of black steaming coffee for the gunsmith. Mac Kelly was gathering up the pieces of the broken chair. The three ranch hands had disappeared out the front door.

"One of 'em was lifting a gun, otherwise I never woulda' shot. Don't ever let it be said that I don't run an exciting joint here," Bert watched as Kelly laid a small Remington derringer onto the bar. Stenson pursed his lips and his eyebrows went up.

"Well, lookie here. People think derringers are for ladies' purses. Like a little toy gun. But don't count them short. These pack a load as deadly as your Colt there, Bert," Stenson picked up the small weapon and checked the cylinders.

"One shot gone, it was loaded," he said as he slammed the cylinder shut. He moved the gun first in his left hand, then in his right. "The handle is a bit worn here. The shooter was right handed."

"He did draw with his right. I saw it," Watley pointed at the little gun. "Bert, you'll want to lock up that gun, unloaded of course."

"I can dismantle it for ya, if ya want. Put it in my gun safe, nice and tight," Goldman said and then thought a minute. He handed the derringer to Stenson.

Stenson took another sip of the coffee, then held up the little gun and motioned to Watley. "You let me know when you need it. I'll unlock it for ya." He gave them more of a grimace than a smile. He left out the rear door.

"If that gang of outlaws is still around these parts, we should notify the local ranches," Watley said and looked thoughtful for a moment.

"Those hands in here, playing cards over at that table. Where'd they go?"

Dunagan spoke up, "They have to be saddling up at the stables. They came in earlier and Thomas put up their horses. They're local boys from Carl Johanson's ranch. Pay day, ya know."

"Mac, see if you can catch up with 'em. Make sure they tell Carl to keep a lookout for suspicious riders," Watley said with a frown. Kelly trotted out the door.

"We don't need no raging gang of outlaws tearing up the countryside."

The next morning Goldman swept out the bar and his broom hit an object stuck in a crevice between planks. A push of the broom sent a silvery, shining needle-like object skittering across the floor. It was an Arkansas toothpick.

*******

Dawn White stood wringing her hands. She paced back and forth in front of the Bradford Hotel. She craned her neck out looking up the dusty road trying to see the stage coming. The pretty dressmaker twisted a small handkerchief in her hands. She had sat with her broken and battered brother as he lay in the bed at the Doc's place. She wiped his brow, fluffed a pillow, and smoothed the quilt. There was nothing else she could do. The feeling of helplessness was crushing her.

Shortly after three o'clock the creaking black stage pulled up in a cloud of dust. Boardman pushed a small step into place and opened the door. Carmella Frisch stepped down and her green eyes saw Dawn up on the hotel steps. She hurried up the steps and the two women hugged. Jackson Frisch walked up the stairs and kissed his sister's cheek and squeezed her hand. The small party walked into the cool lobby. They chatted for a few minutes in the hotel lobby and then followed the porters up to their second floor rooms.

"Mr. Frisch, I would advise against moving him any time soon," Doc Baines said in a low voice as he leaned over Harley Long checking his bandages. He stood up and walked around the foot of the bed. The elderly man lay under an old patchwork quilt, laboring to breathe.

"He has several broken ribs and a severe concussion. He needs bed rest now with someone to attend him."

Carmella sat down on the side of his bed and took his rough, cracked hand in hers. His stained, gnarled fingers with broken nails were a bleak contrast to her soft, pink gentle hands. She saw the folded bandages on the side table, the white porcelain pitcher of water and matching bowl. The scent of alcohol drifted from a cloth hanging over the chair.

"With his age, he hasn't done too well. Before the robbery he got around okay, still rode his horses, but the heavy strength jobs were left to the ranch hands," Doc Baines took off his glasses and frowned slightly, rubbing his eyes.

"Sir, I must tell you. I am not optimistic on his recovery. Elderly patients with rib injuries often develop pneumonia and their health worsens. Please, I want you to prepare yourself for that possibility," Doc said. He made a couple of notes onto the papers at the table, checking the time.

The group stepped into the outer office.

"Doctor, do you think that he will not recover from this? Harley Long has always been a strong man and in good health," Jackson Frisch had a grim look on his face.

"I've been wrong before about the time it takes to heal from a serious wound. People sometimes have remarkable healing determination. But Harley suffers from broken bones, he was shot and whoever did this to him, tried to bury him alive. Sometimes the injuries are too great to overcome, Sir," Doc Baines took off his white doctoring coat and put his black frock jacket on.

"If you wish to bring in your own doctor or a specialist, please do so, with my most appreciative cooperation. Just make sure they hurry as time is wasting here."

Jackson Frisch stood there a moment fidgeting with his hat then looked at Carmella and Dawn. Born in Chicago into a well-to-do family, he studied building and architecture. He built his first hotel at twenty five and sold it at thirty. He was a tall, lean man close to six foot five in height and about one hundred ninety pounds. Frisch kept his white hair trimmed and combed back. He had medium brown eyes, a white mustache and eyebrows lending him that distinguished statesman appearance. Dressed in black slacks, white long sleeved shirt with cufflinks and a suit coat, he could not be mistaken for a local ranch hand, but more as a successful business owner or attorney. Carmella was his only child.

Dawn turned to Frisch. "Merle Doyle, an attorney here in Bradford has some papers for you to sign, Jackson. Power of attorney and such so you can keep the ranch running until Harley is up and around. I am not sure how Harley conducted the ranch business. You will need to speak with William Huddleston over at the bank that has an accounting of the ranch funds."

Dawn put her arm around Carmella and smiled, kissing her cheek. "I am so glad you have come. The weight of caring for him and not knowing what to do has been a heavy responsibility."

Frisch fussed with his cuffs. "Let me go over to Mr. Doyle's office. At least I can take care of keeping the ranch up and running. Will you stay here or go to the hotel?"

"Aunt Dawn, if you could show me what to do for him, I'd like to stay here with him for a while," Carmella said as her pretty green eyes smiled.

"Jackson, go ahead, if you would, please. I have been nervous about the ranch, not knowing what is going on out there. Riley Stephens is a good ranch hand, but I'm not sure if he has any business skills. I'll show Carmella what to do here for Harley," Dawn said with a little smile.

Jackson Frisch looked at Carmella. He did not know how long they would be there or if Carmella realized how big of a job was taking care of her uncle.

"I'd like to have dinner at six at the hotel. We'll talk more then," Dawn said and took in a deep breath and let it out. Frisch kissed Carmella and then Dawn.

"I'll see you both a little later." He closed the door behind himself.

Three strangers also arrived on the stage that day. Addie had just come out of Doc Baines' office and stood on the porch fussing with her gloves. She was anxious to see Dawn's young niece and her brother arrive from San Francisco. As she stood there, she saw first a tall man in a gray duster and black boots step down off of the stage and walked to the rear. After him came another tall man in a black duster with brown boots. The last passenger was a heavier man who wore a buckskin duster, gray mustache, short gray hair under a black broad-brimmed hat. The stagecoach driver tossed down three saddlebags to the men.

Without looking at anyone they walked a short distance past the Doc's office then turned at the town hall. Addie was prepared to bid them good afternoon, but the aloof men walked right on by not noticing her standing there. Addie walked to the end of the porch and peeked around to see where they went. The men walked straight to Bruno Stenson's shop where they closed the previously propped open door.

After purchasing three shotguns, the men walked down to Chick Miller's saloon where they drank a couple of beers and ate plates of food. Near sunset a man on horseback leading three other saddled horses stopped in front of Chick Miller's saloon.

Nobody recognized the man who led in the horses. Nobody remembered if the men said anything aside from ordering drinks and food. Miller did remember they paid in gold coin.

In the darkness, the three men went out, put their shotguns into the saddle sleeves, mounted up and rode out following the first man. Another man taking the air on the hotel porch remembered seeing the men turn their faces away as they trotted past going out of town.

***

Cutter and Wood were taking the last sips of coffee in the hotel restaurant. The little saucer in front of them had the remaining crumbs of the cake they had enjoyed. When the door opened, they looked up and found Addie Watley hurrying over to them.

"Newton, we've been talkin', William and me. Newton, I want to volunteer to teach until y'all get a regular proper teacher. I taught for fifteen years when we lived in Pennsylvania so I know I can do it," Addie said as she patted him on the shoulder, nodding her head, smiling.

"Well, that's wonderful Mrs. Watley, but it's not up to me to decide who the teacher is here. I'm putting up the building, is all," Cutter said and smiled his best to her.

"You are the most kind and generous lady, Ma'am. There is one thing you could do, that would be of great help, too."

"Oh, of course, Newton, what is it?" Addie dabbed her mouth with her handkerchief, her hazel eyes crinkled up in a smile.

"Would you be so kind as to make up a list of supplies they'll need? Like pencils and paper and such?" Newton took her hand in his with a light touch. He had always held a teacher in high regard and had respect and admiration for the fidgeting woman.

"Oh! Of course, I would be happy to. I believe I still have the names and addresses of some folks in Philadelphia and Boston who could send some help, too. I'll get letters out to them this week,' She said with enthusiasm. She squeezed his big hand.

"We want to help, too, Newton. It is a big job so you let us know what we can do for the children." Several townspeople had gathered around their table and were nodding.

Newton smiled at the group astonished at the generosity. "Well, right off the top of my head, I know the teacher is gonna need a nice big desk and the children will need a place to hang up their coats. You bring up the one thing I have given no thought on, and that is what the inside will look like," Cutter said as he wiped his mouth with the soft cloth. He stood to face the group.

"Can we all meet up at the town hall about 6:00pm tonight and work out a plan on what the inside of the classrooms will look like?" Wood slid in his chair and put the napkin over his plate. He reached and shook the hand of one of the store owners with a big smile.

"Now, let me get busy, I have a lot to do with settin' up lesson plans!"

She patted Newton again and bustled away, chattering with two other ladies. Wood and Cutter smiled at each other.

They were the only diners in the hotel dining room. Jackson Frisch sat drinking whiskey as they waited for dinner to be served. Carmella had changed and washed her face and brushed out her red, glossy hair. Still a young girl at twenty two, she possessed the negotiating savvy of a much older woman. Five foot five with the thick, lovely red hair belaying her Irish ancestry, her green eyes darted from her aunt to her father. The small gold circle earrings shined against her white skin.

"Doyle will send the power of attorney request to the court in Santa Fe. There should be no problem with its completion in about ten days," Frisch swirled the amber liquid around inside the small glass, his gaze focused on the liquid.

"I asked Doyle to accompany me out to the ranch on Saturday so I can get an idea of what should be done. I want to talk to the hand, Riley Stephens, to see if he can tell me about what happened," Frisch leaned forward, his arms on the table and his voice low. Dawn and Carmella both nodded, adjusting their cloth napkins.

"Dawn, how well do you know this banker, William Huddleston?"

Dawn looked at her brother and started to frown, then shook her head. "Not very well at all. I confess I don't use the bank here. I still have the majority of my money in San Francisco. I keep only a couple hundred dollars for necessities in the hotel safe with Tommy Boardman. Why do you ask?"

"When I talked to him today, he was hesitant to discuss any of Harley's financial affairs until I had the power of attorney in hand. Some people don't divulge particulars about money and I'm a complete stranger to him so it's understandable," Frisch drummed his fingers on the white tablecloth a few times. "I told him that once I had that document I would need a complete accounting of the ranch as soon as possible."

Dawn lowered her voice and leaned a bit closer over the table. "There is something about William Huddleston I do not like and I'll tell you right now. I do not trust him."

Jackson raised his eyebrows, waiting for her to continue.

"Uncle Harley told me something odd one day about that banker fellow. He thinks he is a big fish but doesn't know he is stuck in a small pond." Dawn was surprised to hear Jackson begin to chuckle, then laugh out loud.

Carmella grinned then hid her smile behind her hand. Dawn could see her trying to suppress a giggle.

The door to the hotel lobby opened and then closed. At the doorway to the dining room stood Newton Cutter and Thomas Wood grinning to each other as if there was a joke between them. Newton saw Dawn hold up her hand motioning them over to the table.

Dawn smiled at the blacksmith and stable master. "Jackson Frisch, may I present Bradford's own blacksmith, Newton Cutter and the man who owns and operates the stables, Thomas Wood." Frisch stood and shook the strong hands of Cutter and Wood.

"Gentlemen, allow me to introduce my daughter, Carmella," Jackson said as he smiled at his daughter. Carmella rose and reached her hand to Thomas Wood who bowed with a smile.

"Good evening, Miss." Wood's eyes crinkled up at the corners as felt her smaller hand in his.

Cutter caught and held her eyes as her hand slid into his. There was the faintest scent of flowers floating around her.

"My pleasure, Miss." She was aware that she was holding her breath and she brought up her eyes taking in the glossy black curly hair, the blue eyes, and the strong jaw. There was a fine, subtle sting running from her hand up through her arm and then washing through her with the speed of lightning. She wanted to stay right there.

"Jackson has come in from San Francisco to handle Harley's ranch until he is able. Carmella and I will share the nursing duties over at Doc Baines for a while," Dawn said with a tired smile.

"Welcome to Bradford. If there is anything we can do for you, please do stop by," Cutter said. He saw a commanding figure of a man in Jackson Frisch. Someone who gave orders and expected them to be obeyed.

"Actually, there is one thing you could help with, Mr. Wood. I'll need a horse while I'm here. Once I get out to the ranch, I'll send yours back."

Frisch paused and turned to look at Carmella with a smile. "Or maybe two back with me. Do you have any available?"

"Oh yes, Sir! Tomorrow morning, when you are ready, I'm happy to saddle for you," Wood winked at Carmella and she grinned.

Dawn smirked. Georgianna arrived with dinner and began serving.

"Enjoy your dinner, Sir, Miss. At your convenience. Be glad to help," Cutter smiled and winked to Dawn who grinned now. Cutter and Wood went over to the far side of the room and sat down for dinner.

"They seem like nice young men. Have they been here in Bradford long?" Frisch asked as he began slicing his steak.

"Six years now. Newton Cutter made a small fortune up in the gold fields outside Bear Valley. He's decided to build a house here close to town. Owns his own successful business, and he's single," Dawn said with a wink at Carmella who laughed.

Carmella twisted around to one side and could see the side of Cutter's head as he talked to Wood. She felt a twinge of excitement humming within her. She had seen men stare at her with an animalistic desire before, but not with this effect. Once more, she wanted to see his beautiful eyes, powerful strength of his figure, and the rich fullness of his mouth.

"Thomas Wood has an uncommon ability in handling horses. I'm sure he was joking one day when he told me that he listened to them and understood them," Dawn said with a grin and raised her eyebrows turning her head slightly, looking at her brother.

Jackson chuckled and took a bite of his steak.

Thomas Wood was looking at the newspaper and did not notice that Cutter had turned around grinning and had caught the eye of Carmella Frisch. He winked.

***

Later that night, the town quieted. Somewhere in the darkness a lone dog howled.

"Doctor Baines? Doctor Baines?" Carmella rapped hard on his bedroom door. After a minute, he opened it up in his nightshirt, rubbing his eyes.

"I can't hear him breathing, Doctor. Please come see to him!" Carmella turned away and hurried down the stairs.

Carmella had lit two more candles and a lantern threw a white light over the bed. Doc Baines listened to the sick man's chest. The gurgling breaths had stopped. Fingers lifted the eyelids and then felt Harley's neck for his pulse which was gone.

"I'm sorry, Miss. He's gone," Doc reached and sat in the wooden chair. He took off his glasses and rubbed his eyes.

Carmella had sat down on the side of the bed and held the old hand of her uncle.

After a moment, she said, "I'm glad he isn't suffering any more. I really don't like seeing anyone in pain and this was torturing him, I'm sure." Her jaw clenched as she struggled to control herself.

Doc Baines looked at Carmella seeing another aspect of the young woman. There was a compassionate, practical person before him and it appeared that not too much knocked her off the saddle.

"You have a good touch, Miss Frisch. If he had ever woken up, he would have been comforted knowing that it was you taking care of him," Doc said as he looked at the girl.

"I'll walk over and get Miss Dawn, if you don't mind stayin' here with him for a few minutes." Carmella dabbed her eyes and nodded.

***

The small church held vase after vase of flowers. The casket was a burnished wood shined into a glossy darkness. Newton Cutter and Thomas Wood sat near the back reflecting on the short time they had known Harley

Long. People filed in to take a seat and whispered to their neighbor.

Cutter looked up and realized that Georgianna Caldwell was handing something to him. He tried to smile at her but ended up squeezing her small hand as he took a small booklet from her. He handed one to Wood and then opened it up to read a bit about the life of Harley Long. On the back cover there was a Native American poem:

> *Do not stand at my bier and weep,*
> *I am not there. I do not sleep,*
> *I am a thousand winds that blow,*
> *I am the diamond glints on snow,*
> *I am the sunlight on ripened grain,*
> *I am the gentle autumn's rain.*
> *When you awaken in the morning's hush,*
> *I am the swift, uplifting rush of*
> *Quiet birds in circled flight.*
> *I am the soft stars that shine at night.*
> *Do not stand at my bier and cry.*
> *I am not there; I did not die.*

Years ago, he had stood beside another grave of another good man. Cutter had been able to bring in the vile men, the rough men and the cold eyed men and see them punished with the full force of the law. And yet, it brought him no solace until the wife of the slain man wrote a letter to Cutter thanking him for his dedication.

Wood urged Cutter to stand and the blacksmith realized that the service had concluded. People started to file out of the church. Cutter saw Frisch escort out Dawn White, completely in black and behind them walked Carmella, supported by Doc Baines. Cutter read the poem again while he waited for people to pass by, then tucking the booklet into his pocket, he stepped out of the church.

The pallbearers came out carrying the casket and slid it into the wagon. Harley would be buried out at his ranch, under an ancient cottonwood. A twist of fate, it would prove to be mere feet away from the location his murders had tried to bury him.

# 3 CHAPTER THREE

It was still dark when the blacksmith woke. To the east there were three stars still twinkling. Newton Cutter slid into his clothes and went down the stairs carrying his boots to the lobby. Closing the door with slow care behind him, he pulled his jacket a little tighter and shoved his hands deep into the pockets and went down the steps into the street.

The little town was quiet and still. Something scurried, running into the bushes between two buildings. The pungent aroma of earth and plants mixed with the familiar scent of horses, leather, and dust. He was used to the early morning stillness and as he walked across the plaza the dim outline of the stables and blacksmith shop came into view. Out to the west gentle rolling hills curved against the dawn sky.

His thoughts turned to Carmella. It was strange, somehow unusual for her to have turned to meet his eyes at the same time he caught them. He had only a few moments with her, yet inside him grew the realization that she was closer to what he had in mind as a life partner. Other women he had known had been in the hunt for other men and once Cutter figured out he didn't fit the bill, he simply moved on.

Cutter had been raised to be responsible, to have his accounts in order and build on a foundation that would provide for his and his family's future. It might have been it had taken him this long to grow up and leave his youthful fantasies behind. He could not deny that he felt a stronger sense to protect than he had years ago. Now he wanted a wife, a woman to protect and provide for and someone who would share the future with him.

There was a flicker of movement in the corral off to the right at the end of town. There were three horses standing in the corral, swishing their tails, one drinking from the water trough. A lone dog came up out of the brush, circled around the corral and trotted off disappearing behind the auction house. Cutter stood still a moment, listening. Shaking his head he started on towards the shop.

The funeral and burying yesterday of Harley Long had pushed the little town into a subdued, hushed behavior. Little conversation on the streets, the saloons deserted. No horses rode through. People stayed in their homes, shopkeepers closed up early and pulled down the blinds. The blacksmith shop would be the first to open up this day and he would be the first to return back to a normal business.

The big, heavy wooden door creaked with his pushing. The hinges protested then finally silenced as the second double door was swung back and was blocked open. The forge still held a dim reddish yellow glow and Cutter shoved sticks of wood into it, building up the fire. He dragged the work cart out and wiped down his tools. Outside, somewhere there was the sound of a horse walking. Newton stepped to the doorway and saw a horse and rider in the graying darkness passing the bank.

There was one less horse in the corral. Cutter opened the stable door and found the small cot in the tack room had its blanket folded at the foot. The cot was still warm.

***

Mayor William Watley stood at the hotel lobby desk waiting while Boardman worked the telegraph in the little office. Watley had sent telegrams to Santa Fe, Denver, Dallas, San Francisco, and Los Angeles seeking any information and assistance with this gang of outlaws. He reached into his vest pocket and lifted out the small round watch and grimaced as a sudden feeling of helplessness washed over him.

Watley had received a letter from the sheriff up in Denver confirming knowledge of outlaws called Luke Iverson, Thornton Glass and Sammy Ramirez. Iverson was considered to be a reckless hothead kid that would fall in with any gang that threw money his way. Thornton Glass was said to be a cold-blooded ruthless murderer who took a sickening pleasure in the pain of others. Sammy Ramirez was a half-Mexican half Apache that flew into animalistic rages resulting in the death of two men in Colorado.

Watley had notified the other five cities that these armed and dangerous men were now terrorizing Southern California and to send help. But no help was offered and none has come. The Mayor's stomach tied into a knot as he realized the town would have to take matters into its own hands.

The lobby door opened and Flint Carlson, Chick Miller and Merle Doyle walked in, taking off their hats.

"Mayor, any news?" Carlson owned the stacked log trading post to the east of Bradford.

"Sorry, men. Not yet. I'm sending out the last one to Los Angeles right now."

Newton Cutter, Clay Dunagan and Thomas Wood walked in through the door and stopped in the lobby looking at the group.

"What's the matter?"

Merle Doyle spoke, "The Mayor just sent out telegrams asking for information and help about these outlaws that have shown up around here."

Mayor Watley interrupted. "Gentlemen, shall we go sit to breakfast and

I'll fill you all in on what I know so far."

Dunagan, Carlson, and Wood shoved several tables together. Georgianna brought out cups and a coffee pot.

Mayor Watley leaned his arms on the table and in a low voice told the men what he knew. "The U.S. Marshal in Santa Fe was shot and killed two weeks ago. They don't have word yet on any appointment for the new Marshal. It looks like we are on our own here. The nearest court is in Denver."

Merle Doyle frowned and drummed his fingers on the tablecloth.

"Have you sent a telegram down to Austin to the Texas Rangers? Chances are, they have information we can use. Those rangers will ride to the ends of the earth to get their man. If any of them are here in California, they could give us a hand."

"That's a long shot, but worth it. I'll get a telegram out to Austin after breakfast."

"I notified Carl Johanson about the robbery at the Long Ranch. He's fought off rustlers, Indians, bears, and coyotes trying to hold onto his stock. All his hands are carrying guns and rifles anyway. For a big ranch, he knows every inch of it and his hands can tell you where every head is grazing," Clay Dunagan was stirring his black coffee.

"The Ladd Ranch hands that were in Goldman's the other night rode back and told Archie Ladd about the trouble. The only problem is that is a big drinkin' crowd up there. If that gang catches 'em late some night, nobody will be in any condition to fight back."

"We have to keep our eyes open for strangers coming in, too," Cutter told them about the cot in the stables tack room and the lone rider headed out of town early that morning.

Georgianna and Tommy Boardman brought out the plates of food. Sliced beef steak, home fried potatoes, and fluffy scrambled eggs as well as a platter full of cornbread. There was a basket of sweet rolls and tortillas. After Georgianna had refilled all their coffee cups she hurried back to the kitchen.

"Does anyone know what is going on with the Long Ranch? We're comin' up on the time of year Harley used to have his horses groomed and shoed. I was countin' on one hundred bales of that sweet clover hay from his bottom fields. I used to buy it from Harley every year," Thomas Wood took a bite of the tender steak and potatoes.

"Jackson Frisch requested power of attorney so he can run the ranch. Next time he comes into town, I'll ask him about the horses and the hay. I'm not sure how many head are still on the ranch, but I'd think he'd want them taken care of. Riley is still out there working so at least he can help out with things." Merle Doyle took a sip of his sweetened coffee.

"Gentlemen, think about stopping by my office sometime this week. To die and not have a will telling what you want to have done with your land, your cattle, well it causes pain to your loved ones. Please. I don't care if all you have is a coffee cup to your name, stop by my office so we can make sure the right person gets that coffee cup when you get put in the ground," Doyle took a bite of his breakfast and sat back eyeing his companions.

Other diners had come into the restaurant. Low conversations had started up. Wood had been watching Georgianna Caldwell go from table to table pouring coffee and taking breakfast orders.

"I've finished up the ranch wagon that Harley had me build for him. I was thinking I'll take it out there on Saturday. It's all paid for and they'll need it for work around the place," Cutter said as he looked at Doyle.

"You see any problem with me delivering it out there?"

"No, not at all. I'm sure that Riley can put it to good use. It will come in handy for the hay season at any rate," Doyle nodded. "How many of those wagons have you built, Newton? Every time I get by your place there's another one standing there."

"Thanks, I'll get it out there on Saturday as early as I can," Cutter said with a smile.

"I've built twenty two now. All of them are almost identical except for some specialty items like a tailgate and such. At least it makes it easy when they break 'em, I already know how to fix 'em."

Georgianna came by and poured more coffee. With one hand, she lifted a couple empty plates and smiled. Had she grown? Did she seem taller today? Cutter was astounded to find that he had looked at Georgianna not as a child now, but as a young girl becoming a young woman. Could that be why Thomas kept watching her. The blacksmith grinned and looked at Thomas who was glaring at him. Cutter laughed to himself and winked at Wood.

"Mr. Mayor," Tommy Boardman handed a piece of paper to Watley. He read for a moment and then handed it to Merle Doyle. "There is a five hundred dollar reward for Thornton Glass come out of Tucson. He's wanted for the murder of a rancher and his son over there," Mayor Watley stood up, pushing back his chair.

"I need to get a telegram off to the Texas Rangers. Let me get back to work on this. I've got to find us some help."

One by one the rest of the group stood up. Napkins and coins were dropped on the table and the last sips of the delicious coffee taken. Georgianna stood at the edge of the kitchen door holding a wide tray at her side watching the group. Thomas Wood caught her eye and winked as he turned to leave.

***

It was a few minutes past one o'clock in the afternoon on a bright, sunny day. There was little wind coming down through the wide, green valley. A flock of birds had landed in the grove of cottonwoods north of town and set to cackling. Two thin dogs padded down in front of the church, then disappeared behind the bank. For such a big man, Angus Tolliver scurried on his toes and he had a quick glance around as he left the telegraph office. Thirty seconds more and half a dozen sets of eyes would have spotted him.

Cutter stepped in the seamstress shop and found Dawn staring off into space, her sewing in her lap. Five days ago, Harley Long succumbed to his injuries from the ranch robbery. He was buried out at his ranch yesterday.

"Miss Dawn?" The dancing sunlight filtered in through the gauzy curtains speckling the carpet with brilliant spots. There was a light scent of fresh coffee in the shop.

Dawn blinked, then put her sewing aside and stood up, smoothing down her long dark gown. When she smiled, Cutter could see her eyes were red-rimmed.

"Newton, pardon me. I'm not the most attentive person today," She said as she took in a deep breath and let it out slowly, gathering herself.

"I came by to see that you were alright, Miss Dawn."

"I'm managing, Newton. It's like a deep, stinging cut inside me right now. The days and weeks will pass. The weeks and months will pass and with time, the pain will begin to fade," she said with a weak smile.

"I'll keep myself busy and go about getting back to the way I was."

"We all lost a good person in our lives, Miss Dawn. I am saddened by your loss. Please accept my condolences. Harley was such a wonderful person and is already missed. Don't hesitate if there is anything we can do for you, your brother, and niece during this difficult time."

"Jackson is a strong man that doesn't let his emotions govern him," Dawn picked up her cup and took a sip of the coffee. "Carmella is a bit more sensitive, as most young girls are. She is alright, for now. She has that big house to take care of now so I am hoping that she will dig into that and get her mind off this grief we all feel. Reverend Thurston spoke with her at length yesterday at the ranch and she's trying to reconcile it all. The pain will lessen day by day. We'll all be alright."

Dawn turned away for a moment and dabbed her eyes. With a determined hard look on her face, she turned back to him. "Harley and I, we had our differences. We argued about stupid things, things that didn't matter, senseless trivial things. Badgering each other was how we showed love for each other."

"He never criticized me, never tried to bully me. He always listened to anything I had to say, no matter how ridiculous," Dawn paused a moment.

Her voice was a whisper, "I've lost that now, Newton. Jackson will leave and go back to San Francisco. The ranch will be sold. My connection here, my reason for being here will be gone."

"I can understand that. My entire family is two thousand miles away in the Carolinas. We write back and forth, but it's not the same as looking in their eyes," Cutter said with a gentle smile.

"I finished up the ranch wagon that Harley wanted built. I'll be delivering it out to the ranch on Saturday. Would you like to ride along and visit for an hour or two?"

"No, but thank you for asking. I'd like to stay around here for a while. Try to get back to my old routine every day," Dawn said. She straightened up and went over to the store shelves. She took down a wrapped parcel, smoothing the paper wrapping.

"If you would be so kind as to deliver this to Carmella for me, Newton. It is a few sewing supplies that she might need out there. Something to keep her hands busy."

The paper rustled as Cutter took it. With care, he put an arm around her and kissed her cheek as he hugged her.

She nodded her head and she watched the door close behind him through teary eyes.

***

It was Saturday and Cutter drove a big ranch wagon along the Hookton Road to deliver it out to the Beatrice Flats Ranch. A big, gray dappled Appaloosa was tied to the back of the wagon trailing along.

Dunagan rode to the left of the wagon on a big Blood Bay. Cole rode on the right on a black horse with a splash of white on its rump. They had come up on the Anderson cutoff leading to the Flint Hills Ranch. Dunagan and Cole were going out to help with moving a herd of longhorns off the hills and down to the valley for the summer.

The blacksmith gestured to the land. "There's a couple of lots available I found out. About a quarter mile to the south of the shop there is a ten acre lot. The deed shows there used to be a house there, but it's gone now. When I saw it, it was covered with scrub brush, sand, cactus, and some sage. But it's near the curve of the river so there would be water if I needed it. And I intend to drill a well anyways." Cutter nodded.

"Landscaping would run you a bit of money keeping a lawn green, I'd imagine," Cole scanned the horizon watching a couple of crows circling something in the grass off to the right ahead.

"Another lot is outside behind Carlson's trading post about two miles there is an old home site. Someone started building a house there years ago and never got past getting two walls up. It has sat that way for many years and would have to be demolished and started over. It's only two acres, though. Bit small for me. That's for sale," Cutter said as he looked at the passing scenery.

"Where's the other lot at?"

"The other lot is on the other side of the river, north of town. I'd have to build my own bridge to get over the river in winter. It is five acres of that rich valley gassy area over there. For someone running a couple head of beef, that is a prime spot. It's also the most expensive at five thousand dollars.

Dunagan about fell of his horse. "Five thousand? Does it come with its own housekeeper or something? Dang that's a lot of money!"

Newton Cutter laughed at Clay. "There was a loan or something on the land and the bank wants its money back at the time of the sale. I'd be payin' off someone else's debt. I'm not too keen on that. It is a beautiful spot, but I'm not going to pay someone's bills."

"You been dealin' with Huddleston at the bank, Newton?" Cole asked as he looked at Cutter.

"Yeah, he was holding the deeds on those parcels."

Cutter turned to look at the man riding on the right hand side. Cole was still a young man at twenty five. Six foot two tall and robust at two hundred pounds, he had clear blue eyes and a laughing smile. There was a small white scar below his left eye and he kept himself clean shaven. Broad shoulders and a powerful chest with big muscular arms, he had won many wrist wrestling contests with little effort.

"Why you ask?"

"There's somethin' odd about that man. I've never been able to figure it out. He approached me one time askin' if I was looking to buy a piece of land and go into ranching. Said he could make me a real nice loan on the land," Cole shook his head wrinkling up his forehead in a frown.

"I didn't like the look in his eye and the way he rubbed his hands together. That gave me a real uneasy feeling. I told him no," Cole said as he looked at Dunagan.

"My pa always told me that when a man comes looking to give you money, run the other way. I took my money out of the bank the next day."

"The hell you did." Cutter was surprised.

"I asked Tommy Boardman to lock it up in the hotel safe for me," Cole said then spit into the dirt. "You do any business with him, Newton, you be sure to have that attorney fella Merle Doyle look everything over before you sign anything."

Cutter grinned at Dawson Cole and made a mock salute. The turnoff for Cole and Dunagan was a few yards ahead.

"You fellas take care around them longhorns now. They can be feisty, mean cusses," Cutter said as he waved. He watched the two men turn and start up the dusty switchback road.

The road ahead of Cutter went up and around the crest of a small hill. There was an old break in the crest where water erosion had worn away the sandy soil. On the other side going downhill the road swerved around an old black outcropping of rock. As Cutter weaved along on the road, his eyes found a slight trail leading down through the rocks, like a footpath or for a single horse.

His thoughts turned once again to Carmella. It would be different this time if he saw her at the ranch. He would have time to spend with her and her father and learn more about them. He was going to make it different this time.

*** 

Late the next morning, Cutter had finished the rear axle to the big freighter standing alongside the shop. It would take both he and Thomas wood to lift it up and brace it so the angle irons and braces could be screwed together. Cutter pursed his lips and nodded. Perhaps after lunch.

A tired Bay horse was walking up the little side street. A tall man rode, hunch shouldered, gripping the saddle horn. He pulled up in front of the blacksmith shop and got down. At least six foot five, a sharp chiseled face and nose, tired eyes with a heavy brow. Cutter saw that he had a fine white line along his right jaw.

"Horse threw a shoe somewhere back. Are you busy or have you got time?" The man spoke with a bit of an accent and Cutter was trying to place it.

"It's four bits for the shoe and a dollar to put it on, mister. There's a bench out back if you want to wait or the hotel is still serving breakfast," Cutter said. He could see this was a tired horse with its head hanging. He looked at the man.

"I'm in no rush, I'll get some breakfast over to the hotel." The man handed two dollars over to Cutter. He touched the brim of his hat, nodded, and turned away. Cutter patted the horse's neck and out of the corner of his eye he saw the man move with a limp, favoring his left side.

Cutter led the horse over to the rail and put on a rope halter and tied it to the post. The Bay was exhausted. Cutter brought over the water bucket and let the horse drink. After filling it three times the horse raised its head with ears pricked and swung around trying to look at the stables.

"Thomas, come out here a minute, would ya'?" As Wood walked around the corner, the big horse nickered to him and pushed its nose toward Wood. The stablemaster smiled and scratched the horse behind the ears as it lowered its head into his chest.

"Horse knows you, eh? Take a look at this," Cutter said. He slid his hand along its back and pointed out wounds. There was a six inch inflammation on the front leg below the knee. On the left front leg there was a jagged edged scar about two inches long. Cutter smoothed his hand over brand on the hip showing two upright diamonds connected with a bar.

"See if that is in your book, would ya?"

Thomas nodded.

With slow care, the blacksmith trimmed and balanced the back left hoof. The reddish orange glow of the shoe was bright in the tongs as Cutter worked to pull out the heel a bit. The hiss and fizzle in the water cooled down the shoe and when he walked back out to the horse, Thomas was holding a bucket of corn and oats feeding the animal.

Wood looked around before he spoke, and then in a hushed tone. "The double diamond brand comes up under three different places. There used to be a big horse ranch over in the valley called The Diamond Bar. Their brand was like this one. There is another ranch north of Monument Hill that used the double diamond brand."

Wood stopped again and looked around." John Ladd has a big ranch up north of Baker Landing. He had bought several head of horses from that ranch over in the valley when it went out of business. He brought them through here on his way back to the ranch. I fed those horses. That's why this one remembers me." Wood grinned and scratched the horse behind its ears.

Wood lowered the bucket and put the water bucket in front of the horse again. Cutter finished tapping the shoe into place and took off his gloves. Wood carried both buckets back to the stables and brought back a damp cloth. After patting the horse's shoulder, he slid the cloth over the mahogany coat wiping the dust and grime away.

"Thomas," Wood said and then looked at Cutter who nodded towards the plaza.

From the edge of the heavy door, they watched the drifter and the lone man from the hotel standing near the town plaza talking. After a moment, Wood stepped back into the shop and Cutter turned back to his workbench and the short, stubby bits of iron.

As the man approached, he cleared his throat. Cutter looked up,

"All done. He's ready to go," He nodded to the stranger. He wanted to know more about the horse. "I did notice there are a couple of healing wounds on his legs there."

Before Cutter could go on, the man cut in, "Yep, maybe that's why he didn't cost very much."

He swung up into the saddle and touched the brim of his hat, turning the horse to walk towards the plaza.

To the casual observer, Thomas Wood and Newton Cutter were seen talking together about something that Wood held in his hand. But in reality they were watching the horse and rider going over to the plaza. As the men were about to turn away, the lone man riding a buckskin came out from behind the auction house and stood talking with the stranger. After a few moments, both men rode out of sight in between the buildings.

"I'll have to talk to John Ladd to see if he has sold any of his stock. A big ranch like that would need quite a few horses and that seemed like a big healthy horse," Wood ran his hand through his hair trying to shake off an uneasy feeling.

"Makes ya' wonder if those two knew each other," Cutter dug his boot toe into the ground as if squishing a bug. He shook his head and went back to his nails.

***

Royal Benning was wary, cautious, and has spent too many years being frightened. It was a feeling he never would speak of to anyone, and in certain moments, acknowledged it to himself. There was something wrong with this whole setup and he suspected another plan was in place that he couldn't see. He furrowed his brow contemplating the past few days and felt uneasy not knowing what was coming.

For several years now, he had thought of himself as a handsome, dangerous, swaggering man who knew the business end of a gun. He was a good shot and carried himself tall and sure of his power. He kept himself in new shirts with shining boots and practiced with his quick hands. He would have to step up his game if he were going to clean up with Angus Tolliver.

From the top of the path, he could see four men huddled in the camp down the dim trail under the trees. There were eight horses standing over in a grassy area. Four saddles were resting among rocks. His horse walked down the trail in open view and in no hurry.

Three of the men were younger than Benning, but one man was older. Closer to fifty and a rough, lantern-jawed man, he had mean black eyes and a long white scar along one cheek and a tied-down gun. The dry lined face, sparse brownish gray hair looked like any number of tired men from the Pecos to Seattle. The older man who was crouched down on the ground near the fire spoke up. "Are you Benning?"

Before Benning could answer, a voice came from between two giant boulders. "Over here, Royal," it was Tolliver.

The two men shook hands and then they crouched around a small fire tucked back in the rocks.

"That's McCullough and his men. McCullough used to work the Ladd

Ranch until old man Ladd stiffed him out of three weeks' pay. He's got a grudge and wants his pay. He wants to join up with us, at least for this deal," Tolliver poured a cup of coffee from the pot sitting in the fire and handed it to Benning.

"They'll go in and take their horses, a few head of cattle. McCullough says there's a strong box in the house with cash and gold, but he's not sure where it is. Those men want their pay of three hundred dollars. They take the risk. We get the rest."

"You sure they won't just take the box and run?" Benning said before he took a swallow of the strong coffee and frowned, looking at Tolliver.

"That's what you're here for. You watch 'em, make sure they don't all get themselves killed taking that box. Make sure that money gets split up the right way," Tolliver paused. "Then you make sure they take their stock and ride."

Angus Tolliver stood up and walked out to the small camp. One of the men was stretched out against his saddle with his hat down over his eyes as if sleeping. Another man had stepped over to the horses and was rubbing one down with handfuls of grass. McCullough looked up from his knife.

"Mr. McCullough, if you'll fill in Benning here on how this will be done, we can get started on getting your pay," the two hard-eyed men looked at each other with their hackles up.

An hour later after much discussion and strategizing, that was the way they left. Right after sundown, a lone man was seen riding out of the small camp and back up over the rocky ridge.

*******

Lily and George Fremont sat together watching the diamond glints off the little stream. The shelter of the Four Wagon Bridge had been a favorite picnic spot of many local residents where they could break their travels and rest a bit. George smiled, munching on his red apple and watched the glorious blonde curly hair of his bride toss about in the breeze. The water babbled along and down farther in a secluded cove their horses were picketed among lush grass.

George lifted his head, turning it first left, then right, and listened. He motioned to Lily to be silent and together they heard the horses begin the long, slow walk across the forty foot long bridge.

"You sure you got the right men to get this job done? Sometimes a grudge gets a man heated up and he makes bone-head mistakes."

"You heard him yourself. There's a strong box somewhere inside that house. McCullough is loon-crazy enough to go in with guns blazin' and clean out the house. Then all we have to do is tear the house apart. Luke and Jim will get the cattle and move them out. The McCullough boys want ten head, but so what."

"McCullough says everyone is going into town for the grange dance. We'll need someone to watch the road." Royal Benning moved his horse another few feet.

"Benning, relax. This is going to be our easiest job around here," Tolliver walked his horse on across the bridge and out onto the road.

Peeking around the bridge abutment, George and Lily saw the three horses walk east up the road, puffs of dust rising from the horse's hooves. They watched without a word, until all three horses had turned into the curve and disappeared.

"George, what does this mean?" Lily trembled, rubbing her hands together. Her eyes were wide and frightened.

George put his arms around Lily. "You pack all this up. I'll run to get the horses. We need to get out of here in case they decide to come back," George's voice was a whisper.

After trotting for twenty minutes, the young couple reined in at the water trough at the gates of Doc Baines Ranch, about twenty two miles from the bridge. George had been careful to watch the back trail in case someone tried to ride up on them. No one was there. It was close to four o'clock in the afternoon when the road led around the roll of a hill into a gap beyond where several large oaks and a couple of tall cottonwoods clustered around the Faraway Inn. The gap was green, pleasant to see and Lily breathed out a sigh of relief. The horses sank their muzzles into the cool water trough.

# 4 CHAPTER FOUR

After Four Wagon Bridge the dusty track curved up around a low hill and through towering granite outcroppings. Most drivers stopped to rest their horses here and took in the wide gravelly expanse where old wagon wheels had sets of tracks and ruts. If a man were to climb up onto one of the big boulders, before him would lay the dry arid desert to the East.

The flatness of the desert went on for miles. Brown earth turned to gray shades and then dissolved into white in the far distance. This was the land where little rain fell, few water wells and life was a very dry existence. Sparse scrub brush appeared more like crusty twigs sticking out of the baked ground dotting the landscape. Farther out the heat waves rose and distorted the view, making a distorted shimmer to the vista. Travelers moving along nearer to sunset would see the distant hills, purple and gray in the graying light.

Good eyes could see the few buildings of old Graystone about half a mile away silent in the desert chill, a forgotten stop. The adobe cracked and crumbling, fallen timbers of rooflines now sunken into the ground and clumps of old sod walls collapsed waiting to be reclaimed by nature.

Tawny sand and brown marbled gullies where sudden floods had pushed the earth up into swirled muddy sculptures. A trio of tumbleweed ran skipping, hopping over the rough terrain pushed by the light breeze.

Williams Creek was a full day's journey north of the Beatrice community and a few yards under thirty five miles to the east of Bradford along an old stagecoach line. The local area was once known for good ranch land and now is expansive grassy meadow between the mesas of Beatrice and Three Corners. The surrounding hills are home to ranchers, assorted wildlife and those shadowy characters that need a no-name existence.

It was an old stagecoach structure situated with its back up against a wide riverbank. Huge old cottonwood trees leaned over it, heavy branches splayed out dropping leaves and twigs onto the roof.

The Faraway Inn was hand built with a heavy river rock façade; a jumbled mass of stones pushed in with mortar like an impenetrable quilt from foundation to roofline. It was a long and low old structure with a single pitched sloped roof, sections of shingles missing and sections in disrepair. The Inn sat in general dilapidation with the six pane windows like blank stares out at the world. The years have not been good to this beloved building. The broad stone porch with five wide-plank steps leads up from the flagstone walk.

The tall chimney of the kitchen is trailing smoke meaning something is cooking. The main room fireplace is sending smoke up its tall chimney. Still sitting there like a huge rock beast sleeping in the evening air. Faraway Inn had always been an important hub of activity for the locals and wanderers passing through. After its stagecoach stop days it became a forgotten social gathering place, only used by locals, and the stage drivers who got off course.

Locals always said that nobody knows who built it, but the elderly folks remember when it was not there. The porch creaked as Lily and George stepped up onto it. A single redwood chair, smooth and glossy from use, perched near the rail, next to an empty planter box. The heavy thick door sported three brass bars stacked vertically above each other about a foot apart. In the center of the door were three interlocking rings, like the metal had been braided and formed into rings. Below that was a familiar carved wooden door pull most patrons used.

The light within was soft and inviting and came from a six-feet-wide log-fired hearth set into the far wall. The air was warm and stale, with the sharp tang of old ale and the mellow aroma of tobacco. Above the hearth hung a painting of twelve robust comrades lifting their steins in cheer. Scattered around were some well-used easy chairs, comfortable sofas, and upholstered benches against the wall.

George and Lily Fremont walked into the Inn, letting their eyes adjust to the dim interior. Amanda approached them and guided the young couple to a table near the fireplace away from the other guests. Chiatane LaCosta brought over a steaming pot of coffee and a couple of heavy mugs. Over plates of chili, beef and biscuits, George and Lily told Chiatane LaCosta and her grandfather, Gianni about the scare at Four Wagon Bridge.

Chiatane poured more coffee for Lily. "We heard about Harley Long being beaten and robbed. Terrible! The poor man! His ranch was robbed and horses and cattle taken. Nobody has come along that said anything about the robbers apprehended. We haven't heard anything about it."

"I have a friend that might be able to help. I'm not sure where he is right now, but I'll try to track him down."

Chiatane tried to smile but grimaced. "I'm not sure what good it will do, but we'll take all the help we can get on this."

Less than a year ago, Chiatane LaCosta had been in the midst of her continental tour of the States. Gianni had written three words to her in a letter:

"Please come home."

Within two weeks she was standing inside the Faraway Inn. Of all the people in the world who would be trusted to continue on the hospitality tradition of the Inn, Gianni wanted his granddaughter to have it.

Taller than most women at five foot eight she had a full figure that gave men reason to stare. She had long dark brown straight hair that she wore up in a ponytail most days. Her flashing brown eyes were rimmed in thick black lashes against her flawless olive complexion. Chiatane had an infectious laugh that crinkled up the corners of her eyes and brought forth brilliant white teeth in a perfect smile.

The old key turned in the lock and the door creaked as it swung open. Chiatane opened the window a bit and dust swirled around in the breeze. A damp rag wiped down the desk and the wooden box cover over the instrument. With care, she lifted off the cover and looked down at the telegraph. Now that the railroad went in five miles south of Williams Creek, the stagecoaches don't stop at this old stop hardly anymore. But the telegraph still worked.

"You got it ready, sweetie?"

Gianni LaCosta walked in behind her and pulled back the wood chair. He eased himself into the chair, moving his stiff knee to one side. Gianni LaCosta had come from Italy in the last century with his wife and children in tow to work on the engineering of the transcontinental railroad. Once a big proud man, he helped the builders survey, stake, measure and conquer that path of the iron horse through to Utah. It was his grand adventure, the once in a lifetime endeavor and spectacle that was life for Gianni.

The thinning gray hair was a little longer now and he wore it swept to the back of his head. The bushy white eyebrows loomed out over his eyes in need of a trimming. The large blue eyes, slightly watery are still alert at eighty-two and missed nothing. The trembling in his hands disappeared once he began sending the message.

"Do you think Henry is out there where he can get this?"

Fingers tested the click clack of the telegraph before twisting the wires and letting the machine come to life.

"Chi, while I'm sendin' this, take Max and Amanda and get the rifles out. We'll clean them up tonight and make sure they're all ready. I'd hate to be caught unloaded for a war if it comes," Papa said as he winked at her. His expert fingers started tapping.

***

Several miles away, the young couple had arrived in Bradford. After unsaddling at the stables, George took Lily's hand and they hurried to the Mayor's office. Addie Watley had been cleaning the offices and came out when she heard Lily's high-pitched teary voice. She found a small glass and poured a glass of wine. Lily sat and drank it while George relayed what they had heard.

"No, they didn't see us down under the bridge. We were sitting on the west side away from them. I would have thought that they could see us when they rode up, but we must have been sittin' far enough back at the right angle," George's voice trembled. He glanced at Lily from time to time, trying to reassure her with a brief smile.

"Addie, write this down, if you would, please," Mayor Watley motioned her to get a pen and paper. Turning to Lily, he smiled and clasped his hands together.

"Take your time, now. Tell us what these men looked like. Describe their horses. Any small thing you can remember."

Close to forty five minutes later, Addie put down the pen and read back the three pages of notes. George and Lily both nodded as they sat together with George's arm around his wife.

"Folks, I know you were headed west, but I'd like you to be my guests at the hotel tonight. In the morning, if you remember any little thing, please come on by in the morning and we'll make it part of the record," Mayor Watley slid the handwritten pages onto a clipboard and set it on his desk.

"They didn't say the name of the ranch or anyone's name aside from that McCullough. If only I could do something. I am helpless knowing someone's ranch is about to be robbed during the dance tomorrow night," Lily's voice was weak. She had turned back at the door as they were leaving. The young woman was on the verge of tears again and George put his arm around her shoulders, guiding her out the door.

Mayor William Watley and his wife, Addie Watley reviewed the notes on the clipboard.

"I need to talk to Bert Goldman, see if he knows anything about a McCullough around here."

He frowned a moment. Addie rubbed her forehead, which she often did when she was nervous.

"My dear, see if you can contact the organizers of the Grange Dance and ask who has replied for the invitations. We've only got a few hours to try to stop this," Watley said as he kissed his wife's cheek. The woman mustered her resolve and nodded with blinking, moist eyes. The Mayor pulled the door shut, locking it behind him.

***

Cutter and Wood sat at the round, rough wood table behind the blacksmith shop enjoying their lunch of warm stew and bread. The sunlight dotted and danced over the surface as the cottonwood waved in the breeze. The savory fragrance of the stew swirled in the air.

"I see you've got a couple of palominos in the corral," Cutter said as he dunked the sourdough into the bowl and leaned for a big bite.

"Yep, there was a note on the door this morning askin' for grooming and feed for two days. Little pouch had five dollars in it so somebody was mighty trustin'," Wood said with raised eyebrows. He nodded towards the corral.

"Nice, gentle horses. I curried them up pretty and they stood there with their eyes closed. Docile. Funny thing about them," Thomas said as he wiped off his mouth with a cloth.

"They got little silver name plates on the sides of their bridles. There's matching name plates on the saddles. Nothing fancy about those saddles either. All the saddle blankets are the same. I rinsed them off and have them drying over the wood rails right now," Thomas drank some water and wiped his mouth off with the back of his hand. For a moment he paused, then looked at Cutter.

"You got time this afternoon to take a look at their shoes? Seems to me that somethin' looks odd about 'em. Like they are the wrong shape or somethin'," Wood said as he bit into a red apple and munched.

"Sure, I'll take a look," Cutter ate another bite of the thick stew. "You're a good cook, Thomas, you'll make a good wife someday!" Cutter grinned as he looked at Wood. The stable man chuckled.

"Excuse me, gentlemen. I'm sorry to disturb your lunch," A tall lean man stood there with one thumb hooked over the waist of his jeans. In his other hand, he was holding a horseshoe. White long sleeved shirt, red neckerchief, black jeans, dusty black boots, and a pair of tied down Colts. This man was not a cowboy or a rancher and made a man look twice at him.

Cutter squinted looking at the tall, lean man. Thick brown wavy hair, deep set brown eyes, clean shaven and close to six foot three. Cutter's brain was working overtime trying to remember where he knew this man. Newton wiped off his mouth and stood up, moving his lunch basket back on the table.

"I'm Henry Elliot. My horse threw a shoe about two miles back," His hand pushed his black hat back and his gaze swung around the little grassy area.

"Ah, yes, Mr. Elliot. Newton Cutter, blacksmith," Newton Cutter had a big grin and reached his hand to Henry Elliot. "I met you last fall out at the Faraway Inn. There had been some trouble there, as I recall."

This was a firm handshake. Cutter was as tall as Elliot but outweighed him by a good thirty pounds. Wood watched the young and older man standing there and mused about how life's path takes a man one way and another path takes a man a whole different way.

Elliot had a sort of lopsided grin on his face looking at the young blacksmith.

"Yes, I remember that. As a matter of fact, I got a telegram from Chiatane La Costa a few days ago that there had been some trouble out in this area. She asked me to come by, if I happened to be near so I'm on my way out there," Elliot held up the shoe.

"Do you have time to get this back onto that horse of mine?"

"Yes, of course. Let me finish up lunch here and I'll get right on it," Cutter nodded, his bright blue eyes shining as he took the horseshoe. He turned the shoe over in his hand, examining it.

"I wasn't aware of any trouble Chi was having out at the Inn. Do you know what's goin' on?" Cutter frowned showing his worry.

"I heard a rumor about a month ago about a gang of outlaws roaming through this area. I didn't think anything of it. Rumors spread like wildfire all the time," Elliot said as he pulled off his leather gloves and gave Cutter a piercing stare.

"Chi wouldn't exaggerate about there bein' trouble down this way," His voice was low, but there was a heavy, strong meaning there.

"Mr. Elliot, one of our local ranchers, Harley Long, was beaten and half-buried about a month ago. Quite a few head of cattle were taken, someone took off with some of the horses, one of his hands tried to stop it and was beaten half to death." Cutter's voice trembled and looked at the ground.

"Harley Long died from it; he never recovered from his wounds. He lived long enough to tell Doc Baines what happened."

Thomas Wood had stepped over to stand next to Cutter. "Harley's ranch hand, Riley Stephens went back to the ranch. You might want to stop out at the ranch and talk to Riley. He'll give you a description of the men who rode in that night."

"Well, thank you, gentlemen, both. After I talk to the Chi, I'll for sure take a ride out to the ranch. But, for now, I'm going to see an old friend and get some lunch at the hotel. I'll be back later," Elliot said as he touched the brim of his hand. He turned away and walked towards the plaza.

"Maybe there's more goin' on than we know about, Thomas. Chiatane ain't one to make up stories," Newton stacked his cup and bowl into the basket and carried it back to the shop. A big bay stood tied to the rail, finely coated in dust. Thomas tossed a bright red apple to Cutter.

"That man, that Henry Elliot," Wood nodded his head towards the plaza. "People say he is faster than greased lightning. A gunfighter. Not someone to get messed up with. Nobody knows where he is from or where he has been. People get shot and die around him."

Newton Cutter put his heavy leather apron on and set the horseshoe onto the edge of the forge. Stepping over to the big horse Cutter twisted the apple in half and fed it the animal. When he looked up, Elliot had disappeared from sight. Cutter had the feeling that life around Bradford was about to get a lot more dangerous.

***

William Huddleston was smug and laughing inside. He was certain that Harley Long's brother, Jackson Frisch, would not pay off the outstanding loan on the ranch. Huddleston would be able to clean up all the gold in that river. Fleeting images of beautiful clothes, fine horses and pretty women filled his mind as he daydreamed about his soon to be had wealth.

"I want paid. My boys got the old rancher off the land, just like we agreed. I want paid," Angus Tolliver said and leaned on Huddleston's desk with both hands. The black eyes were bored into the banker.

The shady banker was not about to allow a common criminal to command him around. He was a banker. Bankers commanded respect and had authority. His lip curled in distaste.

"Mr. Tolliver," Huddleston cleared his throat. "Yes, you got the old man off the ranch, but in doing so, he died. That has caused a greater problem because now I have to get his brother and niece off the land."

Huddleston stood up, pulling down the grimy vest. "They will have to sell the ranch to clear the loan. I wanted that ranch cleared off with no fussin' and your boys made it even more complicated."

Huddleston went to a cabinet and pulled out a folder. He laid it on the desk and opened it. Five hundred dollars in twenty dollar bills were counted out, leaving the folder empty.

"What is on that land that is important to you? What do you know about that land that you aren't telling me?" Tolliver's voice had a question in it. The eyes below the furrowed brow watched the banker.

Without another word, the angry banker picked up his jacket off the hook, went to his office door and stepped out into the darkness, hurrying away.

***

Nineteen miles to the south, an old man awoke to find a hand over his mouth in the gloom of his bedroom. At gunpoint, he was helped out of bed and taken out to the kitchen. Two tall men in dusters and hats stood in the shadows. The frail thin man squinted trying to see them, rubbing his eyes. Then the sound of coins hitting the wood counter drew his attention. Five dollars in gold. More than he had in the past six months. A candle was lit and a written message was placed on the counter. The old man coughed, rubbed his eyes again, then sat down and then little click-clacks started.

***

The next evening was the prime social event for the region. The county grange hall was bedecked for the area's biggest party. The hanging lanterns suspended from the ceiling glowed merrily around the room. Newton Cutter, Thomas Wood, Clay Dunagan, and Dawson Cole stood at the bar drinking, laughing with each other.

"Ah, here we are!" said Jackson Frisch. He admired his daughter in light blue silk with a white delicate, crocheted collar. Her radiant red hair fell in luxurious waves down her back. Tiny diamond earrings sparkled.

Carmella looked at the long, tall white building with the plank steps and broad veranda.

People with drinks were standing in small groups near the rails. Men smoked and women chatted with smiles. The lawn area was rimmed with flaming torches. More lanterns were hung from the porch rafters. The many windows were lit up with a shining light from inside the building. The scent of cooking meats wafted in the air.

"Carmella!" A woman's familiar voice was near.

Carmella turned right around and saw Dawn White on the arm of a tall man, coming towards her with a calm face and relaxed smile. Dawn wore an off shoulder dark green gown with a white lace edging and a green satin choker. This tall man with the intense brown eyes wore a dark blue shirt and a pearl string tie. Carmella commented on the striking couple.

"Miss Dawn, you look so sophisticated tonight!"

"Carmella, Jackson. Please allow me to introduce Henry Elliot, a good friend of mine," she said. Her eyes lifted up smiling. Jackson Frisch and Henry Elliot shook hands. "My brother Jackson Frisch and his daughter, Carmella Joy Frisch."

Carmella smiled and said, "I think you might be the most elegant couple here."

"You look lovely this evening, my dear. That color becomes you," Dawn turned to her right and looked at Elliot.

"Carmella has steady hands and good eye for detailed sewing."

Elliot smiled and nodded.

"Good evening Mr. Frisch, Miss Carmella," Goldman said with a smile. He bowed to Elliot then shook hands with a quiet greeting.

"Be sure to have a look at the dessert table. Many fine tasty treats there, I'd say!" Goldman chuckled.

"It is a broad assortment. The ladies at the church have outdone themselves," Dawn said as she patted her tummy. "If I get near that table, I'll never fit into this dress again!" They all chuckled.

"Aunt Dawn, if you would be so kind as to tell us who some of these people are?" Carmella asked and edged a bit closer to Dawn.

"You know Mayor Watley and his wife Addie over on the far side," Dawn said as she took in a breath.

"I am sure you know the hotelier, Tommy Boardman and Doc Baines standing over by the stairs."

"The man in the blue hat is Clay Dunagan. He works part time as a ranch hand for Mr. Carl Johanson, who is standing next to him in the brown shirt. Clay also works in the Blacksmith Shop with Newton Cutter from time to time."

Henry Elliot had turned to look across the room.

"I'd like to speak with Carl Johanson tonight. I have a couple of questions about the ranch." Frisch said as he turned to look across the room.

"I'll introduce you, if you would like, Mr. Frisch," Elliot looked at Frisch.

"That's very kind of you, Mr. Elliot." Elliot and Frisch walked across the wood plank floor where Dawn saw the men shaking hands.

Dawn looked at Carmella, watching her eyes scan around the room. "The tall blonde young man sitting in the first chair is Martin Ladd and the other young man seated next to him is his younger brother, Harry Ladd." Behind her hand Dawn said, "They are rowdy young men, prone to riding wild horses, having grand adventures on cattle drives and arm wrestling anyone who comes near."

"The younger girl with the long curly hair is Georgianna Caldwell, niece of Tommy Boardman," Dawn said with a sigh and a smile.

"She has learned the fine art of baking rather succulent delicacies. The box of doughnuts on the table are from her hands." Dawn raised her eyebrows with a grin.

Carmella sighed, too. "A talented girl. The only thing I'm good at baking are cookies. I burn everything else."

Dawn laughed.

"I don't see Mr. Cutter or Mr. Wood here," Carmella said as she went up on her toes. She leaned as she tried to see more of the room.

"They are probably in the dining room. I saw them earlier at the bar so I know they are here," Dawn noticed that Carmella brightened up hearing that.

Doctor Woodson Baines had walked up to the pretty women. "I hope you save me a dance tonight, Miss Carmella. I don't dance much anymore, but I would like a whirl around the floor with you," Doc Baines' merry eyes gazed at the pretty girl.

"Of course! I'd love to! Right after I dance with my father," Carmella said with her eyes gleaming.

"I see that he is engrossed talking with Carl Johanson over there." He turned and looked at Dawn and winked at her. "How are things out at the ranch, Miss?"

"I believe we found six horses down in one of the pastures. Riley

Stephens has been diligent about going out and looking for them. A couple of them are riding horses, so I've been saddling up and getting out a bit," Carmella said as she fussed a bit with her gloves.

"Fresh air and exercise are good for everyone. Good for you for getting out there. It is a beautiful place down by that river, for sure," Doc Baines nodded. "Be sure to get a look at the lake. Harley told me once that it was full of fish. I'd like to find the time to catch one sometime."

Doc Baines excused himself and moved away to speak with other people. Dawn continued pointing out certain people who were arriving.

A rather plump, older woman had come into the hall dressed in a dark red dress with white shawl. She looked around and seemed to recognize Dawn and walked over. A tall, thin pale man was behind her.

"Mr. and Mrs. Carlton, please allow me to present my niece, Carmella Frisch," Carmella caught the formal tone in her aunt's voice and straightened up and gave them her most beautiful smile.

"A pleasure to meet you, Miss Frisch. It appears you have a touch of the Irish in you with all that lovely red hair," Mrs. Carlton admired the pretty red hair.

"My mother was from County Cork in Ireland, yes, Ma'am. I was graced with her white skin and red hair," Carmella said with a smile.

Mr. Carlton spoke. "Miss White, we offer our condolences on the recent death of your brother. He was a generous and understanding man and he is already missed."

"Thank you for your kind words, Mr. Carlton," Dawn smiled and nodded. She then turned to look at the woman on his arm.

"Mrs. Carlton, you are looking stunning this evening. Tell me, where did you get your dress?" Mr. Carlton was eyeing the long dessert table while the women talked. He stood gripping his hat, looking around.

At a pause, he said, "My dear, would you like to get to the dining room now and have a bite to eat? I'm sure there are many good dishes awaiting us." Mrs. Carlton smirked and chuckled.

"I swear this man would get up out of his coffin if he smelled pot roast cooking!" They all laughed. Carmella was still giggling as the Carltons walked away.

"Come along, Carmella. Let's go say hello to the Mayor and his wife," Dawn took Carmella's arm and together they turned a few heads walking across the floor to the Mayor.

"Mr. Mayor, Mrs. Watley. I trust you remember my niece, Carmella Frisch," Dawn said. She smiled as Carmella shook the Mayor's hand.

Addie pushed her hand away and hugged the girl, giving her a kiss on the cheek. Carmella chuckled, feeling her skin flush with a rosy hue.

"You ladies are not alone, are you?" Mayor Watley was trying to look stern.

"Ah, no. Jackson and a friend of mine are over talking to Carl Johanson. It looks like they stepped outside to smoke."

Addie Watley leaned a bit closer to Carmella. "I see a number of young men casting glances your way, Miss Carmella. You are not at a loss for admirers, it seems."

Jackson Frisch and Henry Elliot stepped up behind Carmella and Dawn.

"Who is admiring who here?" The ladies laughed with Carmella once again showing a bit of red in her cheeks.

"Mr. Elliot, it's been a while since the last time we met. How have you been, Sir?" Mayor Watley shook Elliot's hand.

"Very well, thank you for asking, Sir. I finished some business in Los Angeles recently and was riding to Denver. I stopped in here to see old friends." He turned and smiled at Dawn who smiled back and slid her hand into his arm.

Addie Watley didn't miss the familiarity and raised and lowered her eyebrows watching them.

Across the room, Thomas Wood had turned around and waved to Carmella. She grinned at him and lifted her hand. She saw Wood say something to someone nearby and then he motioned towards Carmella. She watched and Newton Cutter's curly head appeared and he waved to Carmella.

Her heart leaped and she breathed a bit faster and her face was a big smile.

Dawn exchanged a glance with Jackson and she chuckled at his expression.

Carmella realized that she had been looking for Cutter in the room. Then she held her breath, looking down at her gloves, as the sudden thought that he might have brought someone to the dance tonight.

"Well, ladies, let us go sit and have dinner. I'm famished!" Elliot walked with Dawn, leaning his head talking with her as they moved into the dining room. Jackson escorted Carmella to the hallway. She turned at the door and saw that Newton Cutter was watching her. Her brilliant smile flashed and she felt a drowning liquid heat race from head to toe as she went around the corner.

After dinner, they walked back into the main hall where the musicians were playing tones and tuning their instruments. They saw each other at the same time, actually. His icy bluish brown eyes met her brilliant emerald ones. Carmella stood there holding her breath as Newton Cutter came towards her, smiling. He wore a red shirt and black tailored slacks with black boots. There was a jaunty blue flower pinned to his jacket lapel. His riotous black curly hair was in ringlets around his ears and down over his collar. He began to take off his black gloves as he walked to Carmella.

"Mr. Elliot, good to see you again," Cutter said as he shook hands.

"Good evening Miss Dawn. Mr. Frisch, I'm glad you could join us tonight." His eyes turned to look at Carmella. Cutter smiled and shifted his weight.

"You are looking most beautiful tonight, Miss. Seems like our country air agrees with you," Cutter said with a grin.

"Are you enjoying yourself, Miss Carmella?" He grinned seeing the pretty girl with a rosy flush on her white throat.

"It's always fun to meet new people and see new places. Yes, I'm having a good time so far," she said and looked at the room in general.

Then she turned her eyes back to him. There was a merriment in his eyes and she gripped her gloved hands together. Why did she have these urges? Why was she feeling like this?

"Very good. Enjoy the evening. I hope you save a dance for me!" Cutter made a mock salute and stepped away.

Her eyes followed him. The clatter of a fork on a plate brought her attention back to Dawn, who laughed.

The younger girl grinned and nudged her aunt.

***

Half an hour later the first tuning of the musician's instruments was heard from the main hall.

"Carmella, come dance with your father, then I know Doc Baines has the next one," Frisch had her elbow and helped her to her feet. He turned with a wink to Dawn. "Her dance card is already as long as my arm!"

The music had started with a gentle waltz and couples moved to the floor. Newton Cutter found Thomas Wood standing at the bar at the end of the room and they watched the dancers.

The double doors opened and Gianni LaCosta came in with Chiatane LaCosta on his arm. They were busy greeting people near the door while they removed their coats. Stopping to greet friends, they made their way to the dining room. Jackson had turned Carmella in time to see Newton Cutter take Chiatane in his arms lifting and spinning her around laughing. Then Jackson moved her away and her heart sank a bit.

She danced around the floor with Doc Baines who held her like a glass figurine. He was still insistent on Carmella's talents as a nurse. Her father had talked with Baines about a tentative nursing school in San Francisco organized by a group of doctors. The dance ended with her back at her table. Again, she searched the floor and not seeing Cutter anywhere, sat back dejected.

To the side near the musicians Dawn and Henry Elliot stood along with the dark haired woman who had come in late. She had her arm through

Newton Cutter's arm and was laughing with him. Was this the woman he was in love with? Was this the woman that he wanted to marry? She looked down fussing with her bag. Dawn and Henry Elliot sat down and smiled at her.

"You two dance well together. You've danced together before, haven't you?" Carmella said when she looked up. Dawn laughed and Elliot snickered. The pretty girl was laughing with her aunt when Thomas Wood appeared at the table.

"Miss Carmella, may I have this dance?" He asked in a hopeful tone and Carmella got to her feet nodding with a big smile. She took his arm, proudly smiling. Thomas wore a silky white shirt with cufflinks, slim black slacks, and silver boots. There was a black onyx slider on his tie with a single tiny diamond centered on it. It twinkled back to her in the light.

When the dance ended, Thomas walked Carmella to the punch bowl and they stood laughing together. Thomas Wood had dozens of horse stories and was regaling Carmella with one when Cutter and Chiatane LaCosta walked up to them.

"Miss Carmella Frisch, allow me to introduce you to Chiatane LaCosta. Chi, this is Carmella Frisch."

"Good evening, Miss Frisch," the pretty brunette said with a warm smile. Her dark brown hair hung down her back straight against the midnight blue silk dress. She wore pearls in her earrings and had a single twisted pearl on a gold chain around her neck.

"I see you have snagged the best dancer in the room," Chiatane winked to Thomas Wood. "He's the only one who hasn't stepped on my toes tonight."

"Well, that's because you won't dance with me!" Thomas laughed. Carmella grinned and looked into Newton's eyes for a moment. There was an animalistic magnetism emanating from him and she was in its grasp.

"Would you mind, Miss Frisch, if I stole Mr. Wood here for a spin around the floor? Let's see how good he is tonight on his feet!"

"Please, by all means. I'd like to see this," Carmella said with a big grin.

Thomas took Chiatane's hand and they stepped away to dance.

"Miss LaCosta is a very friendly sort of girl, isn't she?" Cutter said as he refilled Carmella's punch glass and then filled one for himself.

"Yes, she had to be, in her line of work. Gianni LaCosta is her grandfather and he owns the Faraway Inn out to the east of Bradford. She will inherit the Inn when he is gone."

"Oh. That is a big responsibility."

"She learned to walk in the Inn. She's traveled all over America, much like you have. She likes meeting people and she'll need all her strength when Papa is no longer with us." Newton was looking at Carmella's profile seeing the line of her chin and her straight nose.

Newton chose his words and said, "They are a couple of the best friends I have, Carmella. They have helped me out quite a bit and I help them out whenever I can. And that's the way it will stay, after Papa is gone."

Carmella looked up into his beautiful intense blue eyes and she smiled, understanding what he was saying. She gave him a brilliant smile. That rosy flush was back over her face and throat.

When Carmella turned her eyes once again back to the dancers she saw that Thomas Wood was dancing with the young Georgianna Caldwell from the hotel. She held a look of fascination with him, staring up into his eyes. Thomas was smiling and laughing with Georgianna as they moved around the floor. Chiatane LaCosta was dancing with Henry Elliot. His back was straight and he tilted his head chatting as they stepped.

"Would you like to step out and get some air on the porch?" Cutter asked.

"Yes, for a few minutes. That would be nice," Carmella smiled at him. They got their coats and stood at the far end of the wide covered porch. He leaned back against the rail and she stood next to him staring up at the thousands of twinkling stars.

He looked at her and she searched his eyes for several minutes.

When she pulled her eyes away she said, "What are you thinking, Newton Cutter?"

"I'm thinking about you, Miss."

Carmella raised her eyebrows and gazed out into the darkness.

His voice was near her ear. "I like you, Carmella. I'd like to know you better. What do you think?"

She smiled at his question and said, "I would like to know if we can dance without you mashing my toes." Carmella smirked.

And so they danced for more than an hour together, talking, laughing, and gazing at each other with a young fascination.

The last dance started right close to midnight and Henry and Dawn were dancing near to Carmella and Newton. Chiatane LaCosta was dancing with Jackson Frisch. Thomas and Georgianna were hand in hand moving around the floor.

The double doors at the end of the hall slammed open and a battered, bloody man fell to the floor.

"Rick! It's Christopher!" Katherine Ladd exclaimed, her gloved hands over her mouth. Richardson Ladd ran over to the man who had collapsed at the door, lifting his head. It was Christopher Hawkins, the young nephew of Merton Corly, Ladd's ranch hand. Strong arms lifted the young boy so he could sit up. "Christopher! What happened?"

"Mr. Ladd, they shot your brother!" Christopher coughed and wiped blood from his mouth. His left eye was almost swollen shut and his right brown eye was bloodshot. "Uncle Merton and Bob McReynolds took off after them. They came into the barn where I was rubbing down my horse," Christopher held his ribs and coughed in pain again.

"Get home fast, Mr. Ladd. They said they were going to burn the barn!" Already men were running for the door. Doc Baines knelt to attend to Hawkins. Thomas Wood and Bert Goldman were already mounted and riding out.

Cutter, Carmella, Jackson, Dawn and Elliot stood to one side listening. Elliot caught Cutter's eye and motioned his head towards the door.

"I'm sorry, Carmella. I have to get out there and see what I can do to help. I'll find you later," He said with a quick kiss to her cheek.

"Go! And be safe!" She reached up and touched his cheek and smiled. Cutter sprinted for the door with Elliot right behind him.

Addie Watley pushed her sleeves up and organized a cleanup committee in the now quiet Grange. An hour later, after the doors were locked, Frisch drove Dawn and Carmella along with three other ladies back to town in the carriage.

Even before they came through the ranch gates, Cutter, Wood and Watley could see a barn half engulfed in flames. Wood, Goldman and three other men ran for pails and sloshed water onto the flames.

Watley had knelt over the man lying motionless in the yard, and after a moment feeling for a pulse, shook his head. He had been shot in the heart. Richardson Ladd wiped the blood off of Nick Ladd's beaten face smoothing back the gray hair.

Ladd's voice shook. "He told me that he was feeling stiff and tired earlier today and had decided to rest at home tonight. Merton Corly was going to play cards with him."

Ladd clenched a fist to his mouth. Henry Elliot was walking about the yard looking at the ground in the light of a torch.

"There's a revolver over here by this tree. Tracks lead off to the east. Looks like four horses. Stay here, let me go see what I can find," Elliot yelled as he ran to his horse and trotted up around behind the house.

Cutter could see the front door to the big house had been kicked off its hinges and was lying on the porch. Tables and chairs had been overturned. After he checked the house, he came back out to Watley.

Thomas Wood sat down on the front steps. He was covered in soot with black smudges on his face from the fire. "We saved half the barn. There weren't any horses in it, but a couple of saddles and things were scorched. It will take a little work to get rebuilt, but you let me know and I'll give a hand, Mr. Ladd," Wood said as he stood a moment looking down at the man on the ground.

"Well, I'm thankful for you and those men, Thomas. If the hay had been in the barn, it would have gone up like wildfire, so I guess that's one good thing," Richardson Ladd said as he stood up. He walked over to the tree and picked up the revolver.

Watley noticed Ladd frowning as he turned the gun over in his hands. "What is it, Rick?"

The man looked at the gun in Ladd's hand. He lifted the gun and looked at it in the torchlight. "It's a Colt Pocket Navy revolver. This is a new gun. I'd bet even Bruno doesn't have this gun yet." Watley raised his eyebrows and handed the gun to Cutter.

"One of the holdup men must have dropped it," Cutter said and he looked at Ladd. "And I'd guess he would want it back, too."

Watley shook his head and went into the house and lit some candles, then put some coffee on while they waited for Elliot to come back. It was close to dawn and the Mayor was writing notes at a desk when they heard a horse ride into the yard. Merton Corley had been shot through the shoulder and instead of wounding the old horse tamer, it had just made him mad. The horse he led had a man's body over the saddle. Corley pulled the man's legs and let the dead man fall to the ground.

"Both this man's arms are broken and so is his right leg," Watley looked in astonishment at Merton Corley. The horse tamer grunted and gestured as if to dismiss the accusation and walked to the porch.

"Yeah, well, it took some convincing to get him to talk," Corley sneered and sat down on the steps, pulling his shirt away from the bullet wound. "I need a drink."

"Corley, what happened here?" Richardson Ladd was standing in the yard holding a torch looking over the dead man. Watley peered at Corley's wound.

"His name is MacKenzie. He told me he was paid one hundred dollars to help rob the ranch. His cohorts in crime stated there was a safe with gold in the house and all he had to do was open it," Corley said and then paused a minute. He didn't earn his hundred dollars."

Watley interrupted. "I've got to get that bullet out of you, Corley. This is gonna hurt a bit."

"This ain't the first bullet that's been dug outta me, Mr. Mayor. I've still got three in me from the Battle of Wilson's Creek and one from Lexington."

Corley took a deep breath and let it out with a nod. "Just get it out." Cutter and Wood brought their torches and looked at each other in disbelief as Watley worked twenty minutes on the bullet. The big man only groaned once as small pliers dug around in the shoulder. Finally, the big slug came out and he dropped it into Corley's hand.

"MacKenzie said that he was working for a man named Benning. They got a place out at South Landing where they lay low," Corley looked at the slug, then dropped it on the porch. "There was another man that Benning worked for, but they called him the boss, not any name." Corley tried to flex his shoulder and grimaced. He stood up.

He looked at Ladd and then at the ground, fussing with his sleeve. "We had just finished dinner and started to play some cards. We heard the boots on the porch and thought it was Christopher coming in to play with us. Three of 'em kicked in the door and I just had enough time to grab my gun."

Corley wiped his mouth with the back of his hand. He motioned to the dead outlaw. "MacKenzie shot Nick. I got a shot into one of the other guys who screamed and ran back outside. I will say that Nick got a shot off and hit the other man, but I can't be sure. When they started to run, me and Bob McReynolds took out after them. Bob is still out there."

Richardson Ladd scratched his head with a look of sadness and turned away. The sky in the east was beginning to lighten with the dawn when Bob McReynolds rode back into the yard. The men were sitting in chairs on the veranda and they all stood up and walked down the steps as McReynolds got down off his horse.

Ladd looked at the man in the yard. Six foot five, wide shoulders and a shock of black hair hanging in his face. His shirt was soaked in blood with a sleeve half torn off. There was a gash on his forehead that went back up into his hair and he was limping. "My God, man! Are you alright?" McReynolds grimaced as he shifted to his other foot.

"I'm sorry about Nick, Mr. Ladd. He was a good man, fair to the hands," McReynolds said as he wiped his eyes with his sleeve and limped over to the porch. The minute he sat down Doc was swabbing out the gash.

"I chased 'em as far as Four Wagon Bridge. Finally, I got close enough to rope one and pull 'em off his horse. Monique held him tight and I got a few licks in before the man began to listen to reason."

"Who's Monique?" Wood was holding the torch for Watley, looking at the big man.

"My cuttin' horse. She's trained right good and smart. I named her after the prettiest girl in school," McReynolds chuckled. Wood looked away shaking his head.

"He wouldn't hold still and Monique dragged him a good twenty yards before I caught her. He was kinda scratched up but still cussin' and threatenin' me," McReynolds said.

Watley ordered McReynolds to sit. The wounded man groaned as Watley put on a dressing and bandage.

"I finally convinced him to tell me that a man named Benning had paid him to be part of the gang that tried to rob the ranch," McReynolds said as he looked at Richardson Ladd.

"We did good, preparing with the guns and building them fences, Mr. Ladd. It slowed 'em up enough for me to catch up with this man."

Watley gave McReynolds a drink of whiskey and then shook his head and put things back in the house. The Mayor poured himself a drink and sat back down on the veranda. McReynolds walked down to his horse and took something out of his saddlebag.

"I don't think this man will be holdin' up any more ranches, at least for a while." He dropped a bloody parcel on the veranda table.

Richardson Ladd unwrapped the bloody cloth. It was the outlaw's right hand with an ugly, jagged chopped wrist and all the fingers horribly broken. Wood stiffened and gagged as he turned away. Ladd stood up and walked away to the end of the porch.

Corley laughed. "Took some convincing to get him to talk, eh?" McReynolds and Corley were still talking when they walked down through the yard, leading their horses to burned out remains of the barn.

Watley took another drink of whiskey and folded up the cloth around the severed hand. "You employ some interesting men, Mr. Ladd," he said with raised eyebrows.

Richardson Ladd stopped as he was walking through the door of the house.

"Yes, I do. And they are all getting raises first thing in the morning."

***

The first rays of sun were streaming through the timber in the east. The Ladd Ranch started up on the side of the hills right where the mouth of a valley opened broad and flat. It ran all the way into the low hills area near Hookton Road. Two small streams flowed from the hills, one on the east side coursed along a boulder strewn riverbed which fed a man-made dam and another one on the west that had been cleaned and maintained for water to the house. The ranch had good water year round and a lovely green valley.

The house was perched on a leveled out limestone ridge that rose from the hillside. The barns, corrals, bunkhouses, and sheds were kept a little over a mile away nearer the grassy valley. From the wide, spacious veranda the view went on for twenty miles to the west and fifteen to the stand of timber in the east. Nearer the east river there was a change in the grass color where Richardson Ladd had planted clover and alfalfa seed, creating a sweet hay each season.

The timber to the east was a virgin stand and excellent in health. It never had it been harvested or thinned. There were no burrowing insects or disease. Ladd had been approached by four or five timber men offering exorbitant high prices for the timber, but they were all denied the sale. As a boy, Ladd had lived in the Arizona desert and promised himself that as an adult he would always be surrounded by trees. He wanted that timber as it was until his dying day.

It was Cutter who had been sitting in silent fury on the veranda who saw Elliot walk his horse down out of the timber. He woke the other men and they walked down to the yard. He was leading an appaloosa and a big hammerhead roan.

Elliot was grimy with dirty smudges on his face. "They had other horses waiting for them about ten miles east. These two were left loose to wander. Tracks lead off to the east about another ten miles. It looks like they kept right on going, not doubling back," he got down and looked at Thomas Wood.

"Do you recognize either one?" Thomas was running his hand over the appaloosa. It had been shooed recently, but not very well. One of the shoes was on crooked as if it had been done fast. Wood paused a minute before he approached the roan.

"I need a couple apples or carrots. I never approach a hammerhead unless I have food," Wood said with a smile. Cutter ran up the steps of the house and remembered that there was a bowl of apples on the kitchen counter. He brought out the bowl.

The hammerhead flicked its ears forward when it saw Wood break an apple in half and feed a part to the appaloosa. Cutter untied and led it over to the other side of the yard.

"I don't recognize the appaloosa. There is a crooked shoe on its left hind hoof. Someone on a ranch put it on in a hurry. Let's ask if Christopher will recognize it."

"Henry, did this hammerhead try to bite you when you roped him?" Wood tore three apples in half and stood facing Cutter with his left hand held out with the apples, not looking at the horse. The hammerhead nickered and edged around reaching for the apples with its muzzle.

"Sure did. That is one ornery horse. I've never met a roan that was easy to handle either," Elliot was smiling, watching the stable master and the roan.

The roan had eaten all the apples and then nickered again, nuzzling against Wood's chest. Wood chuckled.

"This is one of Harley Long's horses. I had to cut his hooves back before I shooed him. Went through about a dozen apples doin' it, too." He scratched behind the horse's ears.

Wood looked at Cutter. "Jackson and Carmella have one of their horses back."

***

The next afternoon Cutter drove to the Harley Long Ranch delivering the ranch wagon pulled by two of Thomas' horses. He parked right beside the corral near the barn. One of the ranch hands trotted out of the big barn and helped Cutter unhitch the team. Cutter led the horses over to the corral fence, tied them off and lifted the harness off one of the horses and secured it onto the pack of the other horse. Cutter retrieved the saddle and blanket in the back of the wagon and saddled up the bigger appaloosa. He stood there a moment with his hand on the saddle admiring the contrast of the green valley and the bright blue sky.

"Afternoon, Mr. Cutter. What brings you out here to the ranch today?" Clear greenish hazel eyes were shaded with a small slender hand.

"Ma'am. I finished the ranch wagon that Harley asked me to build a couple months ago. It belongs to him or rather now it belongs to the ranch, I 'spose," Cutter gazed over the thick, glossy red hair falling into waves about her shoulders. Carmella wore a white and green flecked gingham dress. Her white, slender neck rose to a strong chin and a bright smile.

"Oh, yes I remember seeing notes in his journal about a new wagon being built."

Carmella saw a tall man, large shoulders, and a slim waist. Her eyes did not miss the muscular arms and all that black curly hair waving in the breeze. Something in his dark eyes held her attention and she struggled to keep her feet still.

"Thank you for bringing it all the way out here. I could have sent in one of the hands for it," Carmella saw the strength in his shoulders as he worked on the saddle. She felt a sudden warm rush up over her cheeks and she lowered her eyes to the dusty hard packed ground. She gripped the folds of her dress for a long slow breath and then brought her eyes back to his form.

"It's no problem, Ma'am. It's a beautiful drive with decent roads and it's good for me to get out of the shop every so often," he said as he stole a glance at Carmella. He could not help but grin, feeling her gaze upon him.

"Would you come up to the house and have coffee? My father is due back soon from Three Corners and I'm not sure if there was anything he needed to speak with you about," Carmella's face lit up with an inviting rosy flush. She had become familiar to the men with whom her father did business. Builders, bankers, politicians, and cattlemen had visited and even if they were strangers, she still held her poise and grace.

Carmella had traveled around the country after her schooling was finished in Boston. She had seen the Montana Territory from the back of a mule, watched a Mexican cowboy rodeo in Sonora and floated down the Columbia River with mountain men.

"That would be right nice, Miss. I'll turn the horses into the corral," Cutter said with a smile. He noted her pretty white smile. Taking the reins he led both horses into the corral. After he shut the gate, he followed

Carmella up towards the ranch house.

Carmella had an easy assured step and Cutter noted the small boot heel mark in the dust.

They had stepped up onto the broad flagstone walkway when they heard a horse trotting up alongside the house. A tall man under a broad brimmed hat pulled up to the rail and got down off the blood bay.

"Father, you are right on time. Do you remember Mr. Cutter of Bradford?"

"Yes, of course, I do remember you, young man. What brings you out to the ranch?"

"Yes, Sir. I finished the ranch wagon that Harley had ordered a while back and I wanted to bring it out to you folks."

Frisch had short white hair combed back with a white mustache and deep brown eyes. He wore black broadcloth slacks, a white long sleeved shirt with cufflinks and a suit coat.

"We were just about to have coffee on the veranda, Father. I'll have Emma bring out some cups," Carmella said as she went up the wide plank steps and disappeared inside the doorway.

Frisch and Cutter sat back into the soft cushioned chairs on the veranda. Close set thick planks spanned thirty feet wide and fifteen feet deep. A heavy post rail went around the edge to the far stairs leading off to the side of the longhouse.

Frisch set his hat down on the big round table and set back gazing out to the grassy valley, swaying and bending in the light wind.

"Harley had some beautiful land here. It's no wonder he preferred being here rather than in town," Frisch took off his gloves and set them next to his hat.

Emma brought out a tray of cups and spoons with a small sugar bowl. She set a shining steel coffee pot on a round brass trivet. Her quick hands picked up the hat and gloves and with a nod went back inside the house. Carmella came out carrying a plate of cookies.

"Emma baked these this morning. They are still soft and fresh," Carmella said with a smile. She glanced into Cutter's eyes and then set out three cups and then poured coffee.

"That Emma is one fine cook. Beef, chicken, or pork, each one prepared better than the first. It's a wonder that Harley didn't weigh three hundred pounds!" Frisch chuckled as he took a sip of his coffee. Carmella sat down across from the two men. Cutter saw delicate tendrils curling around her face and then picked up a cookie, munching.

"Have you decided what to do with the ranch, Mr. Frisch?" Cutter took a sip of the rich coffee and sneaked a look at Carmella.

Frisch nodded and said, "As soon as we figure out how many head and the exact acreage, it will be made ready for sale. I went up and talked to

John Ladd to see if he had any interest in it, but he is in Kansas City right now on business. I intend to write to him and see if there is any interest."

Frisch looked at Cutter over the rim of his cup. "My business and work are in San Francisco. I am an investor in the business and commerce in California. I help folks start up their businesses and become part of the fabric of society. I'm afraid I don't know much about running a big ranching operation like this."

"It is so beautiful here. I hate the idea of it being sold," Carmella said with her eyes looking at Cutter. Cutter frowned at his cookie wondering what she could mean.

"I know Harley had grazing rights on all three sides. Government land, with good running water all year round and it has both cattle and horses on it. He did a lot of culvert and grading work to increase water flow. I remember him talking about the dam he built up on the east side of the valley so the cattle would have water in the dry months of summer," Newton set his cup down and looked at Frisch and Carmella.

"I'd say there aren't many situated ranches here now like the way Harley set up this one. You'd have to ride forty five miles west over the land before you come to the next ranch and that would be Carl Johanson's place," Cutter looked thoughtful.

"How long have you lived around here, Mr. Cutter?" Carmella caught herself staring at his strong jaw, deep eyes, and full mouth.

"Miss, I've been here coming up on three years now. I've finally built up the blacksmith shop. I've got a good lot of customers and I've made some good friends. I'm like you, Mr. Frisch, in that my business is in Bradford. This big land is beautiful, yes," Cutter said as he gazed at Carmella for a moment. "But my plans are for in town."

"What are your plans, young man, if you don't mind me being so bold," Frisch said as he took a sip of coffee.

Carmella listened as she stood and refilled their coffee cups. She nudged the cookie plate towards Cutter with a quick wink. He grinned and turned to Jackson Frisch.

"I've decided to build a house in town, Mr. Frisch. I've got some money set aside and I want a home of my own. But there is a twist to it," Cutter said as he leaned back and rested his arms along the sides of the chair.

"Bradford doesn't have a school. The local children ride for close to fifteen miles to get to the closest school and for some, it is too far. They don't attend.. I want two big rooms on the first floor of the house to work as a school until the town can build a proper school."

Cutter watched Frisch and then looked at the surprised Carmella.

"Why how generous! What a wonderful thing for those children!" Carmella sat up with a big smile. Slender fingers swept a strand of lovely red hair back from her face.

"That is most generous of you, Mr. Cutter. Are you sure you can take on all that responsibility?" Frisch leaned forward resting his forearm on the table and looked at Cutter.

Newton nodded and smiled. "The Mayor's wife was a schoolteacher back east and she has committed to teaching until a regular teacher can be hired. People have been very receptive to the idea and I've gotten a couple offers of help on the project. I'm fairly confident that we'll make it work."

"Who is your builder? Do you have an architect yet? Pardon my enthusiasm, Mr. Cutter, but aside from calves and the state of the water, this is the most interesting thing going on around here," Frisch chuckled and bit into a cookie.

"I need to find an architect, get some plans drawn up, go look at different houses," Cutter shrugged. "I'm sure there are a thousand things I have to do to get started."

"I have an architect in San Francisco that I would suggest to you. I'll write to him and let him know what you are planning and see if he can help you out," Jackson Frisch toyed with his coffee mug and then looked up at Newton Cutter. "Bruno Giordanni. He has designed and built some impressive structures, including my own hotel. He also has done several larger homes in the San Francisco hills. I cannot recommend him enough.

"I would like to talk with him about this project. I'd like to hear his thoughts on what I'd like to do," Cutter said. He turned and looked at Carmella.

"Miss Frisch, have you seen any of Bruno Giordanni's buildings? Do you have an opinion on architecture, Ma'am?"

"Why yes, Sir! I actually live inside one of Mr. Giordanni's buildings. The Vista Del Grande Hotel . Father and Mr. Giordanni designed and built it for my father in San Francisco. Perhaps someday you will visit the grand city of San Francisco and see it," Carmella said with a smirk to Cutter. She winked at her father, who chuckled.

The three of them sat there smiling while their thoughts went in different directions. Out on the distant valley rim several deer stepped out of the timber and into the lush green grass to nibble. Farther to the east a few quail flew up in a rustle of wings. Lazy puff ball clouds floated from the West dragging ragged shadows over the waving valley.

"Well, I've taken up enough of your time this fine day. I want to make it back to Bradford before it gets too late," Cutter said as he moved his chair back and stood. He nodded to Carmella, reaching to shake the strong hand of Frisch.

"I'll be in touch when I hear from Girodanni. You have a safe ride home, Sir."

Frisch stood on the veranda with Carmella leaning against the rail watching Cutter mount up. They saw him lead the team horses and headed for the road. Carmella made a last wave when she saw Cutter turn back to get one more look at the pretty redhead.

***

The following day Carmella came through the seamstress's door and her face lit up seeing Dawn. The seamstress stood and set her embroidery on the small round table. She kissed Carmella's cheek and they hugged.

"I'm glad you decided to come in for a visit. I do get lonely here sometimes. Plus, you and your father are now my only family," Dawn said with a smile. She sat in the overstuffed chair and tried to find where her last stitch left off.

"It's good to get out and ride again. I don't go far. Most times I turn around at the clearing off the Beatrice Road where that big park is at," Carmella said as she took off her coat and laid her scarf on the chair.

"There were ducks floating around on the lake!"

Carmella shook out her long glossy red hair and sat down on a chair, kicking off her shoes.

"Do you know anything else about that poor man that came into the grange dance?"

"Yes, it was Christopher Hawkins, the fifteen year old nephew of one of the ranch hands, Merton Corly," Dawn said as she raised her eyebrows, widening her eyes.

"I was surprised to find out that our young Mr. Hawkins is quite the scrapper and got in a couple of good punches before a bigger man knocked him out."

"Oh my!" Carmella frowned in amazement.

"Henry is out trying to find out more information on the robbery," Dawn said. She pulled the slender needle through the fabric.

"We are to have dinner with him this evening at the hotel and hear the details."

Carmella nodded and sat still for a moment, looking out the window. Dawn glanced at the young girl and then back to her sewing, with a sly smile.

"Did you enjoy the dance, Carmella?" Dawn asked as she searched through her basket trying to find her little scissors.

"Oh yes, I sure did. There were many interesting people there," Carmella said. She watched Dawn hunt around for something.

"Any one person more interesting than the rest? You did dance quite a while with Newton Cutter, I saw," Dawn said with a wink to her niece.

"Yes, I would like to know more about him. What can you tell me, Aunt?" Carmella perked up and leaned her chin onto her hand smiling as she looked at Dawn.

Dawn grinned as she smoothed out her sewing piece.

"Well, you know he owns his own business. And he is the only blacksmith so he has a corner on the market, so to speak. He's building his own house this year, but you already knew about that." Dawn said and then paused a moment, thinking.

"He pretty much stays right around here. I understand that he did some mining up in Northern California and had some sort of business in Denver. I'm not sure of the details. There is not a lot of pretense or posturing to him. He is not trying to impress anyone," Dawn said as she picked up a spool of blue thread.

"He lives in the hotel?" Carmella asked.

"Yes, he and Thomas Wood both do. There are several others that live in the hotel also, like Doctor Baines and Merle Doyle, the attorney. But once his house is built, he will move out of the hotel and into his own home," Dawn said. She stopped and looked at Carmella.

"You live in a hotel, my dear. You must know and understand what it is like."

"What about his other interests, like books, music, art? Do you have any idea what he is like?" Carmella was gesturing to Dawn.

"Well, I have heard him sing and he does so quite well. One night in Chick Miller's saloon Lily was playing the piano and singing an old Irish tune. Newton was leaning on the piano singing right along with her," Dawn said as she smiled at the memory.

"One day the peddler, Mike Cushman, came into town with a huge wagon load of things from up north. Mrs. Watley had found a box of books underneath a rug. He pulled out a book of poems and was reading one out loud. Newton finished the next line in the poem," Dawn said with a grin.

She cut the end of her thread and with a smile said, "He bought the entire box from Mike."

"I believe your father has a good opinion of him, Carmella. He told me himself that Harley's wagon was built by a skilled craftsman. He has built his business using his brain and his strength. There is a lot to be said for someone who has a good head on their shoulders," Dawn said as she tilted her head looking at Carmella, not sure if she heard the last.

"Why don't we go for a nice afternoon stroll and just happen by the shop. We can stop and say hello," Dawn said as she stood with a smile. Carmella laughed and stood, reaching for her coat and scarf.

***

From the edge of the dressmaking shop, Carmella could see the big double wooden doors swung wide and braced open. There was a horse standing at the post and there was movement in the shop. Dawn and Carmella stopped and admired the blooming flowers in the church garden. Addie Watley was sweeping the church steps when they came around the corner so they chatted a moment.

Thomas Wood was leading a horse back to the corral when the two women got to the edge of the plaza.

"Good afternoon ladies," he said with a smile. Wood had on a heavy leather apron that he wore when grooming horses.

"Another lovely lady got new shoes just now."

Wood patted the horse's neck and Carmella scratched the blood bay mare behind her ears. The horse nickered. Carmella laughed. "She's beautiful. How old is she?"

"She's three now. She belongs to Georgianna Caldwell over at the hotel," Wood said as his eyes softened.

"Pretty horse for a pretty girl." He grinned.

Dawn noted that Wood straightened up taller and his smile grew when he said Georgianna's name. She smiled to herself.

"Oh good! Now we have another lady to ride with!" Dawn exclaimed.

Cutter had heard voices and walked nearer the street. He saw Thomas talking with someone and took another step to see who it was. His face lit up in a smile when he saw it was Carmella Frisch and Dawn White.

Carmella's white skin was flawless and the small silver cross on its chain gleamed against the creamy softness. The long red hair fell in shining waves down her back and then she caught sight of him. Her smile faded and she stood still just looking at him. The smile began to creep upon her lips and the green eyes lit up.

"Good afternoon Mr. Cutter," her voice had a slight musical tone to it.

"Miss Carmella, Miss Dawn," His eyes were bright and shining, that curly black hair was in damp ringlets. Carmella felt her feet take a step towards him before she got herself back in control and stopped. Those icy blue eyes bathed over her and again, she could feel that hypnotic draw to him.

Wood was walking the mare over to the corral and Dawn walked over past Carmella and up to Newton.

"Would Clay Dunagan be around this afternoon? I have a little iron project to speak with him about," Dawn said as she turned, amused and watched him tear his eyes away from Carmella.

"Sorry, Miss Dawn. Clay is out at Carl Johanson's place for the next few days. They are trying to get some defenses built in case that gang tries to hit the ranch. Clay went out to give a hand."

Newton looked at Carmella again and then back to Dawn. As long as he looked at Dawn he could think and talk right. When he looked in those green eyes of Carmella, his brain got all confused and fuzzy.

"Is there any news about the men who tried to rob the Ladd Ranch the other night? That poor boy that came into the grange was beaten terribly!" Carmella had taken off one of her gloves and offered her small hand to Cutter. She wore a thin silver bracelet with a heart shaped black onyx stone set in it.

Cutter grinned and took her small hand in his, holding it a second too long. "Chris is pretty bruised up. He's young and Doc says he will recover completely." He released her hand.

"I'm waiting for Henry Elliot to get back so we can hear about what is happening," Dawn made a small frown. She looked back towards the corral and could see Thomas Wood walking back to the shop.

"Henry has been gone since early this morning chasing who knows where. That horse of his is going to be dead tired when he rides in," Dawn said with a smile to Wood who nodded.

"He brought a big appaloosa the other day. Said that he would ride him as soon as his new shoes were put on," Thomas said as he nodded his head towards the stables.

"That big black will get a rest when he takes the other one out."

Thomas went into the shop and through the center door into the stables. Carmella was standing there in the late afternoon sun glinting in her long hair, her mouth open in a smile. Pretty lashes blinked over the green eyes. Cutter took in a deep breath and spoke.

"When will you be going back to the ranch, Miss?" Newton had leaned against the heavy wooden workbench.

"As soon as I can convince my Aunt to come out for a visit. But I can see that Mr. Elliot has much of her attention right now," Carmella said and chuckled.

Dawn flushed a rosy hue across her cheeks.

Dawn took a deep breath to compose herself. "Speaking of Mr. Elliot we should get back and change for dinner. There is no telling at what time he'll ride in and I want to be ready!"

Dawn winked at Carmella.

Dawn turned to Cutter and laid her white gloved hand on his arm. "Please tell Clay to stop by next time you see him, will you, Newton?" She gave him a warm smile, patting his arm. She gave him a quick wink and then turned away. Cutter chuckled.

"Yes, Ma'am, I sure will. You ladies enjoy your dinner tonight. I understand that Miss Georgianna had cooked a delicious pot roast for dinner. Thomas has been drooling over it all afternoon like a wolf," his deep voice laughed.

Her voice was a warm laughter and he enjoyed seeing her eyes light up. When he stepped closer to her, he saw that she gasped in air. He reached for her hand and held it between both of his.

"Good evening, Mr. Cutter."

There was a wonderment in her eyes as she lifted her chin, her smooth full lips parted. Cutter started to bend his head and then stopped as she slid her hand away

"Good evening, Miss." He stood there several minutes watching the two pretty women walk across the plaza. Wood had come out to see what Cutter was doing and saw that he was watching Carmella walk away. He smiled and went around the far side of the shop. When they started to turn the corner, Carmella stopped and looked back to the blacksmith and smiled a brilliant smile tossing her head, then stepped around the corner.

The afternoon stage from Los Angeles headed to Yuma was coming into town. Addie Watley was stepping up onto the porch of the Town Hall when she heard the low rumbling of horses, metal, wood, and leather. Alton Lengford leaned against the rail of the auction house smoking when the stage rolled by trailing a dust cloud. Mrs. Klinger, with her cane making her way out to the riverbank, stopped at the corner of the church to watch the lumbering stage.

The lone man who had stepped down was a bit over six foot, broad in the chest and thick in the shoulders. He was a younger man in his twenties, with scruffy light brown hair and quick watery blue eyes. He stretched for a moment and then chatted with the driver. The tanned, jagged lines on his face should have been on someone much older. The brown scuffed boots raised small puffs of dust as he caught his saddlebags tossed to him by the tender.

There was a big freight wagon parked in front of Carlson's Trading Post and a couple of men were unloading and carrying things into the post. There was a buckboard standing at Bruno Stenson's gun shop and voices were coming from inside. Mrs. Klinger continued on her way in search of wild mint down by the river. Alton Lengford stubbed out his cigarette and went back inside the auction house. Addie Watley remembered something inside the Town Hall and went back inside.

"Do you have any horses for sale, Mister?"

The voice startled Wood who had knelt to pull a leather cord through the rear skirt of a saddle. He had not heard anyone come up and jumped a bit, turning around.

"Pardon me, I didn't mean to startle you."

"No, no. It's alright. I was thinkin' on something too hard, I guess," Wood said as he stood and took off his leather gloves. Smiling, he took a step reaching his hand out.

"Thomas Wood."

The young man smiled and reached to shake Wood's hand. "Reed Vance, Sir." Vance turned to the corral.

"If you'll come with me around back, I've got two for sale right now," Wood said as he gestured to the side and the two men walked around to the back of the stables.

"It's ten dollars for the buckskin, fifteen for the Morgan with the white stockings. Saddles are five dollars and five for the bridle," Wood leaned his arms on the top rail of the corral. Reed Vance whistled twice and both horse's heads came up. The buckskin nickered and walked over to Vance, nosing him.

"Funny how a horse will come when you whistle," Vance said as he patted the horse and scratched behind its ears. The horse softly nickered again.

"Looks like I'm buyin' this one!"

Wood chuckled, watching the horse and the man. "Horses remember people. They remember how they were treated. They remember places, like where water is at or feed."

Half an hour later, the buckskin was saddled up and Vance mounted up. Wood caught sight of the Colts strapped down under the duster. "If you ever want to sell him, bring him back and I'll pay you for him." Vance tipped his hat and turned walking the horse slowly up the street.

***

It was spring. The sun was bright and just comfortably warm. The birds were chattering up in the big cottonwood that loomed over the stables. To the east, the grassy valley swayed in the light breeze and more birds swooped into the green grass looking for a meal. The rolling mountains to the north framed the sky at the horizon with flecks of green. Wood watched the walking horse until it turned the corner at the hotel, then without another thought, went back to his wrestling with the saddle.

Cutter had closed the heavy wood double doors to the blacksmith shop and was rolling the water barrel back to the side. Wood came around the corner of the stables and rolled the other barrel alongside the first.

"Another stranger came into town this afternoon. Reed Vance, he called himself. Bought the buckskin, a saddle and rode out about an hour ago," Thomas sat down on the water barrel looking at Cutter.

"He come in on the stage?" Cutter ran his fingers through his black curly hair, shaking it. Bits of wood scattered to the ground.

"Yeah, he must have. He wasn't covered in dust like he'd been out walking," Wood said and then hesitated a moment.

"He's wearing twin Colts, nice shiny guns strapped down under the duster."

Wood sat in the late afternoon dappled light and told the details to

Cutter.

"I have a mind to let the Mayor or somebody know about this. Considerin' all that has been going' on around here lately," Wood said as he ran his fingers through the black hair then adjusted his gloves.

"That's a good idea. I think we should talk with Henry Elliot on this, too. He seems to be taking an interest in these robberies. He might know something," Cutter said as he nodded.

*******

The evening began to settle in on the surrounding hills. A warm wind swirled bits of dust, rolling dried brush up against the shop. Someone was trying to play the piano over at Goldman's saloon and others were roaring with laughter. A man's voice lifted singing an old campfire cowboy tune and the piano plinked along with him. Under the porch of Bruno Stenson's shop, a dog sat up and began to howl, making the men inside the saloon roar with laughter.

Goldman stood behind the bar pouring coffee for a tall stranger in a black frock coat when Wood and Cutter walked in. It's not a stranger. It's Jackson Frisch.

"Howdy, Mr. Frisch. I didn't know you were in town." The men shook hands. Cutter noticed that the saloon was empty, the floors swept, the long dark burnished bar was polished and clean.

"I wanted to find out if anyone knew anything else on who robbed the ranch. I heard Mr. Goldman here is better than any newspaper so I was listening."

Goldman chuckled. "The only thing we know is that there are three outlaws here in the neighborhood. One of 'em is wanted for murder over in Tucson." Goldman filled in those details for Frisch.

Frisch looks at Wood and Cutter with his eyes narrowed. "Why do you think this is happening here in this area?"

Goldman says, "Well, it could be a couple of reasons. This gang could be on their way to someplace else and we just happened to be in their path. We had that happen a couple of years ago. Snake bellies crawled up from under the rocks and thought this town is an easy knock over."

Cutter took a sip of his coffee. "One or two of them might know this area and have a grudge and want to cause trouble or harm someone. Like a ranch hand that wasn't treated fairly or got shorted on their pay."

Thomas Wood was spinning his spoon around in a circle on the bar. "Harley was one of the fairest, most honest people I've ever known. Riley Stephens already said that he didn't know anyone that had been out to the ranch lately. The Long Ranch isn't a flashy, prosperous sort of place so it's a

73

mystery as to why anyone would want to do this."

"I'd say over this last month, there'd been a dozen strangers come in. Most of them had some sort of business here. The fight the other night was the first time in a couple of weeks I've seen anybody new around,"

Goldman with his arms crossed over his broad chest raised his eyebrows and nodded his head in agreement.

"Maybe Chick Miller knows more about folks bellying up in his place. Tommy Boardman keeps real good track of everyone going in and out."

"What fight? I'm out in the middle of a beautiful valley and missin' out on all the action?!" Frisch chuckled to himself. Goldman grinned and told Frisch the action-packed details of the dust up in the saloon the other night.

Cutter stood there a minute looking at the dark brewed coffee in his cup. He frowned and Jackson Frisch caught it.

"What are you thinking, Mr. Cutter? If you don't mind me askin'," Cutter looked up at Bert Goldman, who frowned at him. Then he looked at Wood, but with a long stare as if not seeing him.

"I'd like to think that I know the people of this town, this community. It's not often a man can say he has friends within a hundred miles, but we do here," Cutter said as he shook his head, grimacing.

"Nobody here is acting any different than they did a month ago. Everything is the same, everyone is the same. There is nothing different that I can see. How about you, Bert?" Goldman looked at him for a moment, his mind working. The bartender picked up the coffee pot and poured Cutter another full cup.

"I'm with you, Newton. We're missing something here, but I couldn't tell you what it is." The four men stood there musing over their own thoughts. The lanterns flickered in moving air casting dancing shadows on the walls. A door slammed somewhere and a lonely dog howled at the moon. Most citizens were in their homes, having dinner with their families, settling in for the long, cool night.

# 5 CHAPTER FIVE

The hinges on the heavy wooden trunk creaked as Cutter lifted the lid. Two small candles flickered on the table next to the bed. The musty smell of old papers and leather drifted out. Cutter made a mental note to get some ground coffee for the smell. The little brass plaque of Wm. Crockett and Co. had begun to blur under the growing patina.

He took out a couple of shirts, jeans and a pair of boots and set them up on the bed. He folded back the leather flap and tucked it down and he lifted out a couple of soft leather folders. The first folder was receipts and invoices from the blacksmith shop along with a twenty dollar bill. He closed it and put the folder aside, picking up the next one.

There is an old crinkled up photograph of a stagecoach with three men standing at the door. There is a huge white tent behind the coach with a sign that read "Whiskey fifty cents". Cutter was in the center wearing a star badge. Cutter smiled and turned the photograph over reading "Oliver, Cutter and Burns 1855." It was the first day Cutter was on the job as sheriff.

Small clippings of newspaper articles fluttered onto the bed from the soft leather folder.

Shortly after noon on February third, a man dressed in all black and wearing a mask entered the First Bank tent carrying a handgun and demanded money. After securing an amount of gold and cash from the teller, the man fled on foot, disappearing into the crowd near a saloon.

Cutter sorted a couple more articles until he stopped at one on May fourth. It was an article about miners being robbed on the way to sell their gold. One of the robbers was identified as an Angus Tolliver. The public was being warned about this man.

The third article of May twentieth gave a physical description. The article behind that was about a bank guard being killed and a gold deposit taken. Witness accounts matched the description of Tolliver as the bank robber. There were other men involved holding guns, but Tolliver was the man directing the robbery.

Cutter had heard Riley Stephen's description and Christopher Hawkins' description. But the most telling description had come from Harley Long who had heard someone yell Tolliver's name during the robbery at the Long Ranch.

Cutter ran his hand through his hair and rubbed his eyes, not wanting to bring the memories back. He was fighting remembering a very painful failing of his that he had hoped was buried forever. But old trouble has a way surfacing and here it was with this man coming into Bradford.

***

It was a little after five o'clock when Cutter leaned in the Mayor's door and then knocked twice to get Watley's attention.

Mayor Watley motioned him to come in as he scribbled a signature to a few documents and laid them aside. "What can I do for you, Newton?"

Henry Elliot followed Cutter into the office and closed the door behind them. Elliot took a seat to the side of the Mayor's desk and Cutter sat down in front of the Mayor and put the little wooden box onto the desk.

"Seven years ago, I was working my gold claim up in Bear Valley. The town was still dozens of tents back then with only the real building being the stagecoach stop. There was no law, no one to keep the peace and crime ran rampant. The beatings, assaults and murders were increasing. There were robberies and killings every day."

"The town decided to set up a sheriff and someone nominated me. To make a long story a little shorter, I ended up wearing a badge and working one end of that town to the other every waking moment," Cutter said as he took in a deep breath and let it out.

"It was a rich area of the country where dozens of men sank shafts down into the earth hitting bedrock. Using picks, shovels and most with their bare hands. They took the gold from the cracks and crevices where it had rested from millennia. They washed it in the creek and then put little sacks, often two or three ounces at time, strapping it onto their bodies to hide for the trip to town to sell it.

"It was a way to pay to continue to look for more gold. It paid for whiskey, women, horses, and it was gold that gave them a life far different from what they left hundreds of miles behind them. Gold had made men do things they wouldn't have done mere weeks before. Hang by rope hundreds of feet about certain death to chop out shiny flakes. Climb hundreds of feet deep into the earth with only the light of a candle reflecting on golden rock. It was an open, pure land until someone found color, then it was like insanity struck."

Cutter paused for a moment. He could feel Watley's eyes on him.

"There was an old man named Jimmy on the other side of the valley working his claim. I met him in one of the saloons one night and he told me a story about a doctor telling him he was going to die. The old man had accepted his fate, gave up, and laid down to wait for the end to come. One day the doctor stopped by and told him that it was too bad that the old codger was going to miss out on the biggest gold strike in the history of the world. I started to laugh and asked Jimmy if that was him in the story and he nodded and said yes. He'd been here two years and hadn't died yet." The three men chuckled.

"Jimmy was one of the men who described this one outlaw that was after the miners. I kept hearing the same description of a man doing the beatings and the robbing of miners for their gold. Twice I had my hands on him but he escaped. It was a mean, cold Friday when I finally got my hands on him.

"I had caught him coming out of a tent. I thought I had him dead to rights. He beat me down with that heavy pistol and got away. The next day I was on my back in the Doc's tent when the citizen's board came in and took my badge. They fired me. Said I couldn't do the job anymore and they put another man in that shot first and asked questions later."

The Mayor leaned his forearms on the desk, his brow made a deep furrow and looked at Elliot for a long moment. Then he looked back at Cutter.

Cutter continued. "A week or so ago I thought that I saw this man. He had met a man out by the auction house. The same man whose horseshoe I had fixed that afternoon. I couldn't be sure until I went back and read the newspaper articles about those robberies and murders years ago.

"I am reasonably sure that this is the same man. He is here in the area and his gang robbed Harley Long's ranch and killed him. Riley Stephens identified three of the men who robbed the ranch and beat both him and Harley. It's the same man. This man is running that gang."

The Mayor squinted at Cutter and shifted in his chair. "What's his name?"

"Tolliver. Angus Tolliver."

"How can you be sure it's him?" Cutter removed the yellowed newspaper articles from the small flat wooden box.

"I'll know when I get a good close look at him," Cutter said as he shifted in the wooden chair. Mayor Watley examined the stacks of the newspaper clippings on his desk. Then he looked at Cutter with his gray eyebrows bristling.

Elliot stood up. "It ain't the dog in the fight that counts, Cutter. It's the fight in the dog that counts. Sounds like you once had plenty of fight in ya. You just didn't have any help is all," Elliot stared hard at Mayor Watley.

Elliot spoke again. "I've heard stories, some rumors about an Angus Tolliver from San Francisco to St. Louis. I get around and listen to these tales taking into consideration the teller. Tolliver brings people in, does a robbery, and then disbands to the majority of the gang, letting them take spoils and loot. He uses other outlaws for his own means, letting them take the fall if they get caught."

"Thomas Wood sold a buckskin to a stranger this morning. By the description of the man and his guns, I'd say Tolliver has called in a gunfighter from somewhere," Elliot rubbed his chin, thoughtful for a moment.

"You'd best notify your bank that this gang may take a chance on robbing it. Make sure the bank is prepared and secure in case this gang turns their attention there."

Elliot took off his black hat and ran a hand over his head, scratching in thought. "If you can, Mr. Mayor, send telegrams to Santa Fe, San Francisco, Los Angeles and Denver asking about wants and warrants for the arrest or capture of Angus Tolliver."

Cutter gathered up the fragile, yellowed newspaper bits and stacked them back into the wooden box. He stood up.

"Thank you, Newton, for coming in and telling me about this. I know that could not have been easy for you," Mayor Watley pushed back from his desk and stood up.

"I'll get those telegrams sent out this evening," He nodded.

"Mr. Elliot, whatever assistance you need on this, you'll have the full cooperation of this office." There was a stern sober look on the Mayor's face.

Dusk had fallen out in the streets of Bradford. The lights of the town flickered in windows. Goldman's saloon was full, the piano was playing and one could hear the sweet voice of Yvette Lang singing about a cowboy and his horse. The graying dusk painted the prairie grass into silvery blades waving in the wind. Cutter watched Elliot walk towards the dressmaking shop where a lantern sat in the window.

*******

The next day there was a letter waiting for Cutter when he and Wood walked into Hotel Bradford for lunch. It was from Jackson Frisch's friend and architect Bruno Giordanni in San Francisco. He was available for Cutter's project and the letter outlined the fees and approximate timetable.

Cutter and Wood lunched on a tender, flavorful honey glazed ham steak and mashed potatoes with a red eye gravy. Wood had read the letter and it laid the white tablecloth.

"I had no idea that architects cost so much," Wood said as he wiped a bit of gravy on his chin. Cutter motioned to it.

Thomas dabbed it away with the soft cloth.

"I'll have to write back to him and explain what I have in mind," Cutter said as he took a bite of the fluffy potatoes in savory gravy. Georgianna had come out to fill their coffee cups. Cutter saw Wood wink at the pretty young girl.

"Mr. Frisch was right kind to recommend an architect. That sure saved you some time," Wood said as he sliced another bite of ham. A plate of hot sourdough biscuits and butter slid onto the table. Georgianna set down a little jar of honey and smiled as she turned away.

After lunch, Cutter stood at the reception desk and wrote out a letter to Mr. Giordanni. He also sent an authorization to Wells Fargo Bank disbursing five hundred dollars for the fee of the architect. Boardman smiled as he added the letters into the leather pouch for the three o'clock stage. A new part of his life, a good part was about to start and these thoughts were running through his head as he and Wood went down the hotel steps and walked back to the shop.

Bradford was a growing small town on the southern edge of California, twenty miles or so from the lonely flat desert of Mexico to the south. Man was claiming more land and now the war-weary masses were moving west to find a place where they could live in peace. The row of wood front buildings faced a dusty but well-kept street in the small town. There was order here and a sense of pride in the community of like-minded people. Cutter was about to put down roots and become a contributing member of this small town society.

The scruffy dog stretched and yawned coming out from under the town hall porch. It perked up its ears hearing a chucking sound and then moved off down the street. To the north in the distance the blackish gray Flint Hills clawed up in jagged peaks like a vicious saw edge. With Piñon trees, little water, and sparse bunch grass, only the fawn colored antelope with their flickering tails grazed there. To the east and west the green rolling hills were still fresh with the morning dew making a pretty contrast to the soft blue sky. The solitary Hookton Road followed along the low rise, twisting, and turning at the edge of the valley. Wide and well-traveled, it was the main road stretching from Four Wagon Bridge in the east to the summit in the Pacific Range leading to San Diego one hundred fifty miles away.

If there had been anyone watching he might have seen a lone rider in the shade of a towering cottonwood standing back off the road, smoke drifting upward from his cigarette. The black horse with a splash of white on its rump stomped a hoof at the flies and swished its tail swatting the biting insects. From up on the ridge came the sound of a walking horse in the loose rock. Then on solid ground, the horse picked its way down the narrow trail and then up a small rise, coming to a stop next to the black horse and its rider. After a few moments, both horses moved on down across the road and then disappeared behind a knoll in the grassy valley.

Nearer the river there was a wider flat place about fifty yards square where the grasses did not creep in and take root. Slight straight ridges no more than five or six inches high were here with some at right angles. Like the old foundation of walls. It was a forgotten place of man being reclaimed by nature. The structure was returning to the wilderness of the valley. The inhabitants had found a place, tried to make a life, but in the end they had moved on and never looked back.

It was at this spot the two riders had stopped. The horses were watered then picketed in the soft grass. The watery blues eyes of Reed Vance stared back up the trail looking for any blowing dust. These were the eyes of a young man out to prove he was superior, out to show that he was tough and fearless. A fast draw and fast thinking had brought him this far and now he held two hundred dollars in gold in his saddlebags for his next piece of work.

"Folks have vouched for you. Given recommendations for, young man," Tolliver said as he knelt digging a stick into the dirt. "You've proven yourself to men I trust and now I know you can get this job done."

The blue eyes looked icy cold at Angus Tolliver. Kingman had told him to watch his back and that Tolliver was not above killing any witnesses. Vance mentally agreed with Kingman now that he had seen and heard Tolliver. He had been told that Tolliver organized the jobs and that the pay was good. It had been presented as a simple dry gulch job, let the man lay where he fell and then ride north and disappear. Vance had a sister north of Las Vegas that he had not seen in a few years and relaxing at the foot of the Spring Mountains for the summer seemed attractive.

"So this happens tomorrow?" Vance asked with a glance at his buckskin grazing.

"You make sure there is no one in the bank before you go in. Close the door and lock it. The banker fella should be alone. The only time he closes the safe is when he closes down the bank for lunch or when he goes home," Tolliver said as he squinted.

"There's a side door. You'll let me in that door and I'll take my time with his office," there was a mean, ugly sneer on Tolliver's face now. "He's holding out on me, keepin' something from me and I'll find it."

Tolliver looked at the young man who was watching the river flow by. "You ride across the river and keep going north. Don't look back. Keep right on going."

This didn't feel right. Vance dug a rock out of the dry earth with his boot heel. That thorny feeling was coming up his back that was his premonition of trouble. Vance had the suspicion that it was this Tolliver that was the trouble. That little town was sleepy, calm, and relaxed. Vance could see that it was not the gold or money in the bank that Tolliver wanted. There was something else. Something that was not a money lust. And that always meant trouble.

Vance knew that Tolliver was watching and pushed his bottom lip out when he nodded. The younger man kept his eyes averted to the water. One of the horses nickered and Vance shot to his feet. Half a mile away on the road, the stagecoach lumbered along headed east. It started up a slight grade and at the top disappeared down the other side.

"Camp out here tonight. Be at the bank tomorrow at eleven and then you'll be on your way," Tolliver stood up dusting off his pants. Tolliver rode away along the road in the tracks of the stage. Vance waited an hour and then he was on his horse going cross country back to Bradford.

Vance waited in the brush behind the back corral of the stables. It was coming up at six o'clock and the young man needed to see that stable man. About ten minutes later, Thomas Wood closed the first door and locked it. Then as he swung the other door, he jumped as Reed Vance was standing behind it. Wood chuckled and shook his head.

"That's the second time you've made me jump, Mr. Vance,"

Vance hesitated a moment, then said. "I apologize, Sir. Can you tell me if you got a lawman in this town? I got some information that I need to pass on."

Vance looked past Wood at the street and saw nothing.

"We don't have a sheriff or Marshall or anything. We all handle our own. Sort of like a peace committee," Wood said.

The stablemaster could see the young man struggling with what he knew. "The blacksmith is on the committee, let me go get him and you can talk to him. He'll know what to do."

A minute later, Cutter came around the edge of the building and approached Vance. "Newton Cutter, Mr. Vance. I unlocked that back door to the tack room. Thomas, take him into the tack room and I'll shut both my doors."

A few moments, Wood came back into the tack room by the backdoor and locked it from the inside. Cutter and Wood looked at Vance who had sat down on a hay bale.

"Mister, your bank is about to get robbed. I was supposed to be the one doin' it. But something is wrong and I ain't takin' the blame for it," Vance said.

His eyes were level and straight as he told them of the meeting with Tolliver. "I don't kill people and someone is fixin' to kill that banker fella."

"Huddleston?" Wood looked at Cutter, perplexed. Ten minutes later, Wood and Cutter knew the details of Tolliver bringing in Vance to kill Huddleston. Cutter had something rolling around in his head, frowning in confusion.

"Mr. Vance, you've redeemed yourself here in bringing this to us. We can stop it now." Cutter's mind was racing about why Tolliver wanted Huddleston dead. Wanted him dead bad enough to pay someone to make it look like a bank holdup.

Vance could see that he needed to explain further. "My horse is out there in the brush. The gold is in the saddlebags. It's blood money and I don't want it. I'm a bit superstitious and it would bring me nothing but trouble. I've done a few things that I ain't proud of in my life and I'll be darned if I'll do another where an innocent man will die."

Vance's voice broke as he scratched his head. "I'd like to wait until dark and then ride north and forget I ever came into this town."

"Thomas, go get that horse and bring it up to the corral. Bring in those saddlebags, please," Cutter said as he looked at Vance.

While Thomas was retrieving the saddlebags, Cutter filled in Vance on what they suspected was a gang run by Tolliver.

"He never said anything about that. Didn't say a word about any robberies or ranches. He is keen on something in the bank office he wanted to find," Vance said with a shake of his head.

The young man felt like he had stepped into the path of a coming stampede. Wood came in the back door and laid the saddlebags on the table. Vance reached in and brought out four small cloth sacks of gold coins.

"Mr. Vance, I'm making a citizen's decision here and giving you a fifty dollar reward for the information you passed on to us," Cutter said as he dropped the coins into Vance's hand.

Vance frowned and looked at Cutter who motioned that it was alright.

"There is one more thing I need you to do. In order to document this so it will hold up in a court of law, I want you to recite this, recite it again for any arrests or legal actions."

Vance acknowledged the request with a nod.

At the end of the next hour, Mayor Watley had taken great care to write out the ten-page statement of Reed Vance. Just past nine o'clock that night, a buckskin carrying a man with watery blue eyes crossed the river and at the top of the next ridge the horse stopped in the darkness. The man turned in the saddle, taking one last look at the small town and then urged his horse on down the other side.

***

The next morning brought the scent of rain. Cutter breathed in the smell and paused to lift his head to get a better scent. He put down his tools and stepped outside the heavy door, looking to the sky. Thick, puffy white clouds floated along in the eastern sky. Cutter walked around to his left and looked west. A bank of gray clouds were crowding the western horizon, wind beginning to swirl the leaves bouncing around.

Off to the right a sudden flash of white light streaked through the sky. Cutter straightened and yelled for Wood to get all the horses inside and lock everything down. Storms could take a day to get to Bradford and some took fifteen minutes.

People were running across the plaza. A woman's hat tumbled end over end catching in a bush. Cutter felt his pulse pounding in his head as he raced to get everything shoved into the blacksmith shop.

At eleven o'clock a distant thundering crash echoed up against the building. The air was full of static electricity and it felt like needles in Cutter's skin. Thomas Wood came running around the door. Thunder was rumbling now closer and there were increasing flashes. Bits of paper rolled by in the street. Trees swayed and twisted in the wind.

The sky now to the west was blackening, tall rolling clouds carrying a torrent of rain heading right for Bradford. Mayor Watley came out and locked the Town Hall doors and hurried away. Alton Lengford closed the doors and then slid shut the storm door to the auction house. He ran down the steps and around the corner.

Most of the citizens were gone from the plaza. One of the shop owners had been struggling to  batten down a shutter and waved as he ran inside. Cutter pushed the lone work cart under the porch roof and set a heavy stone against the wheel.

A great bolt of lightning hit something out in the valley and the ground shook. As Cutter and Wood ran towards the hotel, they could feel first drops of the fury to come. Someone opened the hotel door and the men dashed in as a great sheet of water fell from the dark sky.

The shutters had been closed in time, but several people yelled for help with the upstairs windows. The rain slammed into the building, wind tore at anything loose and the thunder sounded like cannons at the door. A man with a towel ran up the stairs in answer to someone calling.

One of the men brought in an armload of firewood and set it down in the wood bucket. From his room upstairs, Cutter looked out at the water streaming down the window, low clouds heavy in the distance.

***

The next morning Wood and Cutter stepped down off the hotel porch and felt the soft, oozing earth beneath their feet. The earth was dark and wet from the rain. The street looked like churned up mud with puddles still waiting to soak in. The sky was filled with low gray rain clouds floating off to the east. The calm river north of Bradford roiled in a turbulent mass.

One of the big limbs off the cottonwood behind the church had fallen, and lay in splintered pieces near the corner of the building. Small branches were littering the plaza grass. People were standing on the porches and boardwalks looking at the muddied street.

The waxy green leaves and yellow flowers of the creosote bushes were glistening from the water still sitting on the plants. There was an earthy fragrance of loam, sage and wildflowers mixed with the scent of cattle and horses.

"Bruno Giordanni, please allow me to introduce building contractor Richard Vaughn from Beatrice. Mr. Vaughn, the architect for my house, Bruno Giordanni." The two men shook hands and walked over to the long table where the house building plans were unfolded. Cutter watched the two men, familiar immediately.

There were three large sheets showing the house front, back and elevation of the new structure. There were two big rooms in front downstairs, each twenty by thirty which would be the classrooms. There was a parlor and a kitchen downstairs also.

Upstairs were four bedrooms, a sitting room, a larger kitchen, Cutter's study, and library. Two sides of the house had wide verandas and the back of the house had a large flagstone patio.

Cutter was studying the drawings. "Is there room for a stairway to come down into the first floor kitchen? My family' home in North Carolina had a back stairway going down to the kitchen and it was very convenient.

After a moment of studying the plans, Giordanni stood up." If we remove this closet on the first floor and move the pantry over and this second floor closet and about a foot of the sitting room. Yes, I think a narrow kitchen stairs could be built in that space.

Cutter pointed to the first floor drawing. "I'd like to add a wood burning stove in each of the classrooms."

"The elementary school up at Beatrice has a wood burning stove in each classroom. Those kids stay right warm during the winter," Vaughn was nodding as he wrote in his notebook. "I know where a couple of large wood burning stoves are at. I'll run a vent for each one. Good idea."

"I'd say you have a very straight-forward solid house here, Mr. Cutter. I won't say it will be easy to build. No house is easy. But it is not as hard as the Victorians in Boston or San Francisco," Vaughn smiled.

"I agree! Drawing up those Victorians is difficult. They are so popular in San Francisco, there are builders who won't build any other type of house. And they are putting them right smack up against each other in some places," Giordanni sat back in his chair sipping the steaming coffee.

"On what I see here, I would say it will take a good six months to build it. I know I can procure the building supplies nearby. There is only one other house going up in the county that I know of so I should be able to find labor," Vaughn said as he looked at Cutter. The blacksmith had leaned over the details of the second floor.

"I'd propose we start building in about two weeks, unless you have another start date," Vaughn was looking at Cutter.

The curly head nodded. "Papers are signed, money has been paid. I'm waiting on the deed now from Mr. Huddleston over at the bank. He said that it should be here on Friday. We're ready to go the next day."

Vaughn indicated something on one of the drawings and he and Giordanni discussed it between themselves. Both men smiled and nodded to Cutter.

"Gentlemen, I'd like to take you out to the site," Cutter took the last drink of his coffee and stood up.

The shining sun had warmed the day and a couple of doves cooed in a tree. The three men walked about a quarter mile south of town, boots kicking up little bits of dust. Vaughn looked at the old foundation walls and predicted no problems removing those. After an hour, some general measurements had been taken, the ground marked, and the front of the house had been established.

Mayor Watley sat with his wife at the hotel dining table in the corner. "They said the same thing. No help available. Santa Fe is waiting for Washington to send a Marshall, as it is," he sipped his coffee.

"Have you heard from the Texas Rangers yet?" Addie took a bite of her breakfast and watched the worried mayor.

"No. That is the oddest part. Usually they respond faster than any other office, too. But this time, not a word," the Mayor leaned his arm on the table and stared at his meal. "It might be prudent to send them another telegram, see if that gets a response."

The hotel lobby door opened and three people came in. Two small girls ran into the dining room and climbed up into chairs at a table. Their mother and father came in and sat down with the happy chattering girls.

Mayor Watley had the feeling that no matter what he did, it would not be enough to protect the lives of such innocent families as this. He had never received much guidance or information about what to do when calamities happen. It had always been a calm, relaxed town. As he sipped the rich, dark coffee, he resolved that he would try the Rangers again.

"Mr. Cutter?" William Huddleston stood next to the heavy wooden door, looking into the empty blacksmith shop.

"Be right there, just a minute!" Cutter yelled from somewhere in back of the building.

A moment later, Cutter and Wood came out carrying a small stack of eight foot wood planks. They set them down in front of a couple of sawhorses. Cutter wiped his hands of a rag and turned to Mr. Huddleston, who held a large, white envelope.

Mr. Huddleston took a document out of the envelope. It was the deed to Cutter's land. "Congratulations, Mr. Cutter. You are the owner of the parcel now. The deed was recorded in Los Angeles on Monday, just to be certain," Huddleston said with a nod. The banker's face held a quick grimace.

"I sent a letter of confirmation up to your bank in San Francisco, as you directed." Cutter took the document and looked it over. Wood came up and after wiping off his hands, read the deed. He nodded and smiled.

"We need some shovels so we can break ground now!" Wood said with enthusiasm and Cutter laughed with his friend.

"Thank you, Mr. Huddleston for your help on the deed." Cutter said to the banker with a nod.

He saw the banker looking about the shop building. Huddleston rubbed his hands together. The blacksmith had remembered someone talking about outstanding loans tied to deeds handled by the bank. One afternoon, he went to the attorney Merle Doyle to do some research on the one lot he liked for the new house. The deed was free of loans, but for an abandoned lot with no buildings the asking price was high.

Upon Cutter's request, Doyle had written to the owner in South Carolina and made an offer at half the original price and it had been accepted.

"So you are ready to build? Have you found an architect and a builder for your house, Sir? I have a couple reputable experts I could recommend." Darting small dark eyes were shifting from the deed to Cutter and back.

The Bradford bank's fee for processing the sales price had been reduced to near nothing after that lawyer Doyle had gotten involved. Huddleston had made some tentative plans for a couple hundred dollars and now there was no money for any plans.

"My plans were finalized a couple of weeks ago. The builder is getting the supplies ready to ship in. I am anticipating the start this Saturday," Cutter said as he nudged Thomas.

The stablemaster made a few, quick movements to fold the deed up and slid it back into the envelope.

"I'll be sure to send you an announcement of when the construction is completed."

"Thank you, Sir. Good day, Sir," Huddleston's voice was cold and abrupt with stifled anger. It irritated him that he had been excluded from a profitable gain. It was apparent the young blacksmith had money sitting in the bank up in San Francisco and Huddleston could not come up with a way to get at it. As he walked up the street, the banker realized that he had been shut out of the money to be made on building this new house. He clenched his fists and frowned.

Cutter and Wood walked back into the shop.

"I'd say that banker would be a man frustrated at not making a dime off of you, my friend," Wood said with a grin. He tied on his heavy leather apron.

Cutter nodded. "Yep. I took Doyle's advice and when we settled on the negotiated price to be paid for the land, Huddleston was in an uproar that the full original price was reduced. I would say he might have missed out on some sort of commission."

Later that day, Wood and Cutter were seen walking around Cutter's new home site. Talking and gesturing as if trying to fill in the space for each other they walked the footprint of the house and then the boundaries of the five acre lot. That night telegrams went to Giordanni, Vaughn and the Wells Fargo Bank in San Francisco.

# 6 CHAPTER SIX

The following afternoon, Mayor Watley tore open the envelope and took out the single page letter from The Permanent Council, Governor of Texas, Austin, Texas. They knew of no Texas Rangers working in the general vicinity of Bradford, but there was a possibility of a Ranger-at-Large available to take a temporary commission and assist the town. Once they found him, he would order to report to Mayor Watley and provide any and all means for the apprehension of the outlaws.

The Mayor sat back with his shoulders slumped in disappointment. He took in a deep breath and let out the sigh, shaking his head. He rubbed his eyes. Little bits of dust floated in the sunbeam from the window, rising and swirling in a draft. Addie worked a stitch on her needlework in a chair near the hearth. The old leather and wood chair creaked as he leaned on the desk and read the letter again. Petty criminals and common thieves had attacked the Harley Long Ranch and the Ladd Ranch causing life loss and destruction. The gang of outlaws was being masterminded by this Benning and another man that had yet to be discovered. The Mayor had no resources.

Nobody wanted to be sheriff, nobody wanted to take responsibility for taking a life, if needed. Watley stood and went to the door and stepped out into the cool air., The four walls had begun to close in on him. There was a scruffy dog gnawing on a bone under the porch of the auction house. The sound of a hammer ringing against iron came from the blacksmith shop. Goldman was sweeping off the porch chatting with a man sitting on a horse. Watley knew the people in this town and liked them. After living here for four years, he ran for mayor and was astounded to have won by a landslide. He had been trying to find help for his little town, but there was none to be found.

Once a stranger, but now he was an upstanding citizen with the interests of the community at the forefront. He and Addie had become part of this small town and they had flourished here. A criminal gang had dug in like a tick at South Landing and someone had to face the risk and go out there and remove them. Nobody volunteered. William Watley had an ugly sensation that his days of glory were about to come to an end.

When the stage delivered its bag of mail this morning, there were three letters for Henry Elliot. As a weary Elliot stepped into the hotel lobby and closed the door, Tommy Boardman waved to him and handed the letters with a slight smile. Elliot went up the stairs and after he locked the door to his room he opened the first letter.

It was a wedding announcement of Miss Elizabeth Dutton to Mr. Reginald Livingston scheduled for Los Angeles in August. Elliot smiled as he remembered the pretty Elizabeth, or Beth as he had called her. Elliot had not seen her in over a year as he had no intention of marrying into a questionable business enterprise that her father ran with a local criminal element. Rather than speak ill of her father to the young lady, Elliot resolved to go and never return.

The second letter was from the First National Bank of Chicago that had been forwarded from the hotel in Denver. Elliot was happy to see that his railroad investments had been profitable and while not wealthy, he was comfortable.

Elliot pulled off his dusty boots and stripped off his shirt and pants. He washed his face and chest, shaved, and dried off with a soft white towel. He sat on the bed and looked at the last letter from The Permanent Council, Governor of Texas, Austin, Texas. The first page he read, then read again and then laid it face down on the bed. The second page was the list of Texas Rangers who had died in the line of duty. At the bottom, was Woodruff, Francisco. The notation showed he died in the apprehension of a known fugitive in Sonora, Mexico. Henry frowned and grimaced with sorrow of the death of a man who was true and good and had the intelligence of a scholar.

For the next hour, Elliot penned a letter to Maggie Woodruff, Frank's widow. It was important to him to tell Mrs. Woodruff of the friendship and camaraderie that he had shared with her husband. The pages were folded and stuffed into an envelope and he would mail it in care of the Texas Rangers in Austin when he went down to the lobby.

Elliot had dressed and was fastening the cuff of his shirt when he remembered the page lying face down on the bed. He read it again and dropped it once more onto the bed. After he had his black jacket on, Henry picked it up and folded it small and flat, sliding it into the soft leather wallet he carried in his coat pocket. Making sure everything was in its place he stepped out into the hallway and closed the door. He wanted friendly company right now, good conversation and a bite to eat. Knowing what he had to do, knowing what was coming, he wanted another brief taste of a normal life before it all changed forever.

There was an argument going on out at the rails. Someone was waving their hands and another man was saying something indistinguishable. Henry Elliot was stepped back against the corner of the town hall. He could see Newton Cutter perched on the roof of the blacksmith shop. The Bradford Safety committee had been on high alert as they knew someone was going to try to rob the bank.

Elliot could see Carmella Frisch and Dawn White standing on the church steps talking in laughing tones with Addie Watley. It had been a painful few weeks for the seamstress, and Dawn had lately managed to relax. She had begun to enjoy the company of her niece. They were happy, but they were mere steps away from the bank and, in the lawman's eyes, in the line of fire.

Carmella looked around the small town, at the warm sunlit street, the dappled sunlight dancing on the church wall. The cool breeze in the shade of the porch overhang tossed a tendril of hair. She had remarked on what a lovely, peaceful small town it was. Dawn turned to look at the three men arguing and squinted a bit, not recognizing any of them.

"Who are those men?" Addie's voice was irritated at a noisy group of men disturbing her nice afternoon.

From between the church and the bank strode three tall men with weapons in their hands. Dawn gripped Carmella's arm silencing her. Their attention was turned jerkily to the right and a gunshot sounded. The heavier man of the three fell to one knee attempting to lift his weapon. Carmella gasped loudly and Addie tugged her back into the doorway of the church.

From the corner of the town hall a booming fire came from a shotgun and the kneeling man fell against another bigger man, disturbing the man's aim. Another boom from the shotgun showed a growing red stain on the left leg of the smaller, thinner man and he fell into the dusty street.

The wire had only come across this morning of the warrant for the arrest of Jim Caudle, for cattle rustling up in the northern valley and in Nevada. Only an hour later was another wire for the arrest of Frisco Hafton. The man lying face down in the street matched Hafton's description, but Elliot had not had a clear look at the other man. He showed the wires to Cutter and Wood to see if either was recognized.

Elliot's hand was stiff, but he held the Colt and brought it level as Caudle's first shot missed and slammed into the side of the building. Elliot dropped down to one knee and got a shot off making splinters fly from the water trough. Elliot rolled back into the alley and broke open the shotgun, his fingers tightening as they fed shells into the big gun.

Then he was up, running behind the hotel and dodged around the porch of the lawyer's office. Cutter and Wood had started to draw fire and Elliot sprinted around Doyle's office and over behind the dressmaker shop. He leaned far enough around the corner to see the man lying in the street, but not the other shooter.

Wood was yelling something and pointing to the west of town. Cutter and Wood climbed down off the roof and came running up the street to the man lying face down.

"The other one is wounded, but he made it to his horse and rode west," Thomas said as he rolled the man over to see a dark stain was in the dirt underneath him.

"Frisco Hafton."

Elliot went through the dead man's pockets.

"Get over to Doc's and tell him he might be called out to work on a gunshot or two. If he goes, we'll have to follow him to find the other man." Elliot stood up with a wrinkled torn scrap of paper 'Bank 2pm' was scribbled on it.

"Frisco, you are late for your appointment at the bank," Elliot let the scrap of paper fall to the ground. "I need to get the ladies out of the church. Cutter, can you bring over a wagon or a horse so we can load him up? I'd rather the ladies did not see this."

Mayor Watley trotted towards them, his red face sweating.

Cutter ran past him to the blacksmith shop.

"Who is this?" He peered at the man,

"A guy named Frisco Hafton, Mayor," Thomas Wood picked up the scrap of paper and the Mayor read it. "Your wife, Carmella Frisch and Dawn White are in the church, Mr. Mayor.

"Alright, bring him over and we'll put him in the constable's office until we can figure out what to do with him," Watley frowned and grimaced. "Well, it looks like you three have yourselves a reward on this man."

Wood shook his head. "No, no. That money goes to the fund for the new school." He waved his hands to indicate he would not accept any money.

"Thomas is right. Let's make sure the kids have what they need for school."

Elliot saw Cutter bringing a horse trotting up the street. It took a few minutes to get the dead man laid over the horse and over to the little office behind town hall. Wood grabbed a shovel and removed the dark stained dirt from prying eyes. Watley went to the church and rescued the ladies inside.

Elliot hugged Dawn and assured her that he was not hurt or injured, but he was grimy with dirt. Smiling, Elliot informed Carmella that Cutter was just as good and was assisting the Mayor with whatever he needed. Carmella's eyes got big and round when she heard that Thomas Wood and Newton Cutter had been instrumental in stopping a bank robbery.

The bank's doors were closed and locked when Wood went to check. The bank could not have been robbed at any rate as William Huddleston had ridden out of town and was at South Landing checking on his other investment.

Cutter walked through the connecting door to the stables and found Wood wrestling with a saddle skirt. "You need a hand?"

It looked like the saddle was winning the fight. Wood looked up. "No, I'm almost done."

Cutter sat down on the wooden stool and watched Thomas bend and work the leather. His eyes saw but his mind was on another matter.

"What's on your mind?" Thomas had moved the finished saddle to the stand and had a bit of saddle soap on a cloth rubbing it over the stiff leather.

Newton grimaced and shook his head and said, "You'll think I've lost my mind. I want to go out to South Landing and get a look at that hideout. See how many there are. See what we are up against."

Wood's mouth dropped open.

"You ain't goin' out there by yourself, are ya?"

"I will if I have to. But I was sorta hopin' that you'd like a nice midnight ride along with me," Cutter said as he tried to smile.

"Well, I ain't just gonna let you run off out there by yourself, Mr. Cutter," Thomas said with a smirk.

"Can't let you be runnin' off and havin' fun without me." Wood slapped the back of his buddy, grinning.

*******

The night was silent with no sounds. No owls, no rushing wings, no scampering feet, or growls. Cool air like a long drink of a free running mountain spring. The musty smell of earth and sage mingled with the horse and leather scents. Two black horses and riders in black with black saddles. Nothing shiny, nothing bright.

In the darkness the bushes, trees and outcroppings became dim and a shade of charcoal. The thousands of twinkling lights overhead stretched from horizon to horizon so clear and bright a man could hit one with a well-thrown rock. The horses trotted down the twisting, turning clay and gravel lane.

Two hours later, the horses were picketed in a grassy spot, Wood and Cutter were flat on their bellies on a sandy ridge overlooking Kneeland Road and South Landing beyond. Lights burned in the two of the windows of the old stone house. There was a corral about a hundred yards to the east with a lean-to shelter for the horse. It looked like three mounts stood in the corral dozing.

Both Cutter and Wood heard the metallic click at the same time and rolled in opposite directions, scampering across the soft grass. Cutter started to dive behind a mound when something struck a wicked blow on the shoulder. Clawing, he fell sideways, coming down on something hard that crunched. There was another shot and he tried to roll up on his hands but the shoulder would not hold his weight and he fell further.

His ears thundered with a roar and he rubbed his eyes to wipe away the sparkling lights. With care, he edged up over the mound trying to see in the darkness. He dare not call out for Wood. To a distance on his left he heard the boots stomping in the grass. Then behind him there was another sharp splitting crack. Gunshot, then silence.

He must have passed out because the next time he opened his eyes the stars had changed. He was on his back, covered in sandy dirt, and his mouth was dry. He spit out a couple pebbles and sat up. The agony of his left shoulder throbbed and stabbed and he fell over onto his right side, struggling to keep the groan in his throat. His hands were sticky with his own blood.

Wood was out there somewhere and hurt or dead. The camp must have posted a lookout on the ridge. The two men were seen from a mile away. The pain was shooting across his shoulder now. He rolled using his right hand, pushing up so he was in a sitting position. His vision was blurry and he blinked trying to clear it, then shook his head. He guessed that he was about fifty feet from where he and Wood had lain.

Nothing moved. He held his breath to listen for any sound, a match striking, a boot heel crunching in gravel. Nothing. His mouth and throat were dry and he kept spitting out sandy dirt. His temple throbbed. That was when he realized someone had tried to bury him alive.

Using his right hand and legs he managed to get into a crouch and crept along until he arrived back in the grassy ridge. His eyes cleared a bit and about twenty yards away was an odd-shaped mass. He strained harder to see it when it moved.

Every movement shot pain through his shoulder. Cutter crept over nearer and saw the black shirt and pants. Wood! Three more feet and the blacksmith rolled Wood onto his back. Wood groaned and collapsed. Cutter waited for a good ten minutes and then laid down next to Wood.

"Thomas, can you hear me?"

Cutter reached out and held Wood's hand which was slick and sticky with blood.

"Squeeze my hand if you can hear me." The wounded man's grip was shaky and weak.

"I got to get you on a horse and back to Doc Baines. Can you ride?"

Thomas didn't answer but he squeezed harder this time. "I'll go get the horses. I'll come back for ya."

As he crawled over the next hundred feet, Cutter stopped as his hands went over shell casings. Two of them. He shoved them into his pocket and kept going around the knoll and down the slight hill. In the trees a ways over to the left there was movement. A dried branch cracked and dead leaves rustled. He froze waiting for more movement. After ten minutes he started in again creeping towards where the horses were picketed.

Gone! The grass had been clipped, some of it trampled. He fell onto his right side in dejection and cradled his throbbing left arm. The thought of walking all the way back made his shoulder ache that much worse. Then he heard the rhythmic clipping of grass by the horses. Throwing caution to the wind, he clucked twice and one of the horses nickered. Crawling, he found them farther on down the grassy incline. He washed the dirt and sand out his mouth with the canteen.

It took close to half an hour to get both horses up closer to the ridge. Another half hour to drag Wood down the incline. Cutter pushed him up into the saddle only to have him fall back over onto Cutter. Leading the horses back down towards the road, Cutter mounted and began the walk back to the town.

Again, he was jerked awake by the sound of gunfire. He struggled to clear his head and rubbed his eyes. He found Thomas sitting more upright in the saddle ahead of him moving at a trot, leading Cutter's horse. He could feel the cool air hitting his face and he put both hands on the saddle horn and gripped it for balance. His shoulder screamed and there was a river of stickiness down his back. He tasted water in his mouth and he drank.

When he woke it was still dark and the air was much cooler. Thomas's horse was standing to one side of the road, grazing with an empty saddle. Cutter shook his head trying to clear his vision. There was now a constant humming in his head and he rubbed his eyes. In the darkness about fifty feet back lay Wood, half off the road. Off balance and unable to use his left arm, Cutter's feet hit the ground and he fell into the grass, rolling until he came up against something solid.

It was a slow, painstaking journey to get up on his feet and get to the horse for the canteen. His agony was growing and he realized that he must have lost a lot of blood. That was why he was weak. On his knees, cradling his left arm, Cutter crawled along the side of the road back to Wood. He dribbled water into the dry mouth and after a few minutes, Wood responded and groaned.

"Come on, Thomas, we gotta get up and get going."

Newton had gotten to his feet and was struggling to get Wood up. An arm went around Newton's shoulder and he tasted blood from biting his lip. Once upon the horse, Cutter's head throbbed in pain, and his shoulder wound dribbled blood down his back. He tried to figure out which way to go was right but in the end, kept going in the same direction as before.

He was alive and Wood was alive. He knew that he would know what happened, but not here, not in this darkness and not until he made it back to town. The only thing he was sure of is that the shots had come from behind them. Cutter's hand reached down and the rifle was still in the sleeve. He looked back and Wood was still somehow in the saddle, woozy and bobbing like a rag doll.

He jerked awake from the sound of the horses walking through the river. They were north of town and the horses had left the road and found the faster way home. His eyes were dry, hot, and blurry. He rubbed them and looked around to see that some miracle had kept Thomas on his horse.

The fire in his shoulder screamed in lightning pain as he lifted Wood from the saddle and both men fell to the ground. How long he lay where he fell, he did not know. Only then did he know that hands lifted him, a horse nickered, voices murmured and cold cloths. The dark night swirled around and Cutter fell into a blackness.

When Newton opened his eyes, the gingham curtains at the window waved in the breeze. Everything was blurry and his head was a pounding drum. He closed his eyes again, trying to calm the pounding and heard someone come into the room. Another cool cloth on his head and someone wiped off his face. Again, he tried to open his eyes.

"Doc Baines, I think he is waking up!" Dawn's voice. It was Dawn there with him.

Cutter rolled his head and grimaced in pain, groaning.

"Now, Newton, you're gonna have to hold still for a while, Son. You've got a pretty bad knock to the head and some stitches," Doc Baines said as he held Cutter's wrist counting.

"Thomas.."

"Mr. Thomas is in the next room, being fussed over by Miss Georgianna. She cooked up some broth for you boys and has been feeding it to ya for two days now."

Two days. He'd been here for two days. The darkness crept back up around his eyes and he fought to open them and see, but he couldn't fight it. Every so often he could feel a soft damp cloth against his face and felt his body turned and a bandage replaced.

Two men were talking in the room and Cutter struggled to open his eyes. Blurry figures swam. He tried again and blinked hard a couple of times. Wood sat in a chair at the foot of his bed with his head wrapped in a white bandage. He closed his eyes and made a silent thank you to the Creator. The other man was Elliot who was drinking a cup of coffee which smelled really pretty darned good to Cutter.

Henry was looking at Newton as Doc Baines and Dawn White lifted him up to a sitting position. It was tolerable but still brought on a tremendous throbbing.

"A bullet split open your shoulder leaving a long red gash over part of your back. You've also got a pretty deep gash in your head. Both you and Thomas do. I suspect you were both face down and someone tried to put a bullet in the back of your heads."

Doc Baines tried to examine Cutter's eye.

"It's called a concussion where your brain gets shaken around inside your skull. It's gonna hurt for a while. Another week lying in bed and then only limited walking around. I'd say you two are the luckiest gents I know right now," the gruff doctor said. He dismissed Cutter with a wave of his hand. "Like he'll listen to me. Some men have harder heads than others!"

"Your little adventure out to South Landing put the scare into whoever was laying low out there. It's cleared out. Not a soul around. Everyone is long gone," Elliot said with a nod.

Cutter cleared his throat and Dawn gave him a sip of water.

"Thomas, you okay?"

"I will be, but I think I could still use some nursin' by Miss Georgianna," Wood said with a wink.

"Oh I see how you are!"

"Thomas filled me in pretty much on what he remembers but I'd like to hear you tell what happened, Newton," Henry Elliot said.

He had a serious look on his face. For the next half hour, Thomas Wood, Henry Elliot, and Newton Cutter discussed, analyzed, dissected, and traded theories about what happened that night.

Just as Elliot was getting ready to leave, Cutter stopped him.

"How's Carmella?"

Elliot smiled, holding his hat. "She's over at Dawn's resting. She hasn't left your side these last days. I'll send her over later."

After three days of nursing Cutter, Jackson insisted that Carmella return to the Long Ranch. The day had come for buyers to visit and review the property.

Friday morning was clear and bright with only a few scattered clouds. The breeze sent rolling waves through the green grass in the valley. Movement out of the corner of Jackson Frisch's eye made him turn his head. Carmella came out, pulling on her gloves.

"Sure you won't come riding with me? It's a gorgeous day," his daughter had the most beautiful smile.

"You go ahead. I'll sit here and watch you for a while," Jackson winked to her. "Besides, I'm expecting a couple of prospective buyers for the ranch today.

"I'm taking the roan out. We get along together very well and I'd like to see what he can do," she had on a long leather skirt, a light blue blouse and her buckskin jacket. Out of the many pairs of fancy boots she could wear, she always picked the oldest, and the most worn. Jackson chuckled.

***

It had been three days now that Carmella had been back to the ranch. Newton was finally up and around, but still shaky. Thomas Wood and Clay Dunagan were handling the business and things were moving at a snail's pace towards normalcy. Jackson wanted his daughter closer at hand lately.

Frisch sat on the veranda of the ranch watching Carmella ride out in a distant valley. Her bobbing head rose and fell amongst the grass and trees and the exercise had brought back a glowing rosiness to her cheeks. Jackson had been starting to realize that Carmella had feelings for Newton Cutter, but it wasn't until the young man was wounded that he accepted it.

Somehow in his parental thinking, he had imagined Carmella married to a successful banker or businessman in San Francisco, living in a fine house and moving in society. But yet, when he thought about his own life, it had not worked out as his parents imagined it either.

Frisch looked at the cigarette trailing a gray snaking stream up into the air. Cutter was successful, strong, and happy living in a small country town. He had many friends who supported him and he had exhibited an exceptional generosity that gave back to the community. As with most western men, there was more to Newton Cutter than met the eye.

When Carmella came in from her ride a few hours later, she was surprised to find three men seated in the living room at the round table. Charts, graphs, and maps were laid out showing the boundaries and characteristics of the ranch. They stood up and Jackson held out his hand to her.

"My daughter, Carmella," Jackson said, gesturing to his guests.

"This is Ben Davies from the Rocking R Ranch near Santa Fe."

Carmella smiled and pulled off her glove, extending her hand. "How do you do, Mr. Davies?" His rough hand felt like sandpaper against her skin.

"This is Johnny Lipscomb from the McCann Ranch over in the valley."

As they shook hands, Carmella felt an enveloping presence moving from Lipscomb beginning to swirl around her. It was like sand falling down over her skin.

"My pleasure, Miss Frisch." Like a bursting bubble the cloaking feeling was gone. She blinked several times and gave him a pretty smile.

"I believe you know Marty Ladd," Jackson said as he nodded toward the tall, blonde man coming around the edge of the table to greet her.

"I certainly do! Mr. Ladd, it is good to see you again," She clasped his strong firm handshake and held it a moment longer.

"I believe you still owe me a dance, Sir!"

It was a big smile to her. "Yes, ma'am, I believe I do. Perhaps I'll pay my debt at the Summer Ball."

Ladd had clear watery blue eyes below all that thick wavy blonde hair. His white smile was dazzling and he nodded his head.

"Can I get coffee, Father? Or something else?"

"Coffee would be fine, dear."

The men were murmuring a conversation while she put cups and a sugar bowl on the platter. She had folded the cloth for the coffee pot when she heard someone say Cutter's name. She went to stand next to the door out of sight and listened.

Her father was talking. "Bank, general store, a gun shop, assorted saloons and the town hall. There's an auction house of sorts. Thomas Wood owns the stables in partnership with Cutter."

Someone said something but she couldn't make it out.

"Both he and Thomas Wood helped save the barn and offered to come all the way out here to help rebuild. We are pretty much on our own out here and it is a comfort to know folks in town will pitch in to help," Marty Ladd said with a voice that was strong and sure.

They were quiet for a while. After the coffee had been settled in, Carmella grabbed three apples from the bowl and went out the door pulling on her gloves. Her father and his guests were standing on the porch and he was pointing out the view to the valley.

Johnny Lipscomb stepped to the rail and watched Carmella feed an apple to the hammerhead roan.

"You ride a hammerhead, Miss Frisch? Isn't he kind of ornery and mean?"

Lipscomb had that narrow eyed smirk on his grinning face.

Carmella could feel his voice grating on her. Something was off, something not right about him.

"No, not mean, Sir," Carmella said with a nod. She put a foot in the stirrup and vaulted herself into the saddle. She laughed, patting the big horse's neck.

"But I have taught him to bite on command." She waved her hand to her father and trotted the roan down the yard and towards the barn.

Her father stood there chuckling.

"Seems a bit odd for a fine young lady to be riding a hammerhead, Mr. Frisch," Ben Davies took a drag off his cigarette. "You aren't afraid the horse kicking or biting her?"

"He doesn't like men. Riley, the ranch hand can't get close to him. He was Mrs. Long's horse, born and raised. I've heard old horse trainers talk about how hammerhead roans are smart and that they think and have opinions much like people," Frisch said as he shook his head.

"He rushed against the corral fence when I tried to get a look at him the first time he came in. He doesn't like being in the barn. Already kicked two boards down." Davies and Lipscomb laughed.

"It doesn't surprise me that the roan takes to her," Marty Ladd said as he leaned against the rail watching the trotting horse.

"She's even better handling the Percherons." Marty chuckled with

Jackson and did not see Johnny Lipscomb's mouth fall open.

***

The morning had come with a chill. The tall cottonwoods dripped with moisture from the heavy, gray clouds. On the Flint Hills thirty five miles to the north storm clouds gathered. By noon, the wind had come up, tumbling loose bushes and leaves across the now damp road and off into the grass. The heavy limbs of the tree dragged back and forth over the roof of the Faraway Inn.

Gianni "Papa" La Costa stood on the back veranda watching the river get faster and higher. The tumbled boulders in the center of the stream were covered in the rushing water. He breathed in the cool air scented with sage and the musty earth. Folks had lit out for home an hour ago and the saloon and dining room were empty except for two men at the corner table. Papa ran gnarled fingers through the silver hair and watched the water.

Max, the cook, came out wiping his hands on a white towel.

"Dinner is all set up and ready. Beef pot roast with potatoes, carrots, and onions. Amanda is pulling out five loaves of sourdough in a few minutes. There's berry cobbler, apple pie and blueberry cornbread," Max said. He thought for a moment, looking down at his shoes.

"We still have half a pot of chili. Do you want anything else set up?" Max asked as he poured Papa another cup of the steaming coffee.

"No, that's good. Not too many folks will be venturing out. There is a storm comin' in. I'm going to walk down to the stables and make sure everything is alright down there. Chi should be riding in about an hour or so. I'd think she'd be hungry."

Gianni took his heavy, white mug and walked down to the end of the veranda and down the steps.

Max took the pot out to the saloon doorway and held it up to the two men in the saloon. "More coffee, gentlemen?" The taller man held up his cup and Max smiled and went over to fill it.

"There's a good storm rollin' in from the Flint Hills. If either of you need to be somewhere, you might want to ride ahead of that rain," Max said with a smile. "If not, dinner is ready when you are. Just call out!"

"Thank you kindly," the taller man said.

Dark eyes looked at Angus Tolliver and nodded his head. They didn't speak again until the cook was back in the kitchen.

Royal Benning drummed his fingers on the red tablecloth. He was looking at his coffee cup and moved his head left to right with a grimace.

"Caudle made it as far as the valley. There's a doctor over there who doesn't ask too many questions, but I haven't heard anything else. The bank wasn't even open that day. Men got shot and killed on your word, Tolliver," Benning was spinning a spoon around and around with his fingers. "For nothing."

"Where are Everett and Iverson?"

"Iverson rode to Denver after they changed horses. Everett was talking about a stagecoach job going down into Mexico. After all the shooting stopped he packed up and headed south," Benning took a drink of his coffee.

"He said the county is all gunned up and there was nothin' for him here."

They were silent for a moment grinding through what had happened. Everett was right. Every house, every ranch every window now had a gun or a loaded rifle waiting for someone to spit wrong. Unless you are a friend or neighbor, you were one step away from having a bull's eye on your forehead.

The heavy door opened and the wind swirled in. Candles flickered and the fireplace flames danced. Two men came in and Tolliver lifted a hand in greeting. They took off their slickers and hung them next to the door. They hung their damp hats on the stand and walked over to the table.

"What will you have, gentlemen?" Max asked as he stepped behind the bar. He leaned thick muscular arms on the bar and his eyes sized up the newcomers.

"Whiskey for me," the heavier man said with the mustache.

"Coffee, please. Smells good in here, you got food?" the thinner man asked. He sniffed the air with a grin.

"Yes, sir. Dinner is ready when you are. Beef pot roast with potatoes, carrots and onions," Max poured a shot of whiskey and brought it along with an empty cup and the coffee pot to the table. After he left, Tolliver spoke.

"Royal Benning, Ben Davies," Benning nodded to Davies. Davies motioned to the thin man beside him.

"Jag Rossiter, this is the man I was telling you about, Angus Tolliver," Rossiter nodded and sipped his whiskey.

"What do you think?" Tolliver asked as he sat back in the wooden chair.

"Nice ranch. Five thousand acres. A bit pricey though at twenty two thousand. He's selling the timber rights and the mineral rights separate," Davies said with a sneer.

"Beautiful place situated right near a good road. Nice place to run whiteface. His daughter might be the one to inherit that ranch if he can't sell it. She's a feisty one, too. Rides a hammerhead roan used to be her aunt's." Davies chuckled.

"It would be a prime location for you. Good water, standing virgin timber. Davies, I thought you would jump on something like that," Tolliver was frowning at Davies.

"Frisch is a businessman from San Francisco handling the sale of the ranch for the family heirs. By the way he talked and handled himself, I'd see that he will get the price he wants. He'll wait to find the right buyer. I'll take another look at my finances when I get home," Davies said as he ran a hand over the table.

He looked at Tolliver and then at Benning. "I'll be in touch with you by the end of the week."

Max stacked a couple of full bottles behind the bar and started to take the empties into the kitchen.

Davies stood up. "Bartender, can we get that dinner now?"

Max gripped the bottles and smiled.

"Yes, Sir. Step right into the dining room there and we'll set you up. Two for dinner?"

Davies looked at Benning and Tolliver with raised eyebrows. Tolliver shook his head.

Rossiter walked to the dining room rubbing his tummy smelling the scent of good food.

"Smells mighty good," Davies said as he clapped Rossiter's shoulder and they disappeared into the dining room.

"That ranch is startin' to look like a lost cause," Tolliver said and sat there fuming.

His plan to get the gold had begun to fade away. He had made a little over a thousand on the horses and cattle. The Ladd Ranch was a complete bust with hired guns dead and another good hand on the trail to Denver. Now there were snooping folks onto the South Landing so they could not lay low there.

"I don't have anything else lined up around here. I haven't heard of any likely jobs anywhere," Tolliver looked at Benning who was watching the door open up. A pretty brunette had taken off the dripping slicker and shook off the water from her hat. She wore tight denim jeans down over high-heeled boots with small silver spurs and Benning smiled watching her figure move across the floor. She unbuttoned the long white sleeves and began to roll them up she moved past their table towards the kitchen.

"Good evening, gentlemen," she said with a clear voice. That was a beautiful smile and deep brown eyes and lustrous straight hair down her back loose.

Benning grinned. "Ma'am."

Slender silver bracelets jangled as she pushed against the kitchen door and went in.

Benning's mind was racing.

"Gold."

"Gold?" Benning's mind came to a screeching halt and he jerked his head to Tolliver.

"The only people that know there is gold on that ranch is you, me and the banker Huddleston. I told him I was pulling out and heading for greener pastures and he finally admitted why he wanted that ranch enough to kill for it," Tolliver said in a low voice.

His restless fingers lipped the edge of the tablecloth back and forth. Tolliver told Benning how the discovery of gold came about and how the banker was involved.

"That power of attorney is due any day now and Doyle will have the safety deposit box unlocked and then the entire county will know there is gold on that ranch," Tolliver's eyes squinted and he gripped his fists. The vein in his temple throbbed and his face got redder by the second. "The ranch has never been mined. It was a pure accident that Long had even found the nugget. It could have all been ours."

"So all we have to do is follow that stream and find color? Can you see the river from the house?" Benning was sitting up leaning forward on the table.

"Lower your voice," Tolliver warned him with a dark, ugly glare.

"Let's go out to the stable. I want to know more about this," Benning said as he stood up and dropped coins on the table.

"Good night, folks," Max called from behind the bar.

Smiling he waved as the men got their hats and went out the front door. Chiatane came out of the kitchen wrapping a long white apron around her slim figure, as the big door eased shut.

"Did you know those men, Max? Ever see them here before?" Chiatane looked at their table and then at Max.

"No, Miss Chi, I can't say that I've seen them before."

"Did they say who they were? Did you catch a name?"

"Those two in the dining room. The older man's name is Davies. The younger man is Rossiter. These two came in later and sat with those two for about twenty minutes. Then they stepped into the dining room for dinner," Max said as he polished glasses.

Chiatane went over to the table and picked up the coffee cups and glasses along with five dollars. The smooth, tanned forehead frowned and she walked into the kitchen.

Papa had the habit of slipping off to the old tack room in the stables and taking an undisturbed nap from time to time. He had listened to Chi stable her horse, rubbing it down and humming while she forked hay to the mare. He had just started to doze off again when the door opened. He jerked awake, disoriented, and was just about to call out when he heard strange voices.

"So where's the gold at?"

"There is some sort of dam the old man put up over twenty years ago.

It's an earth and timber dam. He found the nugget while digging out for the dam. We find the dam; we find the gold."

"Can you see the dam from the house?"

"I don't know. I never got that close. I was all over that ranch during those three days and I never found any dam. It's there somewhere, but I can't find it."

"So Huddleston knew about the gold, expected us to kill off the old man and he'd get the gold and us to hang."

Papa heard a piece of wood break and swearing. The wall was built with no cracks. It probably did not matter because it was pitch black.

"There are two ranch hands now out there. And that girl is riding around the ranch all the time. I don't need to be crawling around out there and suddenly have that hammerhead come up on me."

Papa was sure that his heart was pounding loud enough for them to hear it. His grip on the side of the cot made his knuckles hurt.

After a while he smelled smoking tobacco and the rustling of leather. Then the big door pushed open and two horses walked out. The door was pushed shut and then the only sound was the rain on the roof and the dripping on the ground.

Papa waited another ten minutes, then walked in between the stalls out to the big door. Nobody was there.

He grabbed a slicker and trotted back to the Inn. The slicker was dropped over the veranda rail and he stood for a minute trying to control the trembling hands. Smiling, Chiatane started to chastise Papa for being out in the weather, but the look on his face stopped her.

His voice was a whisper. "Is anyone in the dining room? Is there anyone in the saloon?"

Chiatane came closer and took his hand.

"What is it, Papa?" he looked at her again, glaring at her. She let go of his arm.

"There are two men eating dinner in the dining room. Uh, a man named Davies and his friend, Rossiter."

"Anyone else?" Max leaned through the doorway and saw them talking quietly. Just as he turned away, Papa called him to come out on the veranda. Papa asked him the same questions and found the two strangers had been in the Inn and had to have been the same ones in the stables.

"What is this about?" Chiatane was starting to get worried. She had never seen Papa so angry and worried at the same time.

To Max, Papa gave directions. "Make sure the men in the dining room get dessert. Don't rush them." The older man's hands were trembling.

"Chi, come with me." Papa took her hand and walked back through the hallway, skirting the far side of the kitchen, and then passed through another door. He stopped before the locked door and fumbled with the key in the dim hallway. After he and Chiatane were inside, he sat her down on the chair.

He told her everything he had heard. He wrote out three words on a slip of paper and guided Chiatane to the little click-clack machine.

"Send this to Henry Elliot, honey." His voice trembled as he pushed the scrap of paper into her hand.

"There's a lot more to Henry than you know, Chi. Send the message." Expert fingers fastened the little wires to the screws. It took her about twenty seconds to send the message to Henry Elliot at the Hotel Bradford.

"Come. Fast. Papa."

Newton sat before the huge fireplace in the hotel lobby with drawings and papers spread before him on the table. It seemed there were a thousand decisions waiting for this house. The cut oak planks for the heavy flooring, flagstones for the walkways and patio, the bricks and river rocks for the fireplaces and then the quarried marble for the kitchens all added up to one huge puzzle.

Contractor Richard Vaughn sat across from him leaning towards a lantern in effort to read a specification. "I've got a construction foreman lined up. Bailey Cook, good man, seen through a couple of big houses over in Los Angeles perched up on the coast," Vaughn said as he nodded, pursing his lips.

"Two carpenters, one is a Master Carpenter and one is a finish carpenter, are due tomorrow by noon if this storm doesn't wash out any roads. I've worked with Bob McNary and Ernie Amundson for going on ten years now and I know they will do a fine job, Newton."

Vaughn lowered his papers and looked over at Cutter. The blacksmith started stacking some of the papers, turning them face down on the table out of sight.

"I've got three local men who need work and have construction experience. I've stood inside the houses, barns, and buildings they have put up and I'm sure they can get this job done. All three of them have kids that will attend this school so they have a vested interest in seeing this done well," Cutter ran his fingers through his hair thoughtfully.

"Mac Kelly, Brett Doyle and Fergie Miller. They'll come in and stay at the hotel during the construction. All of them are from the Beatrice area which is about seventy-five miles southwest of here and too far to ride in every day. Tommie can put them up and at least we'll all be to work on time every day."

Cutter chuckled as he sipped his coffee.

Vaughn nodded and looked at the windows and the darkness beyond. Raindrops hit the window making long, jittery trails down the panel.

It was not such a pleasant conversation in the back room of the bank.

"I'm hearing rumors in town that Benning is now a wanted man. Jim

Caudle is wounded and nowhere to be found. I overheard several women talking behind their fans in the trading post about a gang of outlaws out of the hideout at South Landing," Huddleston shielded his mouth with his gloved hand. The back office of the bank was cloaked in darkness lit by a flickering lamp.

"And now Jackson Frisch has prospective buyers coming in from outta state on the ranch." Tolliver paced back and forth in the small room, gripping his gloves in frustration, the black duster swishing as he turned. The thick boots were muffled in the thin rug and Huddleston glared at Tolliver from behind clasped hands.

"What are you going to do? I don't see how," Tolliver yelled and turned and slammed his fist down on the desk, making small items jump. Huddleston gasped, wide eyed and shrank back making the old wood chair creak and groan.

"Get off my back! I don't know what I'm going to do. I'll think of something, this is too big of a prize to let go of now."

Tolliver started putting on his gloves and gave Huddleston a hard stare. The banker averted his eyes over to the big safe in the corner thankful it had been locked for the night. After a moment, Tolliver straightened up and pulled his hat down lower.

"I'll be in touch."

The lock on the door turned and a gust of wind blew into the office scattering a few loose papers and made the lamp flame dance. Huddleston jumped up and tried to grab the swinging door but it slammed back, knocking over a chair and coat rack. Before shutting it, Huddleston leaned out to see if anyone was around and then shut the door and locked it. The flickering lamp had outlined the two men for a brief moment and there was no one around to see them except for the man smoking in the darkness in the doorway across the alley.

# 7 CHAPTER SEVEN

Someone pounded with a heavy fist on the private residence door of Dawn White. Elliot saw that it was Tommy Boardman and opened the door. Without a word, Tommy handed the folded page to who held it to the light and read it. "Thank you, Tommy," from his pocket he shoved a coin into Tommy's hand and the man drew up the slicker and scurried off into the darkness.

Elliot hurried into the sitting room and struggled into his heavy coat. Dawn looked up from her embroidery and saw the alarm on his face. She tossed the hoop aside and stood up.

"What is it?" There had been several times when he had been called away without prior warning. This was one more. She watched him shove his feet down into his boots.

Elliot kissed her mouth and looked in her eyes. "I promise, I'll come back. One way or another." Then he was gone out into the rainy darkness.

She locked the door and stood at the window trying to see in the black of the night. She caught herself wringing her hands and shook them as if to get the worry out of her. But she had no way of knowing that Elliot raced to the aid of good friends.

Papa made sure there was a stall ready for Elliot's big black horse and that a large lantern inside a metal box was lit at the door. It was closed to midnight when a wet Henry Elliot walked in through the heavy wooden doors of the Faraway Inn. Behind Henry, Max locked the door and blew out the last three candles. Only the glowing coals of the fireplace gave off a red cast into the room. All the interior doors had been shut. If anyone had looked at the Inn from a distance, all they would see was that it was closed for the night.

Max, Amanda and Chiatane sat around one of the dining room tables with steaming coffee cups listening as Papa told what he had heard to Henry. With his trained ear, Elliot asked questions and then Papa told him again what he had heard. At the end of the hour, Henry mounted up a spry buckskin and was galloping in a downpour back to Bradford.

Cutter and Wood stepped into the Mayor's private office at nine o'clock that morning. The smell of damp mustiness permeated the office. While they took off their coats Bert Goldman quietly locked the door behind them. Mayor Watley motioned them to sit in a couple of wooden chairs to the side. Cutter and Wood sat down looking puzzled.

Mayor Watley motioned to Elliot to proceed. "There is gold on the Long Ranch. That's why Harley was murdered. Riley Stephens was supposed to die right along but somebody let him live," Elliot could not mince words.

In a confidential low voice, Elliot told Mayor Watley, Goldman, Wood, and Cutter the details of what Gianni La Costa had heard in the stables at the Faraway Inn. Their mouths dropped open and started firing questions at Elliot who did his best to answer.

"I figure whoever is after that gold has to be out there right now, prowling around snooping for that dam."

Elliot looked at Cutter. "If Jackson or Carmella just happen to take a ride around the ranch, they are in greater danger than before.

Elliot spoke. "I would suggest getting those three someplace safe until the ranch can be searched for these outlaws. But if I know Jackson Frisch the little I do, he'll dig in like a tick and put out all fours."

Wood said, "How are we supposed to get them out of there? And how are we supposed to catch these outlaws?"

Well, Riley has already proved himself to be a brave lad and he can handle a gun. I would say he is the only one who knows where this dam is at on the ranch. We'll need him when we start the search," Goldman said as he rubbed his chin.

Wood turned and looked at Cutter. "Do you remember me telling you there was something odd about that banker Huddleston? I knew there was something not right about him. I wouldn't be surprised if we found him with his pants rolled up wading around that river looking for the gold."

Cutter nodded. "Huddleston tried to buffalo Thomas into a bank deal once. Neither one of us trusts him."

"If any of you know a way, aside from outright kidnapping, to get them off the ranch, you let me know. Jackson is going to be mad as hell once he finds out about this and I don't intend to be anywhere near him then." Elliot was drawing a piece of rawhide through his fingers over and over.

Goldman raised a quizzical brow and said, "Why can't we come out and tell them? They're adults. It's their ranch. Let them make the decision. If it were me out there, I'd want my friends coming to warn me of danger. I'd want help. And I'll tell you another thing,"

Goldman stood up going to stand against the wall.

"If I found out that any of you had tricked me to get me off my ranch, you wouldn't be welcome at my door ever again."

It took another hour of raised voices to finally agree that Elliot, Goldman and Watley would ride immediately to the Harley Long Ranch and lay all the cards out on the table for Jackson and Carmella Frisch.

Cutter and Wood were to stay in town as Newton was still weak and unable to ride the long distance. Wood would make the rounds of the small businesses to see if any strangers had come through. Addie knocked on the door and announced it was time for lunch so the meeting broke up.

***

Carmella looked up at the drifting clumps of cottony white clouds, wispy threads of softness, fat, and round. Over near the river white streaks floated nudged by a breeze. She could see the rich blue to the horizon where the azure sky continued on in all directions with no sign of rain, no feel or scent of rain. The same clouds had been stuck on the ridge all day motionless in the shimmering afternoon heat. She had been sitting here for a couple of hours trying to soak it all in as the new buyers would be coming and she would be leaving.

Her eyes looked at the far hills shimmering in the dull green of desert plants. Small patches and clumps of flowers dotted purple and yellow in amongst a verdant carpet. A clump of trees in the valley swayed in the breeze. The last time she rode out there she had seen where last winter the older trees had fallen making room for young seedlings ready to grow like their predecessors. She smoothed back a strand of curls as her eye followed the line of pine and willow along the foothills aware that the trees always found water.

It was peaceful here with no schedules or timetables or calendars to keep track of. She leaned back in her chair and let her eyes reach as far around the ranch as possible. Twenty head of white faced cattle grazed in contentment by the edge of the trees where the moist grass was sweet. A flock of birds swooped into a clump of wildflowers, raucous chirping, chattering in high excitement, and then streaked back out into a flock in the sky. Riotous clamor flew around overhead and then disappeared in a copse of trees to continue their games. The young girl smiled to herself wondering if this grandeur existed anywhere else.

This was to be sold to the highest bidder. This exact piece of earth would be transferred into the hands of someone who looked for its exact characteristics. Her attention was turned back to the landscape as a jousting duo of crows cackled and barked their displeasure to each other and took turns tugging at branches in the pine tree. The noisy flock of little birds swooped into the huge pine tree and drove out the crows, trilling and cackling in victory over the larger predator. The big pine tree had dropped most of its huge cones a month ago and now a herd of squirrels argued and complained about the bounty. Gliding a piece of the long grass between her fingers, she wondered if she would ever find another peaceful haven like this again.

Two dogs played the biting game, nipping at each other, tackling, chasing, and rolling in the dirt near the barn. Carmella breathed in the earthy smell of sage and wood, warmed from the sun, the distant sound of a horse whinnying and brown cattle grazing. Her eyes spied in the far distance, a horse and rider trotting up and over the knoll headed west on the road that ended at the sea. She had ridden it herself in the stagecoach on the way back to San Francisco earlier in the year. Folks had told her of the arduous journey but she had found it wondrous and fascinating.

The afternoon had slid away from her, the temperature fallen and even the birds had quieted down, finding a roost for the night. The purple, gold and gray of the night sky began to deepen and one final glimmer of red traced across the horizon and a last sunburst highlighted the grove of red oak across the valley. Darkness crept in and claimed the valley. In the dusk, one last bit of wind caught the edge of the U.S. flag on the pole at the barn, ruffling it out, streaming out strong before it relaxed again, the wind now gone and the fabric furled into rest. The smell of the warm earth was replaced with the scent of valley grass, hay, and flowers.

Carmella stood up from her chair and smoothed down her khaki skirt. She picked a burr of her cotton blouse and let the strand of grass fall into the green carpet around her. It was 100 yards back to the ranch house, squat and imposing on the slight ridge. Her boots crunched in the crushed gravel path and she thought about how river rock would look good as a border along it. Without a doubt this beauty would influence the new owner. Her hands rested on the oak timbers of the porch rail as she indulged in one last gaze out into the darkening gloom and then the heavy wooden door closed her in for the night.

***

Amber streaks and pink hues in the eastern sky told of the day coming. The gold faded out and the sliver of clouds wore traces of orange and red as the sun began its trek up into the sky.

Four horses pulling a heavy wagon came up over the ridge in the valley. Heavy wagon covered in a gray canvas and tied crisscross with thick rope. The driver held the horses to a walk where they should be at a trot to meet a schedule. The horses tossed their heads and strained at the reins, wanting to run. The raggedy umbrella wavered over the driver shielding him from the growing heat. The wooden wagon creaked and groaned under its load, bumping along the rough road. In the west, time is money so a freight wagon inching along like this meant one of two things: something important and valuable was on board or something was wrong with the wagon and team. Carmella started to look away but then saw a rider loping along at a good pace and after squinting a bit, taken aback that the rider had looked right at her.

# 8 CHAPTER EIGHT

The big living room of the Harley Long ranch was spacious and comfortable. There was a big desk under one of the side windows used for letters and paying bills. The ledgers were kept on a handy wood shelf under the window along with a dictionary, cattlemen's guides, and a supply of blank paper. The fireplace was nine feet wide with a long wide oak mantle. Pictures and mementos had gathered a slight coat of dust. The river rock stones stretched up to the twelve foot ceilings and dominated the room.

"What sort of thoughts have you given towards marriage, Carmella?" Dawn sat in a leather chair next to a small table with her sewing basket situated in the center.

"I must confess, until I came to Bradford I had thought little of marriage. I sort of supposed that I would meet someone in San Francisco and marry there and settle down. I find now that I feel so comfortable and enjoy this country and the nice people here."

Dawn sat down on the end of the leather sofa and opened her sewing basket. She had a lighter turquoise long blue skirt to hem.

"Your father would like to see you married to a good man and settled with your own family. Every father wants his daughter in a good marriage with respect and love." Dawn watched as Carmella paid close attention to her stitches.

"Was there no one in San Francisco that you were considering? I would imagine there might be several powerful, prosperous men in the city that would want a pretty young woman for a wife."

Carmella looked at Dawn for a moment, with her mind preoccupied. "I guess I treated everyone as a friend. I've held people at arms' length for more than a few years. They were father's business friends and I never thought of them in relation to marriage. There were a few men who were sons of older friends of my mother."

The young woman shook her head.

"I'm sure that if I stayed in San Francisco I'd have a completely different life of dinner parties, the theater and charity functions," she laughed softly. "Much like it has been for the last year or so."

"Newton Cutter has been very attentive to you, Carmella. You seem to enjoy his company."

"I do enjoy his company. He seems like he has a good head on his shoulders. He is a handsome man and a good dancer. What do you know about him, about the man, Auntie?"

Dawn smiled and let her embroidery rest in her lap. She looked at Carmella.

"I have never seen him with any one woman. As far as I know he has no attachments or understanding with any local girls. He has been dedicated and focused on building his business and now is starting to enjoy its success. He has no desire to raise cattle or horses or livestock of any kind."

"I do know one other thing about Newton Cutter that is not generally known in the town. After he has his house built, he intends to marry," Dawn said with raised eyebrows.

Her fingers began to unravel a strand of red thread.

"He was in Goldman's one night and the Mayor was party to his discussion and debate on the finer points of courtship."

Dawn winked and then whispered. "And you know, Addie Watley can't keep a secret to save herself."

Carmella giggled. After a moment she adjusted the fabric looking at the hemline of the skirt. "I met Marty Ladd at the grange dance and then again here when he came down to look at purchasing the ranch. He seems like a rowdier, flamboyant sort of man. I know Father liked him." Carmella leaned back into the cushions with a sigh.

"He is a wealthy young man from his breeding of whiteface cattle. He studied breeding lines from back east at the university and then had the breeding stock shipped from England. Quite an accomplishment for a sixteen year old boy. Shows quite the determination." Dawn smiled.

"The talk in town is that he could outright buy the ranch and run it together with his father's ranch. When his father dies, it would make him the largest landowner in Southern California."

Dawn let silence take over for a moment.

"I would suggest Thomas Wood but he has his eye on Miss Georgianna Caldwell, Tommy Boardman's niece. Besides, I cannot envision my niece as the wife of a stable master. Aren't I horrible?" Dawn said with a grin and looked devious.

"I'd have friends and family here. There is a lot to do. I was fascinated helping Doc Baines with Uncle Harley and Newton and Thomas. I'm looking forward to there being a school with children here, too." She had a thoughtful look on her face.

"You bring up a good point. When Harley died, my reason for living here vanished. Jackson will sell the ranch and he'll go back to San Francisco. I was wondering about moving back to the coast. San Francisco Bay is so beautiful and I am sure I could open a shop there," Dawn said as she looked out the window.

"But if you were married and settled here, I'd stay."

Carmella looked at Dawn and then back to the slender white thread pulling through the fabric.

"What about Mr. Elliot? Has he not mentioned marriage to you? He doesn't even look at anyone else, that I can see," Carmella said as she went into the kitchen and put the pan of water onto the wood stove for tea.

"Henry has different business interests from Chicago to Los Angeles. Sometimes he is gone for months and then one day he is standing at the door. He never talks about what he does, what sort of business he handles."

Dawn frowned and rubbed her eyes.

"I know that what he does is dangerous. He's come in with bandaged ribs and fresh scars from time to time."

She stopped, hearing the shrill whistle of the tea pot and when she looked up her pretty blue eyes were watery.

"Carmella, I cannot suffer another loss in my life. I've lost my husbands, my brother, and many dear friends. I've seen enough violence and brutality to last three lifetimes. If Henry were to ride out one day and never come back, I would wonder what happened, yes. But I would go on as if he was on a grand adventure somewhere. I would always open the door and think it would be him standing there," Dawn's voice trembled and she blinked back tears.

Carmella poured tea into the cups.

"I've never told him that I love him, but I do. I don't intend to love any other man in my remaining years, my dear. It is a little promise that I have made to myself." Dawn said as she took in a deep breath and added a spoonful of sugar to the small china cup. Carmella gazed at her aunt over the rim of the cup. There was a whole other dimension to Dawn White she had never known.

***

The sky was gray and the clouds seemed to be lowering. A gust of wind fluttered curtains and rolled a tumbleweed up against a building. Birds scurried about flitting from the trees to the brush and back, chirping, cackling, and complaining. A door slammed, a voice called out, here and there a dog barked. Horses nickered in the corral, stomping their hooves at the flies. The small town was going about its business.

The blacksmith shop smelled of fresh lumber and coffee from the pot nestled against the forge. The two heavy wooden double doors had been braced open against the gusting wind. Long oak planks rested in two stacks as Cutter trimmed and planed them across two sawhorses, his metal tool peeling off thick slivers. Outside in front of the doors, a long wagon frame sat up on blocks of wood. Seven planks across and fifteen feet long, it would carry five ton for its owner.

A stagecoach had pulled up in front of the hotel and the driver was leaned over the side talking to Tommy Boardman. A shaggy spotted dog laid down, curling up under the edge of the hotel porch with its eyes wary kept on the passersby. There were four horses tied to the rail on the right and three carried heavy saddlebags and bedrolls. The other carried two shotguns on either side.

On the porch of the Town Hall there was a man relaxed in a tipped back wood chair with his hat pulled down over his eyes. A woman's laugh came from a shop. Dunagan slammed the heavy hammer down onto the red glowing iron, curving it around into the bracket for the big axles. The clanging ring carried out over the plaza, bouncing off the church and bringing up the head of the dozing dog under the porch.

Cutter lifted the long board up onto the frame, fitting it into the bracket fresh from the hammer. The ache in his shoulder telling him of its strain. A hammer pounded nails down into the plank securing it to the frame. The dog sat up, scratched, and then trotted around the corner of the hotel. Addie Watley came out of the church and stood looking down the street with a broom in her hands. A puff of dust left the broom as she neared the porch edge. Wood scraped against wood and another plank went up on to the sawhorse.

The door to Doc Baines' office opened and the older man stepped out, closing it behind him. He pulled down his hat and walked over towards the church, his coat edge flapping in the gusty wind. He and Addie talked a few moments, then stepped inside the church. The door to Goldman's opened and a short slender man came out and on the steps he stood looking around. He turned and moved off disappearing behind the Town Hall.

There was not a symmetrical attractiveness or beauty to the small town. Aside from size there was no one building that drew admiring attention. Five buildings were painted, but the rest remained that gray weathered silvery color with faded rusting drips from nails. Cutter felt a nudge at his elbow and turned to see a heavy mug of steaming coffee handed to him. His fingers rubbed against the side of his head and he blinked blue eyes to clear his vision. The two silent men stood in the doorway of the blacksmith shop, looking at their town.

*** 

"I had an interesting talk with Carmella, about love and marriage the other day," Dawn said with a smile. She poured tea for Jackson Frisch. The hotel dining room was empty and the two sat at a quiet corner table. Jackson raised his eyebrows and lowered his newspaper, shiny gold cufflinks brilliant at the white cuff of his shirt. Streams of sunlight came in through the windows and tiny bits of dust danced in the glow.

"Have you two discussed her future about home, husband and family?" Dawn asked and rested her chin on her hand, gazing to Jackson.

Jackson frowned and folded his paper laying it to one side. His eyes scanned the room and leaned closer to Dawn.

"She hasn't said anything to me about anyone in particular, Dawn," Jackson thrummed his fingers on the white linen tablecloth. "There were several eligible men in San Francisco that had expressed interest but nothing ever came of it. I sort of figured she would find someone there and settle down. I always pictured her living in the city in a big house without a care in the world. Her mother would have wanted that for Carmella."

The lobby door opened and a couple crossed the doorway headed for the stairs. A door opened and closed somewhere and some clattering was heard from the kitchen.

"Well, it seems that she has a fondness for our town blacksmith, Newton Cutter. I wasn't so sure of this until we were returning from our stroll past the forge yesterday and I saw for myself," Dawn said as she dabbed the napkin in the corner of her lips. She smiled at her brother.

"There was a mutual attraction there, Jackson. He has no attachments or understanding with any young lady hereabouts and as a local business owner, he is quite eligible," She took a sip of her tea watching her brother.

"Newton, huh? He does seem like a levelheaded young man and he seems to be making a home here in Bradford. I know he does fine work from what I can see. Riley Stephens has been fussing over that freight wagon ever since Newton delivered it," Frisch rubbed the edge of the tablecloth through his fingers.

"I guess we wait and see if they do hit it off and go from there. I am a fish out of water when it comes to my daughter's romances," Jackson said before he took a bite of a sweet roll and smiled at Dawn.

A waiter in his long white apron came out of the kitchen with a tray of cutlery and began setting up tables for the coming lunch. A girl brought out a tray of water goblets and began positioning them on the tables. Through the dining room doorway they could see people standing at the hotel front desk talking with the clerk. The day was showing signs of being a warm one. A light breeze shuffled the leaves on the old oaks in the square and made a ripple in the tall green grass of the valley. Somewhere birds chirped and chattered as a couple of fluffy clouds floated on the horizon.

***

The blacksmith shop had a visitor this afternoon.

"Good afternoon. I am here to see Clay Dunagan, please. I'm Sarah

Merryman," said a small middle-aged woman as she stood in front of Cutter. He had been so engrossed in the rolling iron that he had not heard her approach. There was a horse and wagon standing in the street.

"Yes, Ma'am. I'll go get him for you. I'll be right back," Cutter said as he took off his heavy leather gloves and laid them on the workbench and trotted around to the side of the shop.

"Clay, there is a Mrs. Merryman here to see you."

Dunagan nodded and stood up, brushing off his jeans and walked with Cutter around to the front of the shop.

Her face lit up in a big smile when she saw him. Her water blue eyes matched the drab faded blue denim dress. She tugged at the knitted black shawl around her shoulders. "Howdy Ma'am. Thank you for coming in all this way," Dunagan turned to Newton. "Mrs. Merryman lives over in the valley and it's not a short trip over here." The stablemaster brought a little stool and set it down close to Mrs. Merryman to sit on.

"I'll be right with you, ma'am."

The little woman was now a fidgeting bundle of nerves, shifting on the little stool. Grayish black curls bobbed around from a loose bun and fingers tugged off dark little gloves. She craned around trying to look into the depths of the shop. From the back, Dunagan carried something big and heavy.

"Oh my word! It's beautiful!" It was a custom-made metal fireplace screen. A bouquet of small flowers surrounded by flat curled iron bars. The side frames had forged posts with a braided rope centerpiece. Cutter felt his jaw drop open and stared at the formidable work of art.

The woman was running her bare fingers over the little flower petals and leaves. "It's perfect! It is the exact likeness to the cloth!"

She set down her purse and pulled out a tiny bit of cloth. She held it up and Cutter could see a vase of wildflowers surrounded by curlicues and framed with twisted rods.

"It's perfect! Oh my Lord, you are a true craftsman, Mr. Dunagan!" She clutched his arm with joy and cooed over the screen.

"This is the most marvelous screen I've ever seen!"

Her voice had elevated higher and she choked out a shrill cry of delight.

Dunagan kept quiet watching the woman walk around and around the screen.

"So, do you like it, Ma'am?"

"Oh, I can't wait to see it in my living room! It is exquisite! Fabulous! I'll be the envy of my sewing circle! Would you boys be so kind as to load it into the wagon for me?"

Mrs. Merryman clapped her hands watching Cutter and Dunagan settling the screen into the wagon. They tied it down with several short lengths of rope and spread the large canvas to cover it over.

She wiggled her eyebrows. "To keep it from those prying eyes. I still have to make several stops before I get home and I wouldn't want anyone running off with it."

She nodded, directing them to tuck in the canvas around her prized possession.

The happy woman pulled out a little leather pouch and looked at Dunagan.

"Fifty dollars, as we agreed on."

She beamed as she dropped the payment into Dunagan's hand. Cutter felt his eyes go wide and had to grab the wagon to keep from falling down.

"Thank you, Ma'am. Please let me know if you need anything else," Clay said politely as he helped the woman climb in the seat and handed her the reins.

Stepping back, he touched the brim of his hat and nodded.

She moved out the team and cracked the whip once putting them into a trot down the road.

"How in the world..fifty dollars?!"

Cutter's jaw was still hanging open, staring at Dunagan.

"Thomas Wood, come out here!" Dunagan yelled and turned to Cutter. He held up the little bag wiggling it. Thomas came trotting out.

"What's going on out here?"

"I'm buyin' drinks. I've got a story you won't believe." Dunagan slid his arm around Wood's shoulder and together they walked towards the plaza.

Cutter was incredulous, blinking in the bright sunlight. He slammed both big doors to the blacksmith shop and ran after his friends crossing the green.

# 9 CHAPTER NINE

Cutter's house construction was now well underway. The debris on the site had been hauled away and the old adobe building had been demolished. The surveyor had come in on Monday and laid out the stakes and lines had been driven into the ground as markers for the foundation. Contractor Richard Vaughn had been watching the three men digging through the morning and was getting ready to organize the foundation stones.

"Mr. Vaughn, you wanna come take a look at this, Sir? We've hit something in the digging over here," one of the workmen was waving him over. Down under the surface about three feet a shovel hit something and the man had started digging with a pick.

Vaughn peered into the dugout hole.

"Dig around it and let's see what it is. Come on over boys and let's see if we can get this dug out."

Shovels cut into the dirt bringing up brown earth and gravel. A few minutes later the outlines of the long and wide stone foundation came into view. Vaughn directed the men to clear away as much of the dirt as possible and the sides of a ruined adobe began to show. By the middle of the afternoon broken bottles, clay dishes and charred wooden beams are dug up.

"This is about thirty degrees angled off of the new house foundation. We're going to have to rethink this house placement," Vaughn rubbed his chin looking at the old dug up foundation and the new stakes.

"Uh, someone needs to take a look at this," said one of the digging crew who had stopped to kneel at the end of the trench.

Vaughn and the crew walked over and stared at what had stopped the digging. Next to the wall they saw part of a white skull with two round holes on the side.

"Fergie, drop your shovel and run get Mayor William Watley. I know he will want to see this. Everybody step back and don't touch anything until the Mayor gets here," Vaughn said as he knelt on one knee. "Looks like some poor soul has been here a while."

After Mayor Watley saw the situation, he ordered a wooden box nailed together and the skeleton, the small iron box, and the remaining burial things were taken into the sheriff's office for storage.

"Well, gentlemen, I got telegram that a new U.S. Marshall is coming in from Tucson to look into this problem we're having with these outlaws. He should be here on Saturday and we'll organize a meeting to fill him in on what's going on," Watley said as he pulled his vest down and rubbed his hands together.

"Do you want me to stop with the house construction and wait until the new Marshall arrives? Do you think he will want to see this site?" Vaughn leaned up against a stack of lumber, a light coating of dust on his pants and boots.

"No, you go right on with the construction. Come and get me if you find anything else. I don't need you men out here freezing come winter trying to build a house. I'll start asking the old-timers and see if anyone knows anything about what you found," Mayor Watley reached and shook Vaughn's hand and then started to walk back up to town.

Fergie Miller picked up the axe and moved over near one of the stakes and began another trench. Mac Kelly and Brent Doyle followed along behind Fergie and shoveled out the dirt.

"We've got a foundation of an old adobe house here about five foot deep and about twenty feet square.  I'm not too familiar with this type of construction but it looks like this could be a good cellar for the house if Newton wants us to make use of it," Vaughn paced off the dimensions while Fergie recorded them into a notebook.

"You men take a break while I walk up and talk to Mr. Cutter about this and see what he wants to do," Vaughn slapped the dirt of his pants with his hat and climbed up out of the sunken room.

Vaughn walked over to the shop and stood around a wooden table and unfolded a piece of paper. "It is an old iron box with some heavy clasp on it, long rusted shut. We didn't open it, but when we lifted it out, there was something inside that slid around a bit."

Vaughn took in a deep breath and let it out. Cutter wondered if they had come across an anonymous burial site.

"The thing is, that stone foundation is deep enough down that it would make a comfortable twelve foot by fourteen foot root cellar for winter. It's logical to use it rather than spend the money to excavate and then fill it in," Vaughn had drawn out a simple drawing on a piece of paper and traced his finger around the lines of the foundation.

"You have a good eye, Mr. Vaughn. If I had been left to my own devices, I wouldn't ever have thought about a root cellar," Cutter slid his fingers back through his black, curly hair. "Go ahead and put in the cellar. I'm sure that my wife, whoever she might be, will welcome it at some point." The men chuckled over that and Vaughn gathered up his drawing and shook hands with Cutter and left.

By the time that Vaughn had returned to the home construction site, three local ladies had started setting up a lunch table and upon a spread out gingham tablecloth were laying out chicken, salads, and bread. Vaughn always marveled at the generosity for a work crew by the townspeople.

"We'll put in a double doorway here, and then position stairs over where this cabinet was going to be. That will give them access from inside the house and from outside," Vaughn measured and drew lines showing the foreman where to dig and how to set the doors.

The Mayor had a white napkin tucked into his collar and was feasting on a chicken leg. "Addie, can you have the clerk over at the office start digging through the lots and deeds for the town's buildings. I want to see what was standing here before we started digging," Mayor Watley looked at other plates on the table.

There are no records stored to identify or describe any dwelling that used to be on that site. Boxes, crates and old leather portfolios and a trunk in the attic of the City Hall revealed not a thing about that land. One of the Mexican workmen described that it appeared to be an adobe three room house with a timber vault roof which had been common about twenty miles away. Someone speculated that it might have been the first structure in the town but had collapsed and crumbled away during years of storms.

Cutter and Wood leaned against the bar in Goldman's saloon. It had been a long day with too much activity and too much tension. The burly bartender was busy making a pot of coffee for the set of people who were known to come in around this time of day.

"Well, they've got the entire foundation dug in and we figured out a doorway to the cellar so it looks like I'll be safe if a tornado ever hits," Cutter sipped his whiskey and set the little glass down on the bar. Wood had pulled something out of his pocket and peered at some details. The evening gloom of sunset washed over the small town and a splash of last sunlight bounced on the mirror behind the bar.

A tall, thinner man in a dirty duster walked in and took off his hat and sat down facing the door. He caught the bartender's eye and asked for a bottle of whiskey and a couple of glasses. Bert sat the bottle down and the glasses and told the man it would be five dollars.

"Five dollars? I can get two bottles down the road for five dollars! This don't look like any high class joint to be chargin' five dollars."

The thin man glared at Goldman who picked the bottle back up and had started to turn away.

"Suit yourself, stranger. You can move on down the road."

Goldman gave a sneer and took another step toward the bar. With cat quickness, the thin man grabbed the whiskey bottle back and gave Goldman a shove sending him falling toward the bar. Cutter had turned to see what was happening and caught the man with a strong left to the jaw, sending him sprawling to the floor.

Royal Benning started to speak, and then with a whining cry of inexpressible fury, he hurled himself from the floor. Cutter sprang forward to meet the attack, but even as he jerked up his hands, Benning's body struck him, knocking him back and down. Benning went down with him, and both men rolled over and scrambled to their feet. Benning was fast and light on his feet. With lips distorted in a wicked grimace and he swung. The blow caught Cutter on the side of the face and staggered him, but Cutter clinched his fists, got his footing and threw a sudden left hook missing Benning's jaw. The couple that had been walking past on the boardwalk gasped, stepped to the side and stared.

Benning stepped back, wiping the back of his hand over his mouth and Cutter came up on a lunging dive. As Benning stepped back, his boot turned on a stone twisting his ankle and he fell, taking a wicked swing in the face. There was now a dirty low brown cloud of dust swirling around the street from the fight.

The late afternoon streaks of sunlight stole in between the buildings illuminating the fighters. Both men got up, gauging their enemy, and walked into each other, swinging with both hands. Benning was furious, grunting with each blow landed. Cutter was cautious with his hands up ready for the other's attack.

Cutter reached out and with a quick left grazed Benning's chin and then staggered him with a right. Benning fell back a bit and shook his head hard trying to clear out the cobwebs. The big man gritted his teeth and lunged in, butting with his head. The murmurs of the crowd grew louder with men's voices calling for strategic punches. Cutter raked his face with an elbow and slammed a right to the body and then a sharp, fast left. Cutter jabbed then pushed Benning off to the side and shook him to his heels with a well-placed uppercut.

Benning turned to the left, lunged, and his fingers caught Cutter's shirt, ripping it down the front. He grabbed at Cutter and swung. Both men with feet tangled went to the ground. Now there were over a dozen people standing in amazement on the side of the street, on the boardwalk and at windows watching the two fighters. Benning started to rise then shifted his weight and made a vicious kick at Cutter's head, catching him behind the ear. Cutter threw a handful of dirt into Benning's eyes and scrambled to his feet while the other fought to clear his vision.

When Benning stood up there was a huge gash on his left cheek, dribbling blood, one sleeve was partly torn off and he was coated in the fine gray dust from the street. Cutter's fists were reddened and his forehead was bloody where the boot had grazed him. Two horses tied at the far rail danced, shying away from the fighting men. Almost equal in height, Benning had the lone drifter fighting skills, but years of lifting heavy iron gave Cutter powerful strength. Both men circled with fists up, panting for air.

Benning lunged in and threw a right, and Cutter angled in a left to his mouth that smashed his lips to a pulp. Whirling around, Benning threw a fast right to the chin. Cutter was stunned, his knees wobbling and he backed up, shaking his head. Benning saw his chance and stiffened his shoulders, walked into Cutter swinging fists with a savage hatred. A thin red bloody streak ran from the corner of Benning's mouth. Cutter caught a wicked punch to the side of his head, but with a quick move gripped Benning and tossed him into the side of the water trough.

Benning's high fury had settled into shrewd, fighting moves. Royal Benning was a man who could fight and who liked to fight and had the stamina to win. West of the Mississippi, he had never lost a bare knuckles brawl and had often stated that it would take more than fists to bring him down. In St Louis, Denver, and Santa Fe he had backed up his words and left broken, battered men in his wake. It was rumored that he had beaten a man to death on a trail drive in northern Texas.

Benning waded into Cutter and began a proven punching strategy. He punched hard to the body and was surprised to find the punch blocked. Cutter jabbed a left and then jabbed again. Benning landed one into Cutter's midsection and the man gasped for breath. Cutter clinched with huge, muscled arms and slammed two quick punches into Benning's ribs.

There had been an old fist fighter up in the mining camp outside Sacramento when Cutter was developing his claim. After a playful sparring match between Cutter and another rough and tumble man, the old fighter took Cutter aside and spoke to him. The aging fighter still had an eye for footwork, jabs and uppercuts and precision-taught Cutter how to move, turn and keep balance. In three months Cutter learned the art and science of ring fighting and now standing in the street, he brought all that knowledge to bear with his fists.

Cutter jabbed a left, moved right and jabbed again, glancing a fist off Benning's jaw. Benning turned and landed a punch hard to the body and Cutter gasped for breath. Cutter grimaced and struck Benning on the kidney and Royal's knees buckled. Cutter went after him, swung hard to the ear, and came away with a bloody smear on his fist. Then he smashed his right to the Benning's ribs and stepped back. Benning's eye and lip were swollen and bloody, but the man rose up, took a deep breath, and turned angry eyes on Cutter.

Benning stomped his right foot, feinted his left swing and Cutter stepped in and caught a looping right that knocked him down. He rolled over, saw Benning coming in with a vicious kick, and then hurled himself at Benning's legs. The fighter sprang back and Cutter started up. The sky was showing purples and burnished gold now with streaks of blue hanging at the horizon. The fine dust was everywhere and women had their handkerchiefs over their noses. Benning kicked out, the boot raking Cutter's head but catching his shoulder and knocking him to his knees again.

Benning rushed in and Cutter saw the boot swing back and threw himself against the pivoting leg. Benning saw him coming and slammed a fist into Cutter's ear with lightning speed. Benning groaned in pain and went down in a crashing heap and Cutter rolled away, eying the other man carefully. With bloodied, puffy welts, jagged cuts, and torn flesh, both men rose to their feet. There were gouges in the dirt from boot heels, bits of torn shirt, and the fine gray dust coated everything.

Benning hit Cutter with a swinging right fist, a bone-jarring blow that loosened teeth, and then swung a right to the body. Cutter gasped and backed up. His fist rubbed against his mouth showed smears of blood. Cutter tried to cover but Benning brushed away the fist and struck the blacksmith in the mouth. Benning again swung left and Cutter smashed in on the chin. Benning turned with the blow and tried to shake his head to clear it but could not focus.

Cutter swung a fast left hook and Benning grabbed the arm with both hands, flinging Cutter around, and to the ground. Cutter pushed himself up and came up charging in and Benning threw a high hard one that caught him on the chin. Cutter went to his knees and Benning grabbed him by the shirt and jerked him erect, but Cutter was ready with a smashing uppercut. Benning was stunned, groaning and Cutter punched two hooks to Benning's face and once into his body. The man's knees sagged and Cutter flung him against the boardwalk where he hit with a thud.

Benning tried to rise, staggering, then fell flat. "Drag him out back and put him on those hay bales. I'll have Hank keep an eye on him," Goldman cleaned up the broken bottle.

Two men off the boardwalk came and lifted Benning up, dragged him out around to the back.

"Any idea who he is?" Cutter rubbed his forehead that was red and raw.

"Nope, never seen him in here before. I thought he might be one of those guys working on your house, but he was dressed for the road, not construction," the bartender straightened up the table and a couple of chairs that had been knocked over. The two men came back in and Goldman poured shots for their assistance.

"I heard you had a commotion here, Bert. What is the ruckus?" Mayor Watley stepped into the saloon and walked up to the bar. He saw the disheveled Cutter wiping off his face and said, "What the heck happened to you? Does the other guy look as bad as you do?"

Goldman poured a shot of whiskey into a little glass and eased it over to the Mayor. Watley lifted it in silent cheers and then took a sip.

"Stranger came in, didn't like the price of whiskey and well, Newton here taught him some polite manners. He's out back sleeping comfortably, I would think."

The men chuckled.

"Think I'll have me a look-see at this stranger."

Watley downed his whiskey and Cutter and Wood followed him around the side of the saloon. Gone. Nobody lay there in the scattered hay. The three men looked at each other and shook their heads.

A brown mottled short haired dog trotted down the alley as a cool breeze stirred up the dust. The smell or horses, sage and warm earth was carried on the wind. A party of four headed to the hotel for dinner as the last gleams of sunlight disappeared in the sky over the West.

***

A couple of days had passed with relative quiet and peace for the little town. Wood had sold the pinto along with a saddle and a few doodads. The construction on the house moved along and nearly the entire foundation was done. Cutter had finished planing a long oak plank when he heard voices behind him.

"Good afternoon, Newton Cutter. You remember my niece, Carmella Frisch, don't you?"

Dawn said with an interesting glint in her eye as she glanced at the young woman standing with her.

Cutter turned around, grinned and removed his heavy leather gloves. He looked at the pretty Dawn then let his eyes take a slow walk over Carmella.

"Yes, Ma'am, I do. And let me say again Miss Frisch, I want to offer my condolences for the loss of your uncle," Cutter said.

He straightened up as Carmella's eyes slid down over him. A corner of her mouth curled up and she turned her head taking in all that curly black hair.

Carmella glanced into the interior of the shop at the glowing forge and then back to Cutter, with her eyes wide and appraising. He looked strong, powerful with an assurance, a confidence in himself as a man should. Plus, he looked to be a savvy businessman and she liked that.

Cutter looked at the girl. The afternoon walk had brought a rosy tint to her cheeks. Cutter was becoming aware of her intelligence as a young woman. She had a quick wit and a relaxed smile.

"Thank you, Mr. Cutter. Please, call me Carmella. I wish I would have had more time with him. I do have very fond memories of him."

Carmella fussed with her gloves and then began to look up but then averted her eyes. She had been casting sideways glances at him as if unable to look at him.

"Newton, if you are not busy tomorrow for lunch, please join us at the hotel. I want Carmella acquainted with as many people as possible. She'll be staying out at the ranch for a couple of months and it always helps to have a friendly face around,"

Dawn smiled with a cool look in her eyes as she watched Cutter's reaction.

"I have to make a run out to Carl Johanson's tomorrow, but I can have lunch with you two ladies before I go. " Cutter gave her a brilliant white smile and with his fingers brushed back the dark curls.

"I'm glad you said that, Newton. I have been working on a new tablecloth for Carl and I'd like to send it along with you, if you don't mind?"

Dawn reached over and smoothed a red curl back off of Carmella's face.

"It would be my pleasure, ma'am," Cutter said as he watched the pretty Carmella stroll about for a moment and then winked at Dawn.

"Well, then, we'll see you tomorrow about 12:30 at the hotel. It was good to see you again Newton." Dawn's voice had a smile in it as she slid the gloves with slow care.

Carmella held out her hand to Cutter. It was small in his. "Thank you for letting us interrupt you for a few minutes. I look forward to our lunch tomorrow."

Deep blue eyes glistened and she licked her lips as she turned away. He opened his hand and waited for her to lift hers away and there was a jolt through him as she dragged her nails over his palm.

"See you tomorrow." Cutter watched them go as far as the green grass of the square where Carmella turned and waved before turning the corner. Cutter grinned and began sliding his gloves on.

The rest of the afternoon was busy as horses came in for shoe repairs, some progress on the heavy freight wagon and a delivery from Santa Fe of needed supplies. Gone was the relaxed peace and calm people had known for this area and now everyone was on edge if not downright afraid.

The western sky was shot with purples, crimson, and gold streaks. Wispy clouds trail off to the east lit up with a pink blush. The blackish flint hills in the distant had started to glow in the golden light of the evening. Somewhere out there is a couple of crows, complaining and tussling over a morsel. A pungent, moist smell of earth and sage has come rolling into Bradford, signaling the coming of night.

Newton Cutter had swept away the leaves into a pile out by the lumber pile. He leaned on the handle of the rake as his brilliant eyes looked south, watching gray shadows creep up on the valley. In the distance, he could hear indistinct voices from the town, a door closed, the horses stomped in the corral, a woman laughed.

Cutter took off the leather gloves and carried the rake back inside the workshop. The leather apron found its home on the hook, ready for tomorrow's work. The open lined notebook showed four jobs and several tasks that will need his expert attention. He wrote into the ledger, noting some detail on one of the lines. Deft fingers closed the book and he laid the pen down into the holder. His mind moved back over her blue eyes, the curl of that glorious red hair and her small hands.

Cutter listens to the sound of heavy wooden doors closing together and recognizes the creak of the stables being closed for the night. He ran fingers through the curly hair and shook the dust out of it. Mites floated in the last gleam of light sliding in through a window and then the light faded. The forge had begun to cool. Glowing red embers began to crust over with black charcoal, yet in spots yellow bits of flame danced into life and then spiraled back down into the red heat.

He pushed the heavy wooden door shut into place and his strong arm forced the spike down into the buried pipe. He glided the other door shut and as he slid the wooden slat into its casing, he felt a hand grip his shoulder and squeeze.

Newton Cutter turned to grin at his good friend, Thomas Wood who stood next to him. These last few weeks have been painful, treacherous, and costly. Cutter motioned his chin out to the valley and Thomas took a couple of steps over to the wood pile. The silver traces of evening have come in and taken away most of the green of the grass. Wood cocked his head to the left, frowning as he heard a boy calling for a dog.

The dusky gray sky spanned the horizon. Cutter slapped his hat on

Wood's shoulder and together the two young men walked across the town square. At the hotel, a man was about to enter but stepped back making a grand flourishing bow to the two younger men. With a low laugh, the man began to step into the doorway, he looked at the sky and caught the twinkle of the evening's first star. He took in a deep breath and let it out and looked down as if in thought. The hotel front door closed behind him.

Vaughn walked over to the blacksmith shop the next morning and sat down on the little stool inside the heavy wood doors.

"Newton, one of the framers fell this morning. Hurt his back. Doc Baines says that he needs to rest for a week before getting back to work. He don't want him to wrench it around or hurt it worse."

There was a serious, cold look in Vaughn's eye.

Cutter wiped his hands and frowned a bit, looking at Vaughn. "Alright. You sure he's gonna be okay?"

"I'm not gonna sugar-coat this. There were several rungs on the ladder that appear to have been sawed part way through. When the man stepped his weight on the rung, he fell through it. Tumbled about nine feet down, headfirst. Lucky he didn't break his neck. We checked all the other ladders and they're all fine."

Vaughn scowled at his gloves.

"I want to pay the man for the entire week. I know he has five children to feed and he was counting on pay from this job to take care of his family," Vaughn said and took in a deep breath and let it out.

"Yes, pay him. Let him know he still has a job to come back to," Cutter said as he ran his fingers back through the black curly hair and his blue eyes looked at Vaughn.

Vaughn stood up, shook hands with Newton, and then turned. "Thanks, Newton. This means a lot."

Cutter leaned against the heavy oak door and watched Vaughn walk back to the building site, wondering about rungs on ladders.

From a clump of stubby pines on the slope of the hill, Angus Tolliver squatted down on his heels and observed the ranch below through field glasses. Near the river there were waving fields of green grass that led up to a stand of tall timber on the east side of the beautiful property. There might be a few head of deer up in those trees.

This was the third trip up onto this hill that Tolliver had made over the past couple of weeks. And today he brought Royal Benning along to get a second set of eyes on the prize. Benning was busy tracing a narrow trail that led from the shoulder of the hill down around an old river wash and then disappeared in the grass close to the bottom. He had been careful to step over loose rock rather than leave boot prints in the dirt as he climbed back up to Tolliver.

So here was a ranch with a reputation of housing its own safe and conducting its sales in cash from Texas to California. The Ladd family's reputation spanned to Denver for its fat calves and good Hereford breeding stock. Chances were that Mr. Ladd Senior and sons were inside that big house right now going over some cattle contracts now and scheming their way to a greater fortune. A fortune that Tolliver had decided to take off them.

"Who busted your lip, Benning? Some saloon girl turn down your advances?" Tolliver chuckled and waited for the story.

Benning moved up alongside him. His face looked tired and drawn with a dark cut at the corner of his mouth and another alongside his left eye. He no longer moved catlike but with pain and rigidity, the telltale signs that he had been in a fight.

"I'll be alright, you just never mind about me," he said.

"Looks like a nice ranch down below."

Tolliver squinted through the glasses once more.

"We'll have to take the horses south where nobody asks questions. There is a man in Arizona that is looking for any cattle that will want at least twenty head. The boy's oughtta be able to handle that."

"Yeah, this'll give us some pocket money," Benning said as he pointed to the trail.

"That trail is about a month old. Lots of horses on it coming up and going down."

Benning had seen the remains of an older, wider trail partly hidden amongst rock outcroppings and tufts of grass and brush. Someone had once moved a large number of cattle up this hill.

"It's the perfect opportunity with that big dance coming up. There will be only a couple of hands on the ranch while everyone else is over kicking up their heels at the big shindig," Tolliver handed the glasses to Benning who studied the landscape.

"I want to get a better angle on this," Benning stood up and led the way around to the east, walking down a bit and moving in behind some brush he had seen from higher up. This was undisturbed land, no trails marking up the dirt and no sign that anyone had come through it. At a group of pine trees, he stopped and pointed something out to Tolliver.

"What am I lookin' at here?" Tolliver looked back up the hill and was confounded.

"There is an old trail here where someone pushed cattle up this hill. At first I didn't see it from the top but looking up there, this is the way we'll bring the cattle. Move them into the trees and then out the other side of the hill. Nobody will look for them there," Benning wiped his face with his bandanna.

"Alright, let's get back and get the boys setup on how we are gonna do this. I don't want any last minute surprises and if we are all careful, we can get a nice payday off this."

Benning nodded with his lips pursed in thought. He took one last glimpse through the glasses. Something bright and shiny reflected off something near the big barn and glinted, blinded him. He rubbed his eyes and took another look then ducked. Someone looked in his directions with another set of field glasses.

***

At the blacksmith shop, Cutter wiped the sweat from his face with his bandana and took a deep breath. The three professional construction men were blazing through framing up the walls. He had never seen first-hand the building of a home, except for adobe and sod. Since April, Cutter and Dunagan had forged over a thousand nails and those were gone, set deep into the lumber. It was several minutes after two o'clock on a beautiful bright day when the light breeze swirled dust and leaves about.

The crew chief called out, "Okay men, we're ready to lift."

Cutter, Wood, Dunagan and three other men took positions at the edge of the framed wall lying on the ground. Two more were in position to brace the new upright wall. At the signal all the men gripped the edge and lifted, bringing up the wooden skeleton. Level and plumb were found and wood braces were nailed into place.

Cutter stepped back and watched the hammers fly. Within the hour the other three walls stood, braced, and tied together forming the first floor. The lumber pile was sifted and sorted through. There were still major timbers, trusses, and planks to be raised into place.

"They're fast. They know what they're doing and going to it," Wood said as he took off his glove to rub his right eye.

"I know what you mean. I feel like I'm in the way," Cutter said with a grin. He watched two men carry a long plank into the new building.

"Newton, we're gonna set up the food over here under the tree," Mrs. Watley said as she passed by carrying two big baskets over to a couple of wood tables. Another woman smoothed out a bright cloth over the rough planks.

"Did she make fried chicken?" Wood leaned into Cutter and pretended to be drooling. Cutter laughed and shoved him away.

"I bet she did. I'm hoping Miss Dawn made her rhubarb cobbler, too," Cutter raised his eyebrow and grinned.

Richard Vaughn walked around the corner dragging a tape measure, wrapping it around a spool. He waved to Cutter and went to speak to one of the builders.

Wood nudged Cutter and motioned towards the growing table of food.

Carmella had unpacked a basket of what looked like potato salad and biscuits. She caught Cutter's eye and a rosy blush flooded her face and neck.

Vaughn stood beside Wood. "I doubt my workmen will get anything else done today after they see all that food getting set out."

The construction manager craned his neck to check out the tasty delights.

"Mr. Vaughn, can I see you a minute, Sir?" One of the workmen took Vaughn aside and talked. Then both walked into the structure pointing and gesturing.

"I understand that is the stonemason that is going to start tomorrow on the fireplaces," Cutter said as she motioned to the pile of stones stacked to the far side.

Vaughn came back. "The footings on the fireplaces will go in tomorrow. The measurements are all good and those should go in without a hitch."

He turned to face Cutter with a stern look. "Now remember, you can't build any fires until a full week after the stone goes in." He winked.

"Oh yes. I was telling Thomas that I feel like I'm in the way here. Your men are good, and fast," Cutter said as he nodded.

They watched two men nail a board into place.

"Just like you have your familiar hammers and tongs and such, I have the right men to accomplish what I need done. I trust 'em, I know they'll do it the right way," Vaughn rubbed his chin thoughtfully and said in a quieter voice, "and if they want more work from me, they'll do it the right way."

"Food's ready, gentlemen! Come and get it!" A feminine voice called out.

"Work was called off early today on account of food!" Vaughn did a mock salute and with a wink headed for the food table. Cutter chuckled as Thomas Wood was hot on his heels.

Tool belts were dropped into work carts, hammers stowed into benches and the group of workers shed their tools and were handed brimming plates of food. Cups and glasses of lemonade and iced tea were offered. Bert Goldman backed in a pushcart with a beer keg which was met with a rousing shout of approval.

Standing off to one side in the shade, Cutter felt a small hand slide into his. With a grin he looked into Carmella's eyes and brought her hand up to his lips.

"Everyone is so friendly and caring here. Neighbors helping neighbors," Carmella's shining eyes took in the scene as she squeezed Cutter's hand. "We don't have that in San Francisco. There are so many strangers and people passing through now."

"I've helped most of these people build barns, sheds, fences, let alone houses. We all pretty much rely on each other," Cutter smiled at her and watched the citizens and workmen chatting and munching.

Someone had asked the stonemason a question on the fireplace and Cutter frowned for a moment listening. Then he realized it was a German accent he heard. Amanda Hayes exclaimed a greeting in German and took her plate to sit near the mason.

Cutter and Carmella smiled as they made their way past the new friends chattering together.

Cutter and Carmella sat down at a table where Jackson Frisch was talking with Clay Dunagan about iron sculptures and processes. If there were ever complete opposites, it was these two men. Yet here they sat in the midst of a small town on the western coast of a growing nation, aiding friends, and family in their quest for a home.

Cutter took several minutes to walk through the construction site early the next morning.

The courses of stones had been laid out in a sandy area. Big stones, small stones, dark ones, light ones. Cutter stopped by to look before he got busy with another iron project. Nobody was moving around the site yet. It was still early, a few minutes after seven o'clock. Off in the distance old wagon wheels turned and a horse blew. There was a crow out in the valley circling one area, looking for breakfast.

The kitchen was longer than wider. Twenty feet across the inside wall by fifteen feet to the outside wall. Cutter had asked for the fireplace to be on the same wall as the pump. Someone had told him at one time that was ideal, but he could not remember the source. Hands in pockets, he looked at the stone pile and saw dull purples shot with steely gray, a gun barrel blue with flecks of copper and one reddish stone with black veins running through it.

Cutter had been working the iron for about an hour back at the forge when Thomas Wood walked in and laid down a cloth wrapped parcel. Cutter's hammer paused and watched as Wood pulled back the fabric to reveal a yellowish, moist blueberry muffin. Wood grinned.

"Where'd you get that?" The hammer dropped to the work bench and in three big steps Cutter cradled the fluffy morsel. He sank his teeth in and closed his eyes, savoring the warm sweetness.

"Aunt Dawn," Thomas said as he popped the last of his muffin into his mouth.

"I could smell 'em when I came out of the hotel this morning. I told her I was gonna stand there all day until I got one," Wood said as he laughed.

"She told me if'n I was gonna stand there, I could hold her laundry. Her lady laundry," Cutter and Wood doubled over laughing.

"Your aunt's baking will get her passed through the pearly gates, ya know. She could be a heinous fiend or murdering, insane goblin and she'd still get into heaven," Cutter said as he raised his eyebrows and held up a testimonial right hand.

"She'd show the good Lord that pecan pie and He'd shush her right on through."

Wood wiped his mouth, folded up the soft cloths and waved as he walked back to the stables. Cutter chuckled to himself, thinking about Dawn White. She was masterful in her baked goods. Her pies always won at the fairs. She once paid a man with a rhubarb cobbler for roof repairs on her dress shop. She had only one blemish to her record. She could not make doughnuts. Every man in the county would be on bended knee before her, maybe a couple of the married ones included, if she could make a doughnut.

The wagon wheels were done and leaning against the wall. Four angle irons were ready for the freight wagon. Fifty pounds of ten penny nails nestled in a small wooden box next to the door. Clay had gotten twelve feet of the twenty five foot chain done yesterday. There was a good chance that he would finish that today. Cutter mused about his growing business.

"Mr. Cutter, Sir?" It was one of the construction builders with a worried expression, gripping his hat with grimy hands.

"What is it? What's wrong?" Cutter said as he took off his heavy apron.

"The mason workin' in the house, he had a, well, a stone fell an, well, his fingers maybe his hand, might be broken."

His voice shook with a stammer as he explained that the mason had tried to continue to work with the hand wrapped but couldn't.

"I'll hitch up a wagon and take him…." Cutter stopped and looked past the man and saw a slow walking burly man holding his hand wrapped up, coming towards the shop.

"I'm needing yer Doc, Mr. Cutter. I'm afraid it's broke." His voice trembled as he stopped and unwrapped his swelling hand.

"Let's get you over to Doc Baines. He knows what to do with broken bones, for sure," Cutter said as he led the way while the man grimaced following him.

"Mr. Vaughn ain't here yet and I don't know my way around the town yet. I'm sorry to put to this bother," Cutter could hear muttering behind him.

Doc Baines came around the corner at the same time Newton was getting ready to knock on the door. He stood there a minute looking at the unwrapped hand, grunted a couple times and then opened the door to his office.

"You a drinkin' man, Sir?" Doc hesitated before opening up the large wooden closet.

"Aye, a good German is a good drinker, Sir!" Doc nodded and poured a hefty glass of whisky and handed it to the mason.

"I'll set your hand in about an hour after you drink this. Can't have you trying to swing on me when I get them bones back into place," Doc said with a wink at Cutter.

About ninety minutes later, Cutter lifted and held and pushed and pulled on command by Doc. After the hand was wrapped, a blanket was spread over the snoring man.

"Humph, I know a thirteen year old blonde girl who can hold her liquor better 'n that!" Doc Baines nudged Cutter snickering.

"That hand is gonna be hurting tomorrow. I'm afraid he's off the job for at least three weeks." Doc shook the wild gray hair with his lip out. "I was lookin' forward to seeing that big ole' fireplace, too, Newton. Darned shame."

Cutter leaned up against the doorjamb and took in a deep breath. "Maybe Vaughn knows someone who can fill in."

"Wait a minute. You remember John Ladd's boy, Marty? He's got some masonry work behind him. Spent a summer back in Boston with family laying brick or somethin'," Doc was rummaging around in his desk drawer, shuffling through papers.

"I don't know if he's around, though. He's supposed to be runnin' off to work way up north in Canada." Doc said as he scratched his head.

He looked around his office like he was lost. Doc felt around in his pockets, frowning. Cutter wondered if this was his future.

Finally, Doc leaned on his desk and looked at Cutter. With a quick movement, he took his spectacles off the top of his head and put them on his nose.

"I have to ride out to the ranch after lunch today. I'll take a detour up to the Ladd ranch and see if Marty is able and available. I'll let you know tomorrow, young feller."

Doc shooed Cutter out the door. Cutter waved and shut the door behind himself, chuckling.

When Cutter walked back to the building site, Vaughn was writing into a notebook at the desk he had set up near the lumber pile.

"Doc says the mason's hand has to heal for at least three weeks before he can use it," Cutter said as he sat on the bench and looked at Vaughn still scribbling.

Vaughn stopped, put the pen down and looked at Cutter. "Well, there's about another week of general construction that can be done without the fireplace going up. I know that the mason likes to have the room all to himself when he is puttin' up stone. I'm not sure how fast I can find another mason of his quality."

"I'd like to try a local man if you'd oblige me. One of the local boys has some experience with laying bricks and stonework behind him from back east. Doc is gonna' bring him by tomorrow. Marty is on a ranch about seventy miles out, if he is here this summer." Cutter said as he fidgeted with a small chunk of lumber.

"If he doesn't work out, then we'll look for someone else."

Cutter leaned forward elbows on knees and clasped his hands together. "Ah, Herr Mueller could have a pupil to instruct, eh?" Vaughn had a hearty laugh."Okay, you're on. We'll see how your boy holds up."Vaughn rolled up a set of plans and squeezed Cutter's shoulder then walked into the growing house.

# 11 CHAPTER ELEVEN

The Summer Ball had always been an event for the locals to renew acquaintances, meet new friends and establish business relationships. The punch was good, the whiskey was free, and men stood around the beer keg telling stories and jokes. Cutter paced the rug in the lobby as he waited for Jackson and Carmella to come downstairs. From the window he turned and looked at the figure at the top of the stairs. Carmella was a curvy-shaped girl that came down in a long, off the shoulders green satin dress. Cutter held his breath gazing at her. Behind her Jackson looked smart in his black slacks, white shirt, and string tie with black boots with silver accents.

"Good evening Miss Carmella. Good evening Jackson," Cutter said and tipped his hat in greeting. "Ready for an evening of good folks and dancing?" Carmella's laugh was like rich honey as her eyes lit up. "Only if you promise not to trample my toes, Mr. Cutter. I've been saving these shoes for a special occasion and I don't want them ruined by muddy boots." "Well, we haven't had any rain in a week. I would say your little shoes are safe from mud, Miss. I'm quite sure that most folks are bathed and shaved for the Summer Ball tonight and I'd even go out on a limb and say we're on our best behavior. But there again, you understand how I'll reserve the right to retract that statement later."

Jackson and Carmella laughed. "You will recognize most folks here tonight, but please, let me know if you would like to meet someone. I am happy to make introductions for you," Cutter said as he winked and smiled sideways to Carmella. It was ten miles out to the fairgrounds where the Summer Ball was held each year. On the bandstand there were several local men along with a well-known musical group of players that came over from Beatrice. There was lively music playing from the two violin players, tambourine player, a drummer, one flute player, and three guitar players.

Carmella was an admired vision as she danced with Cutter around the floor. He held her at a distance, not wanting to do the wrong thing.

Jackson came over to their table and took Carmella around the floor.

Thomas Wood stepped to the table and held out an offered hand. "May I have this dance, Miss Frisch?" Carmella nodded and took his hand, stood up, grinning.

Thomas winked to Cutter. "You can't keep all the pretty girls to yourself, buster!" Carmella laughed and they whirled away. After a few moments, Carmella was searching for Cutter with her eyes.

"I think he has thrown you over for another woman," Thomas whispered.

Carmella looked up at him, frowning and Thomas gestured over to the far side of the floor. Cutter was dancing with great care with Mrs. Klinger, whose face was lit up in a big smile. Carmella admired the handsome blacksmith for his sociable charm.

A bit later Cutter and Carmella were strolling around the outside of the festivities admiring the hanging lanterns.

"Has your father decided on selling the ranch or letting it set?" Cutter asked as he admired the small gold locket against the whiteness of her skin.

"I think most of the prices he has been offered are way too low for its worth. Riley Stephens will be left in charge for the time being until a buyer can be found," She frowned a bit, smoothing down her dress.

He pulled Carmella into the manicured garden of azaleas, beneath a sheltering cottonwood. Her face turned up to his with a gentle smile. His arms were strong around her, gripping her and his lips touched hers and melted into welcoming softness. He slid his fingers up into the hair at the back of her head and gripped , holding her in place. Cutter could feel a lightning strike rush through him, a fire in his veins and the intense desire to possess her. Her slender fingers became tangled in his curly black hair and he heard a moan in the back of her throat. The pretty girl pulled back as if stunned and blinked several times.

Carmella took a couple steps back and felt a breeze flow past. It was then she realized that he stood there, watching her actions. Without a word, he held his hand out to her and she took it. Drawing her to him, he folded her into his arms and she laid her head on his shoulder.

"Answer me something, Carmella."

Her voice was low, "Alright."

"A woman doesn't kiss a man like you just kissed me unless she wants more of him. Is it your desire to become mine?" He could see her eyes widen and her lips parted.

He lowered his lips to the back of her neck and ran his tongue in little circles up to her ear. "I'm the sort of man that won't just go in and take something that isn't mine. You'll have to offer yourself to me. You can stay here in my arms or you can step away and I'll move on."

There was a look of hunger in her eyes as she rose on her toes melting her lips to his. He could feel her nails digging into his back. His heart pounded in his chest and his fingers slid into the thick waves at the back of her head and he lifted her off the ground, holding her head as he kissed her.

"I'm on fire. What have you done to me?" His voice was husky as he lowered her to the ground. He lifted a long tendril of the pretty hair back off her shoulder. He smiled and turned to the right and took three steps into the garden.

"I need a woman who will be beautiful for me, keep herself for me and who's only intent to be at my side no matter what. I'm going to be open and honest with you, Carmella. You are a beautiful, desirable woman who will make a man happy. This is not about what I can give you in marriage and in life. There are no bounds, no limits for that. This is about what you are willing to give to me as your husband, your lover and the master of your heart."

Carmella took in a deep breath and said, "I can't answer you now. I feel like I've been hit by lightning. My head is spinning being this close to you right now." It was a whisper.

He nodded and reached for her hand. They walked into the crowded hall. For the remainder of the evening she was never more than an arms' length away from him.

After he delivered Carmella and Jackson back to the Long Ranch, Cutter had plenty of time on the drive home to remember the pretty red hair on bare shoulders, the light in her eyes and the feel of her soft lips. He thought again how she dug her nails into him as she tried to grip him tighter. The tiny silvery twinkling stars overhead spread from horizon to horizon and the tangy sweet smell of sage was carried on the breeze. He had made his desire known to her and now he must wait.

*******

The next morning Cutter made another quiet inspection of the house building site. Three wheelbarrows were parked near the gravel with a shovel leaned up against it. A big pile of dirt had been dumped on the far corner of the lot from excavating the foundation. There were assorted lengths of water pipe lying on the ground off to the back of the house. Three wooden ladders leaned up against the frame. Tool carrying boxes sat idle on a wooden cart. Over on the far side of the building there were the milled planks stacked in high bundles on the grass. There had been constant work on the house and only on Sundays was the site quiet. Cutter stepped around the lot.

Sometimes Cutter thought that he should stay out of the way of the construction progress so he kept his visits to a minimum and after the workers had left for the day.

Last week, Cutter had watched the teams of draft horses bring in the five huge rumbling freight wagons of lumber. The patience and expertise of the drivers put the offload within one foot of the area reserved. Today there was a plumbing contractor turning a die against a pipe preparing for a connection. A long line of pipes lay end to end from the well snaking towards the house. The school and his house would have inside water and every convenience he could think of. Many nights after dinner, he walked alone through the site and around the house thinking of what it might look like, how it would be to live in it and if he would be living alone.

Heavy canvas and leather work gloves hung over a sawhorse inside the door. Next week fifteen thousand bricks would arrive from Tucson. All the doors would arrive from the woodworking shop. More windows were coming. It had taken six strong men making five trips with the wagons to get all the granite slabs from the quarry, exclusively at the watchful eye and direction of Mrs. Klinger. One of the dedicated masons was right now hauling three tons of slab marble back from a little quarry outside of San Francisco, brokered by the same Mrs. Klinger. Cutter wondered about those many pieces of building material all fitting together and becoming a house.

The building contractor advised Cutter to put up a strong fence right on the property line to keep out any grazing cattle that might wander in as well as the deer that could be attracted into the garden. He had yet to decide the type of fence or material. If Giordanni suggested it, Cutter woud approve.

The grounds were flat with two trees. The play area would be almost a full acre of lawn for the school children. Also, a great location for any lawn parties after it became a private home. Cutter stood on the property line lost in thought as he looked at the building.

A twig snapped and Cutter turned around to find Dawn White. "I thought you might want to know that my brother, Jackson, has decided there is no more that he can do out at the ranch right now. He is getting ready to leave and head back to San Francisco next week. His business there needs his attention and he has been avoiding the trip but now he must go,"

Dawn frowned as she fussed with a glove.

"Carmella will be going with him, Newton."

Cutter put down the scraps of wood and rubbed his hands together, looking off into the distance. "You say they are leaving next week?"

"I didn't want it to come as a surprise to you. I know that you and Carmella have struck up a good friendship and I thought you might want to know their plans. At this time Jackson has no plans of returning anytime soon."

Dawn sat down on a bench and looked at Cutter.

"Riley Stevens is going to take care of the ranch and I'll go out from time to time to take a look. When Henry gets back we'll take a ride out there and see what needs to be done," Dawn said as she rubbed her eyes. She squinted and looked at Cutter.

"In some ways I'm glad that he didn't sell the ranch because it was the only thing I have left of Harley. I still hate to think of him as completely gone and it would have deepened my sadness if the ranch had been turned over to strangers," Dawn said with a trembling voice.

She took a deep breath and forced a little smile.

"Dawn, I believe that Carmella is a smart, beautiful young woman and I'm so very. Well, I," Cutter grimaced struggling to find the right words.

He twisted his gloves in his hands.

Birds flitted in and out of the tall grass on the edge of the valley. The scent of wildflowers mixed in with that tangy smell of sage in the air. The sounds of hammers and saws came from inside the growing house.

"She cares for you, Newton, I know she does. She has not said if she would want to live a quiet life in a rural town or if she would prefer living in the city," Dawn said. She watched as Cutter kicked at a clod of dirt and ran a hand through his dark, curly hair.

"Well, my bank is in San Francisco and I could always use that as an excuse, if I needed one," Cutter grinned and winked at Dawn who brightened up a bit.

"Besides, the poets say that absence makes the heart grow fonder." Dawn laughed.

***

Five days later, Dawn and Frisch stood in the lobby chatting as Carmella sorted things from her pockets into her small velvet purse. There were six other passengers taking the stage that day and people generally mingled around, drank coffee, and said their goodbyes. Two small children had climbed up on chairs to look out the window and were chattering about what was going on outside.

The heavy door opened and Newton Cutter walked in. He smiled when he saw them and walked over, removing his hat. He wore a dark charcoal buttoned shirt with a red neckerchief and black jeans and boots. Dark, glossy black curls framed his blue eyes and in his hand was a small, wrapped box with a pink bow. Frisch was amused about how Carmella perked up and she took in a breath when she saw Cutter.

"Miss Dawn, Miss Carmella, Mr. Frisch," Cutter said with a smile and nodded.

"Miss Carmella, a little something to help you remember all of us," Cutter placed the little box into her gloved hands. She searched his eyes then took off the bow and opened the tiny box. Lifting back the tissue papers, she exclaimed as she lifted out a shining, silver pendant about three inches long.

Each silvery horseshoe no bigger than a penny laid end to end with a key clasp were inscribed "Home" "Family" and "God", with a round ring on the end. Frisch took a step closer and peered over her shoulder.

"Oh my heavens! It is so beautiful! You made this, Mr. Cutter?" Her green eyes were incredulous.

"It's for your keys so you won't lose them," Cutter stood relaxed, with his hat down at his side.

"Oh!" Carmella searched in a pocket of her bag and brought out a small key on a strand of leather and handed it to Cutter.

"Would you, please?" Cutter untied the leather and showed Carmella how to expand the ring and slide on the key. Frisch examined the little key holder and finally nodded, smiled, and handed it back to Carmella.

"You are quite the artist for a blacksmith, Mr. Cutter," Frisch shook Cutter's hand and winked.

"Newton, this is lovely. You just might have to make one of those for me," Dawn said as she held it in her hands and read the tiny inscriptions. Her eye crinkled up at the corners when she handed the silver key chain over to Georgianna who held it up to the light for a better look. A sly smile and a wink passed to Cutter from Carmella as she gave his hand a squeeze.

The stagecoach arrived pulled by six horses stirring up a cloud of dust in front of the hotel. The passengers unloaded to get a bite to eat in the hotel and the tenders changed out the teams. Thomas Wood walked the tired horses back down the street headed for the stables softly talking to them like old friends.

Cutter took her bare hand in his as Carmella stepped up into the stage. Cutter shook hands with Frisch and he stepped up into the stage and sat beside Carmella. Three others boarded and the door shut. Brilliant green eyes kept and held brilliant blue eyes until the stage passed out of sight down the long valley road.

"I must say, I'm going to miss this town," Carmella said as she squeezed her father's gloved hand. Frisch squeezed back and his eyes crinkled up in a smile to his daughter. Together they watched the landscape slide by as the stage picked up speed on the long road back to San Francisco.

*******

"Newton! Thomas! Come at once!" Mayor Watley was visibly shaking at the front door of the stables, mopping his forehead with a handkerchief. Scattered shafts of sunlight fell through the giant oak's limbs creating dancing spots of light on the ground as Cutter and Wood trotted around the side of the building up to the Mayor.

"What is it, Mayor? Are you hurt?" Newton saw the alarmed mayor and pulled off his heavy leather gloves. Thomas started to turn the Mayor around looking for a wound.

The mayor shook himself loose from the gripping hands. "No! I'm fine.

I want you to take a look at this wanted flyer for Thornton Glass. This man here, he is standing in Bruno's store right now."

Thomas and Newton looked at the sketch of the man. Wood frowned, gripping the crumpled paper. A classic chiseled jaw and piercing dark eyes stared back at them.

"I only saw him for a second as I walked by, but then I remembered the flyer and .. I think it's him!" The Mayor's voice was starting to rise in urgency. "Quick, I want you to take a look at him."

Watley reached for the flyer and shoved it in his pocket, walking towards the square.

Someone had walked into the auction house letting the heavy door slam behind them. Two scruffy dogs tussled over a raggedy bone under a tree on the grass. Two couples stood near the steps at the hotel with their baggage on the ground next to them. The faint scent of sage and warmed earth carried on the wind.

The three men turned the corner of the square in time to see a heavy man in a grimy brown duster trotting his roan down the street headed out of town. Twin leather scabbards held rifles on each side of the saddle and bigger than usual saddlebags swayed against the animal.

"We're too late." Dejected, Watley cursed under his breath and went into Bruno Stenson's gun shop.

***

Later that afternoon, Cutter frowned and tilted his head back as they sat at the big table behind the blacksmith shop. Dunagan motioned for them to listen. Wood cocked his head and listened for a minute and then pointed at the front of the shop.

"We're back here, Mike. Bring your lunch back and set yourself down," Cutter yelled with a smile.

Local wagon vendor Mike Cushman came toddling around the corner. Cushman put down his lunch tote and took off his hat, seating himself at the round wooden table. Cutter and Wood liked Cushman because he was interesting, nosy, and brought them regular business. The exuberant, chatty vendor irritated Dunagan.

"Mrs. Landry over at Table Bluff needs a fine mesh iron grate. Says she is tired of fried beef all the time. The lady wants to grill it up over an open flame."

Cushman sighed with a dreamy look in his old watery eyes.

They laughed.

"My kinda woman!" Cushman winked. The vendor handed the paper notes to Dunagan.

"I should have this ready on Friday. I'm only workin' on nails for Newt, so this is a welcome change."

Dunagan nodded and tucked the paper into his breast pocket.

"Maybe I'll stop by Table Bluff and have the Widow Landry show me how well it works." Dunagan winked at Cutter who started laughing.

"Well, I am sorry to bring bad news today, gentlemen. Mr. Bob Samuelson up at Freshwater had a stroke about a month ago and now must be fed like a baby. Poor soul. It's hell to have your body quit on ya like that."

They shared their personal stories about getting old.

"Mrs. Emeline Lundy over at Drake's Landing had a fine big baby girl last week. They're calling her Juliana. Big brown eyes and lots of hair. Bug's ear cute, I'd say."

Wood nodded. "I think that is the only new baby around here."

"What's new around here lately? Any news I can pass along?" Cushman tore into a piece of cold fried chicken like a proud carnivore.

"I need you to keep your eyes open for furniture for sale, Mike. I'm gonna need everything," Cutter said. He paused a minute for effect.

"I'm building a house."

"You are? Congratulations, young man! Where at?"

Cutter filled in Cushman on the details and some of the particulars of the construction.

"If I recollect, Mrs. Willoughby over by Four Wagon Bridge was looking for someone to buy her piano. Would you be interested in that? I'm not sure what she wants for it," Cushman bit into an apple and wiped his mouth with the back of his hand.

"The children might like that, singing and all," Wood said. He had been rolling a pebble back and forth on the table.

"I'll let Addie Watley know. The school committee will want to buy a piano. I don't need one, myself, but it would be nice to have one for the children."

"You run across a dinner table and chairs, couple of bed frames, dishes, let me know," Cutter said.

"There is a new furniture store over at Three Corners. Opened up last month. Big freight wagons have been trucking in every blessed thing a woman could want in her house," Cushman said. He held his arms out wide emphasizing the number of things going into the store.

"Sounds like an opportunity. I've got a job over at Three Corners next month. I'll stop by that store and take a look!"

Cutter leaned back against the wall of the blacksmith shop and relaxed a moment.

Cushman stood up and packed his lunch basket up, folding the cloth over itself.

"I'm expecting a box in from my beloved daughter on the three o'clock stage. I want to be there when it rolls into town," Cushman said.

He raised his eyebrows and looked dubious. "There's no telling what that girl will be sending to me".

Cushman waved goodbye and sauntered back across the plaza.

Cutter stood up, excused himself and headed for the house building site.

"How you holdin' up, Marty?" Cutter had climbed up the exposed boards of the back stairs and leaned in to catch Marty measuring something. For the blacksmith, the framing of the second story had gone agonizingly slow.

Boards cut to the wrong length, missing tools left at home and the never ending need for nails caused delays, let alone the building crew's physical problems.

"Little sore, but good so far, Sir," Marty said as he grinned and waved.

"I think we all have carried two ton of brick, stone and rock up those stairs, and we ain't finished yet!" Several courses of stone had been laid out on planks so each row going up the fireplace chimney could be set in order. Seven feet wide and the face went through the roof ending with a massive river rock.

Cutter and Wood had built three mantles for each fireplace in the new home. The first floor kitchen would have the heavy oak mantle and designed to hold cooking tools. The second floor bedroom had a raised hearth with a broad hearthstone for sitting. The men had taken great pains with the cherry wood mantle for the living room.

The plank roof was half done. The workmen scurried back and forth to put on the remaining boards. A big storm headed towards the area and would damage the unfinished house. Pounding hammers echoed through the building and Cutter turned around trying to visualize a completed living room with sofas, chairs, tables, and bookcases.

Cutter walked over to the mason fitting in the fireplace chimney stones.

"You are an artist," he said with admiration to the skilled worker.

Trowels of mortar buttered the top of the heavy stones and then another row was lifted into place. Marty worked in a rhythm moving, reaching, lifting rock, and stone into place.

Cutter knelt to look closer.

"I never in my dreams imagined I would be building my own home, Marty. I sort of figured I would move into a house that had already been built and sort of make it my own, ya know?" Cutter rolled a pebble between his fingers, musing about this huge undertaking.

"That's what I did, Mr. Cutter, I moved into a house my father had built as a young man first married to my mother. It wasn't all that big, but I added onto it here and there. I built on a broad veranda and put a big wide kitchen on the back of the house for my wife. We are comfortable there and we all feel a definite sense of family history," Marty said.

He laughed as he tapped a stone into place.

"If walls could talk, you know," Marty said with a chuckle.

Cutter moved to one side as a bucket of mortar came in and was set onto a bench. He walked over to look out of the window. The afternoon was wearing on. A big freight hauler wagon was unloading wooden crates on the back of the house. Big Percherons stamped in the light dust, shaking their manes, and snorting. A young boy carried an armload of short planks across the yard. The little cloth ribbons waved merrily in the light breeze from the yard stakes.

On the other end of town, people weren't so peaceful.

Chick Miller had warned the shabby man about starting trouble. But he paid no attention, like he didn't hear a word. The drink was too strong for Jim Caudle who had spent his time bragging about how well he could hold his liquor. One remark too many about a passing woman on the boardwalk brought out the chivalrous knight in Dawson Cole.

There was no warning when Dawson Cole swung around with a high elbow and caught Caudle right across his mouth, splitting one of his lips. Caudle stumbled a bit in surprise, lost his balance and fell back, heavy against the water trough and both men struggled to get up. His men were jumpy, spurs jingling, starting to walk towards the fight. Cole glanced at them and then back to the big man that stood in front of him. One of them started to close in, but the loud sound of a shotgun being cocked stopped him in his tracks.

Caudle struck out with a sharp right. An inch or two lower and his fist would have caught Cole's chin and knocked him out. Caudle went up on his toes and sort of scurried to the left in a quick move to evade a swinging left from Cole. The shabby man turned the wrong way and Cole's fist smashed into the right cheekbone that staggered Caudle. He groaned and an angry sneer came over his face, eyes full of vicious hate, and a wild right hand was thrown at Cole. Dawson dodged to the right and caught a glancing blow to the side of his head.

Caudle lowered his shoulder and rushed Cole, caught one leg, and threw him tumbling to the ground and dust flew up in a drifting cloud. Caudle was right on top of him and aimed a wicked knee into Cole's belly, but Dawson was spry and rolled to the right like a cat. Both men had caught their breath and jumped up, crouching with fists clenched. Dawson Cole reached out a right cross and caught Caudle on the ear. Another stiff, straight blow landed on the man's jaw that shook him making his eyes roll.

Caudle was the taller man, and smashed Cole in the face with both fists, and Cole replied with two heavy punches into Caudle's ribs. Toe to toe, neither man avoiding any punches, they stood there for a few moments battering each other. Caudle struck Cole again, on the ear and then people saw a bloody drip down onto his neck. Cole slammed a heavy fist right into the midsection and swung up hard on a left uppercut.

Chick Miller who stood at the boardwalk rail murmured that Caudle had landed more punched. The auctioneer raised his eyebrows and remarked that Cole was a full punch faster than Caudle so it should all even out. Cole then put three fast punches into Caudle's body, doubling him over, making him gasp.

Caudle's hands were bloody as he held them up, the knuckles torn and jagged. Cole swung a wicked left hook and Caudle dodged it. Cole was off balance from the punch and Caudle lifted a boot going for Cole's knee. Cole saw Caudle coming for the kick and reached out grabbing both hands into his shirt and throwing the big man to the side. Caudle tumbled into the dirt and wiped out his eyes, spitting out dirt from his mouth. Cole paused a moment leaning his hands on his knees, panting, never taking his eyes off Caudle.

Caudle grunted, rage in his eyes and rushed up to his feet, and a wild left jab glanced off Cole's jaw. Cole answered with an uppercut that pounded into Caudle. Jim tried to dodge the punch but got caught with a hard jabbing left hand.

Cole was breathing heavy, and stepped to his right, angling for a spot for his punch. Dawson started to throw his right, then stopped and came around with a left hook and smashed Caudle's nose. Caudle grunted and brought three fast jabs into Cole's ribs, staggering him backwards.

Caudle's mouth was red and bloody, his eyes burned with hatred and his fists were bloody all up to the wrists. Both men were cut, oozing from gashes and filthy from the powdery dirt of the street. Cole leaned in a right hand and punched Caudle's cheek before he could get his hands up. Cole dodged and went under the swinging left of Caudle and then brought around a mean right hook, catching Caudle's ribs.

Caudle caught Cole coming in with a right and the bystanders knew that Cole was hurt now. Caudle went in for a vicious punch and caught an elbow up alongside his head making him see stars. Caudle started to rush in from a crouch and grapple Cole but a big boot caught his leg and Caudle rolled down into the dirt. This time Cole didn't wait for Caudle to get back up and rushed him, head down, butting him. Cole's feet went out from under him and down he went.

Caudle scrambled, trying to kick Cole's face, but Dawson sprang up and grabbed the boot and rolled into the man, knocking him down with an elbow into his belly. Caudle rolled away groaning, holding his midsection and came up on one knee, looking for Cole. A heavy left swung for Caudle's chin but he pulled back and came up swinging with a right cross to Cole's face.

Cole ducked fast and put two fast punches into Caudle's ribs and people now saw that Caudle was hurt as well. Caudle backed away, circling trying to decide what to do about Dawson Cole. Finally Caudle moved in bringing a left hook but Cole ducked it and threw another punch into the ribs. Cole was slow to recover and Caudle landed one on Cole's chin and the man went down into the dirt.

Cole was stunned, dazed, and wobbling as he tried to get up. Jim Caudle kicked at Cole's face and Cole barely dodged the boot. Cole stumbled and another boot caught him in the belly and the man groaned falling over next to the boardwalk. Caudle took three steps to jump down onto Cole's stomach with booth heels, but Cole jerked up both knees and kicked hard. The double kick caught him coming down and tumbled him off to the left. He tried to grab Cole with his clawed hand, aiming for his eyes.

Cole grimaced, jerking his face away, panicked and came up in a crouch backing away. Caudle grunted and rushed towards Cole, wildly swinging, punching both fists. Cole was driven back and back, as the big man's fists hammered at Cole's, stumbling backwards, trying to steady himself. Cole was under attack with no chance to ward off Caudle's blows. Cole squatted down low and Caudle in his momentum carried him over the top of Cole. Jim Caudle started to fall, caught himself and both men got up again. Caudle rushed at Cole once again in fury and the right hook caught the edge of Cole's jaw. Cole tried to punch him but blocked the fist. Cole ducked inside of the next punch, lowered his head, and punched three hard fists into Caudle's middle.

Caudle shoved him off and glanced another left off Cole's temple. Cole twisted around and brought up an uppercut crushing into the jaw of Caudle, shaking him hard. Cole swung around and planted his feet, bloody bruised hands held up before him. Caudle sank down into a heap in the dirt, his arms limp, and fists bloody, a wrecked man.

Two trail hands picked up and dragged the unconscious Caudle out behind the saloon and let him fall into the broken bales of straw kept for that sort of occasion. The auctioneer started dropping glinting coins into the outstretched palm of the saloon keeper.

***

The next morning, Addie Watley and Dawn White stood in Newton Cutter's new kitchen looking at the deep cast iron sink finished in white enamel with a tall pump mounted next to it. The construction on Cutter's house had finally progressed so that the functioning kitchen was done. "I am just so pleased that someone had the sense to put a water pump inside a house!"

Mrs. Watley leaned over the white enameled cast iron sink with her gloved hands gripped together.

Dawn nodded and walked around inside the big room looking at the unfinished walls. She could envision a huge sideboard on the far wall holding the dishes, plates, and platter, every kitchen stocked.

Dawn had been musing over Newton Cutter's and Carmella Frisch's new friendship. "Well, as least she will have plenty of room."

"Who will have plenty of room? Who are you talking about, Dawn?" Addie had an alarmed look on her face. She gave Dawn a wide-eyed stare.

Dawn chuckled and looked up at the tall ceiling.

"I mean whoever will be cooking for the children will have plenty of room. I'm just figuring that it would be a woman cooking in here. I had assumed it would be a woman, maybe a mother of one of the children."

Addie murmured agreement with a nod of her head.

Dawn turned away grinning to herself and gazed up at the huge ceiling beams. Tiny bits of dust floated in the sun rays coming in through the tall windows. The heavy wood plank floor was still rough with little piles of wood shavings and chalk marks for finishing.

Mrs. Watley looked a bit stern pressing her lips together but softened a bit upon hearing about the school children.

"I don't know if Mr. Cutter was planning on supplying any of the kitchen items for the first floor. I'm sure we could get them from Mr. Cushman when he comes through. Pots and pans and a big table and some chairs, I imagine."

Dawn White smiled listening to Addie Watley chatter about getting things set up. For Dawn, she could see Carmella standing there in an apron cleaning the dinner dishes as Newton's wife. She smiled to herself and followed Addie into the next big room.

# 12 CHAPTER TWELVE

Brett Doyle had built the cabinets for the house over in the woodworking shop in the old warehouse behind the Bradford Auction House. His eldest son, Jeremy, had been sawing, cutting, and pounding nails alongside Brett for over a month. It was a complete cabinetry shop and there had been talk of Jeremy taking it over as a business next year. The young man had an eye for building furniture. His current project was a writing desk for upstairs landing. The equipment table was organized, saws hung from pegs in the wall and a cloud of wood dust seemed ever present.

Cutter could see nine first floor kitchen cabinets, eight open-shelf cabinets, ten small side tables and assorted chairs. Over to the far side of the building there were a dozen round top stools of varying heights made out of fir. He grinned and realized that these were for the children in the schoolrooms.

Mike Cushman had delivered the four big rolled-up rugs for the bedrooms. Things were moving right along now and on Tuesday the workmen would start bringing up the handmade cabinets and furniture. It was methodical with everything moving at the right speed and the right time. It was all coming together.

The wide plank black oak finished flooring from North Carolina had started going in. Cutter had always liked the black oak flooring in Carl Johanson's big ranch house. A dark elegant hardwood arrived last month on a freighter wagon. It has been stored in a meeting room of the church so it could get acclimated.

Ernie Amundson had laid the flooring in three of the four upstairs bedrooms. The master bedroom fireplace was scheduled to finish the following day if everything went well. Ernie would lay the oak in there, and then the entire second floor would be ready for Cutter to move in.

Mac Kelly had been working on the fireplace in the upstairs kitchen. It stood centered with a raised hearth, iron swinging arms, and impressive in stacked granite on the outside wall with counters to both sides. It took two weeks to build it and it was the first thing someone saw when they walked into the kitchen. Cushman delivered the iron cook stove yesterday and it was finally installed. It was a Chicago model; heavy from its solid construction took four men the better part of an hour to wrestle it up the stairs and another to get it anchored into the brackets.

Wood nudged Cutter and handed him a glass of beer. "Where did you get this, buddy?"

Cutter took a long drink and wiped his mouth with the back of his hand, grinning.

"I have my ways, friend," Wood said as he grinned back. Together, they walked from room to room as Cutter pointed out how furniture would be brought in and about how it would look once he moved in.

"That is up until Carmella, oh uh, your wife arrives and it becomes her house, that is, right?" Wood's eyes crinkled up in laughter.

Cutter sat down on a wooden crate and rubbed his hands together in thought.

"Things have been a bit quiet around town lately. No big shootouts or robberies that I know of. I was talking with Bert earlier and no strangers have been drinking at the saloon."

Cutter told Wood about the visit to Mary Rideout's place and went back over the strange details of the strong box found on the property.

"It is definitely a mystery and I'm not sure if it will ever be solved," Wood said as he collected the beer mugs.

T young men walked down the stairs and out of the quiet, dusty house.

"Hopefully, we'll learn more and maybe get some answers when we get out to her place tomorrow."

Cutter gripped his good friend's shoulder and they walked out onto the broad patio at the back of the house.

***

The following morning had been cool on the ride out east. There were ten deer grazing in the sweet grass near the river. The ranch still ran whiteface cattle and a small herd dotted the green valley.

The maid helped the elderly Mary Rideout into the chair and put a soft pink knitted shawl around her shoulders. Mary's hazel eyes were bright and held a steady gaze. At eighty years old she was still sharp as a tack.

Addie Watley, Dawn White and Cutter sat around her sipping steaming cups of tea.

"Here's what I wrote to you about, Mary," Addie placed the small black box in her hands and opened it. There was a folded black satin handkerchief with embroidered initials of GML. When Mary unfolded the handkerchief there lay the golden chain with an emerald the size of a penny with three small diamonds on each side of it. Mary's hand trembled as she picked up the necklace and a smile came over her lips, lighting up her eyes.

"Minnie Hollister was an acquaintance of my daughter in law, Rose. She'd pass through once a month or so, always on her way to some doin's. She would sing us the latest songs she had heard and tell us about what she saw in her travels. She was wearin' the prettiest dresses and the smartest shoes all the time. She was always so lively, singin' and dancin' all the time."

"People used to pass through all the time. Back when I was just a child, probably seven, maybe eight folks were always comin' and goin' and I never paid no attention to who was there and who wasn't. My mother loved company, bein' out here in the wild country alone. That many years ago, there weren't that many people livin' out here. A store, tradin' post and a couple of saloons. My mother used to let me buy penny candies at the tradin' post on Saturdays."

"Rose and Minnie used to sit for hours and chat about things and people they knew and what far off places were like. Dreaming about far off places. I remember lookin' at that necklace because the light from the fire jumped and sparkled on it. Like there was living green lightning inside the stone. She always wore  it was how I knew it was her. I don't remember ever seein' her without it. She told me laughin' one time, that it was her entire fortune. I didn't understand what she meant by that so I thought she was joking with me. She was that way.

Mary was thoughtful for a moment. "I'd say about the size of a normal woman. She could have been as tall as you, Miss Dawn. She wasn't a heavy or chubby person by any means. Slimmer but not that gaunt, painful skinniness. I don't remember ever seein' her hair up, she liked to wear it long and down. Auburn, yes, that auburn reddish brown color. Rose's hair was that light blonde color and the two of them contrasted together."

"I remember Minnie used to talk about her older sister living somewhere east of here. I do know that she had family, but they didn't live here and I never met any of them."

Mary read the yellowed faded letter.

*'Dear Minnie,*

*I am so sorry that I have not stopped by lately. I have been busy in Denver with some businesspeople. It is so high up in the mountains that it is hard to breathe at times, but the sunsets are the most brilliant I have ever seen. I will be coming back your way in June and plan on staying with you for some time. I have missed you, terribly. I found that thing you have been looking for and I promise to bring it with me.*

*Your affectionate friend, Johnny'*

Mary sat back in the upholstered chair and was very still as she stared at the paper for several moments. Her brows furrowed.

"There was a man named Johnny she spoke of, too. She called him her firecracker. I never saw him. He never came around with her." Mary's eyes read over the letter again and she bit her lip, breathing a little faster.

The older woman blinked her eyes a couple of times and then with a heavy sigh looked at Cutter. "I'm so sorry I can't recall anything else. I wish I could help ya' more." Her twisted fingers folded the letter and set it back inside the box.

Addie spoke up. "Mary, I don't have many memories of your son, Foster. What happened to him? Is he still living?"

Mary rubbed her eyes and smoothed back a few stray hairs. "My dear Foster died a ways back. He got a fever, bad and then the pneumonia took him. After he died, Rose went back to her people back in Tennessee. I never saw my grandchildren again. They don't write or keep in touch. I am sorry to say that I don't know what became of them."

Mary's smile trembled.

Dawn looked about the big living room that had once been the loud, boisterous scene of many a party, anniversary, and celebration. The worn rugs, the heavy drapes and leather furniture bespoke of a time where many men had lived here. "Well, we've taken up enough of your time. We've got a long ride ahead of us, too. Thank you for letting us come out today, Mrs. Rideout, you have been a big help to us" Dawn held the eyes of the older woman for a few moments, then stood up and moved to the door.

Mary struggled to her feet and with the aid of a carved wood cane., She walked them out to the front door.

"I do love having company. Stop by any time. I'll probably be here unless the good Lord calls me to Him," Mary Rideout said with a wink.

Her hand still gave a firm grip.

Addie gave her a little hug and kissed her cheek and then handed the little iron box to Cutter.

"Thank you for all your help, Mrs. Rideout," Cutter said as he leaned and gave the frail woman a light kiss on her wrinkled cheek.

"In a couple of months, the house will be finished and the school will be ready. If you are up to it, would you consider coming in for the party? We'd love to have you be our guest at the celebration."

"Well, I don't know where my dancin' shoes are, but I'd love to be there. Promise me a dance, young man, and I'll see about drivin' in." She smiled with humor and winked to Cutter, who chuckled.

The open carriage bumped along over the dusty road heading west. The afternoon sun heated the big cottonwoods and the verdant valley grass in its warmth. A couple of magpies argued with each other flying overhead. A small herd of Black Angus grazed in the gentle valley silent in the distance.

Addie clasped Dawn's hand and smiled weakly, blinking back stinging tears.

Dawn leaned closer to Addie and said something that only the two ladies were privy to, then they dabbed eyes with handkerchiefs. Cutter driving the carriage was going over Mary's words, not sure if he has any more answers or just more of a mystery. A glance back saw Mary waving from her porch and as he raised his hand vehicle disappeared over the rise.

*******

There was the smell of earth and trees and grass and animals in the air. The long walk from the new house back into town gave someone a chance to clear their mind or get past their worries. The dusty road was uneven in places where the rain runoff formed crusty rivulets in the clay and ridges bulged up.

The shapes of the buildings in town came into view, the blocks separated by narrow alleys and trees. Closer to town the road flattened and became smoother with less washed out cracks and holes. The church looked clean and white in the afternoon light with the shining windows and manicured lawn and garden. It sat at the edge of the grassy valley and small birds flew around in and out of the grass chasing insects. A lone wagon trundled along the winding river road beyond the church and then disappeared over the rise.

Cutter thought about the three wagons sitting alongside the blacksmith shop waiting for wheel repairs and how those will take up the majority of tomorrow morning.

Twenty years ago there used to be a big ranch house on the other side of the river set back on a small knoll. A big two story Victorian built by a prosperous family and suddenly abandoned when the war took the men in the family. About five years ago during a bad storm, the rising river tore out the beam and timber bridge isolating fertile farm and ranch land and that big house. Cutter could just see the roof peak of the house as he crossed the town square. There is not another Victorian house in the town. Cutter frowned. Nobody built another one like, maybe to avoid tragedy.

Cutter's expression was calm and relaxed as he moved on past the bank and saw a parked wagon next to the auction house. His boots are dusty and his wrinkled denim pants were stained from everything he did at work. Cutter gripped his hat and tried to brush off the dust from the day at the bottom steps of the hotel.

Two ladies came out of the doorway and went down the steps, greeting him as they walked away. Cutter paused for a moment and looked around and noticed few people were out. It was the time of day when most were sitting down to dinner, enjoying their families, and trying to relax and rest a bit from the day's activity. Everyone worked except for the elderly and infirm and the end of the day was always welcomed.

Cutter had taken the first step up and a little black buggy turned the corner and halted in front of the church. Cutter brought up his hand to shade his eyes to see a pretty chestnut mare and who might be driving. The church doors were locked and the young boy who waited at the door looked around and saw Cutter. The boy loped over to Cutter and asked a quick question. Cutter motioned him into the hotel. A couple of minutes went by and the young boy came back out and with a smile and a wave to Cutter, ran back to the buggy. Somewhere in his mind Cutter knew who this was but couldn't put a name to a face right then. As fast as he came, the buggy turned back around the corner and disappeared.

Cutter felt the warm evening sun on his face and at the top step he turned to see the dusk trying to push its way in over the valley. The shadow of the low hill let the gray creep ever so much closer to the green landscape. Off in the distance someone whistled hard and loud twice and then dogs barked in answer. He had become used to the responsibility of being town blacksmith and of the commitment he had made to the community. His community. His town. Cutter smiled as his hand pulled the door open and he walked into the chattering lobby of the hotel.

***

William Huddleston leaned back from the window letting the drape fall into place.

"He went on into the hotel. He is not coming over this way."

"Jackson Frisch has long gone back to San Francisco. You have done well to get him off that land. I'll be formatting a writ of abandonment and post it to the Denver courts and with any good luck, I will have complete control over that ranch by the end of the year," the look of smug satisfaction on the face of the banker made the outlaw grimace.

"When can I expect my money, Huddleston? I've got men to pay and bills to settle up and I'd like to do that right quick," Tolliver's voice had a sneer in it.

He turned to the side and made sure his gun was ready.

Always observant, the banker caught the slight movement out of the corner of his eye and stood up, adjusting his vest and jacket. "I'll get your money out of the safe right now and then you can be on your way," Huddleston was careful to keep his hands in sight lest Tolliver decide that he was going for a weapon and ruin his day.

"You never did tell me the reason why you wanted that ranch so bad.

You ain't the type to raise cattle or horses and those hands of yours are too soft to be tending a garden and pullin' weeds." Tolliver hooked his thumbs into his vest pockets and watched the banker's fingers turn the knobs on the safe.

"It is an investment, Mr. Tolliver, and I plan on finding Eastern bankers who are retiring and looking for a quiet ranch to live on in their golden years. It should turn me a tidy sum and allow me to move out of this stagnant backwater. I need to be in a bigger city where my talents can be used," Huddleston said with a smirk. He brought out three stacks of bills and set them on the desk in front of Tolliver.

The banker pushed the heavy iron door shut and turned the knob tumbling the lock. Just as Tolliver had stuffed that last packet of bills into his coat pocket the sound of shattering glass and men yelling came from somewhere outside. The banker jerked upright gripping his hands together, his nerves on edge.

Tolliver chuckled at the nervousness of the banker.

The piano player was plinking along some country tune and pretty Yvette Lang sat on a stool at the edge singing along. Three local men were standing at the bar swapping stories of the day. A card game was played on at the corner table. Fergie Miller and Brett Doyle were getting cleaned out in a card game by a stranger at the far table.

Tommy Boardman stood at the end of the bar, sipping a drink. "He took three dollars off me and I was payin' attention, Hank. Those are good card players and there's no way that he could get all the cards like that."

Hank stepped from around the bar. He held a white towel in his hands, wiping them dry. After watching the game for a few minutes, he walked over to the table.

"We don't allow that sort of play in here, mister. You take yer business somewhere else," Hank Madison said. He had tended bar for Chick Miller for close to ten years. He had seen tricksters, card sharps and outright hustlers looking for a fast buck walk in those doors and now another one sat here.

Madison slammed a heavy fist down on the table, making the cards jump. The other two men rose up and stumbled back against the wall, gripping their coins and cards.

It was a blindside swing at the bartender's head, but the years of being in barroom brawls and fistfights had given Madison light cat feet and he turned. Madison's fist came around with the momentum of his turn and slammed into Jim Caudle's temple. The big man stumbled, shook hard, arms went limp and his knees started to buckle. But not before his hand went for his knife. It caught Madison's sleeve and then Caudle swung the blade in a wicked rip at the bartender's head. Had it found flesh the knife would have carved a devastating gash.

The unmistakable sound of steel sliding over steel filled the room and all eyes turned to look at the metal in Hank Madison's hand. With two fingers of his right hand he held a short piece of metal which he flipped up over the back of his hand, allowing a slender, thin razor sharp blade to emerge. Repositioning his fingers, he flipped it again and slid the handle farther down, creating a long grip on the blade. Madison's eyes were dark and the big man began to step to his left.

"Someone go get Doc Baines. This man is gonna need stitches real fast."

Boots pounded across the rough plank floor and scurried out the side door, leaving it ajar. The piano player sidestepped and closed it, leaning up against it trembling with wide eyes.

Jim Caudle was belligerent with drink, and the knife he held looked huge. But knives were Hank Madison's specialty. Caudle lunged in, but Madison was ready and Caudle howled as a thin red line showed on the back of his hand. Caudle slashed low at Madison again but the bartender lifted a knee and blocked the blade away. Madison stepped in with a quick upswing motion that at first looked like a miss and then brought the blade back down, stepping to the left. Caudle gasped as he arched his back grimacing in pain. A long red streak soaking through the back of Caudle's shirt.

Madison had stepped to his left and Caudle saw the back of Madison's neck and went after it. The big bartender ducked but it wasn't quick enough and a red dribble of blood started from the nick. It was a mean, vicious glare that made the bystanders take a step back. Like a cat, Madison's foot shot out and kicked in Caudle's knee crumpling the man to the floor. Expecting the bartender to go for Caudle's throat, everyone held their breath. But Madison stepped back against the bar, wiped his blade on his jeans, and waited.

Caudle turned to face Madison; the long knife held ready to kill. Madison dragged his sleeve over his face, wiping sweat out of his eyes. If Caudle continued Madison would slice him to pieces.

"I figure you need about a hundred stitches so far, mister. You keep comin' at me, I'll make it so you never hold a knife again," Madison's voice was a hoarse whisper, but with a sure confidence.

Caudle tried to lunge up from the floor, the dull gleam of a knife blade flashing. Madison had his arms down, gripping his own knife and without expression. Without taking his eyes from Caudle, Madison threw the knife to his other hand and spun left along the bar. An ugly wide gash opened up from cheek to jaw on Caudle and his hand came away bloody. Caudle screamed in pain and tried to shrink back against the wall. Stumbling, he dragged a chair between him and the bartender.

Madison took two steps and landed a left hook to Caudle's jaw, stunning the man. A foot hooked Caudle's knee and kicked hard, making Caudle sag.

With lightning quickness Madison stabbed through the back of Caudle's hand, making him scream out in pain. Madison dropped his knife and went to his knees holding his hand against his chest.

Caudle had the look of a cornered, wounded bear. Limping, he inched back with an awkward crawl towards the door.

"This ain't the last you'll be hearin' from Jim Caudle. You'll be somewhere someday without that fancy knife, and then I'll learn ya."

A red gash started to bleed across the top of Caudle's head and he yelped. The gleaming thin knife was embedded in the wall, shuddering from the impact.

"Anytime, anywhere," Madison said and took one step, shifting his weight towards Caudle who struggled to stand.

"Joey, step over to Doc Baines office and tell 'em to set them stitches in good. An' I'm paying for them."

An ugly sneering grin came up on one side of the bartender's face. "I want him real purty for next time."

The door slammed and Joey was gone.

"Next time you come in here, you'll leave in a box. Go crawl back into a hole and lick yer wounds, wounds put there by me, Hank Madison."

The big bartender folded his meaty arms over his chest and glared as Caudle limped out the saloon door.

Everyone let out their breath at the same time, relief flooding the saloon. A curious man wearing spectacles was leaning to get a good look at the shiny slender knife when a strong muscular arm reached past him and took the knife from the wall. With three flashes, the knife folded and slid into Madison's vest pocket.

Mean dark eyes gazed into the saloon from a man standing outside the window. A tall man, black hat in a dark frock coat. Something was muttered and he turned away, walking down the boardwalk and no eyes followed him as he then disappeared between two buildings.

*******

The crunching of gravel made Cutter look up to find Dawn White approaching the blacksmith shop. She wore a pretty lavender and yellow long skirt that fluttered in the light breeze and a long sleeved white eyelet blouse covered with a light cream colored shawl. Dawn was not known for coy small talk or a petty discussion of the weather so Cutter dropped his tools and picked up a damp cloth to wipe off his blackened hands.

"Do you have a minute, Cutter? I'd like to talk to you about something."

Her dark eyes darted about the area. "Where's Thomas, are we alone?"

"He went over to Beatrice to deliver a team this morning. I don't expect him back until later this afternoon, Miss Dawn."

Cutter frowned a bit and wiped his mouth with the back of his hand. "Is there a problem?"

Cutter could see Dawn fussing with her gloves.

"I've got coffee on, if you would like a cup."

Cutter motioned to the inside of the shop and Dawn gently smiled and followed him into the small office area. Dawn sat down on the small wooden stool and he put a steaming mug of strong coffee in front of her. He brought out a small crockery jar of sugar and a silver spoon that he set on top of the jar.

"I'll get to the point, Cutter, I know you are a busy man and I don't want to keep you any longer than necessary."

The spoon dipped into the sugar and Dawn fell into a small, silent daze as she stirred the ebony coffee.

Cutter took a sip of his mug and looked curiously at Dawn.

"No, no, take your time. I needed a break anyways."

"I've had a few, very frank talks with my brother, Jackson, about, well, family matters concerning Carmella before they left for San Francisco."

Dawn took another sip of the hot coffee.

"And, well, Cutter there is no simple way to say this other than Jackson has no objection if you were to ask for Carmella's hand in marriage."

Cutter sat up straight and sloshed his coffee. "What?"

"Carmella adores you, Newton, and you do have several becoming qualities that she finds attractive. You've proven that you can support a family with your blacksmith shop and you are a hard worker. She told me that you were a fine dancer and I knew that already and.."

Dawn averted her eyes and her brow furrowed as she took another sip.

"After growing up in San Francisco, I would have thought that she would want to find a husband and home in the city in the sort of life that she always knew, Dawn. I can see she is a smart, very caring young lady and people here seem to have taken a liking to her. But I am not convinced she can trade balls and fancy dinners for square dancing at the grange, cattle round ups, and picnics in the valley," Cutter said as he crossed his arms and leaned back a bit. His eyes looked out the big wooden doors. A slight wind had come up and were tossing loose leaves across the yard.

"According to your construction superintendent, the house is getting close to finished. I would think it will be done by Christmas and you would probably start moving in, wouldn't you, Newton?"

Dawn had been chatting with Giordani at the hotel when he came in and kept up on how the new building was coming along.

"Marriage and a family is what I want, Dawn, I've made that clear from the start. I wouldn't want her to not have a happy life, to live in happiness and security like she deserves. Besides, how can you be sure that she has not gone home to pick up where she left off with someone?" Cutter stood up and walked over to the doorway and leaned an arm on the door casing, looked out at the yard and valley beyond.

"Because I asked her if she had someone waiting on her back in San Francisco and she said no," Dawn said.

She walked over to Cutter and put her small hand on his arm, looking up at him.

"Many years ago, Cutter, I stepped back away from one of the most wonderful men I had ever met. Someone who took my breath away and made me float on a cloud. But those feelings scared me and I backed away and I settled for someone I had known for many years growing up."

Dawn let her hand fall away and turned to the right. Her hand began to wring the gloves.

"Between you and me, I've wondered all these many days since then what my life would have been like if I had said yes. If I had slid my hand into his what sort of adventures I would have gone on, what people and places I would have seen and what kind of love I would have had. I'll never know and as a silly young girl I missed my opportunity."

Cutter looked at Dawn and realized the level of revealing her personal emotion to get him to understand. There was much at stake not just for him but for Carmella and her family.

"I'll get out of your way and leave you back to your business, Newton. I hope you know that I have the best of intentions in coming to you like this and hope that you give it considerable thought," Dawn said as she settled her shawl.

She smiled and squeezed his arm as she stepped out into the yard, headed towards the town square.

Cutter's eyes followed Dawn until she turned the corner of the City Hall and then he stepped out to the fence of the corral. He had not received any letters from Carmella. He had no way of knowing her state of mind or thoughts. She could have decided to walk away and pursue other relationships in San Francisco. She would decide to belong to him or move on. Thoughts raced through his mind and he kicked a couple of dirt clods smashing them into the broken brown soil with his boot. Someone whistled and a black and brown dog came out of the tall grass bounding to its owner.

The big wood doors were heavy and the left-hand side one was locked into place. Cutter spied a piece of metal and picked it up. It was half of the bracket that had broken earlier during a repair. He tossed it inside the shop to the scrap barrel. He kicked the brace away from the left door and had begun to pull when he heard an odd sound from the plaza.

# 13 CHAPTER THIRTEEN

Someone screamed. Cutter took a couple of steps and tried to hear where it came from. A woman, no, a girl was screaming and a man was yelling. Cutter ran down alongside the City Hall and saw a tall man in a black jacket standing over a young girl clutching her hands to her dress front. It was Georgianna with tears streaming from her eyes and disheveled long blonde hair. And the man standing over her with clenched fists was the same one from the hideout at South Landing. The same one from the wanted posters. It was Royal Benning.

It took Cutter two steps to reach Benning and gripped his shoulder shoving him into the wall. Cutter's fist grazed the side of Benning's head and stunned the big man.

"Get out of here, Georgianna, go get help!"

When Cutter turned back to Benning, he caught a hard left to the chin, stunning him. The blacksmith fell to his knees and shook his head trying to clear his vision. With a quick move, Cutter shifted his weight and swung a left leg around to catch Benning, knocking him to the ground.

As Cutter was about to rise, he suffered a viscous blow to the back of his head. He fell to his left side and tried to roll away. Blurry eyes saw another man help Benning to his feet and hurry into the darkness.

"What in the.." Doc Baines hurried to Cutter and helped the blacksmith to his feet.

"Is Georgianna alright? Is she okay?"

Bert Goldman brought a damp cloth over to Cutter and handed it to him.

"Yeah, she's alright. She made it back to the hotel and everyone over there is in hysterics trying to figure out what happened to her. What happened, Newton?"

"That man I just beat, that man had hit Georgianna, ripped her dress and had forced her down on the ground in the alley."

Cutter was trying to catch his breath, motioning back up the dusty alley. He wiped his face and eyes again.

"That was Royal Benning, the man from the wanted posters." Cutter said with a gasp. He straightened up and grimaced as he felt his ribs, arching his back.

The doctor frowned. "Let's get you into the office so I can get some stitches into your head." Together, the doctor and Goldman steadied Cutter over to the lit doorway across the street.

"Doc, you're making it hurt worse than it was!" Cutter pulled away from Doc Baines' hands and the stinging yellow fluid. The doctor had Cutter sitting on a little stool while he tended to the gash on the side of his head. Bert Goldman, Tommy Boardman, and the Mayor watched Doc fuss over Cutter.

"Hush, my boy. If you this this antiseptic hurts, you're gonna have some trouble with these stitches I'm going to put in," Doc looked down through his spectacles examining the wound.

"Well, it looks like Benning caught her when Georgianna came through the alley from picking up supplies at the trading post. She said that she had recognized him from coming into the hotel once a while back," Boardman said and then paused for a moment.

"She is a quite young, very trusting girl and even though she's strong, she was no match for an outlaw like that. On the other hand, if she would've had her knives on her, it would be Benning that Doc would be stitchin' up here."

Georgianna had learned to butcher beef and filet fine cuts from her father and took special care of a set of German steel knives.

"I will get word over to Santa Fe and the Texas Rangers that Benning has been seen here. I'm not going to bring up Georgianna's name but I'll give them a general description of what has happened," Mayor Watley stated as he made pencil notes in a small notebook.

"I shudder to think what will happen to Benning when Thomas Wood finds out what he did to Georgianna." All faces turned serious and the men looked at each other with a nod.

Cutter flinched again as the first stitch went in and the men teased him for being so sensitive. The medicinal whiskey was administered to Cutter to assuage his pain and to everyone in the room to comfort their strained nerves.

*"My dearest Carmella,*

*I hope my letter finds you well, happy and safe. I hope
your journey home was without event and didn't bring
too much discomfort. I've ridden that stage myself and
know what adventures it can bring."*

Carmella scanned the rest of the writing and found something on page three that stopped her.

*"Newton came to the aid of a young lady here who had
assaulted and knocked down by a roguish fool and
trounced the man. Newton is not much worse for the
wear with a couple of bruises, scrapes and ten stitches on
the side of his head. Not to worry as it will heal fast
and even Newton remarked that Mrs. Klinger's mare
Beauty, gives him a worse kick now and then."*

Carmella lowered the pages onto her lap as she looked up staring off into space. The pretty pink and lavender hues of her French decorated room faded away as she saw the dark curly hair failing forward over his broad forehead and those deep, dark eyes piercing her. She could remember the touch of tracing her fingers along his chin and the sweet pressure of his kiss and strength of his arms around her. It had been a small agony traveling away from him. She held the little silver key fob in her hand for most of the way until she had stowed it into her small purse.

The rest of the letter was about local news of Bradford residents that she had become acquainted with during her stay. Dawn had made a request for lace yardage and Carmella knew the shop where it could be purchased. The young girl started to fold the letter but stopped and read it again. Then she folded up the pages and tucked it into the box with her other letters.

It had only been a few days yet it felt like months had passed. She had tried to keep busy with catching up with her lady friends and going to dinner with her father but she longed to see Newton again. She started reading a book, put it down and started another. She looked but did not see wonderful paintings and drawings at the museums. If it hadn't been for the earthy smells of the seaside a trip down to the bay would have been completely forgotten that she had been there to see the ships.

She sat on the front veranda with tea and a knitted shawl calling out to friends who passed by and chatting with neighbors. But watching the hustle and bustle of wagons, prams and strollers interrupted her thoughts, and after a while she retired to sit on the cushions in the back of the big house.

Her eyes took in the tall, whitewashed fence and the manicured green lawn and prim flower beds that ran around the edge. The cultivated roses in flaming reds and brilliant yellows contrasted against the lilies and bluebells. The tall holly tree was the only growing thing in the lawn that had any resemblance of being wild. She closed her eyes and could see the soft waving green grass at the ranch and the tiny plants that lived at the edge of the river. She had spent time sitting with her sketchbook drawing the birds and letting the water flow over her feet. She drew in a deep breath and smelled the rich earthy tang of sage, honeysuckle, and animals of the ranch. She remembered the children running with their kites on the town square playing and laughing as they found a simple pleasure. She could remember the rise of hills, clusters of boulders and wildflowers dotting the landscape. Above all, she could remember the gold flecks in those eyes.

"Come in for tea, Carmella."

Jackson had leaned out the doorway and had watched her, guessing where her mind was at. He winked as she opened her eyes and looked at him, smiling. She stood up and stretched then blinked her eyes as she looked over the deep green lawn and flowers, then went inside.

***

The small room off the back side of the auction house was usually an office for visiting freight haulers, but tonight it was for a meeting for troublemakers. Frisco Hafton and George Everett were leaning back in wooden chairs against the wall making sure that the dim yellow lantern light didn't reach them.

"You boys are gonna have to step up and help me get this job done. This town is too easy going, nobody is on edge or afraid like they should be. Everyone has a gun and they're ready to use 'em," Tolliver paced back and forth behind the old rickety desk, his heavy brows furrowed together and his black eyes darting.

Frisco Hafton watched Tolliver becoming angrier by the minute. "Last year up in Denver I saw a plan very much like this one cost a man his life. Nobody had a payday, nobody got what they thought they would get. And several men, good professional men, got nothing because the leader of the gang lost his temper and let his personal feelings get the best of him."

"If I hadn't had the sense of mind to think ahead, I would have been on the wrong end of a rope." Hafton touched the brim of his hat and pursed his lips. Everett frowned at the man and Hafton leaned a bit closer and whispered a couple salient details. Everett nodded and sat back in his chair.

"Stop grousing and focus on what we have to do here. Forget about the past, it ain't comin' for you here."

Tolliver slammed his fist down the desk, sneering in frustration.

Everett shrugged.

"I don't see how tearing up flower beds and breaking windows are gonna make people afraid. This town is half asleep all the time and it takes a stampede to even get a crowd bigger than five to turn out."

Everett took out his tobacco pouch from his pocket and started hunting for rolling papers. A sideways glance to Hafton and Everett passed the pouch over.

"On Monday night, I want a couple of old greasy barrels set up against the back of the blacksmith shop. Set 'em on fire. See how that goes over."

Tolliver rubbed his cracked hands together.

"Wednesday, break a couple of windows over at the general store. Tear the front door off this place, for good measure. Friday night I'm gonna make sure my horse does a sweet dance all over that tidy lawn at the church. The flower beds are prime to be torn up. That outta make the old ladies cry." It was a cackling laugh that came out of the dark haired Tolliver.

The two outlaws were quiet, looking at the spot on the floor with the eyebrows raised in disbelief at what they heard. This was supposed to be some sort of genius mastermind in the five western states and he is standing there talking about trampling flower beds.

"There has to be something valuable around this town that we can make off with."

Hafton rubbed his chin.

"Something we can haul off to Santa Fe or San Francisco and sell?"

Everett nodded looking down at the cigarette rolling between his fingers. "Trouble with little towns like these, everybody is poor without two nickels to rub together. Living from cattle sale to picnic." Everett and Hafton snickered at the joke. Tolliver picked up the little glass dish and launched it against the far wall shattering it into a million pieces and the two outlaws jumped to get out of the way. Tolliver kicked the desk, shoving it in anger, mumbling swear words under his breath.

A few moments of silence and quiet went by while the two men glanced sideways at Tolliver. After a few minutes Tolliver took a deep breath and straightened his coat. "There is something about this town. It's under my fingernails and I'm just like a cat with its fur rubbed the wrong way."

The men's eyes open wide and heads tilted. Their ears were hearing talk of a crazy man who has lost his senses and is hell-bent on his own destruction. Hafton lit his cigarette and then lit Everett's who took a drag then cupped it in behind his curled fingers. Too many years out on the open range had taught him to hide all signs of life at night and even though he was indoors, a glowing cigarette could always be seen from a distance.

Everett leaned forward resting his elbows on his knees and looked thoughtful. After studying the floor for a few moments he murmured to Hafton who leans forward to listen. Hafton cocked his head forward and squinted as he listened to Everett's words. The outlaw started to shake his head no, but then stopped as he listened further.

Hafton brought his eyes up and looked at Tolliver, then at Everett.

"Alright. But there's just one thing."

Hafton stretched out his legs and let the cigarette dangle from his fingers. He told them of the Red River Stagecoach holdup last year and that his face still adorned wanted posters in Texas. "I'd bet those Rangers in Laredo haven't forgotten me."

"You never said a word about this Ranger trouble when we met up.

You've got the worst lawmen on your trail and they won't let up."

Tolliver gnashed his teeth and gripped his fists grimacing. He knocked over a chair with anger.

"Now, hold on a minute, hold on now."

Everett stood holding out his hands to try and calm down Tolliver. After a few moments, Tolliver regained his thoughts and leaned his hands onto the desk. Everett let out a deep sigh and talked about a couple of details they hadn't considered.

Hafton nodded, keeping an eye on Tolliver. The outlaw talked about his part and how he would hold up his end of the plan. Something still did not sit well with the gnarled man, but it was something he could live with. Tolliver had cooled off enough to sit up on the edge of the desk and wipe his hand across his mouth while he listened. Once more, the basic details were laid out and finally all three nod their heads in agreement.

Hafton felt the pit of his stomach tense and the desire to get on his horse and keep going until sunrise made him start to shake.

"Now, you ready to pay for all this you signed us up for?" Hafton stood up and cracked the knuckles in his right hand. Tolliver brought out a leather billfold from a pocket inside his heavy coat and pulled a fistful of bills out. He handed it all to Everett and tossed the empty pouch on the desk.

"You do your parts and you'll never have to worry about me being one step closer than those Texas Rangers."

Hafton and Everett shoved the money into their pockets and exchanged a look that perhaps they had made an ugly mistake. Both men touched the brim of their hats and left out the door into the darkness.

Tolliver was left alone and thoughts of mayhem and destruction ran through his mind. He couldn't shrug off the uneasy feeling that the worst was yet to come. He set his jaw in determination that this lousy town would feel his wrath and regret the day he stepped foot in it. But at least this part of the plan was coming together. And he still had one last go-for-broke scheme that he was going to use if all else failed. The darkened room with the yellow flickering lantern was still around him. Somewhere out in the black night a door slammed, someone mounted a hose and it walked down the street.

***

The next morning, Cutter climbed the stairs at his new house and stood before the cast iron tub near the fireplace. The drain had caused some consternation amongst the workers. An argument had broken out regarding the proper way of draining the bathwater down two floors and out across the yard. A humored grin came over his face and the blacksmith made sure there was nobody around. Strong arms lowered the blacksmith into the tub. He leaned back, his legs out with plenty of room. He wondered about having a cold beer in a hot bath.

Three tall double door cedar cabinets were standing on the far wall. A dark wood table was standing over by the window. The rough subfloor was sturdy underneath with no squeaks. The interior walls had been nailed up and were ready for the finish carpenters to come in. The smell of wood drifted all around him. Bits of dust floated in the golden sun streaming through the window.

*******

The dust puffed up in little clouds as Frisco Hafton got down off the horse. Goldman's Saloon looked just as good as any other tavern and he stopped for a minute gazing in the doorway before he walked in. He ordered a beer and a shot of whiskey and started rummaging through his pockets looking at pieces of crumpled paper. This was a tall, lanky man prone to a slight stoop and favored his left leg. He had a lean look to his chiseled face with a larger jaw and sharp cheekbones. The heavy brow and broad forehead were characteristic of his Austrian birth to immigrant parents. As a small child he arrived in Iowa to live a new life in freedom as his father became partners in a trading post on the Iowa frontier. From age six, Hafton started to learn just what men were capable of and that he must take what he can get.

Hafton had the look of a man riding away from something the rest of us wouldn't understand. At six foot five he should have weighed about one hundred pounds more but life on the road did not always guarantee a hot meal. He asked for a pencil and scribbled something down on a torn piece of paper. The saloon keeper averted his eyes once the stringy hair fell away from a deep notch on Hafton's right ear.

The outlaw had been an unruly and dissatisfied as a youngster with small town life. At eighteen, Hafton saddled up two pack horses with supplies, shook his father's hand for the last time and started out on the many miles to the Montana wild country. He took up position as the last rider and headed out over the plains following a wagon train headed west. He was determined to find a new life and make something of himself. The Henry rifle and his silvery Appaloosa mare were the sum total of his wealth and yet he knew there would be more for him out there somewhere.

Outside of Bozeman, he found a rundown abandoned shack and camped out behind it. Over the course of three weeks, he rebuilt the walls, put on a solid roof, and turned the shack into a miner's store. The first year brought in a decent income and he earned a reputation as a fair trader and hospitable allowing travelers to bed down in the grassy valley behind the store.

He rubbed rough knuckles against a long thin white scar on his right jaw and grimacing, took a drink of the rich coffee. The card game in the corner had spawned laughter and it ratted on his nerves. He stood still gripping the wooden counter and turned his eyes to the cracked mirror behind the bar. Seeing no immediate threat, Hafton loosened his grip and a quick look around told him no one had even noticed him. The card players went back to a low key mumbling and Hafton finally stopped holding his breath and went back to trying to relax.

It was late May when a loudmouth dirty blonde kid toting two silver revolvers and a mean-looking little Mexican came into the store. The first bullet whizzed by his head and Hafton fell behind the counter and grabbed his pistol and rolled out to the side shooting. The Mexican hightailed it out the door, grabbing a box of coffee and knocking over three chairs. Hafton got off four shots then felt himself jerked to the left and the sting began to burn in his shoulder and he fell against the counter, grasping, struggling to stay on his feet. The kid leapt over the counter and tucked the money box under his arm. Someone came running in the back door and he felt hands holding him up as he got one last glimpse of terrified eyes and greasy blonde hair running out the front door.

Two days later, Hafton was up on horseback with three rifles, two pistols and a couple hundred rounds of ammunition, along with 50 feet of strong sisal rope. After some misguided directions taking him 80 miles south, Hafton found the Mexican face down in a gully and put two more bullets in him for good measure. At the Last Chance wayside community in northeast Wyoming, Hafton finally found a drunk, blonde fool passed out on a cot behind an old stables and he made sure this idiot would not bother anyone again.

Two of the card players stood up, wobbling from too much whiskey, and hanging on to each other stumbled out the door.

"Mister, you want to join in a game of poker over here?" The elder man pushed his hat back as he shuffled the cards eyeing up Hafton.

"No, not tonight. I thank ya for the offer though," Hafton said with a nod. He took a sip of his beer.

"I'm waiting on a man. You boys go on."

"Aww, come on, just for a couple of hands. Just sit in for a spell while you're waitin' on your partner gets here."

The flush-faced redhead rubbed his eyes and squinted at Hafton.

Hafton shook his head no and held up his open palm hand. "I said no, and I'm not in any state to be playin' cards, so leave me be."

Hafton watched the bartender refill the beer glass and pushed a coin over to the edge. The two poker players groused amongst themselves for a few moments and then the saloon became hushed. Hafton lifted his eyes to the mirror and saw a dark haired man in the doorway. Hafton downed his shot, drank half the beer, and turned to the door, walking up on his toes and together both men disappeared out into the evening grayness.

*******

Clay Dunagan screwed up his brows and squinted again at the paper, twirling the stubby pencil between calloused fingers. Something did not add up and it was hiding from him inside all those ones and twos. Dunagan had been at the ledger for two hours noting facts, figures, and tallies. Business had been good over the summer and he was putting all down in black and white to account for how his hard work had paid off. But the flickering lantern was not bright enough. The stubby pencil needed constant sharpening. Peace and quiet with just the scent of hay, horses and the creaking tick of the iron forge cooling was what Dunagan wanted.

The telegram earlier today said that the freight wagon had busted an axel in Phoenix and that it would be closer to midnight before the load of steel bars would arrive in Bradford. He had several projects he wanted to start next week and those were on hold until that steel arrived. Dunagan was trying to make out the handwriting on a receipt when he heard wood splinter and boards creaking. And it was close, real close. He put down the receipt and turned to the right, trying to listen harder. Someone was trying to break in and Dunagan took a deep breath, gripping a long oak stick with both hands.

George Everett had dropped the heavy iron bar and stepped through the hole into the darkness of the blacksmith shop. As he stepped through he caught the dancing light from a lantern and leaned back in time to feel the wind off slamming oak stick on the door frame. Everett caught himself on the tall gate leading into the stables and pushed off, rushing against Dunagan.

Tools, metal filings and a stack of tiny wood bits flew in every direction as the two men crashed into the woodwork table. The shrieking shatter of the wood tore as the men felt over and Everett reached for one of the broken legs and swung it at Dunagan's head. The horses in the stable began to whinny and stomp, snorting as they became worried of danger. Dunagan caught Everett with a right hand and sent him stumbling backwards down on one knee. He followed that with a knee rammed into the side of Everett's head, but the older man turned away at the last second.

Everett caught the boot as Dunagan tried another kick and pulled the man off balance. Dunagan fell with a thump onto his back. Thunder pounded in Dunagan's head and the world started to go black until he shook the cobwebs out and saw the other man coming at him and rolled away. Dunagan clenched his fists feeling the torn flesh and scraped skin as he swung a left hook. His fist met flesh and the sound of a heavy body falling against a wooden floor was followed by a groan of pain.

Somewhere outside a couple of dogs started growling, barking at the commotion inside the blacksmith shop. Someone yelled and pounded on the big heavy wooden doors that were chained closed for the night.

Everett stood over the crashed wooden rack and felt a trickle of blood stream down his cheek and the ache where Dunagan's boots caught him in the shoulder. He wasn't about to stand around and wait for an officer of the law to start asking uncomfortable questions. Four steps and Everett edged out the back door and around the side of the corral and off into the dark bushes.

Dunagan felt hands lift him and glimpsed flickering lantern light.

"He's got a broken nose, a bad gash on his leg that'll need stitches and he'll have a couple of black eyes tomorrow," Doc Baines said.

He turned Dunagan's chin, making him groan.

"That wood rack would've crushed his ribs if it had fell straight on him."

Bert Goldman peered at Dunagan over the shoulder of the doctor.

"If that dog hadn't started up a ruckus, I wouldn't have known someone was even over at the shop. Glad he did, though. Have to give him a bone or something."

Goldman had half carried, half dragged Dunagan over to the doctor's office and pounded on the door to rouse him.

"Don't know who it was, never seen the man before. But he was a strong troublemaker and hellbent on something in that office, I reckon."

Dunagan held a damp cloth up to the side of his head.

"Someone best get Newton over to the shop so he can get it seen to." Dunagan tried to shift his weight to stand and grimaced in pain.

"Take it easy, Clay. You'll be stayin' here for the next few days."

Doc Baines pushed him back down onto the small cot and watched as Dunagan went limp.

"I'll have to go fetch Newton and have him take a look at the mess in his shop," Goldman wiped his hands on a towel noting the blood from Dunagan's wounds. The night air was colder as the door opened and Goldman stepped out.

# 14 CHAPTER FOURTEEN

People shielded their eyes as the dust from the stagecoach whipped around them. The door opened and a spry, older lady stepped down followed by a young boy in knee pants and a bowler hat. Carmella Frisch put a foot onto the step and Newton Cutter reached for her hand and smiled into her eyes as she climbed down.

"Now how is it you've gotten more beautiful since the last time I saw you, Miss Carmella," He hadn't let go of her hand or rather she had not let go of his yet.

"Yes, you are a pretty girl, but you are going to be covered in dust if you don't get inside right this minute," Dawn White slid her arm through the young girl's and whisked her up the steps and into the hotel.

"Good to see you again, Sir," Cutter gripped the strong hand of Jackson Frisch and caught the three bags unloading off the top of the coach.

"You, too, Newton, though I would hazard a guess to say that Carmella is gladder to see you though."

Frisch winked at the blacksmith and walked up the steps into the hotel.

"I didn't get any letters from her while she was gone so I kind of thought there wasn't much of an attraction there, if you want to know the truth."

Cutter raised his eyebrows.

Frisch laughed and said, "I saw her start and tear up over a dozen sheets of stationary at home. She's got words in her but just can't get them out, I supposed."

Frisch winked at Cutter and they walked into the hotel.

"So you have found a prospective buyer, is that right?" Frisch took off his overcoat and hung on the hook near the door and tucked his gloves into the pockets. He turned to look around the room, always curious of new people to meet.

"A Mr. Vincent Barley. Coming in from out of state. He saw the sales ad in the Denver Post and is looking for a quiet place to run a few head of horses away from everything and everybody."

Frisch sat down next to Dawn and gave her a small kiss on her cheek. Georgianna brought around steaming pots of coffee and sugar and cream. One of the other boys from the kitchen brought out warm, sliced bread with rich creamy butter.

"Folks, I am sorry to interrupt but I need Newton for a moment."

Thomas Wood held his hat in hand and nodded towards Cutter.

"The freight wagon has rolled in and the driver needs to see you."

Georgianna passed behind Wood and slid something into his pocket and smiled as he turned to see her. Wood grinned and winked at the pretty young girl.

"I'll let you get settled in. I'll see you later before you leave for the ranch."

Cutter stood up and smiled at Carmella. He tipped his hat to Jackson Frisch and Dawn and then turned and headed out with Wood.

"That reminds me, can we send a message over to the lawyer so he knows I've arrived, Dawn?" I want to see him when we are done eating and before I go up," Frisch said.

Dawn was savoring a soft piece of fluffy bread and nodded.

"Of course! Georgianna?" Dawn called over the girl and gave her the task of informing the lawyer of their arrival. Georgianna walked into the kitchen where Tommy Boardman was supervising the cooking for the day.

The rest of the afternoon saw Jackson Frisch moving from one meeting to another, writing letters and sending telegrams. He and Merle Doyle walked over to the lawyer's office later that afternoon and a dinner tray was delivered in the evening.

The next day the morning stage had delivered its load of people into the hotel so for the next hour or so there were more people than normal in the dining room. Platters of food and pitchers of water, beer and coffee coursed through the room and there was lively conversation heard. Dinnerware chinked and tableware rattled as patrons enjoyed the savory dishes. Streaming sunlight filtered in through the filmy gauze drapes at the windows.

"Jackson, do you have a moment? I'd like to have a couple words with you alone if you don't mind."

Cutter had come down the stairs in clean black slacks and a long sleeved white shirt and black blazer. He smiled at Carmella who admired him being dressed up so. Cutter stood next to the open door to the small sitting room off the hotel lobby. Frisch nodded and squeezed Carmella's hand. Then he walked into the small room and sat down in a deep leather chair.

"What is on your mind, Newton?"

"I am asking for your daughter's hand in marriage, Jackson. She and I have talked some about the possibility and I felt that before we go any further, I'd best speak to you." Frisch raised his eyebrows and rubbed his chin.

"Well, she was miserable all the time after we returned to San Francisco. I had a feeling it had something to do with you but a daughter doesn't talk easily to her father about her love life." Frisch and Cutter chuckled.

Cutter looked at Frisch. "I had asked her about her life in San Francisco.

I thought she had a clear picture of her city life, being married to someone there. She assured me there was no one that she even considered and that living life in the country would be more suited to her idea of married life."

Cutter looked down at his hands rubbing together remembering the look on Carmella's face when they kissed.

Frisch drummed his fingers on the table. "I like to think that over these last few months I've come to know you quite a bit. I think you and I have gotten along fairly well. I think you and Carmella would do well together. You are both of a good temperament and I know that she will have a comfortable and beautiful home here. If she'll have you, you have my blessing, Newton." Jackson smiled and stood. They smiled and shook hands.

Newton brought out a small square box and opened it and showed a gold band with a solitaire diamond. Frisch raised his eyebrows in admiration and nodded.

"I need a moment with her in private, of course. I'd like to get her thoughts and then come back and make an official offer with all of you here," Cutter said.

"I'll ask her to come in. Take your time, Newton," Frisch squeezed his arm.

"Carmella, would you come in here, please?" Frisch sounded a bit brusque and looked at the ceiling to disguise his excitement. The pretty redhead wiped her mouth and stood up to walk to the office door.

"I'll leave you two alone for a few minutes," Frisch winked to Carmella who looked confused. The door closed and she straightened up and looked down at the floor rubbing her hands together.

Cutter saw that she trembled. He reached and lifted a section of the glossy red hair and let it slide through his fingers.

"Have you thought about what I said at the dance, Carmella?"

"Of course, I have. I feel like I'm floating all the time."

She fussed with the edge of her blouse.

"Look at me, Carmella." Cutter's voice had an imperative in it.

She brought her head up and was at once drowning in icy blue eyes.

"Ask for what you want," he whispered to her.

"I want to be yours. I want to be beautiful for you. I want to stand at your side no matter what and make you exquisitely happy." Her soft voice trembled.

Newton held out his right hand with the palm up.

"Show me your devotion, obedience and commitment, Carmella. Kiss the palm of my hand and then you will be mine," he whispered to her.

Carmella held his rough open palm against her cheek for a moment, then traced a small circle in the center and put one kiss inside the circle. She looked up at him and smiled.

He opened the little box and watched her eyes fill with tears.

Georgianna had to grip the platter of dishes when screams erupted from behind the door. She looked around bewildered at the raised voices.

Tommy Boardman came running out to see if anyone had fallen and looked at Georgianna and then at the door. They looked at each other confused until at last the door opened and Newton and Carmella came out arm in arm.

"Ladies and gentlemen, let me be the first to announce the engagement of my daughter, Carmella to Newton Cutter!"

Jackson Frisch stood and began to applaud.

Rowdy applause broke out and people rushed forward to congratulate the happy couple.

Dawn could not stop her tears of joy and wiped her eyes again and again.

"Mr. Boardman, would you happen to have a bottle of champagne in your fine kitchen?" Jackson Frisch beamed as he watched Carmella showed her ring.

Boardman hustled into the kitchen and returned with several magnums of champagne. Georgianna beamed as she filled the glasses and passed them around to the guests.

"To the happy couple!"

Carmella kissed Jackson's cheek and hugged Dawn who sloshed her champagne.

Cutter kissed her cheek and Carmella whispered something to him just as they sipped.

Boardman whispered to Dawn, "I've kept that champagne on ice for six months! Ever since I first saw them together." The hotelier grinned as Dawn squeezed his arm.

"I just knew, I just knew!"

"I've never had champagne at nine o'clock in the morning, Newton." Carmella held up the cut glass flute and marveled at the little bubbles.

"Me neither, my sweet. This is a first!" Cutter laughed watching Thomas Wood clink his glass to Georgianna's as he held her hand.

The morning wore on with people congratulating them. Together they walked down to the construction site and the workers were granted half a day off in celebration of the engagement. Dawn White and Henry Elliot hosted a luncheon for the engaged couple. After lunch, the couple took a couple horses out and went for a long ride to get some time alone together. A dancing party was thrown together inside the auction house that night and everyone danced, sang, and partied until the wee hours.

The next morning Cole and Wood put on work gloves and started the cleanup at the house construction site. They piled the leftover lumber scraps into a wooden pushcart and it seemed like for every sawn piece of wood there were four others laying around. The carpenters worked fast but this sure did leave a mess in their wake. The scent of fresh cut wood was everywhere and more than one person suffered a splinter in a finger. Work gloves were traded back and forth and the smell of leather permeated hands.

Mayor Watley came to the site to discuss the school organization but had been sidetracked with people on other town matters. They stood around the oak barrel smoking, gesturing, and pointing out in the distance.

Cutter smiled and shook his head as he carried adobe tiles around to the side of the lot. Someone called to him something indistinguishable and he waved a gloved hand and kept going.

Three of the children walked around with magnets on strings to pick up loose nails. There was a prize of pie and milk on behalf of Dawn White for the child who came back with the most nails so the competition was ferocious. Boys brought in buckets of stone pieces and added them to the growing pile. Young girls dragged rakes through the grass contributing to the cleanup effort.

The freight wagon had left a big pile of flagstone from New Mexico. Each one weighed in close to one hundred pounds and the crew blustered and sweated unloading them. The patio behind the house was going to be thirty feet square, suitable for cookouts and parties and such. Cutter could not fathom how such rough stone would be suitable for little bare children's feet but the architect Bruno Giordanni had some sort of finishing technique lined up.

Fall was coming in and the coolness of the evening air told everyone that a change of the season was happening. The hay had been stored and stacked in barns around the county. Serious attention was paid to getting cords of firewood out to remote cabins and bunkhouses for hunters. The community aid committee had been making trips out to visit the older residents and bring supplies and necessities to them. Cutter had volunteered his cargo wagon when they had to move an elderly widow over to the community house in Beatrice.

It had been many months in planning, designing, constructing, fretting, and worrying for Cutter and now before him stood his home. Arms folded across his chest, legs apart and head tilted back, he looked in awe at the built house.

The season had eased into autumn now and the end of the harvest was approaching fast. Folks talked about hope of a good winter for man and beast. Cutter could remember the freezing cold slopes of the mines in winter and wondering if he would wake up from the night's rest. He realized that the sense of belonging, sense of roots had been building this year and this house was the realization.

Fine black borders had been painted in on the window sashes that gave the house a stately appearance. The wide patio glistened from the like sheen of moisture. The magnificent artistry of the wrought iron gates added an elegant touch to remind people that this was still a private home and a functioning school.

But the peace and quiet were about to be shattered.

***

"What happened to you, Omar? Who did this?" Bruno Stenson had eased the bloody young man onto the table in the doctor's office and stepped back out of the way. Doc Baines peered at the boy and turned to Stenson.

"Bring that big light over here. And hold it steady," Doc said. His jacket was tossed to a chair and he started to roll up his sleeves.

"I was taking Annie home out to the Zane Ranch and I thought we could beat the rain. We could see the storm coming and had headed back early. We couldn't so we took shelter under the Eight Mile Bridge to wait it out. It was too wet under there to light a fire and I had no matches to begin with. I unsaddled her horse and wrapped that big blanket around her. While she was climbing up underneath the bridge timbers a bolt of lightning hit close and her horse spooked and took off running.

I started to go after it but it was too dark and I was afraid of leaving her alone so I ran back. That's when I saw him standing there. He and his horse had come down under the bridge just like us."

Doc had cut away the shirt and pressed cloth bandages against the two stab wounds on his chest. Doc motioned Stenson to hold the lantern up higher and Stenson grimaced as he caught sight of the damage.

"I got a good look at him because the lightning hit right then and I saw his face. Dark hair, clean shaven, gray overcoat, gloves. Never seen him before, I swear. But I did see the knife he was holding. I wasn't fast enough, Doc and I slipped in the mud. He got me good, doc."

Johnson started to twist and his emotions caught up with him.

Doc motioned for Stenson to put down the light and help hold down the upset boy.

"Aww, it hurts like hell, Doc. I woke up and he was gone. I looked around and called out for Annie but she didn't come out, she didn't answer."

Stenson leaned on Johnson with his weight as the boy tried to sit up.

"Somebody has to go out and find her, Doc, please. She's out there somewhere and half scared out of her wits and soakin' wet, Doc."

The doctor nodded. "Easy now, Omar. I have to stitch you up and stop this bleedin'. I don't know why you are alive, there is more blood on yer

174

clothes than inside of you right now." Doc poured a little capful of dark liquid and lifted up Johnson's head and forced him to drink it down.

He gave the boy a small sip of water and pressed his fingers into the boy's wrist to monitor the pulse.

The laudanum took immediate effect and Omar Johnson went limp on the table. Doc set to doing fine stitches on both wounds. As the men held Johnson on his side, they could see the liquid darkness that had run off the table and pooled on the floor.

Stenson cringed.

"There's not a lot I can do for him. He's got three, no four stab wounds here and those are deep. I need to sew him up, but it will be twenty-four hours before he would even be strong enough to sit up."

Doc washed off the wounds and cleaned away the muddy grime before his needle went to work.

"If you hadn't seen him ride in, he would have bled to death at my door," Doc wiped off his hands in the bowl and handed the bar of soap to Stenson to clean up with. "Let's get him over onto the cot before you clean up. I don't need him falling off this table if he decides to try and get up in the night."

Doc spread out a dark blanket on the cot and together they lifted the limp, pale boy onto the bed. His breathing was ragged and even in the dim light he was pale.

Stenson sloshed water into the bowl and scrubbed the boy's hands with the little brush. He said,

"I've known William Zane for over 20 years and that girl of his is a real beauty. I hate to think of what he'll do to anyone who harms Annie. I'll ride out to the ranch first light after the rain dies down and let him know what happened."

Bruno Stenson dried his hands off. His jaw clenched and he took in a deep breath as he sat on the corner of the big oak desk. The draft from around the door made the light from candles and lanterns wiggle and dance on the walls.

Bruno rubbed his face and forehead with both hands in anguish.

Doc folded a damp cloth and laid it over Johnson's head, knowing it would probably be the last thing he would do for this poor boy.


***


Cutter squinted at the work order again, frowning. Twenty links of chain between each iron. The blacksmith had been working on setting up the chains for the leg since last week.

Dunagan had made the chain sets of twenty links with slow care and draped them over the work cart. The final connector links were lying inside the forge and shimmered a dull orangey red. Tongs held the curved iron and the heavy hammer forced each link closed and the set was complete. The hissing water steamed up around Dunagan as he swirled them in the barrel. Fifteen done and five to go.

"Have you met the new Marshall yet?" Dunagan was looking at Cutter.

"No, he hasn't been by yet. I think he is still out in the Flint Hills somewhere checking on things," Cutter said as he wrestled another glowing link out of the forge and laid it on the anvil.

Clay looked up a moment, watching the blacksmith work. Cutter lifted the completed chain and irons over to Dunagan who promptly lowered them into the water.

"I've been thinkin' on what you had said a while back, 'bout a wife and family," said the iron worker in a lowered voice.

Cutter looked up, letting the tongs rest on the anvil.

"I'm not getting any younger, ya know. I'm gonna get myself over to see a sweet, widowed lady friend of mine over to Beatrice on Friday." Dunagan smiled to himself and ran a hand through his hair, smoothing it back.

Cutter nodded. Then he grinned big and slapped Dunagan's back, wishing him good luck.

They both chuckled about how stranger things have happened to people.

They work for another couple hours.

Dunagan laid out the wet irons onto the workbench and rubbed them with a mineral oil. The new shipment pulled up on the freight wagon and the men began to unload.

# 15 CHAPTER FIFTEEN

After several hours, the equipment was unloaded into the shop and the paperwork signed and the payment made to the freighter. This was the last piece of equipment that Cutter needed to build up his wagon construction business. A steam powered engine ran belts through pulleys for milling lumber to exact measurements. Cutter had ordered it from Baltimore and it took six months for fabrication and delivery. And so now another chapter of his life would begin.

"Let's stop over at the saloon and have us a drink to celebrate. Carmella can get along without you for an hour or so," Wood said.

He clapped a hand on Cutter's shoulder and grinned to his friend. Cutter nodded and they locked the shop doors and headed across the square.

There was a crowd in the saloon that evening. It must have been a payday somewhere as someone was trying to sing a ditty along with the piano player. Several card games were in progress and people were trying but nobody was hitting the dart board.

Cutter had won one game and won a beer for his trouble. Wood had finished his and was heading back to the bar. As he sidled past a table, he was jostled into the table spilling the drinks of the men who now stood up in haste to avoid getting spilled whiskey all over them.

"I apologize gentlemen, let me get you another drink. I'm a bit clumsy tonight," Wood said and started to signal to the bartender for another round.

"These locals are nothing but a bunch of drunks and lowlife dregs of humanity, boys. Somebody ought to teach you a lesson or two, sonny," Wood had heard the threat in the sneering voice and tensed as he turned and felt the edge of the table hit against his thigh.

Wood lifted the wooden table, forcing it back into the face of Thornton Glass. Wood stepped to the bar taking off his hat and laid it up on the bar in front of the bartender. Men scurried out the door, drinks forgotten and the piano player ducked behind the bar.

With a flourish, the big Irish bartender laid a Colt revolving rifle up on the bar and glared at the patrons.

Glass had gone down hard, but now he was getting up, wiping his mouth with the back of his hand and Wood walked up to him and hit him with a work-hardened fist. The blow caught Glass in the mouth, bloodied his lip and staggered him, but he came back swinging. Wood felt his teeth grating as Glass' punch grazed his jaw and went to his knees. He started up and caught another punch on the left cheek, then a pounding right that split his lower lip. Wood staggered back, kicking a chair out of his way and his back fell against the big wooden bar. Glass's mouth was bloody, his fists clenched.

Thornton Glass was a big, bulky, hulking man who bullied and pushed and beat his way west. His face carried scars from previous fights. A thin white line went from ear to the stubbled chin.

"You're gonna take a beating," he said, "and you'll never forget it. People have tried from St Louis to San Francisco and nobody's ever beaten me."

Glass feinted, and then crossed another right to Wood's jaw. There was a smoky taste in Wood's mouth, and he tasted blood now around a loose tooth. Glass could hit hard and not only that, but he knew how to vary his punches and to fight with his fists. Wood took one step back and took in a deep breath. He eyed the bigger man looking for that one weakness. There were pressed noses against the glass of the saloon looking in. A few brave souls stood against the doorjamb blocking the opening, murmuring.

It takes a strong man to wrestle full grown horses into shoes. Wood muscles rippled under the thin shirt. Wood was strong and nimble, but he lacked fighting experience. Glass feinted as he came at Wood, and rolled to let Thomas's right go by, then smashed him with two furious jabs in the belly. Glass half stepped back then, expecting Wood to fall, but Thomas turned in, threw a stiff left and a fast right that missed. Wood wasn't quick enough and caught a hard left in the mouth, but he twisted with a quick movement, ducked his head and lunged in.

Glass was startled as Wood should have gone down. He tried to side-step and bumped into a table, and Wood smashed into him, knocking the table over and Glass with it. Wood went down onto one knee and rolled to the side flinging what was left of a chair to the far wall. The lowered brow hinted at renewed determination in Wood's face. Glass came up on one knee, wiping his mouth with the back of his hand. It was bloody. The bartender shouted at a cowhand who was moving against the far wall and pointed at him with the big rifle.

Glass waded past a table at Wood and started to reach for Wood with clawed hands. Wood shoved the hands aside and came up with a smashing left hook to the jaw. Glass was tottered sideways and Wood threw an uppercut into the midsection and Glass groaned, stumbling back. Wood had a torn left sleeve and a cut under his eye was beginning to bleed. His knuckles were reddened and sweat covered him.

Like a cat, Glass sprang, a huge fist driving into Wood's stomach. Wood doubled over and Glass readied a vicious right cross, but Wood stomped on the instep and Glass yelped in pain. Wood started to bring up a left cross headed for the jaw, but Glass deflected it and punched hard into Wood's midsection. Wood gasped and fell back. He saw Glass turn his body for a smashing right fist and Wood tried to turn but caught a mean glancing blow, knocking him to the floor.

Wood rolled over and came up on one knee, wiping blood from his eye and Glass sprang for him with reached fingers. Wood pushed himself up fast and lifted a knee into Glass's belly and the big man fell to the floor.

Glass was panting, struggling to catch his breath as he came up on one knee. Wood went into him, hooking a short punch into kidney and then another behind his ear. Glass fell back against the bar sliding closer to the end and the bunch of cowboys there scattered. Dusty sunlight filtered in the windows and folks were shouting out punches from outside. Glass got up and tried to steady his feet, but Wood plunged into him, bringing a roundhouse right to his belly and then hooking a left that missed. Glass threw an elbow to Wood's throat and he clawed at Wood's eyes.

Wood gasped, struggling for air, shaking his head, and blinking his eyes to clear them. Glass jumped him and tried to get him into a big locking hug, but Wood gouged at his eyes and Glass released him. Wood stomped another heel into Glass's left foot and Glass howled in pain. Wood showed a sideways grin as he had found a weak spot. Glass lifted a boot to kick and Wood sidestepped it and grabbed the leg, spinning Glass around. Glass grabbed the bar, catching himself and shoved off bringing a wicked right cross into Wood's jaw. Wood staggered back, seeing stars, and grimaced in pain.

Glass saw that Wood was hurt bad and looked around. He spied a broken chair and lifted it, getting ready to swing at Wood's head. It stopped in midair and Glass turned to see the big bartender had grabbed the chair and jerked it out of Glass' hands. Glass was off balance from the tug and Wood launched a smashing right to Glass' jaw, staggering him. After a split second, Glass came at Wood. He caught smashing punches to the head and belly, but he dug in, tenacious like a stubborn terrier, taking Glass's best shots and smashing back with both hands.

Wood was blinded by a reflected sunbeam caught in the mirror behind the bar. He shook his head, stepped to the left and felt a fist graze his head. Wood turned around and whipped a stunning right into Glass and then an uppercut forcing the big man up against the bar. Glass swung and missed with the left but Wood stepped inside his reach and pounded three fast punches into Glass' midsection. Stepping back, Wood threw a huge right fist to the middle of Glass' forehead and a small cut opened up, blood trickling down into the heavy brow.

Wood could feel himself trembling, tight like a spring and the steely taste of blood was in his mouth. He could feel a drop of blood sliding down his cheek. Glass hauled a huge punch and knocked Wood down. Wood tried to stand, but Glass was punching down into Wood's face and he struggled to turn away from the blows. Wood knew he was in trouble when he felt a hammer-like blow on his ear but pushed with his legs and caught the swinging arm. Wood braced himself and threw Glass hard into the old piano. The crashing tinkling could be heard out into the street. Glass braced himself but when he threw the punch Wood dodged it and caught Glass' chin and then delivered a mean uppercut. Glass was struggling to catch his breath and tried a left hook but Wood was ready and broke his nose flooding his face with blood.

Thornton Glass moved away, trying to wipe off the blood. He kicked a chair out of the way and sneered with a vicious hate at Wood. He jabbed and jabbed again. Glass feinted, hooked a right to the Wood's chin and then swung a left. Wood saw that Glass was at his weakest point in the fight and moved in with a right cross. Glass had been waiting for it and he blocked the heavy punch. He thundered a punch into Wood's mid-section and Wood stomped hard down on Glass' left foot and slammed a hard right into Glass' belly. Glass's knees buckled and he started to fall, and Thomas hit him again with a right to the jaw. Glass fell and Wood caught him by the collar and jerked him upright. It was a vicious slap before the bigger man could fall again. He went down then and lay still.

Two of the men who had been playing cards with Glass, grabbed his arms and dragged him out through the door. Cutter brought over a wet cloth and handed it to Wood for the bleeding cuts on his face. Wood was going to be sore in the morning, but alive at the very least.

The friends walked arm in arm back over to the hotel which was now darkened and quiet with the guests all tucked in their rooms for the night. As Cutter closed and locked his door, he knew life would continue on in the morning.

*******

Folks noticed earlier in the day the big dark clouds out to the south. Many wondered if the wind and rain would  roll in blow by or come full force at the town. The afternoon had been oppressed with warm, moist air. Local mothers complained that it made babies cry. Women remarked their laundry that just wouldn't dry on the line. It had been quite some time since the area had been drenched and the low water level in the river had been discussed at some length. A dispatch rider came into the hotel about 4:00pm and told a story of the valley grass whipping around like wild waves in the ocean and that it was a serious storm coming that could cause damage.

Closer to six o'clock those clouds had crept in closer to the valley and now the townspeople were wringing their hands over the work that had to be done before the rain fell. The wind picked up and it was coming from the southeast direction which meant they were in for a storm. Someone mentioned how the thunder started a few minutes ago. Three men rode in herding three cows with two calves that had wandered grazing over near the river. Wood opened up a stall in the stables and ushered the guests in, locked the gates and bolted the doors after dropping a bale of hair and some grain into the trough.

The first lightning bolt hit the other side of the ridge and echoed like a shot through the valley. Loose windows and doors rattled and somewhere a small child started to cry. Everyone hurried a step faster now. The auctioneer and a couple of his boys lugged the park benches and chairs off the town square and stored them inside the auction house. The town residents moved their rockers and benches off their porches to safety inside and took down their wind chimes.

Away from prying eyes, Bert Goldman lifted the heavy wooden shutters into place along the rigid porch frames along the back of his saloon. He had invested more than a few hundred dollars over the years to upgrade his copper still and he was not about to let a rainstorm put his whiskey business out of commission. He put his fingers to his mouth and whistled twice and his two big Labradors lumbered in wagging their tails.

Ropes, tarps, and canvases were dragged out to the construction site and lumber covered along with larger pieces of equipment. Heavy stone was laid over the top to keep the shelters in place. Board shutters went over the windows of Newton Cutter's house as protection from flying sticks and whatnot. The work crew had thought their workday was over when they bellied up to the bar at the saloon only to be recruited to drag, tote and carry equipment and furniture into the auction house. One of the men spied a lady's bonnet rolling past blown by the wind and he ran to rescue it to the laughter of the others. It was not a good fit.

Tommy Boardman called for all hands on deck to unload the firewood for the kitchen and the rooms and five men raced out the kitchen to start ferrying wood through the hotel. As they stocked each room, the shutters were pulled shut and locked, the windows closed and locked and then the drapes pulled shut. Boardman, like Goldman was not about to let a bit of rain and wind ruin his prize investment.

Addie Watley bustled about the church, checking the locked shutters and windows were secure. The church had the luxury of inside shutters to repel the summer heat, but they worked well at keeping out the rain. The lush hanging baskets of fuchsias and peonies were settled into the front hall so they would avoid becoming flying projectiles in the wind.

Thomas Wood and Newton Cutter pushed the unfinished freight wagon through the back double doors of the blacksmith shop and blocked the wheels so it wouldn't roll away in the storm. Wood swung the right hand door closed and pushed the heavy spike down into the ground. Cutter let the left hand door ease into place and the oak bar came down into iron brackets across the doors locking them together. Two more spikes were stomped down into the dirt to secure the doors due to the oncoming storm.

From the doorway of the bank, William Huddleston looked up at the sky and knew he would never make it home dry. Never one to frequent the hotel, he hunched man moved back inside and bolted the door, drawing the drapes shut. The sliver of light around the windows faded as he retreated into his office near the vault.

The last freight wagon was finally unloaded at the trading post. The clerks put up the tailgate and the driver led the team of Percherons around into the alley. The wagon rolled in under the big deck in the rear. The prized horses had been hand raised to touch and voice command. After the heavy yokes were removed, the giant horses followed the driver like puppies over to the stables. Thomas Wood grinned and called to them by name and the gentle giants tossed their heads and whinnied in recognition. Their size and strength relegated them into the corner stall deep with straw, a bale of hay, a tub of water and a brimming trough of grain. Wood ruffled their manes as he slipped apples to them, admiring the muscled animals.

All twenty stalls in the stables were occupied. The animals bedded down with feed and water for the night. As Wood locked the outside access door, the big pine branches swayed and bounced overhead. Pulling his jacket tighter around him, Wood saw the anxious eyes peering out into the gathering gloom. Everyone knew there would be a big cleanup work crew needed in the morning. A rolling thunderclap began to boom in the distance and more than one person hoped they had everything put away and secure.

Downed tree limbs and branches became firewood the next morning. One of the shutters on the church had torn off in the night and a window was broken. Four chickens were roosting on the inside porch rails at the auction house. The ground, the homes, the buildings were wet and soggy but no lives were lost in the big storm overnight.

The inside of Dawn White's dressmaking shop always enthralled Carmella. So many little boxes, drawers, cabinets, and chests where beautiful treasures were stored. The scent of fresh flowers and rich coffee drifted past her and she drew her feet up under her in an oversized chair.

"So are you thinking a sweetheart neckline, long lace sleeves or all satin with some fancy beading?" Dawn fussed with a little drawer in the tall cabinet selecting several buttons.

"You know, a girl has forever picked out shoes and stockings and coats and hats but it's only once she gets to select her wedding dress," Carmella said as she watched Dawn laying out the buttons and a roll of thin lace on the table.

"Please remember one thing, my dear. This is your wedding dress. Not mine, not your friends, and heaven forbid, not your father's!" Dawn tried to look stern but ended up laughing out loud with Carmella.

Time flew as Dawn measured Carmella, showed her fabrics and pictures of the newest styles from New York and Philadelphia. At times, Carmella seemed a million miles away only to snap back and take up another length of soft intricate lace in distraction.

Dunagan was searching through the stack of iron bar stock alongside the blacksmith shop building laying on a sorter rack. A couple of iron bars fell to the ground and he grumbled, muttering under his breath. Clay has been looking for certain sizes and stood up in exasperation.

Clay paused a minute, looking at the blackened iron bars. "When is the next iron stock comin' in, Newton?" The heavy clang of iron on iron ceased for a second.

"Should be here on Saturday, if the good Lord is willing and the creek don't rise."

Dunagan could hear the young blacksmith chuckling and the clanging iron started up once again.

Dunagan went back into the blacksmith shop and hunched over the workbench looking at his drawing again, making a note with the inky pen. The shipment would have eight pieces of iron for the two big andirons for a local customer. Short six inch legs and a twelve inch upright guard with elaborate ornamentation. A heavy iron ring would be attached about two inches from the top of the guard. Round curled bar stock feet. And the iron worker needed those.

"What are ya' lookin' for, Clay?" Cutter holds long iron tongs down in a water barrel looking at Dunagan.

Dunagan holds up the drawing and supply list. "I need a couple of six inch and a couple of eight inch flat stock and a couple of two inch diameter rings, and a week if ya have one to spare," Dunagan said with a frown.

"Bring that bar stock over here, I'll cut it for ya, I got time right now," Cutter put on the other glove and pumped a bit more air into the forge. Together the two men lifted the heavy iron bar, measured and after a few minutes iron pieces rested on the forge. "You've been working on a big iron job lately, haven't you? The forge is usually a lot colder when I get in here in the mornings," Cutter said as he took a sip of the cold water.

"Yep, I've been working on that set of andirons for a customer late every night this week. The first two I made I had to take apart because I couldn't get the spacing right. The one I did yesterday was lopsided and not strong enough," Dunagan said as he rubbed the calloused hand across his forehead in frustration.

Cutter stood watching Dunagan bend and shape the iron, the artistry of the drawing coming to life in the black metal. The repetition of heating, hammering, and heating again delivered a curled knob foot. Turning, Cutter stepped to the pitcher and poured himself a mug of water and looked out at the plaza.

There was a man in a black frock coat escorting a young girl to over the dress making shop. The little girl had a parasol, walking it along with her and she held his hand. There was a sweet, spicy smell in the air. Sort of like when someone is cooking and the rush of warm meadow air collides with it. Cutter looked off to the south and saw a swirl of dust dancing over the range. Hearing a door close he turned back and saw Mrs. Watley step away from the side door of the church, fussing with her gloves and moving across the plaza.

Newton breathed in the evening air, put his gloves back on and stepped over to the anvil. A couple hours later, the blacksmith hung up his apron, stowed his gloves away and chuckled. He told Dunagan not to work so hard.

The stars were twinkling like diamonds in the crisp night sky. Twin black andirons rested on the sturdy wood plank table inside the blacksmith shop. Dunagan poured over his account book, dimly lit by the old lantern. Not being particularly good with numbers, Dunagan constantly spent more time putting numbers in order than most men. His custom iron work had made him close to five thousand dollars in the last two months and he had put his money into a bank in San Francisco for safekeeping.

A wood crunching sound from the stables brought up Dunagan's head and he frowned listening. The lantern light flickered and danced throwing moving shadows up on the wall over the old desk. Faint muffled voices drifted into the blacksmith shop and Dunagan figured it was someone saddling a horse. What sounded like someone falling to the ground caused Dunagan to walk over to the locked dividing door between the stables and the blacksmith shop to listen.

Wood slid against wood and a horse's hooves walked out of the stables and the heavy door shut, the small beam sliding into place. Dunagan looked out the window into the darkness and saw a figure open and close the corral gate, mount up on the horse and walk around the corner of the blacksmith shop. Dunagan made a note to talk with Thomas Wood in the morning about these goings on.

# 16 CHAPTER SIXTEEN

There were less than a dozen people having a late breakfast in the hotel dining room. Silverware tinkled against plates. The intoxicating aroma of savory, sweet and fresh brewed coffee swirled around the room. The white tablecloths covered each table. The goblets of water shone.

Newton Cutter had sat down with Mayor William Watley and the elderly Mrs. Klinger this morning to get more information about finding the right flagstones for the walkway. Cutter had seen the rough cut stones at the Mayor's house several times. Cutter told them how he wanted stones like those for his new house.

Mrs. Klinger laughed and patted her wrinkled hand on the tablecloth. "Those came from the quarry out at the Flint Hills. There is a huge outcropping of granite out there. There were several times when I packed up a big picnic lunch and had a little party out of it when Mr. Klinger needed stone."

"Your husband was a stone cutter?"

"Oh yes, my dear! He learned as a boy with his father and brothers in Devonshire in England. It was a valuable skill to learn and when he came to America he was quick to learn the local quarry locations.

"I would like to see if that Flint Hills quarry is where my flagstones came from. I have always wanted to get more of those for the walkway along the side," Watley said as he took a sip of his coffee.

"Addie would like a big stone patio for parties and such," he chuckled,

"Gentlemen, hitch up a team and I'll show you the quarry. We can get out there and back before dark. I'm in a mood for a nice ride," Mrs. Klinger said as she wiped her mouth and gestured to Georgianna.

After speaking with her a moment, Georgianna hurried back to the kitchen with a big smile.

To one side, Cutter asked, "Do you know anyone that can cut quarry stone like that?" Cutter looked at Watley.

"Not a soul. I'll stop and ask Bert while you get the carriage. He should know someone," Watley said as he stood. He lifted the hand of Mrs. Klinger.

"You are a gem, my dear!" His lips brushed the back of her hand making her giggle.

The Flint Hills held a unique character that was in sharp contrast to the surrounding countryside. Ten miles to the south was a high, wide rolling mesa blanketed with rose verbena and delicate evening primrose flowers. Patches of brilliant salmon orange scattered amongst green and purple flecked grasses. Sparrows and hawks dove into the thick grasses after vermin and snacks.

"Chester said that centuries ago the flint was pressed into the limestone. Believe it or not, this area was underwater at one time," Mrs. Klinger said. She brought up her hand to shade her eyes as the horses drew the carriage up the grade.

"We have found little fossils of shells out there."

"I'll want to take back a chunk of the flint if we can find any here," She smiled. "I have grandchildren in the east that I'm sure have never seen flint. Plus, I much prefer using flint to start my fires each morning. The spark is much better than using steel."

The carriage stopped in a wide level spot where other wagons and vehicles had worn down the dirt and gravel. Mrs. Klinger guided them about fifty yards down into the quarry.

"The flint is difficult to cut and Chester used twenty or more wedges to get a whole piece to drop out. It will fracture easily, sending shards in every direction, so anyone doing a cut will have to be particularly careful," She said as she pointed out three angled outcroppings surrounded by wispy prairie grass.

Twenty minutes later, Mrs. Klinger stepped up onto a massive granite slab close to fifty feet long and twenty feet wide.

"It looks like someone tried to wedge this one long after Chester stopped working."

She pointed to the edge that showed gouges.

"There was someone here working with a chisel trying to smooth the edge."

"I found another over here," Watley called from the other side of a small rise.

"This looks exactly like the ones I have." Cutter helped Mrs. Klinger skirt around the dirt piles and then she clambered onto another granite slab.

"I believe you are right, Mr. Mayor. I would say this is also the stone where the steps for the bank were cut."

She had knelt and ran fingers over a dark charcoal vein in the stone.

"Well, I found the stones I want. Now I need to find someone to come cut them for me," Cutter said.

He held up a chunk of the rough stone in his hands, turning it over watching the sun glint on the veins. Even in the heat of the day this stone was cool and heavy.

Watley had lugged a bigger chunk of the granite over to the carriage and was wrestling it into the boot. Cutter helped him boost it up and get it situated in the center of the compartment.

Mrs. Klinger had spread out a white tablecloth from the dining room and cold chicken, beef and platter of cheese and fruit were laid out. There were several jars of lemonade, sweetened with a touch of sugar. Watley sat down and began to happily devour a chicken leg.

The Mayor munched happily. "Goldman said Brad Amundson can cut stone. He hasn't seen him in a couple of months. He has a place southeast of Doc Baines' ranch, up a long road," Watley said as he wiped off his mouth.

"Mr. Amundson makes some of the best honey smoked ham I have ever had. Mr. Boardman at the hotel serves it from time to time and I dare say, I make a pig outta myself eatin' it,' ' Mrs. Klinger said with a laugh.

Mrs. Klinger pointed out the flint slabs and Cutter tapped with a hammer to break up a couple of good-sized pieces for her.

As he lifted the flint slabs into the carriage he noticed that she had a far-away look in her watery eyes. He watched her silently realizing that this place held happy memories of times with her late husband and Cutter was hesitant to disturb those.

"There is another place you might want to take a look at, Newton. Up north of San Francisco there is a marble quarry. We made two trips up there many years ago to get marble. Fine white marble with those blackish snaky veins all shot through it. Hints of gold, too. Very pretty to some, but marble is too cold to suit me," she said with a nod.

"Granite will warm up in the sun and keep heat."

She turned to William Watley.

"You ever notice how your granite steppingstones are still warm at midnight? That's because they hold the heat."

Mrs. Klinger fussed with her soft leather gloves for a moment.

"It can be a hundred and ten in the shade and that marble always stays cold." She paused a moment, smirking.

"Never let your lady sit on marble, Newton Cutter."

She winked at him as she stepped up into the carriage. "You always want a warm woman in your hands!"

Watley and Cutter burst out laughing. After the food was stored back into the basket, Cutter helped her into the carriage, still chuckling. As he put his gloves on, his eyes with a fresh view around the silent quarry. He wondered about other stones and slabs that had found new homes in the county.

The carriage bumped along the next few miles until finally they turned west onto the smoother, wider Hookton Road. From this slight grade and continuing on to the river about five miles south were sweeping pastures and fertile river-bottom farmland. For many years local ranchers had stood their herds here for three weeks fattening them ready for market.

Mrs. Klinger's gray blue eyes gazed at the blades of grass bending to the strength of the wind. A flock of birds startled, rose out of the long grass with a cackling alarm, and she smiled at the swift flight.

*******

Dunagan and Cutter had spent the better part of the day mounting and securing the wrought iron garden gates to the fence. They were a mirror image of each other with an arched top rail and varying sized scrollwork in the body. The post hinges were measured and mounted onto the heavy wood blocks. Then the gates were lifted up and the iron dowels slid into the round cylinders. There was a clasping cylinder lock that slid down to grip both gates and kept them still.

The school committee had requested a photographer come in and get some pictures for posterity. There was a group picture of them on the steps and then one of Cutter standing alone looking like a true statesman. The shots that took the longest were the ones of Dunagan and his gates.

Dunagan was moved left and right against the gates, turned backwards and forwards, made to kneel and swing them. At one point, he was sure the photographer was going to ask him to climb up on them and stand. The big burst of light poofed as the picture was taken.

The iron worker watched Cutter posing with the gates. "I always start with about a dozen flat bars of iron in the forge. I use the end of the anvil and the hammer to form the circles and rounds."

Dunagan fidgeted with his hat, shifted from foot to foot. Another flash and Dunagan rubbed his eyes again and hoped his hair was presentable.

"No, if someone wants a certain size, I write down the measurements. Then I decide what fits inside the design," Clay said as he rubbed his chin, looking up at the sky.

"I've tried to draw down a design, but it never looks as good on paper as it does inside my head." Cutter folded his arms across his chest and was amused at the uncomfortable fidgeting of the talented ironworker.

The photographer thanked everyone and packed up his camera and trudged back to the hotel trailing a small group of chattering children. Cutter walked over and shook hands with Dunagan, grinning.

"That wasn't too bad, I guess," Cutter said as he noticed Dunagan had put on his best shirt and cleanest broadcloth pants for the picture taking.

"That was downright impressive, Clay!"

"I hope he didn't get me with my eyes closed. People look so stupid and brainless with their eyes closed in pictures," Dunagan said with a frown and shook his head.

"Well, maybe you'll get some work out of it. If you get just one gate order that would be good, right?" Cutter grinned at the older man.

"True."

"Say, let's run over and get a beer over at Bert's. I'm thirsty!" Dunagan nodded and the two men started out walking up the path headed for town.

Inside the new home and school there was another high level meeting taking place. William and Addie Watley, Dawson Cole, Merle Doyle, and Chick Miller had set up a school committee and had decided the first school classes could start the middle of January. There were still supplies and books to be brought in for the children. Both school rooms were painting a brilliant white. Sunlight flooded in the windows. The beautiful hanging prisms of glass cast streaks of blues, green and reds throughout the room. Brett Doyle had built ten smaller desks and small round stools for the first ten children using the leftover building supplies from the house building. Working on them on and off, it took Doyle about six weeks to make them all with a small shelf where they could store their books and papers.

Thomas Wood went over to him and shook his hand, nodding.

"I didn't know you built desks, Brett," Wood said as he turned the small dark wood desk a bit and then turned it back, looking it over. There was a small round steel bar to be used as a footrest attached to the front.

"Once I got a vision in my head of what they were s'posed to look like, well, I just went from there," Doyle cleared his throat, folding his arms over his chest.

"They're not all the same size. I figured there'd be different ages learnin' here so I made some bigger, some smaller."

Wood clapped him on the shoulder, grinning. "What else you buildin'?"

There were five desks that had lids that lifted, with small hinges fastened inside. The smallest organized at the front of the room, for the younger smaller students. The teacher's shining white desk stood at the front. The school committee had been very generous in supplying papers, slates, and rulers amongst other items for the children.

"I've got a good sized chalkboard coming in on a freight wagon at the end of the week. I dare say that cuss is going to take the three of us to get it mounted up on the wall," Chick Miller said as he sipped his coffee.

"I have no idea how much teachers use chalk so I just ordered fifty pounds of it."

Wood and Doyle burst out laughing, looking at Miller.

"Well, that ought to last them til they graduate, Chick!"

Wood giggled. "Maybe we should buy another chalkboard just so we can use up that chalk!'

Miller grew red in the face and lifted a hand to wave. He stepped out the door.

Addie Watley refilled their cups with steaming hot coffee and motioned them to get a sweet roll, courtesy of Papa LaCosta from Williams. He and his daughter Chianne stood chatting with friends near the big windows. Papa had a knack for making sweet pastries and it made the thirty five mile ride worthwhile to stop at the Inn.

Chick Miller paused as he stepped into his saloon and surveyed the big room. Brett Doyle nodded to the owner.

"Who are those guys? I've never seen 'em before," Chick Miller walked in and poured himself a cup of coffee behind the bar. Two men sat at a corner table in Chick Miller's saloon talking and laughing at each other. The table held three empty beer mugs and a whisky bottle.

"I dunno, but they're a couple of loudmouths," Doyle said as he dragged a damp rag over the bar.

"How long have they been here?" Miller leaned his body against the bar resting his arm along the shiny wood, looking across the saloon.

"'Bout an hour now, steady drinkers. Must've been paid off their jobs and now are drinking up their rent money."

The burly bartender grinned and chuckled as he dried and polished beer mugs.

Across the room, a thin, wiry man leaned back in his chair and had to catch himself before he toppled over. The older, grimy man picked up his saddle bags and strode through the swinging doors, pulling his hat down. "Barkeep, another beer!"

The dirty blonde man stood up and made his way to the bar.

"And I want a clean glass this time," Doyle glared at the man and grit his teeth. Nobody made clean glass remarks around Doyle unless they wanted a bump on their head. "The last one I got looked like it had lipstick on it."

Brett Doyle slammed the beer glass down on the bar and a doubled up right fist backhanded Luke Iverson across the mouth, smashing his lips. Luke Iverson was a big and muscular man who used his considerable power and strength. Doyle, while lighter in weight, he was almost as tall and a man with that wiry tendon strength. His fist did not move Iverson when it bloodied his lips, but Doyle was falling off balance against him, so he threw a left hand at Luke's head. The quick jerk of his head aside and Iverson grabbed Doyle with his huge arms.

Doyle lowered a shoulder and jabbed a right up under Luke's chin, forcing his head back then a quick left and right into the ribs, and shoved him off. Iverson struck out hard and the force knocked Brett Doyle into the bar knocking over several other glasses of patrons hurrying to get out of the way. Iverson charged him like a bull with its head down with an ugly sneer on his face. Doyle pushed himself away from the bar and as he rolled free, smashed a wicked short right cutting Luke's ear into a bloody mess.

Luke was fast and light on his feet like a wily alley cat. He landed another left and right to the head and rushed in again, but Doyle threw an elbow into Iverson's head, thrusting it down to meet Doyle's rising knee. Iverson jerked and staggered back, his nose and mouth a gory wreck.

There were faces at the windows peering in watching the two big men fight. They were standing, smashing, punching with brutal force and the two men lumbered across the room. Doyle was a bigger, heavier man and Iverson the quicker. Blood and sweat flew off each rough punch. People crowded in behind the bar unable to tear their eyes away from the fighting men. Doyle pulled free, taking a couple gasping breaths and slammed Luke Iverson down with a vicious right.

The big man lunged up from the floor, grabbed Doyle around the hips and with a wrenching groan lifted his body clear of the floor, then crashed the struggling man down across a table, which shattered beneath them. Iverson dove at him, but Doyle hit him with a short right to the face, and then heaved him off, rolling him up against the wooden bar. It took a slow moment for the two big men to gain their feet. Both men came up together. Iverson swung a boot for Doyle's knee, and Doyle grabbed with both hands and swung the kicking leg to the side, blocking the kick.

Doyle saw an opening and drew back his right and walked in, smashing left after right to Iverson's face. Luke staggered back, trying to shake off the blows, hesitated for a moment and then charged again. He threw himself against Doyle hard. Doyle hit the floor with a bone-wrenching groan doubled over in pain. Iverson jumped for Doyle's face with his boots but Doyle saw it coming out of the corner of his eye and rolled aside. He managed to get up to one knee in time to meet Iverson's rush. Shirts torn, and faces bloodied, the men grappled, punched, and threw their fists into each other.

Doyle had been pushed back by the larger man's sheer physical power. Backwards he went down the room, struggling to find solid footing on the wooden floor and then Doyle lurched against the bar.

Iverson's eyes widened and he dragged the back of his hand against his mouth, wiping away blood. The big man set himself and twisted his shoulder back, doubling his fist for a finishing strike. Doyle had been watching, playing possum, and lowered himself, throwing a fast, short inside right. A stunning, hammer-like blow to Iverson's belly, stopped the big man, his face contorted up in pain. Doyle caught him with another right, then a left, punching hard and fast. Iverson's body had twisted to the left as he leaned back for a punch and Doyle threw a ripping right hand to Iverson's jaw. Iverson's knee sagged and he began to totter back.

Luke went down. He hit the floor on his knees reaching to grip the bar with one hand. Shaking his head to clear his eyes, he tried to lunge up, clawing at the air, blood blinding his eyes. Doyle was gasping, leaning against the bar pouring beer into a glass and Iverson lunged at him. Doyle turned sideways and gripped Iverson as he rushed in with strong hands, dragging and pulling the man to the door. Doyle drew back and with a heavy boot shoved Iverson out into the dirty dusty street.

Iverson fell, rolling over and struggled to get up but he fell to one side, panting and heaving. The big man lay there gasping as the townspeople peered at him from the wooden boardwalk. Doyle walked back to the bar and slugged down his beer.

"Well, I'll never make Hospitality Manager of the Year for this!" Doyle laughed holding a damp rag to the side of his head.

Miller poured him a shot of whiskey and laughed.

***

An hour later, William Huddleston looked up from his book as Royal Benning and Luke Iverson walked with a split lip and a swelling eye that was closing up fast. The musty-smelling office was dim with stacks of papers and old ledgers piled on the floor. "What's going on out there?"

Royal Benning snickered and said, "Brett Doyle just wiped the floor with your boy here," Benning leaned against the closed door.

"Hey! He ain't lookin' none too pretty either," Iverson said as he rubbed the back of his hand against his mouth.

Huddleston gritted his teeth and clenched his jaw. There was a slow burning rage in the heavy, slow banker, yet he looked at these two toughs and felt that uneasy shake.

"Where's Tolliver?"

"I don't know. But that's not why we're here. Things ain't goin' the way they're supposed to be. Things ain't right here."

"Since we took down that big ranch south of here, all the other ranchers have gunned up, brought in more hands. They're all carrying guns and rifles now."

Iverson shook his head. Fingers probed a cut on the top of his head.

"I need those city folk off that ranch. There's too much at stake here. I can foreclose on that ranch by the end of next week and this will all be over!"

Huddleston slammed his meaty fist down on the desk.

"That Jackson Frisch is holding everything up. Him and his daughter. You gotta scare 'em. Get them off that ranch!"

Huddleston looked at the two men across from him.

"I'll make it a thousand dollars if they're outta there by sundown tomorrow."

Benning laughed and stood up tall, pushing his hat back a bit. "No."

Luke Iverson slouched down into a chair and stared at Huddleston.

Benning looked at Iverson's worn expression and took a step forward. "I don't know what you're up to, banker man, but it's not worth getting shot at."

"Go get them off that ranch for good, run 'em outta there," Huddleston's voice trembled. He wiped his damp forehead and took out a brown envelope. Bills spread out on the desk.

"Word is that the folks have called in Henry Elliot to run a raging gang of outlaws outta town," Benning had put his hands on the edge of the desk and spoke in a low growling voice.

Iverson's eyes had gone wide.

Elliot was fast. Fast and sneaky. He had a way of sneaking up on people and then the next day people were saying' nice words over dirt. Iverson knew he was a turtle stuck in mud compared to the gunfighter.

"I ain't gonna tangle with Henry Elliot. I didn't sign up to get six feet under," Benning said. His eyes were mean and hard under his hat.

"He's a professional, lightning fast. The sort of many you call in at a last resort when even a posse can't get the job done."

After Huddleston had counted the five hundred out, he pushed it across to Benning.

"You get the other half when I am rid of those folks for good."

Benning looked at the money and then his eyes squinted on Huddleston and the bank seemed to shrink back in his chair.

"Pick it up, kid."

Benning motioned to Iverson who reached over and stacked the money and folded it over in his hand.

Huddleston struggled to compose himself as he saw Benning's hand drop to his side, the side near the Colt. There was a significant tremor to the banker's hand as he gathered up the remaining bills and shoved them into the brown envelope.

Benning nodded to Iverson and the young kid stood up.

"Keep that money on you all the time. We won't be wanting to stop for tea when we come to collect the rest."

The door to the alley shut behind the hard men and they didn't stop until they were past the church and out of sight.

Under the shadow of a big oak, Benning turned to Iverson.

"You best keep yourself alive to collect that money, kid. If Elliot comes huntin', you ain't got a chance."

They stopped behind one of the nearly collapsed warehouses on the north side of town, in around some trees where they had tied the horses. Benning rolled a smoke and the flame of the match flickered over the mean dark eyes.

"I don't like it. Not one bit. I've seen what a town'll do to a man who raises a hand to a woman. I ain't killin' no woman."

Iverson's voice was a hissing whisper and his hand dug in his pocket. He counted out Benning's share and handed it over.

"All he said was get 'em off the land. Get them off the ranch. For good. Nothing about no killin', but I can read what he wants," said the outlaw.

Benning cupped the burning ember, flicking bits into the night.

"Load up on ammunition, some food and get some rope ready. Get out to South Landing and get it ready for some guests."

There was a glint in the dark eyes. He said, "Stay there, lay low. No more stupid fights."

The stinging cut on the side of Iverson's mouth irritated the man as he mounted his horse and trotted away.

Huddleston sat behind the desk watching the smoke from the lamp float off into the darkness. His hands could not stop wringing. He could hear branches brushing against the roof, a dog barked off in the distance and the faint smell of wood smoke was in the air. His patience was at an end over this senseless waiting for others to act. If things went according to plan, tomorrow would see the rest of his plan finally be done.

***

The morning was beautiful with birds chattering, bees humming and the gurgling stream crystal clear. Carmella has risen early wanting to have a ride and time to herself to sort out her feelings and thoughts. She wore her long red hair in a ponytail, a brown riding skirt and blue striped blouse. She had tried to rub the dirt off of her short suede boots when the horse nickered and its head went up and she stood up to see a disheveled man in bloody and torn clothing jumping off his horse. Her horse reared and danced sideways in fright.

"What do you want? Who are you?" Carmella started to back away but the man caught her hand.

"You're comin' with me, missy," The man rubbed a gloved hand over his mouth and gripped her wrist.

Carmella drew back and kicked as hard as she could and the man yelled in pain.

"Why you, I oughta," said the man with a sneer.

Carmella's pretty day faded into darkness as Iverson slammed her with a right cross.

Carmella groaned as the pounding began in her head and when she tried to move her hands found them tied tightly together.

An hour later at the hideout, Royal Benning paced the floor.

"Our guest is waking up. Get over to Tolliver and tell him we have her. After I get her cleaned up, we'll start riding for the ranch," Benning took a drag on his cigarette and knelt next to Carmella. Iverson drank down his coffee and grabbed his hat and headed out the door.

"Who are you? What do you want? My father will have your head for this!"

Carmella soon realized yelling made her head throb worse. The old, warped planks of the wooden floor were rough and dirty. It smelled like old grease and human sweat mixed with years of dust. The high ceiling framed in thick, rough beams and tiny windows. A river rock fireplace crackled as burning embers floated above the dying fire.

Benning leaned back in his chair in the kitchen and stared at the girl on the floor in front of the fire. He went to a bowl of water and dipped the edge of a cloth into it and walked back to Carmella. He knelt and swabbed at the bruise but Carmella pushed him away. She saw a tall man, dark hair and dark eyes in faded broadcloth pants and a blue shirt. He lit a cigarette and stared at her for a while with menace in his eyes. As he put on his coat she saw the twin Colts in a holster on the back of the chair.

"You'll see your father soon enough and you can tell him all about this, Miss Frisch," Benning said as he stood. He draped the cloth over the edge of the counter. He poured a cup of water from a pitcher and offered her a drink. She took it and drained it.

"If you think you can ride, we'll head for the ranch now," Benning said as he buckled on the guns and tossed his cigarette into the smoldering fireplace. Only about an hour and half had gone by since Iverson delivered this feisty package, but Benning wasn't going to take any chances on people looking for her.

"I wanna get this over with. Get on your feet."

*******

Thomas Wood held the long heavy tongs in a strong grip while Cutter swung the hammer trying to flatten out the long slender iron rod. The clanging echoed across the plaza. Cutter stood in a light shirt, sweat pouring off his reddened face gripping the twenty pound hammer, breathing heavily. Wood lifted the bar and slid it back into the orangy-red forge.

He turned and found Dawn White standing at the heavy door, fidgeting.

"Newton, have you seen Carmella? I thought she might be headed in from the ranch, but she should have been here over an hour ago."

"No, she hasn't been here," Cutter straightened up.

"She was riding in alone?"

Dawn wiped her nose with a hankie. "I don't know."

Wood shook his head. He frowned and took off his canvas gloves, taking a step towards Dawn. He could see her hands wringing the small gloves into a knot. "We've been working on this axle since early this morning and nobody has come by."

"Mayor Watley hasn't seen her either and I know Jackson had some papers for him. I don't know where she is. She didn't show up at the hotel. Considering the recent trouble around, I want to be protective. I don't want her out alone too much."

Dawn turned and shielded her eyes with her hand looking out over the vacant land south of the shop. A light breeze blew leaves past the doorway and tossed the pretty curls.

"Thomas, run over and ask Bert and Bruno if they have seen her, would ya?"

Cutter looked at Dawn. The ugly, growing sense of alarm had started up in his gut.

"I'll check the auction house and Doc Baines. We'll find her." Cutter reached and squeezed Dawn's hand.

"Best get yourself back over to your shop, Miss Dawn. She might show back up there." Cutter gave Dawn a brief smile and took off running towards the plaza.

Dawn squinted, frowning lowering her head and a single tear traced down her cheek as she turned, hurrying along the hard-packed street.

# 17 CHAPTER SEVENTEEN

Four rowdy trail hands sat sprawled at a table in Chick Miller's Saloon. They had been there for a couple of hours and had become drunk causing problems. Clay Dunagan and Mack Kelley were also drinking in the saloon, discussing horses.

Kelley tried to play a jaunty tune on the old piano only to be derided by the drunk cowboys. The worse he played, the more they yelled and whooped. Brett Doyle had had enough finally and asked them to leave.

"There are other places to drink in this town so just move on. Goodnight, fellas," Doyle said. He turned and took down all the glasses and bottles from the bar and refused to serve them. The cowboys tried to focus to stare at Doyle for a minute.

"Come on, I know a place outside of town where we can bed down. Help me get Charley on his horse."

One of them started to help his friend up out of a chair. Outside they lifted up their drunken friend and laid him across the saddle. Kelly and Dunagan watched them from the saloon doorway as they mounted their horses and headed north out of town.

Meanwhile, there were also four trail hands in Bert Goldman's saloon who also became rather intoxicated and belligerent.

Dawson Cole and Doc Baines had walked in about half an hour ago and chatted with Goldman at the bar. Cole was enjoying a hot steaming cup of coffee and Baines was heading towards being drunk.

At the end of the hour, Bert Goldman also was at the end of his patience and refused to serve the loud bunch. He pointed at the door and in a loud voice suggested that they leave and they managed to stumble out.

One of the cowboys stumbled and bumped into one of the passing horses and the rider kicked him in the head and he fell down. The horse startled and bumped into another horse and caused the other rider to lose his temper and become angry. The cowboy that had fallen to the ground half crawled, half ran through the dark alley between the trading post and the saloon.

Voices shouted recognition about someone and angry words were exchanged. Disparaging names were called. Somebody lost their temper and pistols were drawn with one stray bullet that shattered a City Hall window. Another stray embedded itself in the wall of the saloon. Cole and Doc ducked down and scampered behind the heavy wooden bar.

A man screamed in pain and the sounds of horses racing out of town faded into the night. Cole, Doc Baines, and Goldman emerged from behind the bar and peeked out the windows. The other drunken cowboys stumbled onto their horses and chased after the others.

"Sweet Jesus, I hope nobody needs stitches. I don't think I could see the blasted needle," Doc said as he rubbed his bleary eyes and started to chuckle.

"What else can happen in this little town? Bradford is getting rowdier all the time. The days of a quiet evening around here are long gone," Dunagan said as he scratched his head.

Goldman slapped him on the back.

"Calls for a drink!"

The men laughed, stood up and reached for those pretty shining glasses behind the bar. The afternoon trailed on towards evening with few patrons disturbing the small group. The only other disturbance was several warring factions of crows took up residence in the pine and oak trees on the square and began a series of diving marauds onto each other's branches.

Another birds' eye view of the afternoon saw six miles outside of Bradford to the east where a high mesa overlooked the lower valley. It was quiet here. The sounds of bugs scurrying in the scattered rocks and a couple of buzzards floated in a circle overhead.

Henry Elliot had built a camp under an escarpment of sandstone, warmed it with a small fire and he had lain back with his hat over his eyes watching the shimmering distance.

Elliot had been a hard man living in a hard and lonely land up to this point. He had made his own way, lived on his own terms and while he had his freedom, he had chosen little else. He had ridden a trail herd, prospected for gold and silver, built miles of fences, and killed buffalo. He had managed to stay one step ahead of the law, covered his tracks, and disappeared when others came looking.

And he was tired of it all.

Dawn White had sat herself next to him a few nights ago and looked into his eyes.

"Stay here with me, Henry. Let this become your home. Let me cook for you."

He had listened to her, admiring the dark glints of her eyes and the soft waves of her hair as she brushed it next to the fire.

"I want to build a house and to make a home. I want my own roof and walls. And I want it with you."

Her eyes had searched his face.

"We can have happy years together in our own home, Henry."

Elliot had not said a word but smiled as he looked at the floor. He had known Dawn White for five years now and had always found a reason to come back through Bradford. He had come to see her more and more in this past year, desiring her time and company. Of all the women he had known, it was this cool, intelligent dark-eyed beauty that he kept coming back to. She always gave him room and knew not to ask questions, which was something a man could not find lately in a woman.

The lawman had twelve thousand dollars resting in a small bank in Denver. Another ten thousand in San Francisco. There was a thousand in gold in Santa Fe. He remembered there were almost five thousand sitting in Kansas City where his last trail ride ended. He could live anywhere from New York to San Francisco but after he had thought back over the attributes and detractions from each possibility, his mind came back to this small town and the beautiful seamstress.

Birds whistled and sang out in the brush and the air was fresh and cool. He could smell sage mixed with warm rich earth. Wildflowers made patches of red, yellow, blue, and purple waving in the breeze.

Somewhere deep inside himself he knew this was the time. He had not planned any more work, not put in for jobs or committed to ride with anyone. He would need to contact the lawyer and get papers drawn up and money transferred around. He had been past an abandoned ranch up in the Flint Hills more than a couple of times and never seen anyone around.

There were fruit orchards full of apple and pear trees along with what looked to be a long-neglected and overgrown broad garden plot. He stood up and stretched slowly. From his vantage point he studied the countryside. There was a cluster of tall cacti off to the east with birds flitting in and out. Taking his canteen, he hiked up over the rock lip and down to the trickling stream at the base of the hill.

As he walked back up the trail he heard the running horse. Voices. Easing up over the ridge he looked down at a man struggling with a woman on a trotting horse. He had no desire to get involved with wife problems or sweetheart problems. Until he saw the girl's face. It was Carmella Frisch.

Stepping down out of the brush, Elliot came up behind the horse.

"Put the girl down on the ground, mister."

Benning turned his head to the left hearing the voice and Carmella bit down hard on his ear, grinding her teeth. The horse jumped at the sound and Benning's arm loosened a bit and Carmella tumbled to the ground.

Benning wheeled his horse around and faced the stranger.

"Now what are you buttin' in for, mister? Can you see I'm having a tussle with my lady here?" Benning was wiping his bleeding ear with a handkerchief.

"Miss Frisch, are you alright?"

Carmella had picked up a mesquite limb and had started to swing it at the horse. Her face was streaked with dirt and there were bits of grass and twigs stuck in her long hair. There was a hint of animalistic rage on the young woman.

"He tried to kidnap me!"

The wood slammed into the forequarters of the unsuspecting horse and it began to buck and scream in terror. Benning jerked on the reins, causing the horse whirl faster. With a grunt of surprise, Benning hit the ground and the horse shot down the road in fright.

Benning leaped grabbing for Carmella and she sidestepped him but tripped over a rock and fell as she tried to kick back at her kidnapper. Benning pulled his gun and held it on Carmella, his face contorted in rage.

"As soon as her father hands over the deed to the ranch, we'll let her go. Nobody has to get hurt here, it is just a simple business transaction."

Benning felt his ear, testing to see if it was all still there and saw blood. He looked at his own blood on his hands in amazement.

He scarcely noticed when Elliot came up behind him. He was about to bring up his gun when Carmella threw a handful of dirt and sand into his eyes and scampered deeper into the brush. Elliot kicked Benning's leg and knocked him off balance and then grasped Benning's gun wrist and swung him around, hurling him into the dirt. Benning's body crumpled over an old mesquite stump with a crash. He held his arm and groaned as he struggled to his feet.

Benning had been a knock-down, bare-knuckles fighter for many years. But for the last few of those years, his gun had been his weapon of choice and now his reflexes were slow.

Elliot's kick to his ribs blasted the wind from his lungs and he tried to roll away and catch his breath.

"I've waded across your path one too many times, Benning. I've seen the wrecked lives and bloody bodies behind you. You stop here!"

Benning came up charging, arms spread wide trying to grapple Elliot. Henry stepped to the left a bit and gave Benning an open handed slap against his mouth as he lunged past. Benning started to rise up from the dirt and then looked around hunting for his revolver. With a cry of anguish, he found it held in Carmella's hands aimed right at him.

Elliot shielded his eyes from the low hanging sun and stood there watching Benning.

"Have you ever shot a gun, Miss Frisch?"

There was a decidedly amused tone to Elliot's voice.

Carmella's mouth turned up at the corner in a wicked, shaking grin.

"Yes, sir. Yes, I have. I have had plenty of time to shoot rocks, fence posts, rabbits and even a couple of coyotes lately out at the ranch. Father has been very attentive to my firearm education, you might say. An' shooting this poor excuse for a man can't be much different than shooting rattlesnakes."

She didn't take her eyes off the outlaw. "I'd bet I could take out his kneecap, Mr. Elliot."

Benning gasped and whirled around to look at Elliot. "Henry Elliot? The gunfighter?"

"Well, if he takes more than two steps, Miss Frisch, you go ahead and see if you can take off that kneecap."

Elliot smirked. An unpleasant shrill laugh came from Carmella as Elliot dusted off his pants and adjusted his gloves.

"Who's this 'we' in your plan, Benning? Who is in your gang to kidnap Miss Frisch?"

Elliot had taken the loop off his Colt and stared at Benning.

"And just what do you want with that ranch?"

"Just me an' a couple other guys. We know there is gold somewhere on that ranch, and we're gonna take it!"

Benning grabbed a handful of dirt and flung it at Carmella making her stumble backwards. He lunged for the gun, heard a crashing boom.

Benning screamed holding his left arm with a bloody stump on his gun hand. Benning grabbed the wound and Carmella fired another shot that slammed into his hip.

Elliot quickly scooped the gun from Carmella with a disconcerting smile. "We don't want him dead yet, Miss."

Half an hour later, the unconscious Benning had been tied across the saddle of his horse. Carmella rode double behind Elliot.

"Are you sure your father knows nothing about this gold on the Long Ranch, Miss?"

They had been discussing the gold revelations of Royal Benning.

"I am sure he knows nothing about it. I doubt that he would ever sell the ranch knowing there is gold there," Carmella said as she tugged a twig out of her hair and tossed it away.

"I wonder who else knows about this. Could there be people out on the ranch looking for that gold, Mr. Elliot?"

Henry turned and checked on the unconscious outlaw draped over the saddle of the following horse.

"This is going to make your father's selling decision a bit more complicated," Elliot said as he guided the horses down through a grassy green valley.

The horse picked its way up a low hill on the other side following an old cattle path.

They came three miles later into trees cloaked in evening darkness behind Goldman's saloon. The dog sleeping on the back porch woke up enough to bark once then gave up and settled back down into his nap.

# 18 CHAPTER EIGHTEEN

At the Bradford Hotel, Cutter laid awake in bed as his thoughts tumbled. Anger simmered inside him over the possibility that had been kidnapped. Fear crept into his thoughts about what he was capable of against the men that did this.

Three trusted men had headed out to the ranch to see if she was home. There was no need to panic at this point. His back hurt, his legs hurt and his arms ached from a long day's work and his head was pounding. It had not been an easy road getting his life to where it was now.

Over these last several years, he had surrounded himself with people who knew his worth, trusted him and welcomed him into their homes. He felt appreciated for exactly who he was and offered the same back to the kind folks. Still, there was something nagging at him, eating at him that he couldn't put his finger on.

As a child Cutter was taught at Sunday school that he would cross paths with people who could change his life. People who could change the direction of his life. As he grew older, he had dismissed these as simple platitudes of an elderly person consoling a small child. But here and now Cutter looked at Thomas Wood who had become a valued partner, nearly giving his life for something Cutter wanted.

The big hotel creaked and the window a loose pane rattled. Faint glimmers in the night sky revealed stars shining in the inky darkness. Cutter folded his hands behind his head and tried to relax his aching shoulders. His thoughts told him that he was stronger because he had to be stronger. He was smarter because he had made mistakes and learned from them. He had reached a comfortable level of happiness because he had overcome sadness and disappointment in his life. But an old wound was ripped open again by the appearance and upheaval caused by Angus Tolliver.

He was finishing his new home, had become an appreciated member of the town and community and was about to be married. A new phase, a fresh start of his life was about to begin. As he dozed into a light sleep, Cutter knew he would have to take steps to be rid of Tolliver once and for all. And he would need discreet help and understanding of several people.

Just as Cutter drifted off to sleep, two horses and three riders quietly pulled up to the Sheriff's office and if he had been more awake, Cutter might have heard steel bars locking shut in the distance.

The next morning as Cutter came down the hotel staircase he could hear the raised voices and excited conversation coming from the hotel dining room.

"Do you mean that man roughed her up like this?" A woman screeched in indignation.

"Is this the same brute that caused that big fight over at Goodman's?"

"My poor, dear Carmella! Should you be up and around, I mean, you should be in bed!"

It was packed with people at every table and more standing around the center table. The white tablecloth was covered in breakfast dishes, coffee cups and a platter of ham, bacon, and scrambled eggs. He looked around and found Carmella's eyes and moved over to her side.

"What is going on here? Are you okay, what happened?" Her soft hand was in his and she smiled. His fingers pulled back her red curls and he frowned at the darkening bruise at her temple.

"She'll be alright in a day or two, Newton. Don't be fussing over her now."

Doc Baines looked bleary eyed as he sipped the steaming black coffee.

"Sit, Newton, we have a lot to tell you."

Doc Baines motioned to a chair next to Jackson Frisch.

An hour later, Cutter was incredulous that Harvey Long was killed because of some secret gold on the ranch and that Carmella rode into the line of fire. Tommie Boardman had rushed off a telegram to the Texas Rangers for Mayor Watley. Benning was loudly protesting his capture and imprisonment, but to no avail as the sheriff's office was cold and dark. The Mayor had fired up the wood stove for a bit of heat but it did little to ward off the chill.

Cutter stood and shook Elliot's hand. "I cannot thank you enough, Henry for what you did for Carmella."

The young man smiled at the older and they turned away for just a minute and discussed something under their breath.

Carmella watched them and Jackson watched Carmella watching them.

Elliot touched the brim of his hat. He said, "No Sir, I was just in the right place at the right time and came to the aid of a pretty girl."

He winked at Carmella who made a pronounced wink back to him as he turned to take Dawn White's hand in his arm.

"My dear Miss White, we have things to discuss." Together they walked out of the dining room and out of the hotel.

Doc Baines wiped his mouth and excused himself and left. Georgianna threw caution to the wind and patted Thomas Wood's hand as she poured his refill. The stable master winked at her and whispered something causing a little laugh.

There were more questions about who Benning was working for, what were they planning next and when they were to do it. But Benning was closed-mouthed on any details and stewed in his self-pity in the dark office. A herd of children came by and tossed rocks at the open window in hopes of getting a lucky shot on the outlaw until an adult ran them off.

Tommy Boardman delivered a tray of cold cuts, bread, and a pot of coffee, sliding it under the bottom rail of the cell. There was a stern warning to Benning to not break any of his dishes. Nobody else came by to light a lantern or set up a few candles so Benning laid back on the small cot careful of his bandaged hand in the gloomy darkness. As one plan comes to an end, another starts up and there was nothing he could do right now so he drifted off into a fitful sleep.

***

It took three men to get the huge, wooden box down off the ten o'clock stage in Bradford. It was addressed to Newton Cutter and the return address showed a strange name in San Francisco. A small crowd from the hotel had gathered and were speculating about the contents. Dawn White walked over anxiously and looked it over, tapping it in places and listening.

"I have no idea what it is. Heaven only knows what that girl is up to. They'll be coming in this afternoon so I guess we have to wait," Dawn said with raised eyebrows.

She threw her hands up. Women continued to guess about what was in the wooden crate and the men chuckled over their curious wives. Several small children leaned their ears up to listen for any movement inside.

Later that afternoon, Carmella and Jackson Frisch rode into the town from the ranch. Jackson asked Cutter and Wood to take it over to the house, as it was meant for the new building. A wagon came and the crate was lifted and the short ride to the new house was followed by a curious crowd. Hammers and crowbar wrenched the wood planks from the box and inside was hard-packed straw. A cloth wrapped object was nestled inside and they laid it down with slow care.

Carmella lifted back the folds of cloth and there lay a large oblong stained glass window in brilliant greens, blues, yellows, reds, and oranges. Dawn and Addie gasped at its beauty. It was a window from one of the artisans that Carmella had selected in San Francisco.

"This is our housewarming gift to you, Newton. From my father and me for your new home." Her pretty eyes shone and her arms ached to hold him. Jackson reached and shook Cutter's hand with a big smile.

"We like to think that we are part of this community even though we haven't been here long. What you are doing for the children of this area is most generous and we wanted to add something to that cause, Newton," Frisch said.

He nodded in the direction of the construction site. "Once that is installed, I'd think you'd be ready to move it, young man!"

Jackson Frisch gestured towards the house. Folks exclaimed over the beautiful window and asked Carmella endless questions about the craftsmanship and artistry of the San Francisco creative minds.

Cutter stood there, blinking, speechless at the beautiful window. "I've only ever seen a few of these. The last one I saw was in Baltimore and it was only half this size. This is spectacular!"

Cutter smiled and looked at Frisch and Carmella. "Whenever any of us look at that, we will remember your generosity and friendship."

By five o'clock, Brad Amundson and Fergie Miller had installed the beautiful artwork, fitting it just inside the main living room window upstairs. The light caught it with rays sending colored rays beaming against the white walls and a big smile to Cutter's face.

# 19 CHAPTER NINETEEN

The creaking, old carriage pulled up in front of the water barrel so the horses could drink. A weathered older woman helped a frail, shaking passenger down from the vehicle. Mrs. Mary Rideout had stopped at the Faraway Inn to eat and rest before the remainder of her trip back to Four Wagon Bridge. Seated at the large round table before the fireplace, her twinkling eyes shone as she talked with her old friend, Papa.

"Well, that is what my people tell me, Papa," she said.

Her fine eyebrows wiggled.

"Buried beneath an old adobe wall or floor of some sort. Somebody thought it would never be found."

Papa sat back in the wooden chair stunned that after all these years news and information about Minnie Hollister has been found.

"I remember her stopping by here and that necklace was so extravagant that I told her highway robbers would come looking for her."

Papa smiled, looking down at the worn broad wood plank floor.

"Where is the necklace now? Is it locked up safe?"

Papa was stunned on hearing that after all these years. Memories and flashbacks pour through him as Minnie chatters on.

"Oh yes, it's in the safe at the hotel locked up tight. Mayor Watley asked that attorney fellow, Merle Doyle, to start making inquiries about Minnie's family."

Max brought out pewter platters of meat, potatoes and sat them down. Papa excused himself to return to the back veranda and get his thoughts together. Chiatane shared a cup of coffee with Mary, renewing their acquaintance and then left Mary alone to finish her dinner.

Mary was up early the next morning, the horses and carriage prepared for the day's journey and Papa reached up to grip the old, frail hand in friendship. Max set a basket of sweet rolls and fruit and a container of coffee next to Mary.

Papa watched the horses trot down the dusty road and it was only when Chiatane took his arm that he realized he had been lost in thoughts of Minnie.

The fall air was cooling down more and more each day. Big, fluffy clouds floated overhead in a baby blue sky. Last week a flock of wayward ducks were seen out over the river bottom. Gone was the warm earth smells of summer, the higher temperatures, and the longer daylight hours.

As Papa sat on the huge veranda on the back of the Faraway Inn he knew the river would start to rise with the first rains and the current would run faster. The brown grasses off in the distance would sport a white blanket of snow. He had memories of sitting right here with his arm around Minnie cuddled up under a blanket.

That afternoon, Papa found Henry Elliot digging into a slice of sweet apple pie and chatting with Chiatane on the back porch.

"When you are done there, Henry, I'd appreciate a word in private with you in my office," Papa said with a smile. Elliot nodded back.

Ten minutes later, Elliot leaned back into the buttery leather easy chair and lit a cigarette looking at Papa seated behind his massive desk. The man could see that Papa was sorting his thoughts and waited silently.

Over the next hour, Papa told Elliot the story of how he came to love Minnie Hollister and the mysterious disappearance so many years ago. The night that Minnie left him and rode back to Bradford, Papa had decided to ask Minnie to marry him. Minnie never came back. She had disappeared. Papa searched for her, but never found her. He had wondered all these years. Papa did not know anything else. This was a big puzzle and Henry promised to keep Papa posted as he found new information.

The big roan knew the road and Elliot let the horse have its head and walk on. His thoughts kept trying to form a clear picture about Minnie Hollister and Bradford but there were too many holes. Too many missing bits of what happened.

A pretty woman who was loved went missing. Her necklace was found, dug up from underneath old adobe ruins many years later. Was the skeleton that of Minnie Hollister? The town would never know the whole story.

Dawn looked up from her sewing surprised to find Elliot standing in her parlor with his hat in his hand. She saw the seriousness on his face and motioned for him to sit while she poured coffee. Elliot began to relate the information on Minnie Hollister and Dawn drew back and gazed off into space without seeing.

"Henry, I can fill in some of it, but I'm afraid it's only going to create more questions."

Dawn wrung her hands and fidgeted. She poured herself a small glass of whiskey and handed one to Elliot and took a sip to steady her nerves.

"My late husband, Graham, was fifteen years older than me and had a relationship with Minnie long before he married me. It was in the year before Graham married me that I remember Minnie having a baby boy. I'm not too proud to confess that I always thought that Graham might be the father of that boy. When I brought it up to Graham, he did not admit to it or deny that he could be the child's father. There is no proof."

Dawn refilled their cups and sat back down. For all these years, in Dawn's heart she knew Graham must be the father.

Then Dawn told Elliot about the events of one night in particular, when she found Graham passed out on the floor in their house. He was stupid drunk, bloody, and scratched up, knuckles skinned and covered in dusty dirt. He was never the same after that night. That winter, Graham caught the flu and then pneumonia. He ranted and raved in fitful sleep about someone named Minnie apologizing to her over and over. Graham never recovered and died from his illness. Dawn suspected he died more from grief over Minnie and the child.

"Henry, my imagination back then used to run away with me and I often wondered who this man I had married was. For years afterwards, I knew in my heart beyond a shadow of a doubt that Graham had done something horrible such as killing Minnie and buried her body somewhere. Is it possible that was Minnie's skeleton under all that old adobe house, where Newton is building his new house?"

She had a look at great sadness and anguish on her face and struggled to hold back tears. Elliot made Dawn take a sip of whiskey, held her hand and waited for her to calm down a bit.

"My dear, I'm afraid we will never know the complete story about her. All the people who were near to her or knew her are long gone. The only one who remains is Mary Rideout. I think we should go see her."

Dawn nodded and dabbed her eyes as Elliot wrapped his arms around the seamstress.

"We all have events and situations in our pasts that we would rather not ever see the light of day again. Graham and Minnie are dead and gone and there is nothing we can do now about their lives or do anything to change the past."

Elliot felt Dawn sobbing against his chest as he held her.

"You and I now have the chance to move on from what happened here and have a quiet, happy life of our own," he said with a low voice.

Dawn looked up at Elliot, her lips parted and with tears in her eyes. Elliot stopped her as she started to speak.

"I'm going to rebuild the estate across the river and bring that big Victorian house back to its glory. I'm afraid Newton Cutter has inspired me to put down roots here along with your support and affection, this is what I want to do. That is where we will live, my dear, for many happy years." He kissed her forehead.

Dawn hugged him and kissed him. The couple stepped out onto the broad porch of the dressmaker's shop and gazed to the north where they could glimpse the widow's walk of the old Victorian.

Later that day, Elliot met with Mayor Watley and attorney Merle Doyle to fill them in on what he had learned. They all agreed that there was too much information still missing for any solid conclusion. After Elliot provided his personal documents to the Mayor and the attorney, they drew up a formal request for Elliot to be named executor of Minnie's estate.

The mystery would now be solved. Newton Cutter's building site would be free of controversy and the town would have answers. It would have to be published in the newspaper for a week to see if anyone responded or contested. Tommy Boardman was instructed to place a notice in the papers in Santa Fe, Los Angeles, and San Francisco.

***

The next week went by fast. Finishing touches are underway for the school and nearly all the new furniture has gone into the second floor of Cutter's house. Thomas wood sold three horses and took in another stray that needed some gentle care. Bruno Stenson had a huge freight wagon delivery and restocked for the coming winter. He also bottled up thirty-five glass quarts of whiskey from his still, which was greatly appreciated by Chick Miller and Goldman.

On Saturday, three Texas Rangers rode into town. After a meeting with Mayor Watley, Merle Doyle and Henry Elliot, they cuffed Benning to a horse and rode out for the new Ranger outpost in Los Angeles.

The town of Bradford seemed to have calmed down as the weather cooled. Folks shopped, went to church, picked, and harvested the last of the fruits and vegetables to stock their winter cellars. Cutter looked up from his iron to find Merle Doyle standing in the doorway of the blacksmith shop in the cool sunshine.

"Hey Merle, what can I do for you?"

Cutter smiled and took off his glove. Doyle shook hands with the blacksmith and cleared his throat.

"Nobody responded to either advertisement in San Francisco, Denver or Santa Fe about Minnie Hollister. I'm signing the legal papers today on the case. When you are done for the day, I need you to come witness the opening of the safety deposit box, please," Doyle said as he paused to light his cigarette.

"Oh, of course. I'm happy to. I'm just as curious as the next man in finding out what is inside of it," Cutter said as he rubbed his forehead and leaned against the iron anvil.

"Well, we know that the key that was found in the iron box is a safety deposit box key at the bank. We'll need to open up that box and start dealing with those contents. In these cases, it always brings up more questions so prepare yourself," Doyle said. He touched the brim of his hat and walked out to the street.

That afternoon in Merle Doyle's office, a group of men met and witnessed documents assigning control of the estate to Henry Elliot. They then proceeded over to Bradford Bank and were met by William Huddleston, who was surprised at the visit. Doyle produced the documents to Huddleston and made sure that he understood Henry Elliot was to have access to the safety deposit box.

"Those safety deposit boxes haven't been touched in years. The key might not work." Huddleston gripped his hands together so his knuckles turned white. The blood had been drained out of them. The banker had a forced, uneasy wide mouth smile on his face.

"If you will show us to the box, we'll take our chances, Mr. Huddleston," Elliot said in a stern tone.

He took a step forward and Huddleston scurried towards a pair of old wooden doors with iron bars embedded in them. A key scraped against metal and the creaking doors opened. The dry, dusty odor of old wood and paper dust surrounded them. Huddleston found the box number and as Elliot put in the key, he turned to the banker.

"If you'll give us some privacy, Mr. Huddleston, we do have business to discuss." Doyle said with a raised eyebrow.

The banker held up his hands and backed out of the room.

Elliot lifted out the box and set it on the desk. His motions disturbed a fine layer of dust. When he opened it they found letters, papers and a leather satchel containing a small silver ring and a silver bracelet with a small drop pearl. There was one thousand dollars in cash and a deed to a six-acre parcel of land outside Santa Fe. Elliot asked Doyle to find out information/ownership on the Santa Fe parcel.

"Merle, if you would put this one thousand dollars in your office safe for now, I may need it if we ever find any of Minnie's relatives."

The bundle of bills went into a pouch and Doyle put it into his briefcase. Unfolding one letter, Elliot read it and then handed an envelope to Doyle and asked him to read it.

*Dear Minnie,*

*I hope you are happy and healthy where your travels have taken you. Your son is growing bigger every day and has quite a way with words.*

*I did as you asked and changed his name over to Tolliver and the lawyers will finalize the adoption by the end of the month.*

*My little Angus is the most wonderful child and we are so blessed and thankful to you. Our little home is complete now. I cannot begin to understand the grief and agony it took to deliver him to us.*

*My dear Sister, I hope to see you at Christmastime and remember, our home is your home.*

*With love,*

*Adeline Tolliver'*

"Does this mean that Angus Tolliver is Minnie's son? Do you think he knows?"

Mayor Watley's mouth hung open in surprise. The attorney motioned for them all to keep their voices down.

Merle Doyle lit a cigarette and frowned as he looked over the letter.

"I kind of think from this letter that he was never supposed to know. I'm not sure what kind of havoc will start up when he finds out."

Elliot held another paper showing faded ink handwriting.

"I think she started a letter but never finished it."

*"Dear Graham,*

*I know we can be a happy family together. Please just give us a chance to discover what our future together can be. I can change, we can live anywhere you want. I know that you would love...'*

"Graham? Graham White? Dawn's husband?"

Mayor Watley's eyes were wide.

Elliot let out the breath he had been holding.

"Without revealing any confidences, Graham White was acquainted with Minnie Hollister in the year prior to his marrying Dawn. This was many years ago. I am certain that Mrs. White knew of his prior relationship with Minnie but no details."

Elliot folded the paper and put it in his pocket and that stifled any further speculation.

"Dawn Long Biggelo met Graham White in a Seattle hotel when her then-husband met White for business. According to my research, White was a timberman and a logger who had financial success in felling and selling large tracts of timber across the Pacific Northwest. There are newspaper articles up in Seattle about how Graham White had been in negotiations with Charles Milton Biggelo. They had discussed the timber rights on the gold mine claim being sold to White.

"After Charles Milton Biggelo died, Dawn sold the mine claim to a gold consortium and White negotiated the timber contract, winning millions of feet of timber."

Elliot paused and cleared his throat.

"Dawn made plans to travel to southern California to be nearer her older brother, Harley Long. The Pacific Northwest only reminded her of pain, suffering and the death of her husband and soon after she moved her life to the ranch."

The Mayor sat down hard on a wooden chair.

Elliot continued. " Graham White turned up one day and after a year of courtship, they were married and moved to wherever the timber fell. Suffice it to say, she was happy again and I do know that Harley had discussed felling some of the stands of virgin timber on his ranch with Graham. Nothing ever happened, though."

After a few stunned moments, Elliot spoke. "This is all pretty much public record, but what I have told you or inferred here is confidential. I'll thank you for keeping it to yourselves, with all due respect to the lady."

They all nodded in agreement.

The lawyer tapped a finger on the deposit box.

"Well, gentlemen, I suggest we get away from nosy ears and reconvene in my office in a few minutes."

Doyle replaced the empty safety deposit box and locked it. He handed the key to Elliot who slid it into his vest pocket.

As the wooden doors creaked open, Cutter saw William Huddleston scurry back to his desk in the front of the office.

"Ah, gentlemen. All done? Can I do anything for you?"

The smarmy smile, clasped hands and ingratiating tone of the banker hurried the men towards the door.

"Thank you, Mr. Huddleston. If we need your services, we know where to find you. Good day, sir!"

Merle Doyle touched the brim of his hat and followed the other men out the door.

Huddleston felt his fists clench and teeth grind together in frustration. He cast a look toward the safety deposit box room in despair. He had been excluded from some sort of big deal and he could do nothing. Through the dirty, smudged windows, he saw the men walk across the plaza and disappear into the lawyer's office.

He could feel that this had something to do with Angus Tolliver or that Long Ranch and now he was forced out of the events. Huddleston slammed his fist on the old desk in frustration, making the fine dust puff into a small cloud.

***

The next morning, William and Addie Watley, Dawson Cole, Merle Doyle, and Chick Miller stood back and admired the neat work on the two classrooms. Both school rooms were painted a brilliant white with black trim around the casings, trim, and fixtures. Sunlight flooded in the tall windows. Brett Doyle had just brought in the last of the ten smaller desks and small round stools he had built for the first ten children. Thomas

Wood walked over to him and shook his hand, nodding.

Doc Baines donated a young red oak tree and his ranch hands brought it in and planted it in the northeast corner of the property last Friday. Doc told Cutter that someday children would swing on its limbs and Cutter laughed.

"Some of the best memories I have as a child is climbing trees, Doc. Once I learned that pretty girls liked to be pushed on swings, I never looked back," Cutter said and they laughed together.

Bruno Stenson had brought over three small rose bushes and planted them along the front fence. "These came in from Atlanta, Georgia. I told a friend of mine that the town was workin' on buildin' a school and she sent these. It's amazing that they have stayed alive all this way," Stenson kicked the dirt from the shovel and poured a bucket of water onto the plantings.

Yesterday morning there appeared two big planter boxes of flowers, sitting on the steps from an unknown benefactor. Bret Doyle and Fergie Miller attached them under the windows at the front of the house.

Master Carpenters Bob McNary and Ernie Amundson had built six wood benches in the yard for the children. Each one was being painted a bright color by town folk.

Two large, wood burning stoves from Burlington, New York were installed into each classroom on the bottom floor. Clay Dunagan had assembled the stovepipes and handles over in the blacksmith shop. The flat top would be used to heat a water kettle or keep food warm.

"Are we ready for all the visitors tonight, Mr. Vaughan?" Cutter stepped over to the building contractor studying his checklists.

"Yes, we are, Mr. Cutter. There are a few odds and ends that have to be tidied up outside. Those rugs you wanted for upstairs are sitting on the freight wagon outside. I'll have a couple of the men take them up for you."

Vaughan flipped the sheet over, smiled and made a checkmark and then flipped it back.

Cutter raised his voice to the room.

"Whenever you boys are done here, I'm buying drinks over at Goldman's. Get yourselves over there so we can properly celebrate a job well done."

A boisterous cheer went up from the workers.

Across the square, Bert Goldman had finished washing and polishing his new set of bar glasses. He had waited a month for them to arrive from St. Louis and they all stood gleaming on the shelf behind the bar. He made a mental note to ask the peddler Mike to find him some bigger coffee mugs. For a saloon that was meant for liquor, Goldman's served an unusual amount of coffee every day.

Three men in dusters came in the door, laughing and brushing the dirt off. At the bar, they ordered beers and took them over to the table in the corner.

"Is there any place in town we can get supper, barkeep?" The taller, blonde man picked up his beer and took a sip.

"I've got chili with beans, cornbread and apple pie here, if you want something quick. Otherwise, the hotel dining room serves a right nice steak dinner if you have a mind to eat a bit more," Goldman said. He stopped his cleaning and nodded as he talked.

The dark man took off his black hat and laid it on the chair and spoke up.

"Chili sounds good to me. Lemme finish my beer and relax a bit and then I'll have some chow, boss."

He took a sip of his beer. They all sat down and lowered their voices.

Three fast shots sounded outside and a bullet slammed into the heavy wood planks on the bar front. The three cowboys hit the floor and covered their heads.

Goldman ducked down and grabbed the three empty glass mugs off the bar and took them down with him.

"Who did that? What was that?"

One of the cowboys was trying to peek out the window and tried to keep low to the floor. Running feet along the boardwalk went past the saloon and on down the street. Someone shouted something unintelligible and doors slammed.

"Goldman, you alright in there?"

It was Mayor Watley at the back door. Goldman scurried around and unlocked the door, letting the Mayor sneak in the back.

"Did you see anything?"

Mayor shook his head and tried to grasp his shaking hands.

"My nerves are none too good right now. I'm jittery as a leaf in the wind,"

"Hey, Bruno! You okay over there?"

Goldman laid next to the door and called out. No answer. After a minute, he yelled again. Goldman nearly got hit when Stenson tumbled into the bar rolling with three double-barreled shotguns.

"We're not going down without a fight. Load these up, Bert. I got shells right here." Stenson slid a box of shells over to Goldman. He and the Mayor shoved shells into the rifles.

Goldman called over to the cowboys.

"You boys carryin' guns? You better get 'em ready. This might be the big shoot-out we've been waiting for," Goldman yelled as he slammed the breach shut and jacked the shell into the chamber.

Stenson slid the rifle up onto the bar and peeked over the top.

The blonde cowboy's voice had become a high-pitched screech. "Whatdya' mean, big shoot-out? What kinda town is this?"

He rescued his beer and went to sit up against the wall to enjoy his refreshment.

"This is the kinda town that doesn't suffer idiots and won't put up with fools dragging poppycock to our doorstep, mister. Every man, woman and child is armed with at least a pistol and a rifle now. Heaven take pity on the poor man that rides in here and thinks he can shoot us up," Stenson said as he loaded the shiny Colt revolver.

A voice came from outside.

"Goldman, you okay in there? I'm comin' in now, don't shoot me."

It was Newton Cutter. He and Thomas Wood came in and stopped when they saw the pile of cowboys in the corner. He frowned and then went over to the bar when Stenson, Goldman and the Mayor were pouring shots of whiskey.

"What the heck is goin' on out there, Newton? I've got a new bullet in the front of my bar now. I'm lucky none of my new glassware is broken. Scared the living daylights outta those cowboys."

The bartender pointed at the huddled cowboys in the corner nursing beers.

Mayor Watley put his hands flat on the bar so they wouldn't shake.

"Don't know. The Hotel is shut down and locked up. Addie and Miss Dawn are inside the church and bolted the doors shut. The door to the bank is locked and the drapes are closed. Town has been that way all day."

Cutter slid his rifle onto the bar next to the shotguns.

"You guys ready for war or what? Hey, those are some nice shotguns, Bruno."

Cutter ran his fingers down the barrel of one of the guns.

Stenson smiled and nodded.

Wood had picked one up and was testing the balance and weight in his hands.

"Very nice. These aren't the twenty five cent guns that you find everywhere nowadays," Wood laid the big gun down.

"Okay, you men stop admiring Bruno's new toys and let's find out who is shooting up the town. You men over there, where are your horses at?"

The short man perked up.

"They are over at the stables. Are they still standing, mister?"

He asked and looked at Wood who nodded, smiling.

"They're fine, eating oats and hay. I was just getting ready to rub them down when I heard the shots. I got interrupted."

One by one, the doors started opening and the shutters were drawn back. People started coming outside to see what could be seen. Goldman, Stenson, the Mayor, Cutter and Wood walked out onto the boardwalk and looked up and down the street.

The afternoon sun hung in the sky like molasses and a flock of quail lifted up squabbling out of the tall grass to the south outside town. A dog wandered by headed for the plaza. A faint delicious cooking smell drifted on the light breeze. It was a mystery.



lifted up squabbling out of the tall grass to the south outside town. A dog wandered by headed for the plaza. A faint delicious cooking smell drifted on the light breeze. It was a mystery.

Several hours later, the five horseshoes were done and eight more were sitting in the glowing coals ready for the anvil. Cutter had just turned the shoe with the heavy pincers and a shot rang out. The bullet flew past his head. Cutter dropped the shoe and pincers diving for the other side of the anvil. Another shot slamming into the sidewall of the blacksmith shop. Thomas Wood came running in and dove down next to Cutter.

"Who is that? They aiming at you?" Another shot rang out and Wood crouched and ran for the back of the shop. He and Cutter took out their rifles and both pistols as another shot ricocheted off the anvil. Wood in a crouch ran from the stables to the far side of the corral and stopped behind a water trough.

The roar of a shotgun firing boomed across the plaza. Wood shattered and a man screamed.

Merle Doyle was at the corner window of his upstairs office hidden in shadow. He fired off two shots towards the church and sent one man limping behind the corral.

"I think there's four of 'em out there."

Another figure in the office slipped out the door. The sound of a rifle being cocked echoed.

Elliot had been standing near the church considering recent events between himself and a certain seamstress when gunshots rang out. He leaped behind the big oak and knelt hidden by the lush flower bed to scan the town. He had heard four shots but could not determine how many guns were smoking. He had no way of knowing who had been out on the street at the time of the shots, but knew that Dawn was locked in her store, now dark.

He grimaced and shook his head. Stupid foolish people tended to make stupid foolish decisions and while Elliot checked for his ammunition he knew this night someone would die.

Bruno Stenson's big shotgun put a good-sized hole in the side of the auction house, just missing one of the outlaws. Wood winged the outlaw's leg with a rifle and saw him drag himself into the tall grass near the river. An outlaw got off a shot from the corner of the church and then scampered around the side, only to fall back from a point-blank shot.

"I count three, Mr. Stenson," Elliot yelled.

That caused grins on Cutter's and Wood's faces. Elliot ducked down and ran around the other side of the church. He felt a deep sting in his shoulder and fell down into the brushy grass next to the river. His glove showed that he bled from his wound. Keeping low he crept alongside the lawyer's office and with a key, eased into Dawn's little shop and relative safety.

Cutter ran around the edge of the Mayor's office and inched along until he cleared an old tumbled-down warehouse. When he crept into the alleyway he found it already occupied by a dark duster and wide black hat.

Cutter picked up a stone and tossed it, hitting the right shoulder of the man lurking in the shadows. When he wheeled around, Cutter saw that it was Angus Tolliver. Rage boiled over in Tolliver and he rushed toward Cutter with arms raised as if he were to strangle with his bare hands.

Cutter's left hand smashed Tolliver over the eye as they crashed together. Tolliver was stunned and Cutter quickly drew out his narrow pliers and plunged them into the left shoulder as Tolliver spun around.

Tolliver stumbled back, an anguished cry coming from him and as he fought to gain his balance, he fumbled the little silver gun and it fell into the dust. Cutter ran to kick it away and slashed at the outstretched leg, gouging through the denim pant as he turned. The blacksmith wiped away the splash of blood from the cut over his eye. Tolliver tried to throw an arm out to slap away the weapon as his leg soaked with blood. Cutter stepped away about six feet and casually looked around to see if this bloody dance had brought any attention and so far they were relatively alone.

Tolliver dragged himself over to the alley way. He braced himself sitting up and wiped the back of his grimy, bloody hand across his mouth, mean dark eyes glaring at one man he did not want to see.

"This isn't going to work for you anymore, Tolliver. I remember you, and you are done here. One way or another, right here, right now, tonight. You are going outta here in handcuffs or a pine box."

Cutter's voice was a growl as he shifted his weight to one foot and leaned back into the shadow.

Tolliver breathed fast, nearly panting as he tried to find where his gun had fallen, knowing it was his only chance. His shoulder ached and he could feel a trickle of blood sliding down his side.

"You aren't going anywhere, except maybe to jail if you survive this, so just sit there and listen."

Tolliver's voice was a sneer. "Why should I listen to you? You're part of this lousy little town, aren't you?"

Cutter knelt and rested his arms on his legs, clasping his hands together. He studied the wounded outlaw in front of him.

"All these years I've felt that you and I had unfinished business. Now I get my chance to close it for once and for all. I've learned a little about you, Tolliver," Cutter said with a grimace as his fingers wiped away blood from his cheek.

"I've been following your thievery, your killings, your robberies and your petty lies. You used to be quite the big name ranging the western territories, but now here you are. Broken down, bleeding, your partners in crime are running for the hills if not the next state. And what do you have to show for it?"

Tolliver grunted, and rolled up onto one knee, still gripping the blood-soaked thigh. He had to get to that gun that was in the darkness behind him. But Cutter was three feet ahead of him and like a cat swooped the gun up in his hand. The heavy boot stomped on the outstretched fingers and made Tolliver swear as bones crunched. The outlaw cradled his hand against his chest and leaned back, teeth clenched.

There was a small crowd gathering around the other end of the alley and Cutter carefully stepped back into the shadow, watching to see who would come in between the buildings. Some men shouted and the crowd hurried away.

When he looked back at Tolliver, the man was face-down in the dirt, passed out so Cutter stepped over and patted him down. He found a bundle of papers tied with string and quickly shoved that into a pocket of his coat. Cutter stooped and gripped the unconscious man and half carried half dragged him over to Doc Baines where the door was already open and the doctor was rolling up his sleeves.

"Who is this? I heard somebody was shot!?"

Doc peered over his glasses.

"He is Angus Tolliver, Doc and soon to be captured prisoner of the Texas Rangers and I'd be much obliged if you would keep him alive for a few more minutes."

Cutter unfolded the Santa Fe wanted poster and held it out for the doctor to see.

Doc frowned a moment and then reached for his heavy bag and motioned Cutter to bring the bleeding man into the back room.

"We might want to keep him away from the prying eyes of those who like to look, hmm?"

Twenty minutes later, Doc had put in thirty stitches into the leg and put a bandage around the broken fingers. Cutter sat in the corner on a stool turning the sharp pliers over and over in his hands watching the doctor do his work.

"He's more dead than alive, Newton."

Excited voices called to the doctor from the front office and he rushed out, shutting the door behind himself. Tolliver stirred and Cutter gripped the front of his shirt pulling him up off the table and slapped him hard, making his groggy eyes fly open.

"You're gonna answer some questions and then you are going to get some answers before you leave this world, Tolliver, so pay attention."

Cutter pulled up a chair and rubbed his hands together as he began to speak in a lowered voice. Little by little Tolliver's expression went from doubting to astonishment. After ten minutes his eyes half closed and Cutter leaned forward and heard the deathbed confession of the dying man. The blacksmith sat still as he listened, his eyes riveted to a spot on the floor and his mind racing.

Twenty minutes later, Cutter walked out from the back room and saw Thomas Wood and Bruno Stenson watching Doc put stitches into a gunshot wound on Clay Dunagan. Carmella went to Cutter and laid her hand on his arm. After he reassured her that everything was okay, he smiled and gave her a hug.

"Newton! Oh my gosh! What happened to you? You've been in a fight and you've got a nasty cut."

Carmella's voice was going higher and higher as tears gathered in her eyes.

"Miss Carmella, I need to have a few words with these men now. Would you kindly wait for me over at the hotel? I won't be long, I promise." Cutter kissed her forehead and put an arm around her shoulders.

Carmella could see that it was serious as he attempted a smile.

"Of course." Carmella cleared her throat and squeezed Cutters right hand with a concerned smile.

She shut the wooden door behind herself and let out her breath she had been holding. She gripped her hands together to keep them from shaking.

All eyes looked at Cutter as he sat down on the corner of the big oak desk. "Take a seat, gentlemen, this is going to take a bit."

Cutter told them a few more details about how he came across Angus Tolliver and that he never forgot a wrong that had been done. He told them the story of tracking an outlaw from Wyoming down through Denver and about how he escaped justice in Santa Fe. Cutter had cornered him using a sharp horseshoeing tool in an alley here in Bradford. There was no doubt, it was Angus Tolliver.

Dunagan started to get off the exam table. "Where is he? I'd like to whoop the snot right outta him."

Doc shoved Dunagan back down on the table while he finished bandaging the shoulder.

"Sit back down there or you're gonna need more stitches, young man!"

Dunagan saw the long needle and decided to sit back and mind the doctor's orders. Bruno Stenson chuckled.

"So where is he, Cutter? What happened?"

"Angus Tolliver could never prove he was the son of Minnie Hollister. He remembered as a small boy of Minnie wearing the emerald necklace. Minnie's sister changed the boy's name from Andrew Hollister to Angus

Tolliver, her married name and adopted him legally."

Cutter rolled his head around trying to loosen the muscles.

"Minnie's sister confessed on her deathbed his real identity to Angus. Tolliver had been looking for traces of Minnie ever since."

Doc Baines had paused to stare at Cutter.

The blacksmith continued.

"Somewhere along the line Angus came to believe that someone in Bradford killed Minnie, but there was no trace of her ever being there. Not until the necklace and skeleton were dug up. Nobody could prove that Minnie was murdered. There was no proof that Minnie is dead."

Dunagan said, "That was all he had to go on? No wonder he was half crazy."

Mouths hung open and eyes got wide hearing this information.

"It was Angus and his gang that raided Harley Long's ranch and it was the gold on the ranch that was the ultimate goal."

Cutter rubbed his forehead and ran a muddy hand back through his hair while he waited for the speculation to die down.

"Somebody needs to get the Mayor and Henry Elliot. I'm afraid there is another job to be done tonight," Cutter said and then cleared his throat and rubbed his chin.

"It was William Huddleston at the bank that paid Tolliver to raid the ranch. Huddleston wanted to scare Harley off the ranch so he could get the gold."

The doctor stood to wipe his hands.

"I still don't understand about where this gold came from."

Doc Baines poured shots of whiskey, first for Dunagan and then for the rest of the men.

"There was an assay done on the ranch for the timber valuation two years ago. The documents came through the bank as part of the assay and when gold was found, Huddleston hid them. I'll bet that banker has them locked up tight in that vault in the bank."

Dunagan asked, "Do you think Harley knew about the gold?"

Cutter shook his head.

"Huddleston's scheme was a ploy so Tolliver could wreak his vengeance on the town he felt killed his mother."

Cutter stood up and ran his hand through his hair, shaking dust out and then tried to straighten his torn shirt.

Doc helped Dunagan put on a shirt and they stepped out into the night air.

Cutter went straight over to the hotel and to the welcoming arms of Carmella Frisch. Clay Dunagan headed for the little cot in the back room of the stables. Bruno Stenson, the Mayor and Henry Elliot, after a bit of ruckus, escorted the now ex-banker William Huddleston into a cold dark cell later that night. Somewhat bruised and battered but with all his bones intact.

Later that night, Carmella and Cutter stood on the front veranda of the hotel breathing in the cool night air, her slender hand enveloped in his. He brought it up to his lips and kissed the back of it and looked in her eyes.

"After all that's happened here in this town, how will everyone ever get back to the way things used to be, Newton?" Her eyes glistened, her lips apart and moist as she gazed up to him.

"Some people will simply live on; some people won't be able to get past the trauma and upheaval of this and will die. And then some," he said in a low whisper. He leaned his head and lightly brushed his lips against hers.

"Some will never be the same."

# ABOUT THE AUTHOR

I can still see the ridge going through the valley where the rail tracks used to be. Now, there is nobody around that still remembers the train actually going through the valley up to pick up freight racks of timber or bring down passengers from Falk. But there are still some of the old buildings standing where the train used to stop and drop off people and pick up others before heading into Eureka.

When I travel up through the hills and out across the desert I find those same old deserted buildings, left to crumble and so very desolate. There have been musings about what used to be there, what life was like and how at one time this was the place to be and live. When I write, I tell about the places I have seen, what it smelled like, the sounds and then fit in the people who might have enjoyed life there.

If that doesn't sound good, then how about I have got to get all these people out of my head.

I am a dog lover, writer, and author of western fiction and science fiction novels as well as business books.

With several years writing short stories, poetry, and novellas, I have developed a unique story-telling technique on how people get into bad situations.

I have a master's degree from the University of Phoenix. My travels have taken me to the nooks and crannies of Mexico and Europe to broaden her historical knowledge.

Now retired from the professional recruiting business, I live and work out of my home within eyesight of Mt. Hood in Portland, Oregon. I spend my free time building chain link fences with my husband.

# SIGN UP FOR MY AUTHOR NEWSLETTER

GET A FREE STORY AND EXCLUSIVE GINGER WHELIHAN MATERIAL

Building a relationship with my readers is the very best thing about writing. I occasionally send newsletters with details on new releases, special offers, and other bits of news relating to my books.

And if you sign up to the mailing list, I'll send you:

1. A copy of the supplemental Ginger Whelihan story, Twenty-Five Hours

2. A copy of the unpublished Chester Gayton story, Knitted Green Socks.


You can get these stories, for free, by signing up at

https://www.leeanneweltschauthor.com

# OTHER BOOKS BY THE AUTHOR

Please visit your favorite ebook retailer to discover other books
by Lee Anne Wonnacott Weltsch

From Windy Ridge to the Flint Hills
Iron and Rawhide
Nick Stolter
Rage at Rancho Del Oro
The Man from Marvessa
Coming Soon:  Tarragon